THE TURMOIL

Harper's Modern Classics

THE TURMOIL

BY

BOOTH TARKINGTON

EDITED BY

ELIZABETH W. BAKER, Ph.D.
Professor of English, Mary Washington College
Fredericksburg, Va.

AND

MARY V. BAKER, A.B.
Teacher of English, Woodrow Wilson High School
Dallas, Texas

HARPER & BROTHERS PUBLISHERS

New York and London

~~~~~~

THE TURMOIL

~~~~~~

CONTENTS

~~~~~~

THE NOVEL AS AN INTERPRETATION
OF AMERICAN LIFE

THE POPULARITY OF NOVELS. Novels are read at the present time in greater numbers than any other form of literature, except possibly short-stories. They are produced and read more now than at any previous time since the novel form was invented, more than two hundred years ago. Such enduring and growing popularity has its foundation in the fact that novels give us three important things which everybody needs: entertainment, insight into human nature, and an understanding of the institutions of civilized society which we find about us.

NOVELS AS A SOURCE OF ENTERTAINMENT. Novels supply us with delightful entertainment for our leisure hours. If we spend our leisure time in sports, dancing, shows, or travel, we must have specially prepared grounds, or expensive dress and a large bank account, or favorable weather for the enjoyment of that kind of recreation. But if we choose to read a good novel, we can, for a small sum, in any place, and independently of the weather or of company, spend our time in a kind of enjoyment which takes us out of ourselves, thus affording us true recreation, and at the same time gives us a permanent benefit, a part of which we may be able to pass on to our friends.

NOVELS AS A HELP IN UNDERSTANDING HUMAN NATURE. Besides providing us with diversion, novels help us to a better understanding of ourselves and our fellow men. A knowledge of human nature is one of the most valuable assets which any one can possess. If we are able to realize how other people think about things, how they feel, to what motives they respond, why they act as they do in any given case, we shall enjoy our associations with them much more than we otherwise could. We shall be able to get along with them in a smoother and pleasanter way, avoiding misunderstandings and friction. We shall be able to sympathize with their point of view, and to smile at peculiarities and weaknesses instead of condemning them.

But, you may ask, why not get this knowledge of human nature at first hand from the real people with whom we associate, rather than through a book? The answer is that the first-hand method is better so far as it is practical. But it takes longer, and the amount of knowledge is so limited that it must be supplemented by reading. The acquaintance of one person does not extend to a very large circle. Books can introduce us to a much greater number. Our friends, moreover, are mostly persons much like ourselves, brought up to about the same habits, tastes, and general social standards. They use the same language, wear the same kind of clothes, and have the same kind of things happen to them. We cannot get a very wide outlook upon life by associating with those who are alike in all these points. But through novels we may become acquainted with those who live in different parts of our own country, or in foreign lands, and with the people of past times. We may count among our acquaintance the manufacturer who lives among the snows and mountains of Vermont, where the eaves of the houses are sheared away to admit all possible sunlight, and also the ranchman of Arizona, who cools himself under eaves a yard wide. We may know the point of view of the factory girl of New York's East Side, and that of the lady of the Old South. We may know Frenchmen and English, Chinese and Poles, from earliest history, through the adventurous Age of Discoveries, to our own age, the most adventurous and wonderful of all.

Novels have other advantages over first-hand observation. They can present to us a complete span of human life, so that we can trace the changes in the characters to their causes, see the effects of decisions, and estimate the worth of conduct. They can also give a more complete revelation of character than can be got through the study of a real person. No one reveals all of himself to any one friend. This one calls out the serious side, that one the playful, nonsense-loving aspect of his character. One stimulates energy, while another arouses a play of the imagination. The author of a good novel acts toward his characters like all of these friends combined into one, and shows all sides of their natures.

Novels, again, can give us a wider range of experiences than can be had at first hand by any single person. Through reading we can outwit the savage with the Indian scout who helped to mark out the path for the pioneer settler. We can sail the stormy Atlantic with the sea captain of the old pirate days. We can rope longhorns with the now almost extinct cowboy, or cross the snows of Alaska behind a dog-team. We can dance with the colonial lady, or toil with the hired girl on the prairies of Iowa, as they set traditions of refinement, of industry, or of steadfastness for later generations.

NOVELS AS INTERPRETERS OF AMERICAN DEVELOPMENT. In addition to helping us to spend our leisure time pleasantly and profitably, and revealing to us the springs of human conduct, novels are of value in interpreting to us the very complex civilization with which we find ourselves surrounded. Novels of America show colonial life in its three most picturesque phases—the frontier, with its Indians and its heroic scouts and pioneer women, portrayed in the novels of Cooper; Puritan New England, set forth with subtle power in Hawthorne's studies of conscience; and Southern plantation life, told with the charm and color of rapid action in the novels of Johnston.

They preserve for us a picture of the great Western migration—that vast movement of population such as the world has never seen before or since, when, between 1800 and 1870, the great Central Plains and the Mississippi Valley received a stream of settlers from the more thickly populated Eastern states. Such novels as those of Herbert Quick, Willa Cather, and Margaret Wilson show this Westward movement in the light of adventure and romance which illuminate weak and strong alike.

Novels like Owen Wister's *Virginian* and Stewart Edward White's *Gold* immortalize for us the early West, which, from 1849 to 1890, remained the wild and free frontier.

Other novels present to us the period, just as adventurous in a different way, when, between 1870 and 1900, the great industries of the nation began to be organized. This was a time of rapid transformation. A nation which had been agricultural was in a single generation made into one which was primarily industrial. Steam and the use of machinery revolutionized living conditions. During this period, men of powerful imagination and great foresight, seeing within their reach natural resources of stupendous magnitude—iron, copper, coal, oil, cotton from millions of acres, boundless forests—began, with a boyish exuberance, daring, and delight, to manufacture these raw materials into steel and machinery, lumber, paper, cloth, and a thousand other commodities demanded by a rapidly growing population. Competition was unlimited. The great organizers of industry went each his own way regardless of any one else. Wealth gave them power which they sometimes used and frequently abused. Readjustment to the new conditions made by the use of machinery threw hand laborers out of work, creating conditions of poverty unknown in the earlier agricultural age. Great cities sprang up, untrammeled and spontaneous, products of the mammoth struggle to conquer the raw material furnished by nature.

THE BACKGROUND OF "THE TURMOIL." In the region known as the old Northwest Territory, and in the Middle West, the population of eight of the leading cities increased, from 1870 to 1900, from a total of about 700,000 to more than 3,250,000—nearly 500 per cent. The value of manufacturers nearly trebled from 1870 to 1890, and from 1890 to 1900 increased by over a billion dollars.

This enormous growth in population and in industrial organization, while it laid the foundation for later prosperity and better standards of living, was accompanied by neglect of sanitation, beauty, and most of the elements of higher civic life which make a city a desirable place in which to live. In Chicago, for instance, the lake front, which should have been one of the greatest assets of the city for health and beauty, was permitted to be occupied by railroads, and became a source of ugliness and grime. Pittsburgh was ravaged by typhoid fever, which took from its citizens every year about $540,000 in loss of wages and cost of sickness, and more than 4,000 lives.

The era of the rapid growth of the great industrial centers, before the awakening of a civic consciousness, is the time in which Tarkington's *The Turmoil* is set, and just such a city as Chicago or Pittsburgh is its scene. One of the industrial promoters and his son are the principal characters. The father, James Sheridan, revels in the bigness, the growth, the grime, and the attendant confusion; while his son, Bibbs, abhors what his father loves, and longs for a world of art and beauty.

The story shows the reconcilement of the opposing viewpoints through the mediation of Mary Vertrees, and points to a succeeding age, when American cities began to express still another aspect of American genius, and to lead the world in civic splendor and loveliness.

BOOTH TARKINGTON

Booth tarkington of Indianapolis, who is by many literary critics considered the leading American novelist, began his literary career, it is said, by dictating stories to a long-suffering sister before he could write. His admiration for the outlaw, Jesse James, and for the novelist, G. P. R. James, led to his writing plays which were acted in the barn, and which usually began: "It was dusk, and four horsemen were seen riding over the top of the hill."

James Whitcomb Riley and Meredith Nicholson were fellow-townsmen of Tarkington's, and gave the boy their friendship. The three took long walks together, during which the boy Tarkington listened to the men's "moonings," and after which he joined with them in the enjoyment of midnight suppers of pie, watermelon, coffee, and Welsh rarebits.

Tarkington himself tells the story of his first call upon a girl.

"Another young man and I decided one afternoon that we had arrived at the time of life when we should go make a formal call upon a girl. We put on our best clothes, went to the house, and rang the bell. She let us in, smiling, cordial, and much more at ease than we were. We sat on a sofa, facing her, and I just couldn't relax. I didn't dare even lean back. If there had been a lull in the conversation, I don't know what I should have done. No matter what was said, both callers gave an enforced, embarrassed laugh. 'How's your mother?' 'Oh, she's well, thank you. Ha, ha, ha!'

"Then, when we started to leave, backing out the front door, having a terrible time trying to end the conversation— 'Come again!' 'Oh, we'll be glad to! Thank you. Ha, ha, ha!'

"Finally, in backing off, one of us tripped over a metal foot scraper on the stone steps, and we both fell backwards. But we got up laughing—forced laughs. That is, until the door was closed. Then each said to the other, 'You blamed fool, that was your fault!' "

After attending Phillips Exeter Academy, Tarkington went to Purdue University, where he remained two years before entering Princeton. He says that these college years were the happiest and most successful of his life. In addition to engaging in many student activities, writing, composing music, and acting, he stood well in his classes.

His favorite song was "Danny Deever," and his classmates at Princeton always called upon him to sing it as the climax of the fun and the stunts which they enjoyed on the steps of Nassau Hall on spring evenings. He tried to elude the seniors, but they always wanted Tark's song. The following "Rondel" was written about him:

> The same old Tark—just watch him shy
> Like hunted thing, and hide, if let,
> Away behind his cigarette
> When "Danny Deever" is the cry.
> Keep up the call, and by and by
> We'll make him sing, and find he's yet
> The same old Tark.
> No "Author Leonid," we spy
> In him, no cultured ladies' pet;
> He just drops in, and so we get
> The same old song, and gently guy
> The same old Tark—just watch him shy!

This same modesty is still a part of the successful writer.

Upon his return to Indianapolis after his graduation, he began real work, and although he spoke of it as "fussin' with literachoor," he also said: "Writing is a trade, and, like any other trade, it must be learned. We must serve our apprenticeship; but we must work it out alone. There are no teachers.

We must learn by failure and by repeated efforts how the thing is done."

Tarkington continued his efforts to write for years before achieving recognition, even though the gross return for five years of work was only $22.50. Few people realized his seriousness. According to rumors, his principal business was gallant courtesy to every visiting petticoat of quality.

In 1895, when *Life* accepted one of his drawings, Tarkington thought that at last his work as an artist had been recognized; but, as the same magazine later returned thirty-one drawings, he quit drawing and kept on writing.

The editor of a magazine accepted *Cherry,* but lacked the courage to publish it until *Monsieur Beaucaire* appeared in *McClure's Magazine*. *Monsieur Beaucaire* was, it is said, a great disappointment to Tarkington's old friend Riley, who had no use for princelings and perukes. He read no more of Tarkington's works until, in some way, a copy of *The Flirt* fell into his hands. In this book he found no "pretty sprigs of European nobility," and so sat up half the night to finish it, and was over at Tarkington's before breakfast the next morning to say how much he liked it.

Tarkington had been writing short stories some time before he tried a full-sized book. Although many of them, including *Monsieur Beaucaire,* had been rejected, and he had no idea that his novel would be printed, he nevertheless wrote a novel. He says he would have written it just the same if he had been sure that it would never be published. It was, however, accepted by McClure, and *The Gentleman from Indiana* became our novelist's first success.

Tarkington says that until he struck Indiana subjects he had no real success. The state of Indiana is not the whole world to Tarkington, and yet he spends half his year in Indianapolis. Upon being asked why, he answered, "I belong here. I am a part of it, and it is a part of me. I understand it, and it understands me. I should be out of touch with what I know best if I did not spend at least part of each year in Indianapolis."

Tarkington prefers the country for fun, but can work best in the city. In Indianapolis, one writer says, Tarkington lives like a hermit. With food brought in to him, a platter of fruit always at hand, a big silver pitcher of water always within reach, he works, as old man Sheridan said of his son, "like a gorilla." He emerges for an hour or two in the afternoon for a drive or a walk before dinner with the family, then back to the drawing board table, the pile of pencils, and the yellow manuscript paper. His habits of work in the country are much the same, but the effort is not so continuous. The author spends his summers at Seawood, the "House that Penrod built," at Kennebunkport. His study at Seawood is a large room two stories high, with windows on one side only, facing north, and placed so high that he can see only the sky when he sits at the large table which is his desk. Ostensibly this is his work table. Tarkington really does his writing at the drawing board on a little gallery that runs along one end of the room. The gallery is reached by a narrow winding staircase, from which a door opens into his small bedroom. One is reminded of Scott's study at Abbottsford. Scott, too, could work late and then go to bed without disturbing anyone.

Tarkington likes to travel, and is especially fond of Rome, Naples, the Island of Capri, and Sicily.

He tells entertainingly of his experiences abroad—one especially, a balloon ascension, which he describes in a letter to his nephews, to whom he signs himself "your exalted Uncle." "Well," he concludes, "I know you envy me now as much as you admire me. Think of having an Uncle who has been up in a real balloon! It isn't every boy that has that kind of an Uncle. Next time I go up (and I am going up because I have your interests at heart!) I want to take Papa John, but somehow I think we'll have to be diplomatic about it until we have come down safely. I would like to be the only relative of you that has ever been up in a balloon, yet I am willing to give you a

Grandfather, too, who has been as great a help to you as your Uncle. I admit it is a great sacrifice, but I can see what a great benefit it will be to you to have not only an Uncle but a Grandfather in the balloon business. Still, for the present you have an Uncle who has been up in a balloon—to say nothing of an Aunt who has dropped a hat on the top of the Eiffel Tower."

One biographer of the Indiana writer has said that never, in all his going from place to place, even in France where he was said to be one of the craziest Frenchmen of the whole lot, has Tarkington been anything but "the man from home."

He speaks with pride of his country, but deplores its preoccupation with Riches and Bigness. In *The Turmoil* he tells of a city where wealth is loved better than cleanliness, where citizens have lost their old neighborliness and simplicity in their rush for money, where Bigness is the only god known; a place where poetry, truth, and beauty are almost forgotten.

William Allen White says that Tarkington's novels depict us Americans as we are—raw, strong, selfish, with a certain raucous and often gargantuan laughter at the finer amenities of civilization. But, he adds, they depict us always with love, with an understanding heart, with a dynamic faith in our arrival at some useful destiny in the loving purpose of a wise and patient God.

TO THE TEACHER

THE best results can be reached in the teaching of *The Turmoil* when the approach is made through free discussion rather than by means of formal reports or tests. While superficial reading is not to be encouraged, keep in mind that the end to be sought is not exact information, but enjoyment with appreciation. Encourage your students instead to refer to footnotes whenever they come to a word or an expression whose meaning is not clear from the context. Let the students express their opinions freely. Under your guidance they will correct one another's mistaken impressions and build up truer ideals. A book shared with others through reading aloud or discussion yields double value and enjoyment.

When your pupils have finished the study of *The Turmoil,* if they have taken pleasure in the book, and have gained an interest strong enough to impel them to read further, you will have succeeded in reaching the most important object of teaching a novel in high school.

In addition, let us hope that they will have developed a more intelligently sympathetic attitude toward those whose viewpoints are different from their own, and that their eyes will have been opened to see some of the powerful forces moving in our American life and giving it its peculiar character.

THE TURMOIL

CHAPTER ONE

THERE is a midland city in the heart of fair, open country, a dirty and wonderful city nesting dingily in the fog of its own smoke. The stranger must feel the dirt before he feels the wonder, for the dirt will be upon him instantly. It will be upon him and within him, since he must breathe it, and he may care for no further proof that wealth is here better loved than cleanliness; but whether he cares or not, the negligently tended streets incessantly press home the point, and so do the flecked and grimy citizens. At a breeze he must smother in whirlpools of dust, and if he should decline at any time to inhale the smoke he has the meager alternative of suicide.

The smoke is like the bad breath of a giant panting for more and more riches. He gets them and pants the fiercer, smelling and swelling prodigiously. He has a voice, a hoarse voice, hot and rapacious trained to one tune: "Wealth! I will get Wealth! I will make Wealth! I will sell Wealth for more Wealth! My house shall be dirty, my garment shall be dirty, and I will foul my neighbor so that he cannot be clean—but I will get Wealth! There shall be no clean thing about me: my wife shall be dirty and my child shall be dirty, but I will get Wealth!" And yet it is not wealth that he is so greedy for: what the giant really wants is hasty riches. To get these he squanders wealth upon the four winds, for wealth is in the smoke.

Not quite so long ago as a generation, there was no panting giant here, no heaving, grimy city; there was but a pleasant big town of neighborly people who had understanding of one another, being, on the whole, much of the same type. It was a leisurely and kindly place—"homelike," it was called—and when the visitor had been taken through the State Asylum for the Insane and made to appreciate the view of the cemetery from a little hill, his host's duty as Baedeker was done. The good burghers were given to jogging comfortably about in phaetons or in surreys for a family drive on Sunday. No one was very rich; few were very poor; the air was clean, and there was time to live.

But there was a spirit abroad in the land, and it was strong here as elsewhere—a spirit that had moved in the depths of the American soil and labored there, sweating, till it stirred the surface, rove the mountains, and emerged, tangible and monstrous, the god of all good American hearts—Bigness. And that god wrought the panting giant.

In the souls of the burghers there had always been the profound longing for size. Year by year the longing increased until it became an accumulated force: We must Grow! We must be Big! We must be Bigger! Bigness means Money! And the thing began to happen; their longing became a mighty Will. We must be Bigger! Bigger! Bigger! Get people here! Coax them here! Bribe them! Swindle them into coming, if you must, but get them! Shout them into coming! Deafen them into coming! Any kind of people; all kinds of people! We must be Bigger! Blow! Boost! Brag! Kill the fault-finder! Scream and bellow to the Most High: Bigness is patriotism and honor! Bigness is love and life and happiness! Bigness is Money! We want Bigness!

They got it. From all the states the people came; thinly at first, and slowly, but faster and faster in thicker and thicker swarms as the quick years went by. White people came, and black people and brown people and yellow people; the Negroes came from the South by the thousands and thousands, multiplying by other thousands and thousands faster than they could die. From the four quarters of the earth the people came, the broken and the unbroken, the tame and the wild—Germans, Irish, Italians, Hungarians, Scotch, Welsh, English, French, Swiss, Swedes, Norwegians, Greeks, Poles, Russian Jews, Dalmatians, Armenians, Rumanians, Bulgarians, Servians, Persians, Syrians, Japanese, Chinese, Turks, and every hybrid that these could propagate. And if there were no Eskimos nor Patagonians, what other human strain that earth might furnish failed to swim and bubble in this crucible? [1]

With Bigness came the new machinery and the rush; the streets began to roar and rattle, the houses to tremble; the pavements were worn under the tread of hurrying multitudes. The old, leisurely, quizzical look of the faces was lost in something harder and warier; and a cockney type began to emerge discernibly—a cynical young mongrel, barbaric of feature, muscular and cunning; dressed in good fabrics fashioned apparently in imitation of the sketches drawn by newspaper comedians. The female of his kind came with him—a pale girl, shoddy and a little rouged; and they communicated in a nasal argot, mainly insolences and elisions. Nay, the common speech of the people showed change: in place of the old midland vernacular, irregular but clean, and not unwholesomely drawling, a jerky dialect of coined metaphors began to be heard, held together by *gunnas* and *gottas* and much fostered by the public journals.

The city piled itself high in the center, tower on tower for a nucleus, and spread itself out over the plain, mile after mile; and in its vitals, like benevolent bacilli contending with malevolent in the body of a man, missions and refuges offered what resistance they might to the saloons and all the hells that cities house and shelter. Temptation and ruin were ready commodities on the market for purchase by the venturesome; highwaymen walked the streets at night and sometimes killed; snatching thieves were busy everywhere in the dusk; while housebreakers were a common apprehension and frequent reality. Life itself was somewhat safer from intentional destruction than it was in medieval Rome during

[1] A container for heating and fusing chemicals; here used figuratively to mean the great industrial center to which members of various races were attracted and in which they were amalgamated.

a faction war—though the Roman murderer was more like to pay for his deed—but death or mutilation beneath the wheels lay in ambush at every crossing.

The politicians let the people make all the laws they liked; it did not matter much, and the taxes went up, which is good for politicians. Law-making was a pastime of the people; nothing pleased them more. Singular fermentation of their humor, they even had laws forbidding dangerous speed. More marvelous still, they had a law forbidding smoke! They forbade chimneys to smoke and they forbade cigarettes to smoke. They made laws for all things and forgot them immediately; though sometimes they would remember after a while, and hurry to make new laws that the old laws should be enforced—and then forget both new and old. Wherever enforcement threatened Money or Votes—or wherever it was too much bother—it became a joke. Influence was the law.

So the place grew. And it grew strong.

Straightway when he came, each man fell to the same worship:

> Give me of thyself, O Bigness:
> Power to get more power!
> Riches to get more riches!
> Give me of thy sweat that I may sweat more!
> Give me Bigness to get more Bigness to myself,
> O Bigness, for Thine is the Power and the Glory! And
>   there is no end but Bigness, ever and for ever!

CHAPTER TWO

THE Sheridan Building was the biggest skyscraper; the Sheridan Trust Company was the biggest of its kind, and Sheridan himself had been the biggest builder and breaker and truster and buster under the smoke. He had come from a country cross-roads, at the beginning of the growth, and he had gone up and down in the booms and relapses of that period; but each time he went down he rebounded a little higher, until finally, after a year of overwork and anxiety—the latter not decreased by a chance, remote but possible, of recuperation from the former in the penitentiary—he found himself on top, with solid substance under his feet; and thereafter "played it safe." But his hunger to get was unabated, for it was in the very bones of him and grew fiercer.

He was the city incarnate. He loved it, calling it God's country, as he called the smoke Prosperity, breathing the dingy cloud with relish. And when soot fell upon his cuff he chuckled; he could have kissed it. "It's good! It's good!" he said, and smacked his lips in gusto. "Good, clean soot; it's our life-blood, God bless it!" The smoke was one of his great enthusiasms; he laughed at a committee of plaintive housewives who called to beg his aid against it. "Smoke's what brings your husbands' money home on Saturday night," he told them, jovially. "Smoke may hurt your little shrubberies in the front yard some, but it's the catarrhal climate and the adenoids that starts your chuldern coughing. Smoke makes the climate better. Smoke means good health: it makes the people wash more. They have to wash so much they wash off the microbes. You go home and ask your husbands what smoke puts in their pockets out o' the pay-roll—and you'll come around next time to get me to turn out more smoke instead o' chokin' it off!"

It was Narcissism [1] in him to love the city so well; he saw his reflection in it; and, like it, he was grimy, big, careless, rich, strong, and unquenchably optimistic. From the deepest

[1] Narcissus, in Greek mythology, was the son of a river god and a nymph. Because he rejected the love of the nymph Echo, he drew upon himself the vengeance of the gods and was forced to fall in love with his own image reflected in the waters of a spring.

of his inside all the way out he believed it was the finest city in the world. "Finest" was his word. He thought of it as his city as he thought of his family as his family; and just as he profoundly believed his city to be the finest city in the world, so did he believe his family to be—in spite of his son Bibbs— the finest family in the world. As a matter of fact, he knew nothing worth knowing about either.

Bibbs Sheridan was a musing sort of boy, poor in health, and considered the failure—the "odd one"—of the family. Born during that most dangerous and anxious of the early years, when the mother fretted and the father took his chance, he was an ill-nourished baby, and grew meagerly, only lengthwise, through a feeble childhood. At his christening he was committed for life to "Bibbs" mainly through lack of imagination on his mother's part, for though it was her maiden name, she had no strong affection for it; but it was "her turn" to name the baby, and, as she explained later, she "couldn't think of anything else she liked *at all!*" She offered this explanation one day when the sickly boy was nine and after a long fit of brooding had demanded some reason for his name's being Bibbs. He requested then with unwonted vehemence to be allowed to exchange names with his older brother, Roscoe Conkling Sheridan, or with the oldest, James Sheridan, Junior, and upon being refused went down into the cellar and remained there the rest of that day. And the cook, descending toward dusk, reported that he had vanished; but a search revealed that he was in the coal-pile, completely covered and still burrowing. Removed by force and carried upstairs, he maintained a cryptic demeanor, re- fusing to utter a syllable of explanation, even under the lash. This obvious thing was wholly a mystery to both parents; the mother was nonplussed, failed to trace and connect; and the father regarded his son as a stubborn and mysterious fool, an impression not effaced as the years went by.

At twenty-two, Bibbs was physically no more than the outer

scaffolding of a man, waiting for the building to begin inside
—a long-shanked, long-faced, rickety youth, sallow and hol-
low and haggard, dark-haired and dark-eyed, with a peculiar
expression of countenance; indeed, at first sight of Bibbs
Sheridan a stranger might well be solicitous, for he seemed
upon the point of tears. But to a slightly longer gaze, not
grief, but mirth, was revealed as his emotion; while a more
searching scrutiny was proportionately more puzzling—he
seemed about to burst out crying or to burst out laughing, one
or the other, inevitably, but it was impossible to decide which.
And Bibbs never, on any occasion of his life, either laughed
aloud or wept.

He was a "disappointment" to his father. At least that was
the parent's word—a confirmed and established word after his
first attempt to make a "business man" of the boy. He sent
Bibbs to "begin at the bottom and learn from the ground up"
in the machine-shop of the Sheridan Automatic Pump Works,
and at the end of six months the family physician sent Bibbs
to begin at the bottom and learn from the ground up in a
sanitarium.

"You needn't worry, mamma," Sheridan told his wife.
"There's nothin' the matter with Bibbs except he hates work
so much it makes him sick. *I* put him in the machine-shop,
and I guess I know what I'm doin' about as well as the next
man. Ole Doc Gurney always was one o' them nutty alarm-
ists. Does he think I'd do anything 'd be bad for my own
flesh and blood? He makes me tired!"

Anything except perfectly definite health or perfectly definite disease was incomprehensible to Sheridan. He had a
genuine conviction that lack of physical persistence in any
task involving money must be due to some subtle weakness of
character itself, to some profound shiftlessness or slyness. He
understood typhoid fever, pneumonia, and appendicitis—one
had them, and either died or got over them and went back to
work—but when the word "nervous" appeared in a diagnosis

he became honestly suspicious: he had the feeling that there was something contemptible about it, that there was a nigger in the wood-pile somewhere.

"Look at me," he said. "Look at what *I* did at his age! Why, when I was twenty years old, wasn't I up every morning at four o'clock choppin' wood—yes! and out in the dark and the snow—to build a fire in a country grocery store? And here Bibbs has to go and have a *doctor* because he can't— Pho! it makes me tired! If he'd gone at it like a man he wouldn't be sick."

He paced the bedroom—the usual setting for such parental discussions—in his nightgown, shaking his big, grizzled head and gesticulating to his bedded spouse. "My Lord!" he said. "If a little, teeny bit o' work like this is too much for him, why, he ain't fit for anything! It's nine-tenths imagination, and the rest of it—well, I won't say it's deliberate, but I *would* like to know just how much of it's put on!"

"Bibbs didn't want the doctor," said Mrs. Sheridan. "It was when he was here to dinner that night, and noticed how he couldn't eat anything. Honey, you better come to bed."

"Eat!" he snorted. "Eat! It's work that makes men eat! And it's imagination that keeps people from eatin'. Busy men don't get time for that kind of imagination; and there's another thing you'll notice about good health, if you'll take the trouble to look around you, Mrs. Sheridan: busy men haven't got time to be sick and they don't *get* sick. You just think it over and you'll find that ninety-nine per cent. of the sick people you know are either women or loafers. Yes, ma'am!"

"Honey," she said again, drowsily, "you better come to bed."

"Look at the other boys," her husband bade her. "Look at Jim and Roscoe. Look at how *they* work! There isn't a shiftless bone in their bodies. Work never made Jim or Roscoe sick. Jim takes half the load off my shoulders already. Right now there isn't a harder-workin', brighter business man in this city than Jim. I've pushed him, but he give me something to push *against*. You can't push 'nervous dyspepsia'! And look at Roscoe; just *look* at what that boy's done for himself, and barely twenty-seven years old—married, got a fine wife, and ready to build for himself with his own money, when I put up the New House for you and Edie."

"Papa, you'll catch cold in your bare feet," she murmured. "You better come to bed."

"And I'm just as proud of Edie, for a girl," he continued, emphatically, "as I am of Jim and Roscoe for boys. She'll make some man a mighty good wife when the time comes. She's the prettiest and talentedest girl in the United States! Look at that poem she wrote when she was in school and took the prize with; it's the best poem I ever read in my life, and she'd never even tried to write one before. It's the finest thing I ever read, and R. T. Bloss said so, too; and I guess he's a good enough literary judge for me—turns out more advertisin' liter'cher than any man in this city. I tell you she's smart! Look at the way she worked me to get me to promise the New House—and I guess you had your finger in that, too, mamma! This old shack's good enough for me, but you and little Edie 'll have to have your way. I'll get behind her and push her same as I will Jim and Roscoe. I tell you I'm mighty proud o' them three chuldern! But Bibbs—" He paused, shaking his head. "Honest, mamma, when I talk to men that got *all* their boys doin' well and worth their salt, why, I have to keep my mind on Jim and Roscoe and forget about Bibbs."

Mrs. Sheridan tossed her head fretfully upon the pillow. "You did the best you could, papa," she said, impatiently, "so come to bed and quit reproachin' yourself for it."

He glared at her indignantly. "Reproachin' myself!" he snorted. "I ain't doin' anything of the kind! What in the name o' goodness would I want to reproach myself for? And it wasn't the 'best *I* could,' either. It was the best *anybody* could! I was givin' him a chance to show what was in him and make a man of himself—and here he goes and gets 'nervous dyspepsia' on me!"

He went to the old-fashioned gas-fixture, turned out the light, and muttered his way morosely into bed.

"What?" said his wife, crossly, bothered by a subsequent mumbling.

"More like hook-worm, I said," he explained, speaking louder. "*I* don't know what to do with him!"

CHAPTER THREE

BEGINNING at the beginning and learning from the ground up was a long course for Bibbs at the sanitarium, with milk and "Zwieback" as the basis of instruction; and the months were many and tiresome before he was considered near enough graduation to go for a walk leaning on a nurse and a cane. These and subsequent months saw the planning, the building, and the completion of the New House; and it was to that abode of Bigness that Bibbs was brought when the cane, without the nurse, was found sufficient to his support.

Edith met him at the station. "Well, well, Bibbs!" she said, as he came slowly through the gates, the last of all the travelers from that train. She gave his hand a brisk little shake, averting her eyes after a quick glance at him, and turning at once toward the passage to the street. "Do you think they ought to 've let you come? You certainly don't look well!"

"But I certainly do look better," he returned, in a voice as slow as his gait; a drawl that was a necessity, for when Bibbs tried to speak quickly he stammered. "Up to about a month ago it took two people to see me. They had to get me in a line between 'em!"

Edith did not turn her eyes directly toward him again,

after her first quick glance; and her expression, in spite of her, showed a faint, troubled distaste, the look of a healthy person pressed by some obligation of business to visit a "bad" ward in a hospital. She was nineteen, fair and slim, with small, unequal features, but a prettiness of color and a brilliancy of eyes that created a total impression close upon beauty. Her movements were eager and restless: there was something about her, as kind old ladies say, that was very sweet; and there was something that was hurried and breathless. This was new to Bibbs; it was a perceptible change since he had last seen her, and he bent upon her a steady, whimsical scrutiny as they stood at the curb, waiting for an automobile across the street to disengage itself from the traffic.

"That's the new car," she said. "Everything's new. We've got four now, besides Jim's. Roscoe's got two."

"Edith, you look—" he began, and paused.

"Oh, *we*'re all well," she said, briskly; and then, as if something in his tone had caught her as significant, "Well, *how* do I look, Bibbs?"

"You look—" He paused again, taking in the full length of her—her trim brown shoes, her scant, tapering, rough skirt, and her coat of brown and green, her long green tippet and her mad little rough hat in the mad mode—all suited to the October day.

"How do I look?" she insisted.

"You look," he answered, as his examination ended upon an incrusted watch of platinum and enamel at her wrist, "you look—expensive!" That was a substitute for what he had intended to say, for her constraint and preoccupation, manifested particularly in her keeping her direct glance away from him, did not seem to grant the privilege of impulsive intimacies.

"I expect I am!" she laughed, and sidelong caught the direction of his glance. "Of course I oughtn't to wear it in the daytime—it's an evening thing, for the theater—but my day

wrist-watch is out of gear. Bobby Lamhorn broke it yesterday; he's a regular rowdy sometimes. Do you want Claus to
help you in?"

"Oh no," said Bibbs. "I'm alive." And after a fit of panting
subsequent to his climbing into the car unaided, he added,
"Of course, I have to *tell* people!"

"We only got your telegram this morning," she said, as
they began to move rapidly through the "wholesale district"
neighboring the station. "Mother said she'd hardly expected
you this month."

"They seemed to be through with me up there in the
country," he explained, gently. "At least they said they were,
and they wouldn't keep me any longer, because so many
really sick people wanted to get in. They told me to go home
—and I didn't have any place else to go. It'll be all right,
Edith; I'll sit in the woodshed until after dark every day."

"Pshaw!" She laughed nervously. "Of course we're all of us
glad to have you back."

"Yes?" he said. "Father?"

"Of course! Didn't he write and tell you to come home?"
She did not turn to him with the question. All the while she
rode with her face directly forward.

"No," he said; "father hasn't written."

She flushed a little. "I expect *I* ought to 've written sometime, or one of the boys—"

"Oh no; that was all right."

"You can't think how busy we've all been this year, Bibbs.
I often planned to write—and then, just as I was going to,
something would turn up. And I'm sure it's been just the
same way with Jim and Roscoe. Of course we knew mamma
was writing often, and—"

"Of course!" he said, readily. "There's a chunk of coal
fallen on your glove, Edith. Better flick it off before it smears.
My word! I'd almost forgotten how sooty it is here."

"We've been having very bright weather this month—for

us." She blew the flake of soot into the air, seeming relieved.

He looked up at the dingy sky, wherein hung the dis-consolate sun like a cold tin pan nailed up in a smoke-house by some lunatic, for a decoration. "Yes," said Bibbs. "It's very gay." A few moments later, as they passed a corner, "Aren't we going home?" he asked.

"Why, yes! Did you want to go somewhere else first?"

"No. Your new driver's taking us out of the way, isn't he?"

"No. This is right. We're going straight home."

"But we've passed the corner. We always turned—"

"Good gracious!" she cried. "Didn't you know we'd moved? Didn't you know we were in the New House?"

"Why, no!" said Bibbs. "Are you?"

"We've been there a month! Good gracious! Didn't you know—" She broke off, flushing again, and then went on hastily: "Of course, mamma's never been so busy in her life; we *all* haven't had time to do anything but keep on the hop. Mamma couldn't even come to the station to-day. Papa's got some of his business friends and people from around the *old*-house neighborhood coming to-night for a big dinner and 'house-warming'—dreadful kind of people—but mamma's got it all on her hands. She's never sat down a *minute;* and if she did, papa would have her up again before—"

"Of course," said Bibbs. "Do you like the new place, Edith?"

"I don't like some of the things father *would* have in it, but it's the finest house in town, and that ought to be good enough for me! Papa bought one thing I like—a view of the Bay of Naples in oil that's perfectly beautiful; it's the first thing you see as you come in the front hall, and it's eleven feet long. But he would have that old fruit picture we had in the Murphy Street house hung up in the new dining-room. You remember it—a table and a watermelon sliced open, and a lot of rouged-looking apples and some shiny lemons, with two dead prairie-chickens on a chair? He bought it at a furniture-store years and years ago, and he claims it's a finer picture than any they saw in the museums, that time he took mamma to Europe. But it's horribly out of date to have those things in dining-rooms, and I caught Bobby Lamhorn giggling at it; and Sibyl made fun of it, too, with Bobby, and then told papa she agreed with him about its being such a fine thing, and said he did just right to insist on having it where he wanted it. She makes me tired! Sibyl!"

Edith's first constraint with her brother, amounting almost to awkwardness, vanished with this theme, though she still kept her full gaze always to the front, even in the extreme ardor of her denunciation of her sister-in-law.

"*Sibyl!*" she repeated, with such heat and vigor that the name seemed to strike fire on her lips. "I'd like to know why Roscoe couldn't have married somebody from *here* that would have done us some good! He could have got in with Bobby Lamhorn years ago just as well as now, and Bobby 'd have introduced him to the nicest girls in town, but instead of that he had to go and pick up this Sibyl Rink! I met some awfully nice people from her town when mamma and I were at Atlantic City, last spring, and not one had ever even heard of the Rinks! Not even *heard* of 'em!"

"I thought you were great friends with Sibyl," Bibbs said.

"Up to the time I found her out!" the sister returned, with continuing vehemence. "I've found out some things about Mrs. Roscoe Sheridan lately—"

"It's only lately?"

"Well—" Edith hesitated, her lips setting primly. "Of course, I always did see that she never cared the snap of her little finger about *Roscoe!*"

"It seems," said Bibbs, in laconic protest, "that she married him."

The sister emitted a shrill cry, to be interpreted as contemptuous laughter, and, in her emotion, spoke too impulsively: "Why, she'd have married *you!*"

"No, no," he said; "she couldn't be that bad!"

"I didn't mean—" she began, distressed. "I only meant— I didn't mean—"

"Never mind, Edith," he consoled her. "You see, she couldn't have married me, because I didn't know her; and besides, if she's as mercenary as all that she'd have been too clever. The head doctor even had to lend me the money for my ticket home."

"I didn't mean anything unpleasant about *you*," Edith babbled. "I only meant I thought she was the kind of girl who was so simply crazy to marry somebody she'd have married anybody that asked her."

"Yes, yes," said Bibbs; "it's all straight." And, preceiving that his sister's expression was that of a person whose adroitness has set matters perfectly to rights, he chuckled silently.

"Roscoe's perfectly lovely to her," she continued, a moment later. "Too lovely! If he'd wake up a little and lay down the law, some day, like a *man,* I guess she'd respect him more and learn to behave herself!"

" 'Behave'?"

"Oh, well, I mean she's so insincere," said Edith, characteristically evasive when it came to stating the very point to which she had led, and in this not unique of her sex.

Bibbs contented himself with a non-committal gesture. "Business is crawling up the old streets," he said, his long, tremulous hand indicating a vasty structure in course of erection. "The boarding-houses come first and then the—"

"That isn't for shops," she informed him. "That's a new investment of papa's—the 'Sheridan Apartments.' "

"Well, well," he murmured. "I supposed 'Sheridan' was almost well enough known here already."

"Oh, we're well enough known *about!*" she said, impatiently. "I guess there isn't a man, woman, child, or nigger baby in town that doesn't know who we are. But we aren't in with the right people."

"No!" he exclaimed. "Who's all that?"

"Who's all what?"

"The 'right people.'"

"You know what I mean: the best people, the old families —the people that have the real social position in this town and that know they've got it."

Bibbs indulged in his silent chuckle again; he seemed greatly amused. "I thought that the people who actually had the real what-you-may-call-it didn't know it," he said. "I've always understood that it was very unsatisfactory, because if you thought about it you didn't have it, and if you had it you didn't know it."

"That's just bosh," she retorted. "They know it in this town, all right! I found out a lot of things, long before we began to think of building out in this direction. The right people in this town aren't always the society-column ones, and they mix around with outsiders, and they don't all belong to any one club—they've taken in all sorts into all their clubs —but they're a clan, just the same; and they have the clan feeling and they're just as much We, Us and Company as any crowd you read about anywhere in the world. Most of 'em were here long before papa came, and the grandfathers of the girls of my age knew each other, and—"

"I see," Bibbs interrupted, gravely. "Their ancestors fled together from many a stricken field, and Crusaders' blood flows in their veins. I always understood the first house was built by an old party of the name of Vertrees who couldn't get along with Dan'l Boone,[1] and hurried away to these parts because Dan'l wanted him to give back a gun he'd lent him."

Edith gave a little ejaculation of alarm. "You mustn't repeat that story, Bibbs, even if it's true. The Vertreeses are

---

[1] Daniel Boone, a native of Pennsylvania, was a noted Indian scout and pioneer, most of whose feats of marksmanship and daring were connected with Kentucky.

the best family, and of course the very oldest here; they were an old family even before Mary Vertrees's great-great-grandfather came west and founded this settlement. He came from Lynn, Massachusetts, and they have relatives there *yet*—some of the best people in Lynn!"

"No!" exclaimed Bibbs, incredulously.

"And there are other old families like the Vertreeses," she went on, not heeding him; "the Lamhorns and the Kittersbys and the J. Palmerston Smiths—"

"Strange names to me," he interrupted. "Poor things! None of them have my acquaintance."

"No, that's just it!" she cried. "And papa had never even heard the name of Vertrees! Mrs. Vertrees went with some anti-smoke committee to see him, and he told her that smoke was what made her husband bring home his wages from the pay-roll on Saturday night! *He* told us about it, and I thought I just couldn't live through the night, I was so ashamed! Mr. Vertrees has always lived on his income, and papa didn't know him, of course. They're the stiffest, most elegant people in the whole town. And to crown it all, papa went and bought the next lot to the old Vertrees country mansion—it's in the very heart of the best new residence district now, and that's where the New House is, right next door to them—and I must say it makes their place look rather shabby! I met Mary Vertrees when I joined the Mission Service Helpers, but she never did any more than just barely bow to me, and since papa's break I doubt if she'll do that! They haven't called."

"And you think if I spread this gossip about Vertrees the First stealing Dan'l Boone's gun, the chances that they *will* call—"

"Papa knows what a break he made with Mrs. Vertrees. I made him understand that," said Edith, demurely, "and he's promised to try and meet Mr. Vertrees and be nice to him. It's just this way: if we don't know *them,* it's practically no

use in our having built the New House; and if we *do* know
them and they're decent to us, we're right with the right
people. They can do the whole thing for us. Bobby Lamhorn
told Sibyl he was going to bring his mother to call on her
and on mamma, but it was weeks ago, and I notice he hasn't
done it; and if Mrs. Vertrees decides not to know us, I'm
darn sure Mrs. Lamhorn 'll never come. That's *one* thing
Sibyl didn't manage! She *said* Bobby offered to bring his
mother—"

"You say he is a friend of Roscoe's?" Bibbs asked.

"Oh, he's a friend of the whole family," she returned, with
a petulance which she made an effort to disguise. "Roscoe
and he got acquainted somewhere, and they take him to the
theater about every other night. Sibyl has him to lunch, too,
and keeps—" She broke off with an angry little jerk of the
head. "We can see the New House from the second corner
ahead. Roscoe has built straight across the street from us, you
know. Honestly, Sibyl makes me think of a snake, sometimes—the way she pulls the wool over people's eyes! She
honeys up to papa and gets anything in the world she wants
out of him, and then makes fun of him behind his back—
yes, and to his face, but *he* can't see it! She got him to give her
a twelve-thousand-dollar porch for their house after it was—"

"Good heavens!" said Bibbs, staring ahead as they reached
the corner and the car swung to the right, following a bend
in the street. "Is that the New House?"

"Yes. What do you think of it?"

"Well," he drawled, "I'm pretty sure the sanitarium's about
half a size bigger; I can't be certain till I measure."

And a moment later, as they entered the driveway, he
added, seriously:

"But it's beautiful!"

CHAPTER FOUR

IT WAS gray stone, with long roofs of thick green slate. An architect who loved the milder "Gothic motives" had built what he liked: it was to be seen at once that he had been left unhampered, and he had wrought a picture out of his head into a noble and exultant reality. At the same time a landscape-designer had played so good a second, with ready-made accessories of screen, approach and vista, that already whatever look of newness remained upon the place was to its advantage, as showing at least one thing yet clean under the grimy sky. For, though the smoke was thinner in this direction, and at this long distance from the heart of the town, it was not absent, and under tutelage of wind and weather could be malignant even here, where cows had wandered in the meadows and corn had been growing not ten years gone.

Altogether, the New House was a success. It was one of those architects' successes which leave the owners veiled in privacy; it revealed nothing of the people who lived in it save that they were rich. There are houses that cannot be detached from their own people without protesting: every inch of mortar seems to mourn the separation, and such a house— no matter what be done to it—is ever murmurous with regret, whispering the old name sadly to itself unceasingly. But the New House was of a kind to change hands without emotion. In our swelling cities, great places of its type are useful as financial gauges of the business tides; rich families, one after another, take title and occupy such houses as fortunes rise and fall—they mark the high tide. It was impossible to imagine a child's toy wagon left upon a walk or driveway of the New House, and yet it was—as Bibbs rightly called it— "beautiful."

What the architect thought of the "Golfo di Napoli," which

hung in its vast gold revel of rococo frame against the gray wood of the hall, is to be conjectured—perhaps he had not seen it.

"Edith, did you say only eleven feet?" Bibbs panted, staring at it, as the white-jacketed twin of a Pullman porter helped him to get out of his overcoat.

"Eleven without the frame," she explained. "It's splendid, don't you think? It lightens things up so. The hall was kind of gloomy before."

"No gloom now!" said Bibbs.

"This statue in the corner is pretty, too," she remarked. "Mamma and I bought that." And Bibbs turned at her direction to behold, amid a grove of tubbed palms, a "life-size," black-bearded Moor,[1] of a plastic composition painted with unappeasable gloss and brilliancy. Upon his chocolate head he wore a gold turban; in his hand he held a gold-tipped spear; and for the rest, he was red and yellow and black and silver.

"Hallelujah!" was the sole comment of the returned wanderer, and Edith, saying she would "find mamma," left him blinking at the Moor. Presently, after she had disappeared, he turned to the colored man who stood waiting, Bibbs's traveling-bag in his hand. "What do *you* think of it?" Bibbs asked, solemnly.

"Gran'!" replied the servitor. "She mighty hard to dus'. Dus' git in all 'em wrinkles. Yessuh, she mighty hard to dus'."

"I expect she must be," said Bibbs, his glance returning reflectively to the black bull beard for a moment. "Is there a place anywhere I could lie down?"

"Yessuh. We got one nem spare rooms all fix up fo' you, suh. Right up staihs, suh. Nice room."

He led the way, and Bibbs followed slowly, stopping at in-

[1] Member of a dark-skinned, hybrid race of mixed Arab and Berber blood, found in the states of North Africa.

tervals to rest, and noting a heavy increase in the staff of
service since the exodus from the "old" house. Maids and
scrubwomen were at work under the patently nominal direction of another Pullman porter, who was profoundly enjoy
ing his own affectation of being harassed with care.

"Ev'ything got look spick an' span fo' the big doin's to-
night," Bibbs's guide explained, chuckling. "Yessuh, we got
big doin's to-night! Big doin's!"

The room to which he conducted his lagging charge was
furnished in every particular like a room in a new hotel; and
Bibbs found it pleasant—though, indeed, any room with a
good bed would have seemed pleasant to him after his journey. He stretched himself flat immediately, and having replied "Not now" to the attendant's offer to unpack the bag,
closed his eyes wearily.

White-jacket, racially sympathetic, lowered the window-
shades and made an exit on tiptoe, encountering the other
white-jacket—the harassed overseer—in the hall without.
Said the emerging one:

"He mighty shaky, Mist' Jackson. Drop right down an' shet
his eyes. Eyelids all black. Rich folks gotta go same as anybody else. Anybody ast me if I change 'ith 'at ole boy—No,
suh! Le'm keep 'is money; I keep my black skin an' keep
out the ground!"

Mr. Jackson expressed the same preference. "Yessuh, he
look tuh me like somebody awready laid out," he concluded.
And upon the stairway landing, near by, two old women, on
all-fours at their work, were likewise pessimistic.

"Hech!" said one, lamenting in a whisper. "It give me a
turn to see him go by—white as wax an' bony as a dead fish!
Mrs. Cronin, tell me: d'it make ye kind o' sick to look at
um?"

"Sick? No more than the face of a blessed angel already in
heaven!"

"Well," said the other, "I'd a b'y o' me own come home

t' die once—" She fell silent at a rustling of skirts in the cor-
ridor above them.

It was Mrs. Sheridan hurrying to greet her son.

She was one of those fat, pink people who fade and contract with age like drying fruit; and her outside was a true
portrait of her. Her husband and her daughter had long ago
absorbed her. What intelligence she had was given almost
wholly to comprehending and serving those two, and except
in the presence of one of them she was nearly always absent-
minded. Edith lived all day with her mother, as daughters do;
and Sheridan so held his wife to her unity with him that she
had long ago become unconscious of her existence as a thing
separate from his. She invariably perceived his moods, and
nursed him through them when she did not share them; and
she gave him a profound sympathy with the inmost spirit
and purpose of his being, even though she did not comprehend it and partook of it only as a spectator. They had known
but one actual altercation in their lives, and that was thirty
years past, in the early days of Sheridan's struggle, when, in
order to enhance the favorable impression he believed himself to be making upon some capitalists, he had thought it
necessary to accompany them to a performance of "The Black
Crook." But she had not once referred to this during the last
ten years.

Mrs. Sheridan's manner was hurried and inconsequent;
her clothes rustled more than other women's clothes; she
seemed to wear too many at a time and to be vaguely troubled by them, and she was patting a skirt down over some
unruly internal dissension at the moment she opened Bibbs's
door.

At sight of the recumbent figure she began to close the
door softly, withdrawing, but the young man had heard the
turning of the knob and the rustling of skirts, and he opened
his eyes.

"Don't go, mother," he said. "I'm not asleep." He swung

his long legs over the side of the bed to rise, but she set a hand on his shoulder, restraining him; and he lay flat again.

"No," she said, bending over to kiss his cheek, "I just come for a minute, but I want to see how you seem. Edith said—"

"Poor Edith!" he murmured. "She couldn't look at me. She—"

"Nonsense!" Mrs. Sheridan, having let in the light at a window, came back to the bedside. "You look a great deal better than what you did before you went to the sanitarium, anyway. It's done you good; a body can see that right away. You need fatting up, of course, and you haven't got much color—"

"No," he said, "I haven't much color."

"But you will have when you get your strength back."

"Oh yes!" he responded, cheerfully. *"Then* I will."

"You look a great deal better than what I expected."

"Edith must have a great vocabulary!" he chuckled.

"She's too sensitive," said Mrs. Sheridan, "and it makes her exaggerate a little. What about your diet?"

"That's all right. They told me to eat anything."

"Anything at all?"

"Well—anything I could."

"That's good," she said, nodding. "They mean for you just to build up your strength. That's what they told me the last time I went to see you at the sanitarium. You look better than what you did then, and that's only a little time ago. How long was it?"

"Eight months, I think."

"No, it couldn't be. I know it ain't *that* long, but maybe it was longer 'n I thought. And this last month or so I haven't had scarcely even time to write more than just a line to ask how you were gettin' along, but I told Edith to write, the weeks I couldn't, and I asked Jim to, too, and they both said they would, so I suppose you've kept up pretty well on the home news."

"Oh yes."

"What *I* think you need," said the mother, gravely, "is to liven up a little and take an interest in things. That's what papa was sayin' this morning, after we got your telegram; and that's what 'll stimulate your appetite, too. He was talkin' over his plans for you—"

"Plans?" Bibbs, turning on his side, shielded his eyes from the light with his hand, so that he might see her better. "What—" He paused. "What plans is he making for me, mother?"

She turned away, going back to the window to draw down the shade. "Well, you better talk it over with *him*," she said, with perceptible nervousness. "He better tell you himself. I don't feel as if I had any call, exactly, to go into it; and you better get to sleep now, anyway." She came and stood by the bedside once more. "But you must remember, Bibbs, whatever papa does is for the best. He loves his chuldern and wants to do what's right by *all* of 'em—and you'll always find he's right in the end."

He made a little gesture of assent, which seemed to content her; and she rustled to the door, turning to speak again after she had opened it. "You get a good nap, now, so as to be all rested up for to-night."

"You—you mean—he—" Bibbs stammered, having begun to speak too quickly. Checking himself, he drew a long breath, then asked, quietly, "Does father expect me to come down-stairs this evening?"

"Well, I think he does," she answered. "You see, it's the 'house-warming,' as he calls it, and he said he thinks all our chuldern ought to be around us, as well as the old friends and other folks. It's just what he thinks you need—to take an interest and liven up. You don't feel too bad to come down, do you?"

"Mother?"

"Well?"

"Take a good look at me," he said.

"Oh, see here!" she cried, with brusque cheerfulness. "You're not so bad off as you think you are, Bibbs. You're on the mend; and it won't do you any harm to please your—"

"It isn't that," he interrupted. "Honestly, I'm only afraid it might spoil somebody's appetite. Edith—"

"I told you the child was too sensitive," she interrupted, in turn. "You're a plenty good-lookin' enough young man for anybody! You look like you been through a long spell and begun to get well, and that's all there is to it."

"All right. I'll come to the party. If the rest of you can stand it, I can!"

"It 'll do you good," she returned, rustling into the hall. "Now take a nap, and I'll send one o' the help to wake you in time for you to get dressed up before dinner. You go to sleep right away, now, Bibbs!"

Bibbs was unable to obey, though he kept his eyes closed. Something she had said kept running in his mind, repeating itself over and over interminably. "His plans for you—his plans for you—his plans for you—his plans for you—" And then, taking the place of "his plans for you," after what seemed a long, long while, her flurried voice came back to him insistently, seeming to whisper in his ear: "He loves his chuldern—he loves his chuldern—he loves his chuldern"—"you'll find he's always right—you'll find he's always right—" Until at last, as he drifted into the state of half-dreams and distorted realities, the voice seemed to murmur from beyond a great black wing that came out of the wall and stretched over his bed—it was a black wing within the room, and at the same time it was a black cloud crossing the sky, bridging the whole earth from pole to pole. It was a cloud of black smoke, and out of the heart of it came a flurried voice whispering over and over, "His plans for you—his plans for you—his plans for you—" And then there was nothing.

He woke refreshed, stretched himself gingerly—as one might have a care against too quick or too long a pull upon a frayed elastic—and, getting to his feet, went blinking to the window and touched the shade so that it flew up, letting in a pale sunset.

He looked out into the lemon-colored light and smiled wanly at the next house, as Edith's grandiose phrase came to mind, "the old Vertrees country mansion." It stood in a broad lawn which was separated from the Sheridans' by a young hedge; and it was a big, square, plain old box of a house with a giant salt-cellar atop for a cupola. Paint had been spared for a long time, and no one could have put a name to the color of it, but in spite of that the place had no look of being out at heel, and the sward was as neatly trimmed as the Sheridans' own.

The separating hedge ran almost beneath Bibbs's window —for this wing of the New House extended here almost to the edge of the lot—and, directly opposite the window, the Vertreeses' lawn had been graded so as to make a little knoll upon which stood a small rustic "summer-house." It was almost on a level with Bibbs's window and not thirty feet away; and it was easy for him to imagine the present dynasty of Vertreeses in grievous outcry when they had found this retreat ruined by the juxtaposition of the parvenu intruder. Probably the "summer-house" was pleasant and pretty in summer. It had the look of a place wherein little girls had played for a generation or so with dolls and "housekeeping," or where a lovely old lady might come to read something dull on warm afternoons; but now in the thin light it was desolate, the color of dust, and hung with haggard vines which had lost their leaves.

Bibbs looked at it with grave sympathy, probably feeling some kinship with anything so dismantled; then he turned to a cheval-glass beside the window and paid himself the dubious tribute of a thorough inspection. He looked the mir-

ror up and down, slowly, repeatedly, but came in the end to
a long and earnest scrutiny of the face. Throughout this cryptic séance his manner was profoundly impersonal; he had
the air of an entomologist intent upon classifying a specimen,
but finally he appeared to become pessimistic. He shook his
head solemnly; then gazed again and shook his head again,
and continued to shake it slowly, in complete disapproval.

"You certainly are one horrible sight!" he said, aloud.

And at that he was instantly aware of an observer. Turning quickly, he was vouchsafed the picture of a charming
lady, framed in a rustic aperture of the "summer-house" and
staring full into his window—straight into his eyes, too, for
the infinitesimal fraction of a second before the flashingly
censorious withdrawal of her own. Composedly, she pulled
several dead twigs from a vine, the manner of her action con-
veying a message or proclamation to the effect that she was in
the summer-house for the sole purpose of such-like pruning
and tending, and that no gentleman could suppose her presence there to be due to any other purpose whatsoever, or that,
being there on that account, she had allowed her attention to
wander for one instant in the direction of things of which she
was in reality unconscious.

Having pulled enough twigs to emphasize her unconsciousness—and at the same time her disapproval—of everything in
the nature of a Sheridan or belonging to a Sheridan, she descended the knoll with maintained composure, and sauntered
tow l a side-door of the country mansion of the Vertreeses.
An elderly lady, bonneted and cloaked, opened the door and
came to meet her.

"Are you ready, Mary? I've been looking for you. What
were you doing?"

"Nothing. Just looking into one of Sheridans' windows,"
said Mary Vertrees. "I got caught at it."

"Mary!" cried her mother. "Just as we were going to call!
Good heavens!"

"We'll go, just the same," the daughter returned. "I suppose those women would be glad to have us if we'd burned their house to the ground."

"But *who* saw you?" insisted Mrs. Vertrees.

"One of the sons, I suppose he was. I believe he's insane, or something. At least I hear they keep him in a sanitarium somewhere, and never talk about him. He was staring at himself in a mirror and talking to himself. Then he looked out and caught me."

"What did he—"

"Nothing, of course."

"How did he look?"

"Like a ghost in a blue suit," said Miss Vertrees, moving toward the street and waving a white-gloved hand in farewell to her father, who was observing them from the window of his library. "Rather tragic and altogether impossible. Do come on, mother, and let's get it over!"

And Mrs. Vertrees, with many misgivings, set forth with her daughter for their gracious assault upon the New House next door.

CHAPTER FIVE

MR. VERTREES, having watched their departure with the air of a man who had something at hazard upon the expedition, turned from the window and began to pace the library thoughtfully, pending their return. He was about sixty; a small man, withered and dry and fine, a trim little sketch of the elderly dandy. His lambrequin [1] mustache—relic of a forgotten Anglomania [2]—had been profoundly black, but

[1] A lambrequin is a piece of ornamental drapery or a short hanging, attached to a mantel or a shelf.

[2] Over-fondness for things that are English, or an imitation of them by a person not English.

now, like his smooth hair, it was approaching an equally sheer whiteness; and though his clothes were old, they had shapeliness and a flavor of mode. And for greater spruceness there were some jaunty touches: gray spats, a narrow black ribbon across the gray waistcoat to the eye-glasses in a pocket, a fleck of color from a button in the lapel of the black coat, labeling him the descendant of patriot warriors.

The room was not like him, being cheerful and hideous, whereas Mr. Vertrees was anxious and decorative. Under a mantel of imitation black marble a merry little coal-fire beamed forth upon high and narrow "Eastlake" bookcases[3] with long glass doors, and upon comfortable, incongruous furniture, and upon meaningless "woodwork" everywhere, and upon half a dozen Landseer engravings[4] which Mr. and Mrs. Vertrees sometimes mentioned to each other, after thirty years of possession, as "very fine things." They had been the first people in town to possess Landseer engravings, and there, in art, they had rested, but they still had a feeling that in all such matters they were in the van; and when Mr. Vertrees discovered Landseers upon the walls of other people's houses he thawed, as a chieftain to a trusted follower; and if he found an edition of Bulwer Lytton[5] accompanying the Landseers as a final corroboration of culture, he would say, inevitably, "Those people know good pictures and they know good books."

[3] Named for the designer, Sir Charles Eastlake (1793–1865). The case had a cornice top and two open shelves in the upper half. Narrow strips of cut leather across the front of the shelves kept the dust from the books and added beauty to the case. The lower half was divided into two parts, door-covered cabinets and open shelves. Eastlake used oak or unpolished mahogany for his bookcases.

[4] Engravings made by Thomas Landseer, the eldest brother of the English painter, Sir Edwin Landseer. The engraver's interpretation of Sir Edwin's pictures has made them known throughout the world.

[5] A prominent figure of the nineteenth century in the political, social, and literary life of England. As a writer, he is best known for the play *Richelieu,* and the historical novel *The Last Days of Pompeii.*

The growth of the city, which might easily have made him a millionaire, had ruined him because he had failed to understand it. When towns begin to grow they have whims, and the whims of a town always ruin somebody. Mr. Vertrees had been most strikingly the somebody in this case. At about the time he bought the Landseers, he owned, through inheritance, an office-building and a large house not far from it, where he spent the winter; and he had a country place—a farm of four hundred acres—where he went for the summers to the comfortable, ugly old house that was his home now, perforce, all the year round. If he had known how to sit still and let things happen he would have prospered miraculously; but, strangely enough, the dainty little man was one of the first to fall down and worship Bigness, the which proceeded straightway to enact the rôle of Juggernaut [6] for his better education. He was a true prophet of the prodigious growth, but he had a fatal gift for selling good and buying bad. He should have stayed at home and looked at his Landseers and read his Bulwer, but he took his cow to market, and the trained milkers milked her dry and then ate her. He sold the office-building and the house in town to buy a great tract of lots in a new suburb; then he sold the farm, except the house and the ground about it, to pay the taxes on the suburban lots and to "keep them up." The lots refused to stay up; but he had to do something to keep himself and his family up, so in despair he sold the lots (which went up beautifully the next year) for "traction stock" that was paying dividends; and thereafter he ceased to buy and sell. Thus he disappeared altogether from the commercial surface at about the time James Sheridan came out securely on top; and Sheridan, until Mrs. Vertrees called upon him with her "anti-smoke" committee, had never heard the name.

[6] A Hindu deity, worshipped in India, whose image, dragged through the streets, was formerly believed to crush to death the devotees who flung themselves in its way.

Mr. Vertrees, pinched, retired to his Landseers, and Mrs. Vertrees "managed somehow" on the dividends, though "managing" became more and more difficult as the years went by and money bought less and less. But there came a day when three servitors of Bigness in Philadelphia took greedy counsel with four fellow-worshipers from New York, and not long after that there were no more dividends for Mr. Vertrees. In fact, there was nothing for Mr. Vertrees, because the "traction stock" henceforth was no stock at all, and he had mortgaged his house long ago to help "manage somehow" according to his conception of his "position in life"—one of his own old-fashioned phrases. Six months before the completion of the New House next door, Mr. Vertrees had sold his horses and the worn Victoria and "station-wagon," to pay the arrears of his two servants and re-establish credit at the grocer's and butcher's—and a pair of elderly carriage-horses with such accoutrements are not very ample barter, in these days, for six months' food and fuel and service. Mr. Vertrees had discovered, too, that there was no salary for him in all the buzzing city—he could do nothing.

It may be said that he was at the end of his string. Such times do come in all their bitterness, finally, to the man with no trade or craft, if his feeble clutch on that slippery ghost, Property, shall fail.

The windows grew black while he paced the room, and smoky twilight closed round about the house, yet not more darkly than what closed round about the heart of the anxious little man patrolling the fan-shaped zone of firelight. But as the mantel clock struck wheezily six there was the rattle of an outer door, and a rich and beautiful peal of laughter went ringing through the house. Thus cheerfully did Mary Vertrees herald her return with her mother from their expedition among the barbarians.

She came rushing into the library and threw herself into a deep chair by the hearth, laughing so uncontrollably that tears were in her eyes. Mrs. Vertrees followed decorously, no mirth about her; on the contrary, she looked vaguely disturbed, as if she had eaten something not quite certain to agree with her, and regretted it.

"Papa! Oh, oh!" And Miss Vertrees was fain to apply a handkerchief upon her eyes. "I'm *so* glad you made us go! I wouldn't have missed it—"

Mrs. Vertrees shook her head. "I suppose I'm very dull," she said, gently. "I didn't see anything amusing. They're most ordinary, and the house is altogether in bad taste, but we anticipated that, and—"

"Papa!" Mary cried, breaking in. "They asked us to *dinner!*"

"What!"

"And I'm *going!*" she shouted, and was seized with fresh paroxysms. "Think of it! Never in their house before; never met any of them but the daughter—and just *barely* met her—"

"What about you?" interrupted Mr. Vertrees, turning sharply upon his wife.

She made a little face as if positive now that what she had eaten would not agree with her. "I couldn't!" she said. "I—"

"Yes, that's just—just the way she—she looked when they asked her!" cried Mary, choking. "And then she—she realized it, and tried to turn it into a cough, and she didn't know how, and it sounded like—like a squeal!"

"I suppose," said Mrs. Vertrees, much injured, "that Mary will have an uproarious time at my funeral. She makes fun of—"

Mary jumped up instantly and kissed her; then she went to the mantel and, leaning an elbow upon it, gazed thoughtfully at the buckle of her shoe, twinkling in the firelight.

"*They* didn't notice anything," she said. "So far as they were concerned, mamma, it was one of the finest coughs you ever coughed."

"Who were 'they'?" asked her father. "Whom did you see?"

"Only the mother and daughter," Mary answered. "Mrs. Sheridan is dumpy and rustly; and Miss Sheridan is pretty and pushing—dresses by the fashion magazines and talks about New York people that have their pictures in 'em. She tutors the mother, but not very successfully—partly because her own foundation is too flimsy and partly because she began too late. They've got an enormous Moor of painted plaster or something in the hall, and the girl evidently thought it was to her credit that she selected it!"

"They have oil-paintings, too," added Mrs. Vertrees, with a glance of gentle pride at the Landseers. "I've always thought oil-paintings in a private house the worst of taste."

"Oh, if one owned a Raphael or a Titian!"[7] said Mr. Vertrees, finishing the implication, not in words, but with a wave of his hand. "Go on, Mary. None of the rest of them came in? You didn't meet Mr. Sheridan or—" He paused and adjusted a lump of coal in the fire delicately with the poker. "Or one of the sons?"

Mary's glance crossed his, at that, with a flash of utter comprehension. He turned instantly away, but she had begun to laugh again.

"No," she said, "no one except the women, but mamma inquired about the sons thoroughly!"

"Mary!" Mrs. Vertrees protested.

"Oh, most adroitly, too!" laughed the girl. "Only she couldn't help unconsciously turning to look at me—when she did it!"

"Mary Vertrees!"

"Never mind, mamma! Mrs. Sheridan and Miss Sheridan neither of *them* could help unconsciously turning to look at me—speculatively—at the same time! They all three kept looking at me and talking about the oldest son, Mr. James Sheridan, Junior. Mrs. Sheridan said his father is very anxious

---

[7] Two of the foremost painters of the Italian Renaissance, at the height of their fame about the year 1500.

'to get Jim to marry and settle down,' and she assured me that 'Jim is right cultivated.' Another of the sons, the youngest one, caught me looking in the window this afternoon; but they didn't seem to consider him quite one of themselves, somehow, though Mrs. Sheridan mentioned that a couple of years or so ago he had been 'right sick,' and had been to some cure or other. They seemed relieved to bring the subject back to 'Jim' and his virtues—and to look at me! The other brother is the middle one, Roscoe; he's the one that owns the new house across the street, where that young black-sheep of the Lamhorns, Robert, goes so often. I saw a short, dark young man standing on the porch with Robert Lamhorn there the other day, so I suppose that was Roscoe. 'Jim' still lurks in the mists, but I shall meet him to-night. Papa—" She stepped nearer to him so that he had to face her, and his eyes were troubled as he did. There may have been a trouble deep within her own, but she kept their surface merry with laughter. "Papa, Bibbs is the youngest one's name, and Bibbs—to the best of our information—is a lunatic. Roscoe is married. Papa, does it have to be Jim?"

"Mary!" Mrs. Vertrees cried, sharply. "You're outrageous! That's a perfectly horrible way of talking!"

"Well, I'm close to twenty-four," said Mary, turning to her. "I haven't been able to like anybody yet that's asked me to marry him, and maybe I never shall. Until a year or so ago I've had everything I ever wanted in my life—you and papa gave it all to me—and it's about time I began to pay back. Unfortunately, I don't know how to do anything—but something's got to be done."

"But you needn't talk of it like *that!*" insisted the mother, plaintively. "It's not—it's not—"

"No, it's not," said Mary. "I know that!"

"How did they happen to ask you to dinner?" Mr. Vertrees inquired, uneasily. "'Stextrawdn'ry thing!"

"Climbers' hospitality," Mary defined it. "We were so very

cordial and easy! I think Mrs. Sheridan herself might have done it just as any kind old woman on a farm might ask a neighbor, but it was Miss Sheridan who did it. She played around it awhile; you could see she wanted to—she's in a dreadful hurry to get into things—and I fancied she had an idea it might impress that Lamhorn boy to find us there to-night. It's a sort of house-warming dinner, and they talked about it and talked about it—and then the girl got her courage up and blurted out the invitation. And mamma—" Here Mary was once more a victim to incorrigible merriment. "Mamma tried to say yes, and *couldn't!* She swallowed and squealed—I mean you coughed, dear! And then, papa, she said that you and she had promised to go to a lecture at the Emerson Club to-night, but that her daughter would be delighted to come to the Big Show! So there I am, and there's Mr. Jim Sheridan—and there's the clock! Dinner's at seven-thirty!"

And she ran out of the room, scooping up her fallen furs with a gesture of flying grace as she sped.

When she came down, at twenty minutes after seven, her father stood in the hall, at the foot of the stairs, waiting to be her escort through the dark. He looked up and watched her as she descended, and his gaze was fond and proud—and profoundly disturbed. But she smiled and nodded gaily, and, when she reached the floor, put a hand on his shoulder.

"At least no one could suspect me to-night," she said. "I *look* rich, don't I, papa?"

She did. She had a look that worshipful girl friends bravely called "regal." A head taller than her father, she was as straight and jauntily poised as a boy athlete; and her brown hair and her brown eyes were like her mother's, but for the rest she went back to some stronger and livelier ancestor than either of her parents.

"Don't I look too rich to be suspected?" she insisted.

"You look everything beautiful, Mary," he said, huskily.

"And my dress?" She threw open her dark velvet cloak, showing a splendor of white and silver. "Anything better at Nice next winter, do you think?" She laughed, shrouding her glittering figure in the cloak again. "Two years old, and no one would dream it! I did it over."

"You can do anything, Mary."

There was a curious humility in his tone, and something more—a significance not veiled and yet abysmally apologetic. It was as if he suggested something to her and begged her forgiveness in the same breath.

And upon that, for the moment, she became as serious as he. She lifted her hand from his shoulder and then set it back more firmly, so that he should feel the reassurance of its pressure.

"Don't worry," she said, in a low voice and gravely. "I know exactly what you want me to do."

CHAPTER SIX

IT was a brave and lustrous banquet; and a noisy one, too, because there was an orchestra among some plants at one end of the long dining-room, and after a preliminary stiffness the guests were impelled to converse—necessarily at the tops of their voices. The whole company of fifty sat at a great oblong table, improvised for the occasion by carpenters; but, not betraying itself as an improvisation, it seemed a permanent continent of damask and lace, with shores of crystal and silver running up to spreading groves of orchids and lilies and white roses—an inhabited continent, evidently, for there were three marvelous, gleaming buildings: one in the center and one at each end, white miracles wrought by some inspired craftsman in sculptural icing. They were models in miniature, and they represented the Sheridan Building, the Sheridan

Apartments, and the Pump Works. Nearly all the guests recognized them without having to be told what they were, and pronounced the likenesses superb.

The arrangement of the table was visibly baronial. At the head sat the great Thane,[1] with the flower of his family and of the guests about him; then on each side came the neighbors of the "old" house, grading down to vassals and retainers—superintendents, cashiers, heads of departments, and the like—at the foot, where the Thane's lady took her place as a consolation for the less important. Here, too, among the thralls and bondmen, sat Bibbs Sheridan, a meek Banquo,[2] wondering how anybody could look at him and eat.

Nevertheless, there was a vast, continuous eating, for these were wholesome folk who understood that dinner meant something intended for introduction into the system by means of an aperture in the face, devised by nature for that express purpose. And besides, nobody looked at Bibbs.

He was better content to be left to himself; his voice was not strong enough to make itself heard over the hubbub without an exhausting effort, and the talk that went on about him was too fast and too fragmentary for his drawl to keep pace with it. So he felt relieved when each of his neighbors in turn, after a polite inquiry about his health, turned to seek livelier responses in other directions. For the talk went on with the eating, incessantly. It rose over the throbbing of the orchestra and the clatter and clinking of silver and china and glass, and there was a mighty babble.

"Yes, sir! Started without a dollar." . . . "Yellow flounces on the overskirt—" . . . "I says, 'Wilkie, your department's got to go bigger this year,' I says." . . . "Fifteen per cent. turnover in thirty-one weeks." . . . "One of the biggest men

---

[1] The name by which minor nobles were known in Anglo-Saxon times, meaning literally *heroic warrior*.

[2] In Shakespeare's play *Macbeth*, Banquo was slain treacherously by Macbeth. His ghost appears at the coronation feast to mock and threaten Macbeth.

in the biggest—" . . . "The wife says she'll have to let out my pants if my appetite—" . . . "Say, did you see that statue of a Turk in the hall? One of the finest things I ever—" . . . "'Not a dollar, not a nickel, not one red cent do you get out o' me,' I says, and so he ups and—" . . . "Yes, the baby makes four they've lost, now." . . . "Well, they got their raise, and they went in big." . . . "Yes, sir! Not a dollar to his name, and look at what—" . . . "You wait! The population of this town's goin' to hit the million mark before she stops." . . . "Well, if you can show me a bigger deal than—"

And through the interstices of this clamoring Bibbs could hear the continual booming of his father's heavy voice, and once he caught the sentence, "Yes, young lady, that's just what did it for me, and that's just what 'll do it for my boys— they got to make two blades o' grass grow where one grew before!" It was his familiar flourish, an old story to Bibbs, and now jovially declaimed for the edification of Mary Vertrees.

It was a great night for Sheridan—the very crest of his wave. He sat there knowing himself Thane and master by his own endeavor; and his big, smooth, red face grew more and more radiant with good will and with the simplest, happiest, most boylike vanity. He was the picture of health, of good cheer, and of power on a holiday. He had thirty teeth, none bought, and showed most of them when he laughed; his grizzled hair was thick, and as unruly as a farm laborer's; his chest was deep and big beneath its vast façade of starched white linen, where little diamonds twinkled, circling three large pearls; his hands were stubby and strong, and he used them freely in gestures of marked picturesqueness; and, though he had grown fat at chin and waist and wrist, he had not lost the look of readiness and activity.

He dominated the table, shouting jocular questions and railleries at every one. His idea was that when people were having a good time they were noisy; and his own additions to the hubbub increased his pleasure, and, of course, met the warmest encouragement from his guests. Edith had discovered that he had very foggy notions of the difference between a band and an orchestra, and when it was made clear to him he had held out for a band until Edith threatened tears; but the size of the orchestra they hired consoled him, and he had now no regrets in the matter.

He kept time to the music continually—with his feet, or pounding on the table with his fist, and sometimes with spoon or knife upon his plate or a glass, without permitting these side-products to interfere with the real business of eating and shouting.

"Tell 'em to play 'Nancy Lee'!" [3] he would bellow down the length of the table to his wife, while the musicians were in the midst of the "Toreador" [4] song, perhaps. "Ask that fellow if they don't know 'Nancy Lee'!" And when the leader would shake his head apologetically in answer to an obedient shriek from Mrs. Sheridan, the "Toreador" continuing vehemently, Sheridan would roar half-remembered fragments of "Nancy Lee," naturally mingling some Bizet with the air of that uxorious tribute.

"Oh, there she stands and waves her hands while I'm away!
"A sail-er's wife a sail-er's star should be! Yo ho, oh, oh!
"Oh, Nancy, Nancy, Nancy Lee! Oh, Na-hancy Lee!

"Hay, there, old lady!" he would bellow. "Tell 'em to play 'In the Gloaming.' *In the gloaming, oh, my darling, la-la-lum-tee—* Well, if they don't know that, what's the matter with 'Larboard Watch, Ahoy'? *That's* good music! That's the kind o' music *I* like! Come on, now! Mrs. Callin, get 'em singin' down in your part o' the table. What's the matter you folks down there, anyway? Larboard watch, ahoy!

"What joy he feels, as—ta-tum-dum-tee-dee-dum steals.
La-a-r-board watch, ahoy!"

[3] A rollicking sailor song written by Michael Maybrick, under the pen name of Stephen Adams.

[4] A song from *Carmen*, an opera written by a French composer, Bizet.

No external bubbling contributed to this effervescence: the
Sheridans' table had never borne wine, and, more because of
timidity about it than conviction, it bore none now; though
"mineral waters" were copiously poured from bottles wrapped,
for some reason, in napkins, and proved wholly satisfactory
to almost all of the guests. And certainly no wine could have
inspired more turbulent good spirits in the host. Not even
Bibbs was an alloy in this night's happiness, for, as Mrs.
Sheridan had said, he had "plans for Bibbs"—plans which
were going to straighten out some things that had gone
wrong.

So he pounded the table and boomed his echoes of old
songs, and then, forgetting these, would renew his friendly
railleries, or perhaps, turning to Mary Vertrees, who sat near
him, round the corner of the table at his right, he would become autobiographical. Gentlemen less naïve than he had paid
her that tribute, for she was a girl who inspired the autobiographical impulse in every man who met her—it needed
but the sight of her.

The dinner seemed, somehow, to center about Mary Vertrees and the jocund host as a play centers about its hero and
heroine; they were the rubicund king and the starry princess
of this spectacle—they paid court to each other, and everybody paid court to them. Down near the sugar Pump Works,
where Bibbs sat, there was audible speculation and admiration. "Wonder who that lady is—makin' such a hit with the
old man." "Must be some heiress." "Heiress? Golly, I guess
I could stand it to marry rich, then!"

Edith and Sibyl were radiant: at first they had watched
Miss Vertrees with an almost haggard anxiety, wondering
what disastrous effect Sheridan's pastoral gaieties—and other
things—would have upon her, but she seemed delighted with
everything, and with him most of all. She treated him as if
he were some delicious, foolish old joke that she understood
perfectly, laughing at him almost violently when he bragged

—probably his first experience of that kind in his life. It enchanted him.

As he proclaimed to the table, she had "a way with her." She had, indeed, as Roscoe Sheridan, upon her right, discovered just after the feast began. Since his marriage three years before, no lady had bestowed upon him so protracted a full view of brilliant eyes; and, with the look, his lovely neighbor said—and it was her first speech to him—

"I hope you're very susceptible, Mr. Sheridan!"

Honest Roscoe was taken aback, and, "Why?" was all he managed to say.

She repeated the look deliberately, which was noted, with a mystification equal to his own, by his sister across the table. No one, reflected Edith, could imagine Mary Vertrees the sort of girl who would "really flirt" with married men—she was obviously the "opposite of all that." Edith defined her as a "thoroughbred," a "nice girl"; and the look given to Roscoe was astounding. Roscoe's wife saw it, too, and she was another whom it puzzled—though not because its recipient was married.

"Because!" said Mary Vertrees, replying to Roscoe's monosyllable. "And also because we're next-door neighbors at table, and it's dull times ahead for both of us if we don't get along."

Roscoe was a literal young man, all stocks and bonds, and he had been brought up to believe that when a man married he "married and settled down." It was "all right," he felt, for a man as old as his father to pay florid compliments to as pretty a girl as this Miss Vertrees, but for himself—"a young married man"—it wouldn't do; it wouldn't even be quite moral. He knew that young married people might have friendships, like his wife's for Lamhorn; but Sibyl and Lamhorn never "flirted"—they were always very matter-of-fact with each other. Roscoe would have been troubled if Sibyl had ever told Lamhorn she hoped he was susceptible.

"Yes—we're neighbors," he said, awkwardly.

"Next-door neighbors in houses, too," she added.

"No, not exactly. I live across the street."

"Why, no!" she exclaimed, and seemed startled. "Your mother told me this afternoon that you lived at home."

"Yes, of course I live at home. I built that new house across the street."

"But you—" She paused, confused, and then slowly a deep color came into her cheek. "But I understood—"

"No," he said; "my wife and I lived with the old folks the first year, but that's all. Edith and Jim live with them, of course."

"I—I see," she said, the deep color still deepening as she turned from him and saw, written upon a card before the gentleman at her left, the name, "Mr. James Sheridan, Jr." And from that moment Roscoe had little enough cause for wondering what he ought to reply to her disturbing coquetries.

Mr. James Sheridan had been anxiously waiting for the dazzling visitor to "get through with old Roscoe," as he thought of it, and give a bachelor a chance. "Old Roscoe" was the younger, but he had always been the steady wheel-horse of the family. Jim was "steady" enough, but was considered livelier than Roscoe, which in truth is not saying much for Jim's liveliness. As their father habitually boasted, both brothers were "capable, hard-working young business men," and the principal difference between them was merely that which resulted from Jim's being still a bachelor. Physically they were of the same type: dark of eyes and of hair, fresh-colored and thick-set, and though Roscoe was several inches taller than Jim, neither was of the height, breadth, or depth of the father. Both wore young business men's mustaches, and either could have sat for the tailor-shop lithographs of young business men wearing "rich suitings in dark mixtures."

Jim, approving warmly of his neighbor's profile, perceived her access of color, which increased his approbation. "What's

that old Roscoe saying to you, Miss Vertrees?" he asked.
"These young married men are mighty forward nowadays,
but you mustn't let 'em make you blush."

"Am I blushing?" she said. "Are you sure?" And with that
she gave him ample opportunity to make sure, repeating with
interest the look wasted upon Roscoe. "I think you must be
mistaken," she continued. "I think it's your brother who is
blushing. I've thrown him into confusion."

"How?"

She laughed, and then, leaning to him a little, said in a tone
as confidential as she could make it, under cover of the uproar, "By trying to begin with him a courtship I meant for
you!"

This might well be a style new to Jim; and it was. He supposed it a nonsensical form of badinage, and yet it took his
breath. He realized that he wished what she said to be the
literal truth, and he was instantly snared by that realization.

"By George!" he said. "I guess you're the kind of girl that
can say anything—yes, and get away with it, too!"

She laughed again—in her way, so that he could not tell
whether she was laughing at him or at herself or at the nonsense she was talking; and she said:

"But you see I don't care whether I get away with it or not.
I wish you'd tell me frankly if you think I've got a chance to
get away with *you?*"

"More like if you've got a chance to get away *from* me!"
Jim was inspired to reply. "Not one in the world, especially
after beginning by making fun of me like that."

"I mightn't be so much in fun as you think," she said, regarding him with sudden gravity.

"Well," said Jim, in simple honesty, "you're a funny girl!"

Her gravity continued an instant longer. "I may not turn
out to be funny for *you.*"

"So long as you turn out to be anything at all for me, I expect I can manage to be satisfied." And with that, to his own

surprise, it was his turn to blush, whereupon she laughed again.

"Yes," he said, plaintively, not wholly lacking intuition, "I can see you're the sort of girl that would laugh the minute you see a man really means anything!"

"'Laugh'!" she cried, gaily. "Why, it might be a matter of life and death! But if you want tragedy, I'd better put the question at once, considering the mistake I made with your brother."

Jim was dazed. She seemed to be playing a little game of mockery and nonsense with him, but he had glimpses of a flashing danger in it; he was but too sensible of being out-classed, and had somewhere a consciousness that he could never quite know this giddy and alluring lady, no matter how long it pleased her to play with him. But he mightily wanted her to keep on playing with him.

"Put what question?" he said, breathlessly.

"As you are a new neighbor of mine and of my family," she returned, speaking slowly and with a cross-examiner's severity, "I think it would be well for me to know at once whether you are already walking out with any young lady or not. Mr. Sheridan, think well! Are you spoken for?"

"Not yet," he gasped. "Are you?"

"*No!*" she cried, and with that they both laughed again; and the pastime proceeded, increasing both in its gaiety and in its gravity.

Observing its continuance, Mr. Robert Lamhorn, opposite, turned from a lively conversation with Edith and remarked covertly to Sibyl that Miss Vertrees was "starting rather pic-turesquely with Jim." And he added, languidly, "Do you suppose she *would?*"

For the moment Sibyl gave no sign of having heard him, but seemed interested in the clasp of a long "rope" of pearls, a loop of which she was allowing to swing from her fingers, resting her elbow upon the table and following with her eyes

he twinkle of diamonds and platinum in the clasp at the end
of the loop. She wore many jewels. She was pretty, but hers
was not the kind of prettiness to be loaded with too sump-
uous accessories, and jeweled head-dresses are dangerous—
hey may emphasize the wrongness of the wrong wearer.

"I said Miss Vertrees seems to be starting pretty strong with
im," repeated Mr. Lamhorn.

"I heard you." There was a latent discontent always somewhere in her eyes, no matter what she threw upon the surface
o cover it, and just now she did not care to cover it; she
ooked sullen. "Starting any stronger than you did with
Edith?" she inquired.

"Oh, keep the peace!" he said, crossly. "That's off, of
course."

"You haven't been making her see it this evening—pre-
isely," said Sibyl, looking at him steadily. "You've talked to
ner for—"

"For Heaven's sake," he begged, "keep the peace!"

"Well, what have you just been doing?"

"'Sh!" he said. "Listen to your father-in-law."

Sheridan was booming and braying louder than ever, the
orchestra having begun to play "The Rosary," to his vast
content.

"*I count them over, la-la-tum-tee-dum,*" he roared, beating
he measures with his fork. "*Each hour a pearl, each pearl
ee-dum-tum-dum—* What's the matter of all you folks?
Why'n't you *sing?* Miss Vertrees, I bet a thousand dollars
ou sing! Why'n't—"

"Mr. Sheridan," she said, turning cheerfully from the ardent
im, "you don't know what you interrupted! Your son isn't
ised to my rough ways, and my soldier's wooing frightens
him, but I think he was about to say something important."

"I'll say something important to him if he doesn't!" the
ather threatened, more delighted with her than ever. "By
gosh! if I was his age—or a widower right *now—*"

"Oh, wait!" cried Mary. "If they'd only make less noise!
I want Mrs. Sheridan to hear."

"She'd say the same," he shouted. "She'd tell me I was
mighty slow if I couldn't get ahead o' Jim. Why, when I was
his age—"

"You must listen to your father," Mary interrupted, turning
to Jim, who had grown red again. "He's going to tell us how
when he was your age, he made those two blades of grass
grow out of a teacup—and you could see for yourself he
didn't get them out of his sleeve."

At that Sheridan pounded the table till it jumped. "Look
here, young lady!" he roared. "Some o' these days I'm either
goin' to slap you—or I'm goin' to kiss you!"

Edith looked aghast; she was afraid this was indeed "too
awful," but Mary Vertrees burst into ringing laughter.

"Both!" she cried. "Both! The one to make me forget the
other!"

"But which—" he began, and then suddenly gave forth such
stentorian trumpetings of mirth that for once the whole table
stopped to listen. "Jim," he roared, "if you don't propose to
that girl to-night I'll send you back to the machine-shop with
Bibbs!"

And Bibbs—down among the retainers by the sugar Pump
Works, and watching Mary Vertrees as a ragged boy in the
street might watch a rich little girl in a garden—Bibbs heard.
He heard—and he knew what his father's plans were now.

CHAPTER SEVEN

Mrs. vertrees "sat up" for her daughter, Mr. Vertrees having retired after a restless evening, not much soothed
by the society of his Landseers. Mary had taken a key, insist-
ing that he should not come for her and seeming confiden-

that she would not lack for escort; nor did the sequel prove her confidence unwarranted. But Mrs. Vertrees had a long vigil of it.

She was not the woman to make herself easy—no servant had ever seen her in a wrapper—and with her hair and her dress and her shoes just what they had been when she returned from the afternoon's call, she sat through the slow night hours in a stiff little chair under the gaslight in her own room, which was directly over the "front hall." There, book in hand, she employed the time in her own reminiscences, though it was her belief that she was reading Madame de Rémusat's.[1]

Her thoughts went backward into her life and into her husband's; and the deeper into the past they went, the brighter the pictures they brought her—and there is tragedy. Like her husband, she thought backward because she did not dare think forward definitely. What thinking forward this troubled couple ventured took the form of a slender hope which neither of them could have borne to hear put in words, and yet they had talked it over, day after day, from the very hour when they heard Sheridan was to build his New House next door. For—so quickly does any ideal of human behavior become an antique—their youth was of the innocent old days, so dead! of "breeding" and "gentility," and no craft had been more straitly trained upon them than that of talking about things without mentioning them. Herein was marked the most vital difference between Mr. and Mrs. Vertrees and their big new neighbor. Sheridan, though his youth was of the same epoch, knew nothing of such matters. He had been chopping wood for the morning fire in the country grocery while they were still dancing.

[1] A noted beauty of the court of Napoleon I, and an intimate friend of Josephine, Napoleon's wife. Since her husband was a Chamberlain of Napoleon's, she was acquainted with the intimate life of the court and left an account of it in her *Memoirs*, published in 1879.

It was after one o'clock when Mrs. Vertrees heard steps and the delicate clinking of the key in the lock, and then, with the opening of the door, Mary's laugh and, "Yes—if you aren't afraid—to-morrow!"

The door closed, and she rushed up-stairs, bringing with her a breath of cold and bracing air into her mother's room. "Yes," she said, before Mrs. Vertrees could speak, "he brought me home!"

She let her cloak fall upon the bed, and drawing an old red-velvet rocking-chair forward, sat beside her mother, after giving her a light pat upon the shoulder and a hearty kiss upon the cheek.

"Mamma!" Mary exclaimed, when Mrs. Vertrees had expressed a hope that she had enjoyed the evening and had not caught cold. "Why don't you ask me?"

This inquiry obviously made her mother uncomfortable. "I don't—" she faltered. "Ask you what, Mary?"

"How I got along and what he's like."

"Mary!"

"Oh, it isn't distressing!" said Mary. "And I got along so fast—" She broke off to laugh; continuing then, "But that's the way I went at it, of course. We *are* in a hurry, aren't we?"

"I don't know what you mean," Mrs. Vertrees insisted, shaking her head plaintively.

"Yes," said Mary, "I'm going out in his car with him to-morrow afternoon, and to the theater the next night—but I stopped it there. You see, after you give the first push, you must leave it to them while *you* pretend to run away!"

"My dear, I don't know what to—"

"What to make of anything!" Mary finished for her. "So that's all right! Now I'll tell you all about it. It was gorgeous and deafening and teetotal. We could have lived a year on it. I'm not good at figures, but I calculated that if we lived six months on poor old Charlie and Ned and the station-wagon and the Victoria, we could manage at least twice as long on the cost of the 'house-warming.' I think the orchids alone would have lasted us a couple of months. There they were, before me, but I couldn't steal 'em and sell 'em, and so—well, so I did what I could!"

She leaned back and laughed reassuringly to her troubled mother. "It seemed to be a success—what I could," she said, clasping her hands behind her neck and stirring the rocker to motion as a rhythmic accompaniment to her narrative. "The girl Edith and her sister-in-law, Mrs. Roscoe Sheridan, were too anxious about the effect of things on me. The father's worth a bushel of both of them, if they knew it. He's what he is. I like him." She paused reflectively, continuing, "Edith's 'interested' in that Lamhorn boy; he's good-looking and not stupid, but I think he's—" She interrupted herself with a cheery outcry: "Oh! I mustn't be calling him names! If he's trying to make Edith like him, I ought to respect him as a colleague."

"I don't understand a thing you're talking about," Mrs. Vertrees complained.

"All the better! Well, he's a bad lot, that Lamhorn boy; everybody's always known that, but the Sheridans don't know the everybodies that know. He sat between Edith and Mrs. Roscoe Sheridan. *She's* like those people you wondered about at the theater, the last time we went—dressed in ball-gowns; bound to show their clothes and jewels *some*where! She flatters the father, and so did I, for that matter—but not that way. I treated him outrageously!"

"Mary!"

"That's what flattered him. After dinner he made the whole regiment of us follow him all over the house, while he lectured like a guide on the Palatine.[2] He gave dimensions and costs, and the whole b'ilin' of 'em listened as if they thought he intended to make them a present of the house. What he

[2] One of the seven hills of Rome, on which legend says Romulus built his city and on which the palaces of the Caesars stood.

was proudest of was the plumbing and that Bay of Naples panorama in the hall. He made us look at all the plumbing— bath-rooms and everywhere else—and then he made us look at the Bay of Naples. He said it was a hundred and eleven feet long, but I think it's more. And he led us all into the ready-made library to see a poem Edith had taken a prize with at school. They'd had it printed in gold letters and framed in mother-of-pearl. But the poem itself was rather simple and wistful and nice—he read it to us, though Edith tried to stop him. She was modest about it, and said she'd never written anything else. And then, after a while, Mrs. Roscoe Sheridan asked me to come across the street to her house with them—her husband and Edith and Mr. Lamhorn and Jim Sheridan—"

Mrs. Vertrees was shocked. "'Jim'!" she exclaimed. "Mary, *please*—"

"Of course," said Mary. "I'll make it as easy for you as I can, mamma. Mr. James Sheridan, Junior. We went over there, and Mrs. Roscoe explained that 'the men were all dying for a drink,' though I noticed that Mr. Lamhorn was the only one near death's door on that account. Edith and Mrs. Roscoe said they knew I'd been bored at the dinner. They were ob- jectionably apologetic about it, and they seemed to think *now* we were going to have a 'good time' to make up for it. But I hadn't been bored at the dinner, I'd been amused; and the 'good time' at Mrs. Roscoe's was horribly, horribly stupid."

"But, Mary," her mother began, "is—is—" And she seemed unable to complete the question.

"Never mind, mamma, *I*'ll say it. Is Mr. James Sheridan, Junior, stupid? I'm sure he's not at all stupid about business. Otherwise— Oh, what right have I to be calling people 'stupid' because they're not exactly my kind? On the big dinner-table they had enormous icing models of the Sheridan Building—"

"Oh no!" Mrs. Vertrees cried. "Surely not!"

"Yes, and two other things of that kind—I don't know what. But, after all, I wondered if they were so bad. If I'd been at a dinner at a palace in Italy, and a relief or inscription on one of the old silver pieces had referred to some great deed or achievement of the family, I shouldn't have felt superior; I'd have thought it picturesque and stately—I'd have been impressed. And what's the real difference? The icing is temporary, and that's much more modest, isn't it? And why is it vulgar to feel important more on account of something you've done yourself than because of something one of your ancestors did? Besides, if we go back a few generations, we've all got such hundreds of ancestors it seems idiotic to go picking out one or two to be proud of ourselves about. Well, then, mamma, I managed not to feel superior to Mr. James Sheridan, Junior, because he didn't see anything out of place in the Sheridan Building in sugar."

Mrs. Vertrees's expression had lost none of its anxiety pending the conclusion of this lively bit of analysis, and she shook her head gravely. "My dear, dear child," she said, "it seems to me— It looks— I'm afraid—"

"Say as much of it as you can, mamma," said Mary, encouragingly. "I can get it, if you'll just give me one key-word."

"Everything you say," Mrs. Vertrees began, timidly, "seems to have the air of— It is as if you were seeking to—to make yourself—"

"Oh, I see! You mean I sound as if I were trying to force myself to like him."

"Not exactly, Mary. That wasn't quite what I meant," said Mrs. Vertrees, speaking direct untruth with perfect unconsciousness. "But you said that—that you found the latter part of the evening at young Mrs. Sheridan's unentertaining—"

"And as Mr. James Sheridan was there, and I saw more of him than at dinner, and had a horribly stupid time in spite of that, you think I—" And then it was Mary who left the deduction unfinished.

Mrs. Vertrees nodded; and though both the mother and daughter understood, Mary felt it better to make the understanding definite.

"Well," she asked, gravely, "is there anything else I can do? You and papa don't want me to do anything that distresses me, and so, as this is the only thing to be done, it seems it's up to me not to let it distress me. That's all there is about it, isn't it?"

"But nothing *must* distress you!" the mother cried.

"That's what I say!" said Mary, cheerfully. "And so it doesn't. It's all right." She rose and took her cloak over her arm, as if to go to her own room. But on the way to the door she stopped, and stood leaning against the foot of the bed, contemplating a threadbare rug at her feet. "Mother, you've told me a thousand times that it doesn't really matter whom a girl marries."

"No, no!" Mrs. Vertrees protested. "I never said such a—"

"No, not in words; I mean what you *meant*. It's true, isn't it, that marriage really is 'not a bed of roses, but a field of battle'? To get right down to it, a girl could fight it out with anybody, couldn't she? One man as well as another?"

"Oh, my dear! I'm sure your father and I—"

"Yes, yes," said Mary, indulgently. "I don't mean you and papa. But isn't it propinquity that makes marriages? So many people say so, there must be something in it."

"Mary, I can't bear for you to talk like that." And Mrs. Vertrees lifted pleading eyes to her daughter—eyes that begged to be spared. "It sounds—almost reckless!"

Mary caught the appeal, came to her, and kissed her gaily. "Never fret, dear! I'm not likely to do anything I don't want to—I've always been too thorough-going a little pig! And if it *is* propinquity that does our choosing for us, well, at least no girl in the world could ask for more of *that!* How could there be any more propinquity than the very house next door?"

She gave her mother a final kiss and went gaily all the way to the door this time, pausing for her postscript with her hand on the knob. "Oh, the one that caught me looking in the window, mamma, the youngest one—"

"Did he speak of it?" Mrs. Vertrees asked, apprehensively.

"No. He didn't speak at all, that I saw, to any one. I didn't meet him. But he isn't insane, I'm sure; or if he is, he has long intervals when he's not. Mr. James Sheridan mentioned that he lived at home when he was 'well enough'; and it may be he's only an invalid. He looks dreadfully ill, but he has pleasant eyes, and it struck me that if—if one were in the Sheridan family"—she laughed a little ruefully—"he might be interesting to talk to sometimes, when there was too much stocks and bonds. I didn't see him after dinner."

"There must be something wrong with him," said Mrs. Vertrees. "They'd have introduced him if there weren't."

"I don't know. He's been ill so much and away so much —sometimes people like that just don't seem to 'count' in a family. His father spoke of sending him back to a machine-shop of some sort; I suppose he meant when the poor thing gets better. I glanced at him just then, when Mr. Sheridan mentioned him, and he happened to be looking straight at me; and he was pathetic-looking enough before that, but the most tragic change came over him. He seemed just to die, right there at the table!"

"You mean when his father spoke of sending him to the shop place?"

"Yes."

"Mr. Sheridan must be very unfeeling."

"No," said Mary, thoughtfully, "I don't think he is; but he might be uncomprehending, and certainly he's the kind of man to do anything he once sets out to do. But I wish I hadn't been looking at that poor boy just then! I'm afraid I'll keep remembering—"

"I wouldn't." Mrs. Vertrees smiled faintly, and in her smile there was the remotest ghost of a genteel roguishness. "I'd keep my mind on pleasanter things, Mary."

Mary laughed and nodded. "Yes, indeed! Plenty pleasant enough, and probably, if all were known, too good—even for me!"

And when she had gone Mrs. Vertrees drew a long breath, as if a burden were off her mind, and, smiling, began to undress in a gentle reverie.

CHAPTER EIGHT

EDITH, glancing casually into the "ready-made" library, stopped abruptly, seeing Bibbs there alone. He was standing before the pearl-framed and golden-lettered poem, musingly inspecting it. He read it:

FUGITIVE

I will forget the things that sting:
  The lashing look, the barbèd word.
I know the very hands that fling
  The stones at me had never stirred
To anger but for their own scars.
  They've suffered so, that's why they strike.
I'll keep my heart among the stars
  Where none shall hunt it out. Oh, like
These wounded ones I must not be,
  For, wounded, I might strike in turn!
So, none shall hurt me. Far and free
  Where my heart flies no one shall learn.

"Bibbs!" Edith's voice was angry, and her color deepened suddenly as she came into the room, preceded by a scent of violets much more powerful than that warranted by the actual bunch of them upon the lapel of her coat.

Bibbs did not turn his head, but wagged it solemnly, seeming depressed by the poem. "Pretty young, isn't it?" he said. "There must have been something about your looks that got the prize, Edith; I can't believe the poem did it."

She glanced hurriedly over her shoulder and spoke sharply, but in a low voice: "I don't think it's very nice of you to bring it up at all, Bibbs. I'd like a chance to forget the whole silly business. *I* didn't want them to frame it, and I wish to goodness papa'd quit talking about it; but here, that night, after the dinner, didn't he go and read it aloud to the whole crowd of 'em! And then they all wanted to know what other poems I'd written, and why I didn't keep it up and write some more, and if I didn't, why didn't I, and why this and why that, till I thought I'd die of shame!"

"You could tell 'em you had writer's cramp," Bibbs suggested.

"I couldn't tell 'em anything! I just choke with mortification every time anybody speaks of the thing."

Bibbs looked grieved. "The poem isn't *that* bad, Edith. You see, you were only seventeen when you wrote it."

"Oh, hush up!" she snapped. "I wish it had burnt my fingers the first time I touched it. Then I might have had sense enough to leave it where it was. I had no business to take it, and I've been ashamed—"

"No, no," he said, comfortingly. "It was the very most flattering thing ever happened to me. It was almost my last flight before I went to the machine-shop, and it's pleasant to think somebody liked it enough to—"

"But I *don't* like it!" she exclaimed. "I don't even understand it—and papa made so much fuss over its getting the prize, I just hate it! The truth is I never dreamed it 'd get the prize."

"Maybe they expected father to endow the school," Bibbs murmured.

"Well, I had to have something to turn in, and I couldn't write a *line!* I hate poetry, anyhow; and Bobby Lamhorn's always teasing me about how I 'keep my heart among the stars.' He makes it seem such a mushy kind of thing, the way he says it. I hate it!"

"You'll have to live it down, Edith. Perhaps abroad and under another name you might find—"

"Oh, hush up! I'll hire some one to steal it and burn it the first chance I get." She turned away petulantly, moving to the door. "I'd like to think I could hope to hear the last of it before I die!"

"Edith!" he called, as she went into the hall.

"What's the matter?"

"I want to ask you: Do I really look better, or have you just got used to me?"

"What on earth do you mean?" she said, coming back as far as the threshold.

"When I first came you couldn't look at me," Bibbs explained, in his impersonal way. "But I've noticed you look at me lately. I wondered if I'd—"

"It's because you look so much better," she told him, cheerfully. "This month you've been here's done you no end of good. It's the change."

"Yes, that's what they said at the sanitarium—the change."

"You look worse than 'most anybody *I* ever saw," said Edith, with supreme candor. "But I don't know much about it. I've never seen a corpse in my life, and I've never even seen anybody that was terribly sick, so you mustn't judge by me. I only know you do look better, I'm glad to say. But you're right about my not being able to look at you at first.

You had a kind of whiteness that— Well, you're almost as thin, I suppose, but you've got more just ordinarily pale; not that ghastly look. Anybody could look at you now, Bibbs, and not—not get—"

"Sick?"

"Well—almost that!" she laughed. "And you're getting a better color every day, Bibbs; you really are. You're really getting along splendidly."

"I—I'm afraid so," he said, ruefully.

"'Afraid so'! Well, if you aren't the queerest! I suppose you mean father might send you back to the machine-shop if you get well enough. I heard him say something about it the night of the—" The jingle of a distant bell interrupted her, and she glanced at her watch. "Bobby Lamhorn! I'm going to motor him out to look at a place in the country. Afternoon, Bibbs!"

When she had gone, Bibbs mooned pessimistically from shelf to shelf, his eye wandering among the titles of the books. The library consisted almost entirely of handsome "uniform editions": Irving, Poe, Cooper, Goldsmith, Scott, Byron, Burns, Longfellow, Tennyson, Hume, Gibbon, Prescott, Thackeray, Dickens, De Musset, Balzac, Gautier, Flaubert, Goethe, Schiller, Dante, and Tasso. There were shelves and shelves of encyclopedias, of anthologies, of "famous classics," of "Oriental masterpieces," of "masterpieces of oratory," and more shelves of "selected libraries" of "literature," of "the drama," and of "modern science." They made an effective decoration for the room, all these big, expensive books, with a glossy binding here and there twinkling a reflection of the flames that crackled in the splendid Gothic fireplace; but Bibbs had an impression that the bookseller who selected them considered them a relief, and that white-jacket considered them a burden of dust, and that nobody else considered them at all. Himself, he disturbed not one.

There came a chime of bells from a clock in another part of the house, and white-jacket appeared beamingly in the doorway, bearing furs. "Awready, Mist' Bibbs," he announced. "You' ma say wrap up wawm f' you' ride, an' she cain' go with you to-day, an' not f'git go see you' pa at fo' 'clock. Aw ready, suh."

He equipped Bibbs for the daily drive Dr. Gurney had commanded; and in the manner of a master of ceremonies unctuously led the way. In the hall they passed the Moor, and Bibbs paused before it while white-jacket opened the door with a flourish and waved condescendingly to the chauffeur in the car which stood waiting in the driveway.

"It seems to me I asked you what you thought about this 'statue' when I first came home, George," said Bibbs, thoughtfully. "What did you tell me?"

"Yessuh!" George chuckled, perfectly understanding that for some unknown reason Bibbs enjoyed hearing him repeat his opinion of the Moor. "You ast me when you firs' come home, an' you ast me nex' day, an' mighty near ev'y day all time you been here; an' las' Sunday you ast me twicet." He shook his head solemnly. "Look to me mus' be somep'm mighty lami*dal* 'bout 'at statue!"

"Mighty what?"

"Mighty lami*dal!*" George burst out laughing. "What *do* 'at word mean, Mist' Bibbs?"

"It's new to me, George. Where did you hear it?"

"I nev' *did* hear it!" said George. "I uz dess sittin' thinkum to myse'f an' she pop in my head—'lami*dal*,' dess like 'at! An' she soun' so good, seem like she *gotta* mean somep'm!"

"Come to think of it, I believe she does mean something. Why, yes—"

"Do she?" cried George. "*What* she mean?"

"It's exactly the word for the statue," said Bibbs, with conviction, as he climbed into the car. "It's a lami*dal* statue."

"Hiyi!" George exulted. "Man! Man! Listen! Well, suh,

she mighty lami*dal* statue, but lami*dal* statue heap o' trouble to dus'!"

"I expect she is!" said Bibbs, as the engine began to churn; and a moment later he was swept from sight.

George turned to Mist' Jackson, who had been listening benevolently in the hallway. "Same he aw-ways say, Mist' Jackson—'I expec' she is!' Ev'y day he try t' git me talk 'bout 'at lami*dal* statue, an' aw-ways, las' thing *he* say, 'I expec' she is!' You know, Mist' Jackson, if he git well, 'at young man go' be pride o' the family, Mist' Jackson. Yessuh, right now I pick 'im fo' firs' money!"

"Look out with all 'at money, George!" Jackson warned the enthusiast. "White folks 'n 'is house know 'im heap longer 'n you. You the on'y man bettin' on 'im!"

"I risk it!" cried George, merrily. "I put her all on now— ev'y cent! 'At boy's go' be flower o' the flock!"

This singular prophecy, founded somewhat recklessly upon gratitude for the meaning of "lami*dal*," differed radically from another prediction concerning Bibbs, set forth for the benefit of a fair auditor some twenty minutes later. Jim Sheridan, skirting the edges of the town with Mary Vertrees beside him, in his own swift machine, encountered the invalid upon the highroad. The two cars were going in opposite directions, and the occupants of Jim's had only a swaying glimpse of Bibbs sitting alone on the back seat—his white face startlingly white against cap and collar of black fur—but he flashed into recognition as Mary bowed to him.

Jim waved his left hand carelessly. "It's Bibbs, taking his constitutional," he explained.

"Yes, I know," said Mary. "I bowed to him, too, though I've never met him. In fact, I've only seen him once—no, twice. I hope he won't think I'm very bold, bowing to him."

"I doubt if he noticed it," said honest Jim.

"Oh, oh!" she cried.

"What's the trouble?"

"I'm almost sure people notice it when I bow to them."

"Oh, I see!" said Jim. "Of course they would ordinarily, but Bibbs is funny."

"Is he? How?" she asked. "He strikes me as anything but funny."

"Well, I'm his brother," Jim said, deprecatingly, "but *I* don't know what he's like, and, to tell the truth, I've never felt exactly like I *was* his brother, the way I do Roscoe. Bibbs never did seem more than half alive to me. Of course Roscoe and I are older, and when we were boys we were too big to play with him, but he never played anyway, with boys his own age. He'd rather just sit in the house and mope around by himself. Nobody could ever get him to *do* anything; you can't get him to do anything now. He never had any *life* in him; and honestly, if he is my brother, I must say I believe Bibbs Sheridan is the laziest man God ever made! Father put him in the machine-shop over at the Pump Works—best thing in the world for him—and he was just plain no account. It made him sick! If he'd had the right kind of energy—the kind father's got, for instance, or Roscoe, either—why, it wouldn't made him sick. And suppose it was either of them —yes, or me, either—do you think any of us would have stopped if we *were* sick? Not much! I hate to say it, but Bibbs Sheridan 'll never amount to anything as long as he lives."

Mary looked thoughtful. "Is there any particular reason why he should?" she asked.

"Good gracious!" he exclaimed. "You don't mean that, do you? Don't you believe in a man's knowing how to earn his salt, no matter how much money his father's got? Hasn't the business of this world got to be carried on by everybody in it? Are we going to lay back on what we've got and see other fellows get ahead of us? If we've got big things already, isn't it every man's business to go ahead and make 'em bigger? Isn't it his duty? Don't we always want to get bigger and bigger?"

"Ye-es—I don't know. But I feel rather sorry for your brother. He looked so lonely—and sick."

"He's gettin' better every day," Jim said. "Dr. Gurney says so. There's nothing much the matter with him, really—it's nine-tenths imaginary. 'Nerves'! People that are willing to be busy don't have nervous diseases, because they don't have time to imagine 'em."

"You mean his trouble is really mental?"

"Oh, he's not a lunatic," said Jim. "He's just queer. Sometimes he'll say something right bright, but half the time what he says is 'way off the subject, or else there isn't any sense to it at all. For instance, the other day I heard him talkin' to one of the darkies in the hall. The darky asked him what time he wanted the car for his drive, and anybody else in the world would have just said what time they *did* want it, and that would have been all there was to it; but here's what Bibbs says, and I heard him with my own ears. 'What time do I want the car?' he says. 'Well, now, that depends—that depends,' he says. He talks slow like that, you know. 'I'll tell you what time I want the car, George,' he says, 'if you'll tell *me* what you think of this statue!' That's exactly his words! Asked the darky what he thought of that Arab Edith and mother bought for the hall!"

Mary pondered upon this. "He might have been in fun, perhaps," she suggested.

"Askin' a darky what he thought of a piece of statuary—of a work of art! Where on earth would be the fun of that? No, you're just kind-hearted—and that's the way you *ought* to be, of course—"

"Thank you, Mr. Sheridan!" she laughed.

"See here!" he cried. "Isn't there any way for us to get over this Mister and Miss thing? A month's got thirty-one days in it; I've managed to be with you a part of pretty near all the thirty-one, and I think you know how I feel by this time—"

She looked panic-stricken immediately. "Oh no," she protested, quickly. "No, I don't, and—"

"Yes, you do," he said, and his voice shook a little. "You couldn't help knowing."

"But I do!" she denied, hurriedly. "I do help knowing. I mean— Oh, wait!"

"What for? You do know how I feel, and you—well, you've certainly *wanted* me to feel that way—or else pretended—"

"Now, now!" she lamented. "You're spoiling such a cheerful afternoon!"

" 'Spoiling' it!" He slowed down the car and turned his face to her squarely. "See here, Miss Vertrees, haven't you—"

"Stop! Stop the car a minute." And when he had complied she faced him as squarely as he evidently desired her to face him. "Listen. I don't want you to go on, to-day."

"Why not?" he asked, sharply.

"I don't know."

"You mean it's just a whim?"

"I don't know," she repeated. Her voice was low and troubled and honest, and she kept her clear eyes upon his.

"Will you tell me something?"

"Almost anything."

"Have you ever told any man you loved him?"

And at that, though she laughed, she looked a little contemptuous. "No," she said. "And I don't think I ever shall tell any man that—or ever know what it means. I'm in earnest, Mr. Sheridan."

"Then you—you've just been flirting with me!" Poor Jim looked both furious and crestfallen.

"Not one bit!" she cried. "Not one word! Not one syllable! I've meant every single thing!"

"I don't—"

"Of course you don't!" she said. "Now, Mr. Sheridan, I want you to start the car. Now! Thank you. Slowly, till I finish what I want to say. I have not flirted with you. I have deliberately courted you. One thing more, and then I want you to take me straight home, talking about the weather all the way. I said that I do not believe I shall ever 'care' for any man, and that is true. I doubt the existence of the kind of 'caring' we hear about in poems and plays and novels. I think it must be just a kind of emotional *talk*—most of it. At all events, I don't feel it. Now, we can go faster, please."

"Just where does that let me out?" he demanded. "How does that excuse you for—"

"It isn't an excuse," she said, gently, and gave him one final look, wholly desolate. "I haven't said I should never marry."

"What?" Jim gasped.

She inclined her head in a broken sort of acquiescence, very humble, unfathomably sorrowful.

"I promise nothing," she said, faintly.

"You needn't!" shouted Jim, radiant and exultant. "You needn't! By George! I know you're square; that's enough for me! You wait and promise whenever you're ready!"

"Don't forget what I asked," she begged him.

"Talk about the weather? I will! God bless the old weather!" cried the happy Jim.

CHAPTER NINE

THROUGH the open country Bibbs was borne flying between brown fields and sun-flecked groves of gray trees, to breathe the rushing, clean air beneath a glorious sky —that sky so despised in the city, and so maltreated there, that from early October to mid-May it was impossible for men to remember that blue is the rightful color overhead.

Upon each of Bibbs's cheeks there was a hint of something almost resembling a pinkishness; not actual color, but undeniably its phantom. How largely this apparition may have been the work of the wind upon his face it is difficult to calculate, for beyond a doubt it was partly the result of a lady's bowing to him upon no more formal introduction than the circumstance of his having caught her looking into his window a month before. She had bowed definitely; she had bowed charmingly. And it seemed to Bibbs that she must have meant to convey her forgiveness.

There had been something in her recognition of him unfamiliar to his experience, and he rode the warmer for it. Nor did he lack the impression that he would long remember her as he had just seen her: her veil tumultuously blowing back, her face glowing in the wind—and that look of gay friendliness tossed to him like a fresh rose in carnival.

By and by, upon a rising ground, the driver halted the car, then backed and tacked, and sent it forward again with its nose to the south and the smoke. Far before him Bibbs saw the great smudge upon the horizon, that nest of cloud in which the city strove and panted like an engine shrouded in its own steam. But to Bibbs, who had now to go to the very heart of it, for a commanded interview with his father, the distant cloud was like an implacable genius issuing thunderously in smoke from his enchanted bottle, and irresistibly drawing Bibbs nearer and nearer.

They passed from the farm lands, and came, in the amber light of November late afternoon, to the farthermost outskirts of the city; and here the sky shimmered upon the verge of change from blue to gray; the smoke did not visibly permeate the air, but it was there, nevertheless—impalpable, thin, no more than the dust of smoke. And then, as the car drove on, the chimneys and stacks of factories came swimming up into view like miles of steamers advancing abreast, every funnel with its vast plume, savage and black, sweeping to the horizon, dripping wealth and dirt and suffocation over league on league already rich and vile with grime.

The sky had become only a dingy thickening of the soiled air; and a roar and clangor of metals beat deafeningly on Bibbs's ears. And now the car passed two great blocks of long brick buildings, hideous in all ways possible to make them hideous; doorways showing dark one moment and lurid the next with the leap of some virulent interior flame, revealing blackened giants, half naked, in passionate action, struggling with formless things in the hot illumination. And big as these shops were, they were growing bigger, spreading over a third block, where two new structures were mushrooming to completion in some hasty cement process of a stability not over-reassuring. Bibbs pulled the rug closer about him, and not even the phantom of color was left upon his cheeks as he passed this place, for he knew it too well. Across the face of one of the buildings there was an enormous sign: "Sheridan Automatic Pump Co., Inc."

Thence they went through streets of wooden houses, all grimed, and adding their own grime from many a sooty chimney; flimsy wooden houses of a thousand flimsy whimsies in the fashioning, built on narrow lots and nudging one another crossly, shutting out the stingy sunlight from one another; bad neighbors who would destroy one another root and branch some night when the right wind blew. They were only waiting for that wind and a cigarette, and then they would all be gone together—a pinch of incense burned upon the tripod of the god.[1]

Along these streets there were skinny shade-trees, and here and there a forest elm or walnut had been left; but these were dying. Some people said it was the scale; some said it was the smoke; and some were sure that asphalt and "improving" the streets did it; but Bigness was in too Big a hurry to bother much about trees. He had telegraph-poles and

---

[1] Reference is made here to the custom in ancient Greece of burning spices and fragrant gums on the tripod, or three-legged altar, in the temple of Apollo at Delphi.

telephone-poles and electric-light poles and trolley-poles by the thousand to take their places. So he let the trees die and put up his poles. They were hideous, but nobody minded that; and sometimes the wires fell and killed people—but not often enough to matter at all.

Thence onward the car bore Bibbs through the older parts of the town where the few solid old houses not already demolished were in transition: some, with their fronts torn away, were being made into segments of apartment-buildings; others had gone uproariously into trade, brazenly putting forth "show-windows" on their first floors, seeming to mean it for a joke; one or two with unaltered façades peeped humorously over the tops of temporary office buildings of one story erected in the old front yards. Altogether, the town here was like a boarding-house hash the Sunday after Thanksgiving; the old ingredients were discernible.

This was the fringe of Bigness's own sanctuary, and now Bibbs reached the roaring holy of holies itself. The car must stop at every crossing while the dark-garbed crowds, enveloped in maelstroms of dust, hurried before it. Magnificent new buildings, already dingy, loomed hundreds of feet above him; newer ones, more magnificent, were rising beside them, rising higher; old buildings were coming down; middle-aged buildings were coming down; the streets were laid open to their entrails and men worked underground between palisades, and overhead in metal cobwebs like spiders in the sky. Trolley-cars and long interurban cars, built to split the wind like torpedo-boats, clanged and shrieked their way round swarming corners; motor-cars of every kind and shape known to man babbled frightful warnings and frantic demands; hospital ambulances clamored wildly for passage; steam-whistles signaled the swinging of titanic tentacle and claw; riveters rattled like machine-guns; the ground shook to the thunder of gigantic trucks; and the conglomerate sound of it all was the sound of earthquake playing accompani-

ments for battle and sudden death. On one of the new steel
buildings no work was being done that afternoon. The building had killed a man in the morning—and the steel-workers
always stop for the day when that "happens."

And in the hurrying crowds, swirling and sifting through
the brobdingnagian [2] camp of iron and steel, one saw the
camp-followers and the pagan women—there would be work
to-day and dancing to-night. For the Puritan's dry voice is but
the crackling of a leaf underfoot in the rush and roar of the
coming of the new Egypt.

Bibbs was on time. He knew it must be "to the minute" or
his father would consider it an outrage; and the big chronom-
eter in Sheridan's office marked four precisely when Bibbs
walked in. Coincidentally with his entrance five people who
had been at work in the office, under Sheridan's direction,
walked out. They departed upon no visible or audible suggestion, and with a promptness that seemed ominous to the
new-comer. As the massive door clicked softly behind the
elderly stenographer, the last of the procession, Bibbs had a
feeling that they all understood that he was a failure as a
great man's son, a disappointment, the "queer one" of the
family, and that he had been summoned to judgment—a
well-founded impression, for that was exactly what they understood.

"Sit down," said Sheridan.

It is frequently an advantage for deans, schoolmasters, and
worried fathers to place delinquents in the sitting-posture.
Bibbs sat.

Sheridan, standing, gazed enigmatically upon his son for a
period of silence, then walked slowly to a window and stood
looking out of it, his big hands, loosely hooked together by
the thumbs, behind his back. They were soiled, as were all

[2] Gigantic. The reference is to Swift's *Gulliver's Travels,* in which Gulliver
visits the land of the Brobdingnags, a giant people who have everything in
proportion to their own size.

other hands down-town, except such as might be still damp from a basin.

"Well, Bibbs," he said at last, not altering his attitude, "do you know what I'm goin' to do with you?"

Bibbs, leaning back in his chair, fixed his eyes contemplatively upon the ceiling. "I heard you tell Jim," he began, in his slow way. "You said you'd send him to the machine-shop with me if he didn't propose to Miss Vertrees. So I suppose that must be your plan for me. But—"

"But what?" said Sheridan, irritably, as the son paused.

"Isn't there somebody you'd let *me* propose to?"

That brought his father sharply round to face him. "You beat the devil! Bibbs, what *is* the matter with you? Why can't you be like anybody else?"

"Liver, maybe," said Bibbs, gently.

"Boh! Even ole Doc Gurney says there's nothin' wrong with you organically. No. You're a dreamer, Bibbs; that's what's the matter, and that's *all* the matter. Oh, not one o' these *big* dreamers that put through the big deals! No, sir! You're the kind o' dreamer that just sets out on the back fence and thinks about how much trouble there must be in the world! That ain't the kind that builds the bridges, Bibbs; it's the kind that borrows fifteen cents from his wife's uncle's brother-in-law to get ten cent's worth o' plug tobacco and a nickel's worth o' quinine!"

He put the finishing touch to this etching with a snort, and turned again to the window.

"Look out there!" he bade his son. "Look out o' that window! Look at the life and energy down there! I should think *any* young man's blood would tingle to get into it and be part of it. Look at the big things young men are doin' in this town!" He swung about, coming to the mahogany desk in the middle of the room. "Look at what *I* was doin' at your age! Look at what your own brothers are doin'! Look at Roscoe! Yes, and look at Jim! I made Jim president o' the Sheridan Realty Company last New-Year's, with charge of every inch o' ground and every brick and every shingle and stick o' wood we own; and it's an example to any young man—or ole man, either—the way he took ahold of it. Last July we found out we wanted two more big warehouses at the Pump Works—wanted 'em quick. Contractors said it couldn't be done; said nine or ten months at the soonest; couldn't see it any other way. What 'd Jim do? Took the contract himself; found a fellow with a new cement and con- crete process; kept men on the job night and day, and stayed on it night and day himself—and, by George! we begin to *use* them warehouses next week! Four months and a half, and every inch fireproof! I tell you Jim's one o' these fellers that make miracles happen! Now, I don't say every young man can be like Jim, because there's mighty few got his ability, but every young man can go in and do his share. This town is God's own country, and there's opportunity for any- body with a pound of energy and an ounce o' gumption. I tell you these young business men I watch just do my heart good! *They* don't set around on the back fence—no, sir! They take enough exercise to keep their health; and they go to a baseball game once or twice a week in summer, maybe, and they're raisin' nice families, with sons to take their places sometime and carry on the work—because the work's got to go *on!* They're puttin' their life-blood into it, I tell you, and that's why we're gettin' bigger every minute, and why *they're* gettin' bigger, and why it's all goin' to keep *on* gettin' bigger!"

He slapped the desk resoundingly with his open palm, and then, observing that Bibbs remained in the same impassive attitude, with his eyes still fixed upon the ceiling in a con- templation somewhat plaintive, Sheridan was impelled to groan. "Oh, Lord!" he said. "This is the way you always were. I don't believe you understand a darn word I been sayin'! You don't *look* as if you did. By George! it's dis- couraging!"

"I don't understand about getting—about getting bigger,"

said Bibbs, bringing his gaze down to look at his father placatively. "I don't see just why—"

"What?" Sheridan leaned forward, resting his hands upon the desk and staring across it incredulously at his son.

"I don't understand—exactly—what you want it all bigger for?"

"Great God!" shouted Sheridan, and struck the desk a blow with his clenched fist. "A son of mine asks me that! You go out and ask the poorest day-laborer you can find! Ask him that question—"

"I did once," Bibbs interrupted; "when I was in the machine-shop. I—"

"Wha'd he say?"

"He said, 'Oh, hell!'" answered Bibbs, mildly.

"Yes, I reckon he would!" Sheridan swung away from the desk. "I reckon he certainly would! And I got plenty sympathy with him right now, myself!"

"It's the same answer, then?" Bibbs's voice was serious, almost tremulous.

"Damnation!" Sheridan roared. "Did you ever hear the word Prosperity, you ninny? Did you ever hear the word Ambition? Did you ever hear the word *Progress?*"

He flung himself into a chair after the outburst, his big chest surging, his throat tumultuous with guttural incoherences. "Now then," he said, huskily, when the anguish had somewhat abated, "what do you want to do?"

"Sir?"

"What do you *want* to do, I said."

Taken by surprise, Bibbs stammered. "What-what do-I—what—"

"If I'd let you do exactly what you had the whim for, what would you do?"

Bibbs looked startled; then timidity overwhelmed him—a profound shyness. He bent his head and fixed his lowered eyes upon the toe of his shoe, which he moved to and fro upon the rug, like a culprit called to the desk in school.

"What would you do? Loaf?"

"No, sir." Bibbs's voice was almost inaudible, and what little sound it made was unquestionably a guilty sound. "I suppose I'd—I'd—"

"Well?"

"I suppose I'd try to—to write."

"Write what?"

"Nothing important—just poems and essays, perhaps."

"That all?"

"Yes, sir."

"I see," said his father, breathing quickly with the restraint he was putting upon himself. "That is, you want to write, but you don't want to write anything of any account."

"You think—"

Sheridan got up again. "I take my hat off to the man that can write a good ad," he said, emphatically. "The best writin' talent in this country is right spang in the ad business to-day. You buy a magazine for good writin'—look on the back of it! Let me tell you I pay money for that kind o' writin'. Maybe you think it's easy. Just try it! *I've* tried it, and *I* can't do it. I tell you an ad's got to be written so it makes people do the hardest thing in this world to *get* 'em to do: it's got to make 'em give up their *money!* You talk about 'poems and essays.' I tell you when it comes to the actual skill o' puttin' words together so as to make things *happen,* R. T. Bloss, right here in this city, knows more in a minute than George Waldo Emerson [3] ever knew in his whole life!"

"You—you may be—" Bibbs said, indistinctly, the last word smothered in a cough.

"Of *course* I'm right! And if it ain't just like you to want

[3] Mr. Sheridan says George, meaning Ralph Waldo Emerson, usually considered the greatest American essayist.

to take up with the most out-o'-date kind o' writin' there is!
'Poems and essays'! My Lord, Bibbs, that's *women's* work!
You can't pick up a newspaper without havin' to see where
Mrs. Rumskididle read a paper on 'Jane Eyre,' or 'East
Lynne,'[4] at the God-Knows-What Club. And 'poetry'! Why,
look at Edith! I expect that poem o' hers would set a pretty
high-water mark for you, young man, and it's the only one
she's ever managed to write in her whole *life!* When I wanted
her to go on and write some more she said it took too much
time. Said it took months and months. And Edith's a smart
girl; she's got more energy in her little finger than you ever
give me a chance to see in your whole body, Bibbs. Now
look at the facts: say she could turn out four or five poems a
year and you could turn out maybe two. That medal she got
was worth about fifteen dollars, so there's your income—
thirty dollars a year! That's a fine success to make of your
life! I'm not sayin' a word against poetry. I wouldn't take ten
thousand dollars right now for that poem of Edith's; and
poetry's all right enough in its place—but you leave it to the
girls. A man's got to do a man's work in this world."

He seated himself in a chair at his son's side and, leaning
over, tapped Bibbs confidentially on the knee. "This city's
got the greatest future in America, and if my sons behave
right by me and by themselves they're goin' to have a
mighty fair share of it—a mighty fair share. I love this
town. It's God's own footstool, and it's made money for me
every day right along, I don't know how many years. I
love it like I do my own business, and I'd fight for it as
quick as I'd fight for my own family. It's a beautiful town.
Look at our wholesale district; look at any district you want
to; look at the park system we're puttin' through, and the
boulevards and the public statuary. And she grows. God! how

---

[4] *Jane Eyre* is a novel published in 1847 by an English writer, Charlotte
Brontë. *East Lynne* is a melodramatic novel written by another English woman,
Mrs. Henry Wood, and published in 1861.

she grows!" He had become intensely grave; he spoke with solemnity. "Now, Bibbs, I can't take any of it—nor any gold nor silver nor buildings nor bonds—away with me in my shroud when I have to go. But I want to leave my share in it to my boys. I've worked for it; I've been a builder and a maker; and two blades of grass have grown where one grew before, whenever I laid my hand on the ground and willed 'em to grow. I've built big, and I want the buildin' to go on. And when my last hour comes I want to know that my boys are ready to take charge; that they're fit to take charge and go *on* with it. Bibbs, when that hour comes I want to know that my boys are big men, ready and fit to take hold of big things. Bibbs, when I'm up above I want to know that the big share I've made mine, here below, is growin' bigger and bigger in the charge of my boys."

He leaned back, deeply moved. "There!" he said, huskily. "I've never spoken more what was in my heart in my life. I do it because I want you to understand—and not think me a mean father. I never had to talk that way to Jim and Roscoe. They understood without any talk, Bibbs."

"I see," said Bibbs. "At least I think I do. But—"

"Wait a minute!" Sheridan raised his hand. "If you see the least bit in the world, then you understand how it feels to me to have my son set here and talk about 'poems and essays' and such-like fooleries. And you must understand, too, what it meant to start one o' my boys and have him come back on me the way you did, and have to be sent to a sanitarium because he couldn't stand work. Now, let's get right down to it, Bibbs. I've had a whole lot o' talk with ole Doc Gurney about you, one time another, and I reckon I understand your case just about as well as he does, anyway! Now here, I'll be frank with you. I started you in harder than what I did the other boys, and that was for your own good, because I saw you needed to be shook up more'n they did. You were always kind of moody and mopish—and you needed work that 'd keep you on the jump. Now, why did it make you sick instead of brace you up and make a man of you the way it ought of done? I pinned ole Gurney down to it. I says, 'Look here, ain't it really because he just plain hated it?' 'Yes,' he says, 'that's it. If he'd enjoyed it, it wouldn't 'a' hurt him. He loathes it, and that affects his nervous system. The more he tries it, the more he hates it; and the more he hates it, the more injury it does him.' That ain't quite his words, but it's what he meant. And that's about the way it is."

"Yes," said Bibbs, "that's about the way it is."

"Well, then, I reckon it's up to me not only to make you do it, but to make you like it!"

Bibbs shivered. And he turned upon his father a look that was almost ghostly. "I can't," he said, in a low voice. "I can't."

"Can't go back to the shop?"

"No. Can't like it. I can't."

Sheridan jumped up, his patience gone. To his own view, he had reasoned exhaustively, had explained fully and had pleaded more than a father should, only to be met in the end with the unreasoning and mysterious stubbornness which had been Bibbs's baffling characteristic from childhood. "By George, you will!" he cried. "You'll go back there and you'll like it! Gurney says it won't hurt you if you like it, and he says it 'll kill you if you go back and hate it; so it looks as if it was about up to you not to hate it. Well, Gurney's a fool! Hatin' work doesn't kill anybody; and this isn't goin' to kill you, whether you hate it or not. I've never made a mistake in a serious matter in my life, and it wasn't a mistake my sendin' you there in the first place. And I'm goin' to prove it—I'm goin' to send you back there and vindicate my judgment. Gurney says it's all 'mental attitude.' Well, you're goin' to learn the right one! He says in a couple more months this fool thing that's been the matter with you 'll be disappeared completely and you'll be back in as good or better condition than you were before you ever went into the shop. And right then is when you begin over—right in that same shop! Nobody can call me a hard man or a mean father. I do the best I can for my chuldern, and I take the full responsibility for bringin' my sons up to be men. Now, so far, I've failed with you. But I'm not goin' to keep *on* failin'. I never tackled a job *yet* I didn't put through, and I'm not goin' to begin with my own son. I'm goin' to make a *man* of you. By God! I am!"

Bibbs rose and went slowly to the door, where he turned. "You say you give me a couple of months?" he said.

Sheridan pushed a bell-button on his desk. "Gurney said two months more would put you back where you were. You go home and begin to get yourself in the right 'mental attitude' before those two months are up! Good-by!"

"Good-by, sir," said Bibbs, meekly.

CHAPTER TEN

BIBBS's room, that neat apartment for transients to which the "låmidal" George had shown him upon his return, still bore the appearance of temporary quarters, possibly because Bibbs had no clear conception of himself as a permanent incumbent. However, he had set upon the mantelpiece the two photographs that he owned: one, a "group" twenty years old—his father and mother, with Jim and Roscoe as boys—and the other a "cabinet" of Edith at sixteen. And upon a table were the books he had taken from his trunk: *Sartor Resartus, Virginibus Puerisque, Huckleberry Finn,* and *Afterwhiles*. There were some other books in the trunk—a large one, which remained unremoved at the foot of the bed, adding to the general impression of transiency. It contained nearly all the possessions as well as the secret life of Bibbs Sheridan, and Bibbs sat beside it, the day after his interview with his father, raking over a small collection of manuscripts in the top tray. Some of these he glanced through dubiously, finding little comfort in them; but one made him smile. Then he shook his head ruefully indeed, and ruefully began to read it. It was written on paper stamped "Hood Sanitarium," and it bore the title, "Leisure."

A man may keep a quiet heart at seventy miles an hour, but not if he is running the train. Nor is the habit of contemplation a useful quality in the stoker of a foundry furnace; it will not be found to recommend him to the approbation of his superiors. For a profession adapted solely to the pursuit of happiness in thinking, I would choose that of an invalid: his money is time and he may spend it on Olympus.[1] It will not suffice to be an amateur invalid. To my way of thinking, the perfect practitioner must be to all outward purposes already dead if he is to begin the perfect enjoyment of life. His serenity must not be disturbed by rumors of recovery; he must lie serene in his long chair in the sunshine. The world must be on the other side of the wall, and the wall must be so thick and so high that he cannot hear the roaring of the furnace fires and the screaming of the whistles. Peace—

Having read so far as the word "peace," Bibbs suffered an interruption interesting as a coincidence of contrast. High voices sounded in the hall just outside his door; and it became evident that a woman's quarrel was in progress, the parties to it having begun it in Edith's room, and continuing it vehemently as they came out into the hall.

"Yes, you *better* go home!" Bibbs heard his sister vociferating, shrilly. "You better go home and keep your mind a little more on your *husband!*"

"Edie, Edie!" he heard his mother remonstrating, as peacemaker.

"You see here!" This was Sibyl, and her voice was both acrid and tremulous. "Don't you talk to me that way! I came here to tell Mother Sheridan what I'd heard, and to let her

[1] A lofty peak on the boundary between Thessaly and Macedonia. It was believed by the ancient Greeks to be the home of the gods, where their assemblies and feasts were held.

tell Father Sheridan if she thought she ought to, and I did it for your own good."

"Yes, you did!" And Edith's gibing laughter tooted loudly. "Yes, you did! *You* didn't have any other reason! *Oh* no! *You* don't want to break it up between Bobby Lamhorn and me because—"

"Edie, Edie! Now, now!"

"Oh, hush up, mamma! I'd like to know, then, if she says her new friends tell her he's got such a reputation that he oughtn't to come here, what about his not going to *her* house. How—"

"I've explained that to Mother Sheridan." Sibyl's voice indicated that she was descending the stairs. "Married people are not the same. Some things that should be shielded from a young girl—"

This seemed to have no very soothing effect upon Edith. "'Shielded from a young girl'!" she shrilled. "You seem pretty willing to be the shield! You look out Roscoe doesn't notice what kind of a shield you are!"

Sibyl's answer was inaudible, but Mrs. Sheridan's flurried attempts at pacification were renewed. "Now, Edie, Edie, she means it for your good, and you'd oughtn't to—"

"Oh, hush up, mamma, and let me alone! If you dare tell papa—"

"Now, now! I'm not going to tell him to-day, and maybe—"

"You've got to promise *never* to tell him!" the girl cried, passionately.

"Well, we'll see. You just come back in your own room, and we'll—"

"No! I *won't* 'talk it over'! Stop pulling me! Let me *alone!*" And Edith, flinging herself violently upon Bibbs's door, jerked it open, swung round it into the room, slammed the door behind her, and threw herself, face down, upon the bed in such a riot of emotion that she had no perception of Bibbs's presence in the room. Gasping and sobbing in a passion of tears, she beat the coverlet and pillows with her clenched fists. "Sneak!" she babbled aloud. "Sneak! Snake-in-the-grass! Cat!"

Bibbs saw that she did not know he was there, and he went softly toward the door, hoping to get away before she became aware of him; but some sound of his movement reached her, and she sat up, startled, facing him.

"Bibbs! I thought I saw you go out awhile ago."

"Yes. I came back, though. I'm sorry—"

"Did you hear me quarreling with Sibyl?"

"Only what you said in the hall. You lie down again, Edith. I'm going out."

"No; don't go." She applied a handkerchief to her eyes, emitted a sob, and repeated her request. "Don't go. I don't mind you; you're quiet, anyhow. Mamma's so fussy, and never gets anywhere. I don't mind you at all, but I wish you'd sit down."

"All right." And he returned to his chair beside the trunk. "Go ahead and cry all you want, Edith," he said. "No harm in that!"

"Sibyl told mamma—*oh!*" she began, choking. "Mary Vertrees had mamma and Sibyl and I to tea, one afternoon two weeks or so ago, and she had some women there that Sibyl's been crazy to get in with, and she just laid herself out to make a hit with 'em, and she's been running after 'em ever since, and now she comes over here and says *they* say Bobby Lamhorn is so bad that, even though they like his family, none of the nice people in town would let him in their houses. In the first place, it's a falsehood, and I don't believe a word of it; and in the second place I know the reason she did it, and, what's more, she *knows* I know it! I won't *say* what it is— not yet—because papa and all of you would think I'm as crazy as she is snaky; and Roscoe's such a fool he'd probably quit speaking to me. But it's true! Just you watch her; that's all I ask. Just you watch that woman. You'll see!"

As it happened, Bibbs was literally watching "that woman."

Glancing from the window, he saw Sibyl pause upon the pavement in front of the old house next door. She stood a moment, in deep thought, then walked quickly up the path to the door, undoubtedly with the intention of calling. But he did not mention this to his sister, who, after delivering herself of a rather vague jeremiad upon the subject of her sister-in-law's treacheries, departed to her own chamber, leaving him to his speculations. The chief of these concerned the social elasticities of women. Sibyl had just been a participant in a violent scene; she had suffered hot insult of a kind that could not fail to set her quivering with resentment; and yet she elected to betake herself to the presence of people whom she knew no more than "formally." Bibbs marveled. Surely, he reflected, some traces of emotion must linger upon Sibyl's face or in her manner; she could not have ironed it all quite out in the three or four minutes it took her to reach the Vertreeses' door.

And in this he was not mistaken, for Mary Vertrees was at that moment wondering what internal excitement Mrs. Roscoe Sheridan was striving to master. But Sibyl had no idea that she was allowing herself to exhibit anything except the gaiety which she conceived proper to the manner of a casual caller. She was wholly intent upon fulfilling the sudden purpose that brought her, and she was no more self-conscious than she was finely intelligent. For Sibyl Sheridan belonged to a type Scriptural in its antiquity. She was merely the idle and half-educated intriguer who may and does delude men, of course, and the best and dullest of her own sex as well, finding invariably strong supporters among these latter. It is a type that has wrought some damage in the world and would have wrought greater, save for the check put upon its power by intelligent women and by its own "lack of perspective," for it is a type that never sees itself. Sibyl followed her impulses with no reflection or question—it was like a hound on the gallop after a master on horseback. She had not even the instinct to stop and consider her effect. If she wished to make a certain impression she believed that she made it. She believed that she was believed.

"My mother asked me to say that she was sorry she couldn't come down," Mary said, when they were seated.

Sibyl ran the scale of a cooing simulance of laughter, which she had been brought up to consider the polite thing to do after a remark addressed to her by any person with whom she was not on familiar terms. It was intended partly as a courtesy and partly as the foundation for an impression of sweetness.

"Just thought I'd fly in a minute," she said, continuing the cooing to relieve the last doubt of her geniality. "I thought I'd just behave like *real* country neighbors. We are almost out in the country, so far from down-town, aren't we? And it seemed such a *lovely* day! I wanted to tell you how much I enjoyed meeting those nice people at tea that afternoon. You see, coming here a bride and never having lived here before, I've had to depend on my husband's friends almost entirely, and I really 've known scarcely anybody. Mr. Sheridan has been so engrossed in business ever since he was a mere boy, why, of course—"

She paused, with the air of having completed an explanation.

"Of course," said Mary, sympathetically accepting it.

"Yes. I've been seeing quite a lot of the Kittersbys since that afternoon," Sibyl went on. "They're really delightful people. Indeed they are! Yes—"

She stopped with unconscious abruptness, her mind plainly wandering to another matter; and Mary perceived that she had come upon a definite errand. Moreover, a tensing of Sibyl's eyelids, in that moment of abstraction as she looked aside from her hostess, indicated that the errand was a serious one for the caller and easily to be connected with the slight but perceptible agitation underlying her assumption of cheerful ease. There was a restlessness of breathing, a restlessness of hands.

"Mrs. Kittersby and her daughter were chatting about some of the people here in town the other day," said Sibyl, repeating the cooing and protracting it. "They said something that took *me* by surprise! We were talking about our mutual friend, Mr. Robert Lamhorn—"

Mary interrupted her promptly. "Do you mean 'mutual' to include my mother and me?" she asked.

"Why, yes; the Kittersbys and you and all of us Sheridans, I mean."

"No," said Mary. "We shouldn't consider Mr. Robert Lamhorn a friend of ours."

To her surprise, Sibyl nodded eagerly, as if greatly pleased. "That's just the way Mrs. Kittersby talked!" she cried, with a vehemence that made Mary stare. "Yes, and I hear that's the way *all* you old families here speak of him!"

Mary looked aside, but otherwise she was able to maintain her composure. "I had the impression he was a friend of yours," she said; adding, hastily, "and your husband's."

"Oh yes," said the caller, absently. "He is, certainly. A man's reputation for a little gaiety oughtn't to make a great difference to married people, of course. It's where young girls are in question. *Then* it may be very, very dangerous. There are a great many things safe and proper for married people that might be awf'ly imprudent for a young girl. Don't you agree, Miss Vertrees?"

"I don't know," returned the frank Mary. "Do you mean that you intend to remain a friend of Mr. Lamhorn's, but disapprove of Miss Sheridan's doing so?"

"That's it exactly!" was the naïve and ardent response of Sibyl. "What *I* feel about it is that a man with his reputation isn't at all suitable for Edith, and the family ought to be made to understand it. I tell you," she cried, with a sudden access of vehemence, "her father ought to put his foot down!"

Her eyes flashed with a green spark; something seemed to leap out and then retreat, but not before Mary had caught a glimpse of it, as one might catch a glimpse of a thing darting forth and then scuttling back into hiding under a bush.

"Of course," said Sibyl, much more composedly, "I hardly need say that it's entirely on Edith's account that I'm worried about this. I'm as fond of Edith as if she was really my sister, and I can't help fretting about it. It would break my heart to have Edith's life spoiled."

This tune was off the key, to Mary's ear. Sibyl tried to sing with pathos, but she flatted.

And when a lady receives a call from another who suffers under the stress of some feeling which she wishes to conceal, there is not uncommonly developed a phenomenon of duality comparable to the effect obtained by placing two mirrors opposite each other, one clear and the other flawed. In this case, particularly, Sibyl had an imperfect consciousness of Mary. The Mary Vertrees that she saw was merely something to be cozened to her own frantic purpose—a Mary Vertrees who was incapable of penetrating that purpose. Sibyl sat there believing that she was projecting the image of herself that she desired to project, never dreaming that with every word, every look, and every gesture she was more and more fully disclosing the pitiable truth to the clear eyes of Mary. And the Sibyl that Mary saw was an overdressed woman, in manner half rustic, and in mind as shallow as a pan, but possessed by emotions that appeared to be strong—perhaps even violent. What those emotions were Mary had not guessed, but she began to suspect.

"And Edith's life *would* be spoiled," Sibyl continued. "It would be a dreadful thing for the whole family. She's the very apple of Father Sheridan's eye, and he's as proud of her as he is of Jim and Roscoe. It would be a horrible thing for him to have her marry a man like Robert Lamhorn; but he doesn't *know* anything about him, and if somebody doesn't tell him, what I'm most afraid of is that Edith might get his consent and hurry on the wedding before he finds out, and then it would be too late. You see, Miss Vertrees, it's very difficult for me to decide just what it's my duty to do."

"I see," said Mary, looking at her thoughtfully. "Does Miss Sheridan seem to—to care very much about him?"

"He's deliberately fascinated her," returned the visitor, beginning to breathe quickly and heavily. "Oh, she wasn't difficult! She knew she wasn't in right in this town, and she was crazy to meet the people that were, and she thought he was one of 'em. But that was only the start that made it easy for him—and he didn't need it. He could have done it, anyway!" Sibyl was launched now; her eyes were furious and her voice shook. "He went after her deliberately, the way he does everything; he's as cold-blooded as a fish. All he cares about is his own pleasure, and lately he's decided it would be pleasant to get hold of a piece of real money—and there was Edith! And he'll marry her! Nothing on earth can stop him unless he finds out she won't *have* any money if she marries him, and the only person that could make him understand that is Father Sheridan. Somehow, that's got to be managed, because Lamhorn is going to hurry it on as fast as he can. He told me so last night. He said he was going to marry her the first minute he could persuade her to it—and little Edith's all ready to be persuaded!" Sibyl's eyes flashed green again. "And he swore he'd do it," she panted. "He swore he'd marry Edith Sheridan, and nothing on earth could stop him!"

And then Mary understood. Her lips parted and she stared at the babbling creature incredulously, a sudden vivid picture in her mind, a canvas of unconscious Sibyl's painting. Mary beheld it with pity and horror: she saw Sibyl clinging to Robert Lamhorn, raging, in a whisper, perhaps—for Roscoe might have been in the house, or servants might have heard. She saw Sibyl entreating, beseeching, threatening despairingly, and Lamhorn—tired of her—first evasive, then brutally letting her have the truth; and at last, infuriated, "swearing" to marry her rival. If Sibyl had not babbled out the word "swore" it might have been less plain.

The poor woman blundered on, wholly unaware of what she had confessed. "You see," she said, more quietly, "whatever's going to be done ought to be done right away. I went over and told Mother Sheridan what I'd heard about Lamhorn—oh, I was open and aboveboard! I told her right before Edith. I think it ought all to be done with perfect frankness, because nobody can say it isn't for the girl's own good and what her best friend would do. But Mother Sheridan's under Edith's thumb, and she's afraid to ever come right out with anything. Father Sheridan's different. Edith can get anything she wants out of him in the way of money or ordinary indulgence, but when it comes to a matter like this he'd be a steel rock. If it's a question of his will against anybody else's he'd make his will rule if it killed 'em both! Now, he'd never in the world let Lamhorn come near the house again if he knew his reputation. So, you see, somebody's got to tell him. It isn't a very easy position for me, is it, Miss Vertrees?"

"No," said Mary, gravely.

"Well, to be frank," said Sibyl, smiling, "that's why I've come to you."

"To *me!*" Mary frowned.

Sibyl rippled and cooed again. "There isn't *anybody* ever made such a hit with Father Sheridan in his life as you have. And of course we *all* hope you're not going to be exactly an outsider in the affairs of the family!" (This sally with another and louder effect of laughter.) "And if it's *my* duty, why, in a way, I think it might be thought yours, too."

"No, no!" exclaimed Mary, sharply.

"Listen," said Sibyl. "Now suppose I go to Father Sheridan with this story, and Edith says it's not true; suppose she says Lamhorn has a good reputation and that I'm repeating irresponsible gossip, or suppose (what's most likely) she loses her temper and says I invented it, then what am I going to do? Father Sheridan doesn't know Mrs. Kittersby and her daughter, and they're out of the question, anyway. But suppose I could say: 'All right, if you want proof, ask Miss Vertrees. She came with me, and she's waiting in the next room right now, to—"

"No, no," said Mary, quickly. "You mustn't—"

"Listen just a minute more," Sibyl urged, confidingly. She was on easy ground now, to her own mind, and had no doubt of her success. "You naturally don't want to begin by taking part in a family quarrel, but if *you* take part in it, it won't be one. You don't know yourself what weight you carry over there, and no one would have the right to say you did it except out of the purest kindness. Don't you see that Jim and his father would admire you all the more for it? Miss Vertrees, listen! Don't you see we *ought* to do it, you and I? Do you suppose Robert Lamhorn cares the snap of his finger for her? Do you suppose a man like him would *look* at Edith Sheridan if it wasn't for the money?" And again Sibyl's emotion rose to the surface. "I tell you he's after nothing on earth but to get his finger in that old man's money-pile, over there, next door! He'd marry *anybody* to do it. Marry Edith?" she cried. "I tell you he'd marry their nigger cook for *that!*"

She stopped, afraid—at the wrong time—that she had been too vehement, but a glance at Mary reassured her, and Sibyl decided that she had produced the effect she wished. Mary was not looking at her; she was staring straight before her at the wall, her eyes wide and shining. She became visibly a little paler as Sibyl looked at her.

"After nothing on earth but to get his finger in that old man's money-pile, over there, next door!" The voice was vulgar, the words were vulgar—and the plain truth was vulgar! How it rang in Mary Vertree's ears! The clear mirror had caught its own image clearly in the flawed one at last.

Sibyl put forth her best bid to clench the matter. She offered her bargain. "Now don't you worry," she said, sunnily, "about this setting Edith against you. She'll get over it after a while, anyway, but if she tried to be spiteful and make it uncomfortable for you when you drop in over there, or managed so as to sort of leave you out, why, *I*'ve got a house, and Jim likes to come there. I don't *think* Edith *would* be that way; she's too crazy to have you take her around with the smart crowd, but if she *did,* you needn't worry. And another thing —I guess you won't mind Jim's own sister-in-law speaking of it. Of course, I don't know just how matters stand between you and Jim, but Jim and Roscoe are about as much alike as two brothers can be, and Roscoe was very slow making up his mind; sometimes I used to think he actually never *would*. Now, what I mean is, sisters-in-law can do lots of things to help matters on like that. There's lots of little things can be said, and lots—"

She stopped, puzzled. Mary Vertrees had gone from pale to scarlet, and now, still scarlet indeed, she rose, without a word of explanation, or any other kind of word, and walked slowly to the open door and out of the room.

Sibyl was a little taken aback. She supposed Mary had remembered something neglected and necessary for the instruction of a servant, and that she would return in a moment; but it was rather a rude excess of absent-mindedness not to have excused herself, especially as her guest was talking. And, Mary's return being delayed, Sibyl found time to think this unprefaced exit odder and ruder than she had first considered it. There might have been more excuse for it, she thought, had she been speaking of matters less important—offering to do the girl all the kindness in her power, too!

Sibyl yawned and swung her muff impatiently; she examined the sole of her shoe; she decided on a new shape of heel; she made an inventory of the furniture of the room, of the rugs, of the wall-paper and engravings. Then she looked at her watch and frowned; went to a window and stood looking out upon the brown lawn, then came back to the chair she had abandoned, and sat again. There was no sound in the house.

A strange expression began imperceptibly to alter the planes of her face, and slowly she grew as scarlet as Mary—scarlet to the ears. She looked at her watch again—and twenty-five minutes had elapsed since she had looked at it before.

She went into the hall, glanced over her shoulder oddly; then she let herself softly out of the front door, and went across the street to her own house.

Roscoe met her upon the threshold, gloomily. "Saw you from the window," he explained. "You must find a lot to say to that old lady."

"What old lady?"

"Mrs. Vertrees. I been waiting for you a long time and I saw the daughter come out, fifteen minutes ago, and post a letter, and then walk on up the street. Don't stand out on the porch," he said, crossly. "Come in here. There's something it's come time I'll have to talk to you about. Come in!"

But as she was moving to obey he glanced across at his father's house and started. He lifted his hand to shield his eyes from the setting sun, staring fixedly. "Something's the matter over there," he muttered, and then, more loudly, as alarm came into his voice, he said, "What's the matter over there?"

Bibbs dashed out of the gate in an automobile set at its highest speed, and as he saw Roscoe he made a gesture singularly eloquent of calamity, and was lost at once in a cloud of dust down the street. Edith had followed part of the way down the drive, and it could be seen that she was crying bitterly. She lifted both arms to Roscoe, summoning him.

"By George!" gasped Roscoe. "I believe somebody's dead!"

And he started for the New House at a run.

CHAPTER ELEVEN

S HERIDAN had decided to conclude his day's work early that
afternoon, and at about two o'clock he left his office with
a man of affairs from foreign parts, who had traveled far for
a business conference with Sheridan and his colleagues. Herr
Favre, in spite of his French name, was a gentleman of Ba-
varia. It was his first visit to our country, and Sheridan took
pleasure in showing him the sights of the country's finest city.
They got into an open car at the main entrance of the Sheridan Building, and were driven first, slowly and momentously,
through the wholesale district and the retail district; then
more rapidly they inspected the packing-houses and the stock-
yards; then skirmished over the "park system" and "boulevards"; and after that whizzed through the "residence section"
on their way to the factories and foundries.

"All cray," observed Herr Favre, smilingly.

"'Cray'?" echoed Sheridan. "I don't know what you mean.
'Cray'?"

"No white," said Herr Favre, with a wave of his hand toward the long rows of houses on both sides of the street. "No
white lace window-curtains; all cray lace window-curtains."

"Oh, I see!" Sheridan laughed indulgently. "You mean
'gray.' No, they ain't, they're white. I never saw any gray
ones."

Herr Favre shook his head, much amused. "There are *no*
white ones," he said. "There is no white *anything* in your
city; no white window-curtains, no white house, no white
peeble!" He pointed upward. "Smoke!" Then he sniffed the
air and clasped his nose between forefinger and thumb.
"Smoke! Smoke ef'rywhere. Smoke in your insites." He tapped his chest. "Smoke in your lunks!"

"Oh! *Smoke!*" Sheridan cried with gusto, drawing in a deep breath and patently finding it delicious. "You *bet* we got smoke!"

"Exbensif!" said Herr Favre. "Ruins foliage; ruins fabrics. Maybe in summer it iss not so bad, but I wonder your wifes will bear it."

Sheridan laughed uproariously. "They know it means new spring hats for 'em!"

"They must need many, too!" said the visitor. "New hats, new all things, but nothing white. In München we could not do it; we are a safing peeble."

"Where's that?"

"In München. You say 'Munich.'"

"Well, I never been to Munich, but I took in the Mediterranean trip, and I tell you, outside o' some right good scenery, all *I* saw was mighty dirty and mighty shiftless and mighty run-down at the heel. Now comin' right down *to* it, Mr. Farver, wouldn't you rather live here in this town than in Munich? I know you got more enterprise up there than the part of the old country I saw, and I know *you're* a live business man and you're associated with others like you, but when it comes to *livin'* in a place, wouldn't you heap rather be here than over there?"

"For me," said Herr Favre, "no. Here I should not think I was living. It would be like the miner who goes into the mine to work; nothing else."

"We got a good many good citizens here from your part o' the world. *They* like it."

"Oh yes." And Herr Favre laughed deprecatingly. "The first generation, they bring their Germany with them; then, after that, they are Americans, like you." He tapped his host's big knee genially. "You are patriot; so are they."

"Well, I reckon you must be a pretty hot little patriot yourself, Mr. Farver!" Sheridan exclaimed, gaily. "You certainly stand up for your own town, if you stick to sayin' you'd rather live there than you would here. Yes, *sir!* You sure are some patriot to say *that*—after you've seen our city! It ain't reasonable in you, but I must say I kind of admire you for it; every man ought to stick up for his own, even when he sees the other fellow's got the goods on him. Yet I expect way down deep in your heart, Mr. Farver, you'd rather live right here than any place else in the world, if you had your choice. Man alive! this is God's country, Mr. Farver, and a blind man couldn't help seein' it! You couldn't stand where you do in a business way and *not* see it. Soho, boy! Here we are. This is the big works, and I'll show you something now that 'll make your eyes stick out!"

They had arrived at the Pump Works; and for an hour Herr Favre was personally conducted and personally instructed by the founder and president, the buzzing queen bee of those buzzing hives.

"Now I'll take you for a spin in the country," said Sheridan, when at last they came out to the car again. "We'll take a breezer." But, with his foot on the step, he paused to hail a neat young man who came out of the office smiling a greeting. "Hello, young fellow!" Sheridan said, heartily. "On the job, are you, Jimmie? Ha! They don't catch you *off* of it very often, I guess, though I do hear you go automobile-ridin' in the country sometimes with a mighty fine-lookin' girl settin' up beside you!" He roared with laughter, clapping his son upon the shoulder. "That's all right with me—if it is with *her!* So, Jimmie? Well, when we goin' to move into your new warehouses? Monday?"

"Sunday, if you want to," said Jim.

"No!" cried his father, delighted. "Don't tell me you're goin' to keep your word about dates! That's no way to do contractin'! Never heard of a contractor yet didn't want more time."

"They'll be all ready for you on the minute," said Jim. "I'm going over both of 'em now, with Links and Sherman, from foundation to roof. I guess they'll pass inspection, too!"

"Well, then, when you get through with that," said his father, "you go and take your girl out ridin'. By George! you've earned it! You tell her you stand high with *me!*" He stepped into the car, waving a waggish farewell, and, when the wheels were in motion again, he turned upon his companion a broad face literally shining with pride. "That's my boy Jimmie!" he said.

"Fine young man, yes," said Herr Favre.

"I got two o' the finest boys," said Sheridan, "I got two o' the finest boys God ever made, and that's a fact, Mr. Farver! Jim's the oldest, and I tell you they got to get up the day before if they expect to catch *him* in bed! My other boy, Roscoe, he's always to the good, too, but Jim's a wizard. You saw them two new-process warehouses, just about finished? Well, *Jim* built 'em. I'll tell you about that, Mr. Farver." And he recited this history, describing the new process at length; in fact, he had such pride in Jim's achievement that he told Herr Favre all about it more than once.

"Fine young man, yes," repeated the good Münchner, three-quarters of an hour later. They were many miles out in the open country by this time.

"He is that!" said Sheridan, adding, as if confidentially: "I got a fine family, Mr. Farver—fine chuldern. I got a daughter now; you take her and put her anywhere you please, and she'll shine up with *any* of 'em. There's culture and refinement and society in this town by the car-load, and here lately she's been gettin' right in the thick of it—her and my daughter-in-law, both. I got a mighty fine daughter-in-law, Mr. Farver. I'm goin' to get you up for a meal with us before you leave town, and you'll see—and, well, sir, from all I hear the two of 'em been holdin' their own with the best. Myself, I and the wife never had time for much o' that kind o' doin's, but it's all right and good for the chuldern; and my daughter

she's always kind of taken to it. I'll read you a poem she wrote
when I get you up at the house. She wrote it in school and
took the first prize for poetry with it. I tell you they don't
make 'em any smarter 'n that girl, Mr. Farver. Yes, sir; take
us all round, we're a pretty happy family; yes, sir. Roscoe
hasn't got any chuldern yet, and I haven't ever spoke to him
and his wife about it—it's kind of a delicate matter—but it's
about time the wife and I saw some gran'-chuldern growin'
up around us. I certainly do hanker for about four or five
little curly-headed rascals to take on my knee. Boys, I hope,
o' course; that's only natural. Jim's got his eye on a mighty
splendid-lookin' girl; lives right next door to us. I expect you
heard me joshin' him about it back yonder. She's one the ole
blue-bloods here, and I guess it was a mighty good stock—to
raise *her!* She's one these girls that stand right up and look
at you! And pretty? She's the prettiest thing you ever saw!
Good size, too; good health and good sense. Jim 'll be just
right if he gets her. I must say it tickles *me* to think o' the
way that boy took ahold o' that job back yonder. Four months
and a half! Yes, sir—"

He expanded this theme once more; and thus he continued
to entertain the stranger throughout the long drive. Darkness
had fallen before they reached the city on their return, and it
was after five when Sheridan allowed Herr Favre to descend
at the door of his hotel, where boys were shrieking extra editions of the evening paper.

"Now, good night, Mr. Farver," said Sheridan, leaning
from the car to shake hands with his guest. "Don't forget I'm
goin' to come around and take you up to— Go on away, boy!"

A newsboy had thrust himself almost between them, yell-
ing, "Extry! Secon' Extry. Extry, all about the horrable acci-
dent. Extry!"

"Get out!" laughed Sheridan. "Who wants to read about
accidents? Get out!"

The boy moved away philosophically. "Extry! Extry!" he shrilled. "Three men killed! Extry! Millionaire killed! Two other men killed! Extry! Extry!"

"Don't forget, Mr. Farver." Sheridan completed his interrupted farewells. "I'll come by to take you up to our house for dinner. I'll be here for you about half-past five to-morrow afternoon. Hope you 'njoyed the drive much as I have. Good night—good night!" He leaned back, speaking to the chauffeur. "Now you can take me around to the Central City barber-shop, boy. I want to get a shave 'fore I go up home."

"Extry! Extry!" screamed the newsboys, zigzagging among the crowds like bats in the dusk. "Extry! All about the horrable acci*dent!* Extry!" It struck Sheridan that the papers sent out too many "Extras"; they printed "Extras" for all sorts of petty crimes and casualties. It was a mistake, he decided, critically. Crying "Wolf!" too often wouldn't sell the goods; it was bad business. The papers would "make more in the long run," he was sure, if they published an "Extra" only when something of real importance happened.

"Extry! All about the hor'ble *ax*'nt! Extry!" a boy squawked under his nose, as he descended from the car.

"Go on away!" said Sheridan, gruffly, though he smiled. He liked to see the youngsters working so noisily to get on in the world.

But as he crossed the pavement to the brilliant glass doors of the barber-shop, a second newsboy grasped the arm of the one who had thus cried his wares.

"Say, Yallern," said this second, hoarse with awe, "'n't chew know who that *is?*"

"Who?"

"It's *Sheridan!*"

"Jeest!" cried the first, staring insanely.

At about the same hour, four times a week—Monday, Wednesday, Friday, and Saturday—Sheridan stopped at this

shop to be shaved by the head barber. The barbers were Negroes, he was their great man, and it was their habit to give
him a "reception," his entrance being always the signal for a
flurry of jocular hospitality, followed by general excesses of
briskness and gaiety. But it was not so this evening.

The shop was crowded. Copies of the "Extra" were being
read by men waiting, and by men in the latter stages of treatment. "Extras" lay upon vacant seats and showed from the
pockets of hanging coats.

There was a loud chatter between the practitioners and
their recumbent patients, a vocal charivari which stopped
abruptly as Sheridan opened the door. His name seemed to
fizz in the air like the last sputtering of a firework; the barbers stopped shaving and clipping; lathered men turned their
prostrate heads to stare, and there was a moment of amazing
silence in the shop.

The head barber, nearest the door, stood like a barber in a
tableau. His left hand held stretched between thumb and
forefinger an elastic section of his helpless customer's cheek,
while his right hand hung poised above it, the razor motionless. And then, roused from trance by the door's closing, he
accepted the fact of Sheridan's presence. The barber remembered that there are no circumstances in life—or just after it
—under which a man does not need to be shaved.

He stepped forward, profoundly grave. "I be through with
this man in the chair one minute, Mist' Sheridan," he said,
in a hushed voice. "Yessuh." And of a solemn Negro youth
who stood by, gazing stupidly, "You goin' *resign?*" he demanded in a fierce undertone. "You goin' take Mist' Sheridan's coat?" He sent an angry look round the shop, and the
barbers, taking his meaning, averted their eyes and fell to
work, the murmur of subdued conversation buzzing from
chair to chair.

"You sit down *one* minute, Mist' Sheridan," said the head
barber, gently. "I fix nice chair fo' you to wait in."

"Never mind," said Sheridan. "Go on get through with your man."

"Yessuh." And he went quickly back to his chair on tip toe, followed by Sheridan's puzzled gaze.

Something had gone wrong in the shop, evidently. Sheridan did not know what to make of it. Ordinarily he would have shouted a hilarious demand for the meaning of the mystery, but an inexplicable silence had been imposed upon him by the hush that fell upon his entrance and by the odd look every man in the shop had bent upon him.

Vaguely disquieted, he walked to one of the seats in the rear of the shop, and looked up and down the two lines of barbers, catching quickly shifted, furtive glances here and there. He made this brief survey after wondering if one of the barbers had died suddenly, that day, or the night before; but there was no vacancy in either line.

The seat next to his was unoccupied, but some one had left a copy of the "Extra" there, and, frowning, he picked it up and glanced at it. The first of the swollen display lines had little meaning to him:

Fatally Faulty. New Process Roof Collapses Hurling Capitalist to Death With Inventor. Seven Escape When Crash Comes. Death Claims—

Thus far had he read when a thin hand fell upon the paper, covering the print from his eyes; and, looking up, he saw Bibbs standing before him, pale and gentle, immeasurably compassionate.

"I've come for you, father," said Bibbs. "Here's the boy with your coat and hat. Put them on and come home."

And even then Sheridan did not understand. So secure was he in the strength and bigness of everything that was his, he did not know what calamity had befallen him. But he was frightened.

Without a word, he followed Bibbs heavily out through the still shop, but as they reached the pavement he stopped short and, grasping his son's sleeve with shaking fingers, swung him round so that they stood face to face.

"What—what—" His mouth could not do him the service he asked of it, he was so frightened.

"Extry!" screamed a newsboy straight in his face. "Young North Side millionaire insuntly killed! Extry!"

"Not—*Jim!*" said Sheridan.

Bibbs caught his father's hand in his own.

"And *you* come to tell me that?"

Sheridan did not know what he said. But in those first words and in the first anguish of the big, stricken face Bibbs understood the unuttered cry of accusation:

"Why wasn't it you?"

CHAPTER TWELVE

STANDING in the black group under gaunt trees at the ceme-
tery, three days later, Bibbs unwillingly let an old, old thought become definite in his mind: the sickly brother had buried the strong brother, and Bibbs wondered how many million times that had happened since men first made a word to name the sons of one another. Almost literally he had buried his strong brother, for Sheridan had gone to pieces when he saw his dead son. He had nothing to help him meet the shock, neither definite religion nor "philosophy" definite or indefinite. He could only beat his forehead and beg, over and over, to be killed with an ax, while his wife was helpless except to entreat him not to "take on," herself adding a continuous lamentation. Edith, weeping, made truce with Sibyl and saw to it that the mourning garments were beyond criticism. Roscoe was dazed, and he shirked, justifying himself

curiously by saying he "never had any experience in such matters." So it was Bibbs, the shy outsider, who became, during that dreadful little time, the master of the house; for as strange a thing as that, sometimes, may be the result of a death. He met the relatives from out of town at the station; he set the time for the funeral and the time for meals; he selected the flowers and he selected Jim's coffin; he did all the grim things and all the other things. Jim had belonged to an order of Knights, who lengthened the rites with a picturesque ceremony of their own, and at first Bibbs wished to avoid this, but upon reflection he offered no objection—he divined that the Knights and their service would be not precisely a consolation, but a satisfaction to his father. So the Knights led the procession, with their band playing a dirge part of the long way to the cemetery; and then turned back, after forming in two lines, plumed hats sympathetically in hand, to let the hearse and the carriages pass between.

"Mighty fine-lookin' men," said Sheridan, brokenly. "They all—all liked him. He was—" His breath caught in a sob and choked him. "He was—a Grand Supreme Herald."

Bibbs had divined aright.

"Dust to dust," said the minister, under the gaunt trees; and at that Sheridan shook convulsively from head to foot. All of the black group shivered, except Bibbs, when it came to "Dust to dust." Bibbs stood passive, for he was the only one of them who had known that thought as a familiar neighbor; he had been close upon dust himself for a long, long time, and even now he could prophesy no protracted separation between himself and dust. The machine-shop had brought him very close, and if he had to go back it would probably bring him closer still; so close—as Dr. Gurney predicted—that no one would be able to tell the difference between dust and himself. And Sheridan, if Bibbs read him truly, would be all the more determined to "make a man" of him, now that there was a man less in the family. To Bibbs's knowledge, no one and nothing had ever prevented his father from carrying through his plans, once he had determined upon them; and Sheridan was incapable of believing that any plan of his would not work out according to his calculations. His nature unfitted him to accept failure. He had the gift of terrible persistence, and with unflecked confidence that his way was the only way he would hold to that way of "making a man" of Bibbs, who understood very well, in his passive and impersonal fashion, that it was a way which might make, not a man, but dust of him. But he had no shudder for the thought.

He had no shudder for that thought or for any other thought. The truth about Bibbs was in the poem which Edith had adopted: he had so thoroughly formed the over-sensitive habit of hiding his feelings that no doubt he had forgotten—by this time—where he had put some of them, especially those which concerned himself. But he had not hidden his feelings about his father where they could not be found. He was strange to his father, but his father was not strange to him. He knew that Sheridan's plans were conceived in the stubborn belief that they would bring about a good thing for Bibbs himself; and whatever the result was to be, the son had no bitterness. Far otherwise, for as he looked at the big, woeful figure, shaking and tortured, an almost unbearable pity laid hands upon Bibbs's throat. Roscoe stood blinking, his lip quivering; Edith wept audibly; Mrs. Sheridan leaned in half collapse against her husband; but Bibbs knew that his father was the one who cared.

It was over. Men in overalls stepped forward with their shovels, and Bibbs nodded quickly to Roscoe, making a slight gesture toward the line of waiting carriages. Roscoe understood—Bibbs would stay and see the grave filled; the rest were to go. The groups began to move away over the turf; wheels creaked on the graveled drive; and one by one the carriages filled and departed, the horses setting off at a walk. Bibbs gazed steadfastly at the workmen; he knew that his father kept looking back as he went toward the carriage, and that was a thing he did not want to see. But after a little while there were no sounds of wheels or hoofs on the gravel, and Bibbs, glancing up, saw that every one had gone. A coupé had been left for him, the driver dozing patiently.

The workmen placed the flowers and wreaths upon the mound and about it, and Bibbs altered the position of one or two of these, then stood looking thoughtfully at the grotesque brilliancy of that festal-seeming hillock beneath the darkening November sky. "It's too bad!" he half whispered, his lips forming the words—and his meaning was that it was too bad that the strong brother had been the one to go. For this was his last thought before he walked to the coupé and saw Mary Vertrees standing, all alone, on the other side of the drive.

She had just emerged from a grove of leafless trees that grew on a slope where the tombs were many; and behind her rose a multitude of the barbaric and classic shapes we so strangely strew about our graveyards: urn-crowned columns and stone-draped obelisks, shop-carved angels and shop-carved children, poising on pillars and shafts, all lifting—in unthought pathos—their blind stoniness toward the sky. Against such a background Bibbs was not incongruous, with his figure, in black, so long and slender, and his face so long and thin and white; nor was the undertaker's coupé out of keeping, with the shabby driver dozing on the box and the shaggy horses standing patiently in attitudes without hope and without regret. But for Mary Vertrees, here was a grotesque setting—she was a vivid, living creature of a beautiful world. And a graveyard is not the place for people to look charming.

She also looked startled and confused, but not more startled and confused than Bibbs. In "Edith's" poem he had declared his intention of hiding his heart "among the stars"; and in his boyhood one day he had successfully hidden his body in the coal-pile. He had been no comrade of other boys or of girls, and his acquaintances of a recent period were only a few fellow-invalids and the nurses at the Hood Sanitarium. All his life Bibbs had kept himself to himself—he was but a shy onlooker in the world. Nevertheless, the startled gaze he bent upon the unexpected lady before him had causes other than his shyness and her unexpectedness. For Mary Vertrees had been a shining figure in the little world of late given to the view of this humble and elusive outsider, and spectators sometimes find their hearts beating faster than those of the actors in the spectacle. Thus with Bibbs now. He started and stared; he lifted his hat with incredible awkwardness, his fingers fumbling at his forehead before they found the brim.

"Mr. Sheridan," said Mary, "I'm afraid you'll have to take me home with you. I—" She stopped, not lacking a momentary awkwardness of her own.

"Why—why—yes," Bibbs stammered. "I'll—I'll be de— Won't you get in?"

In that manner and in that place they exchanged their first words. Then Mary without more ado got into the coupé, and Bibbs followed, closing the door.

"You're very kind," she said, somewhat breathlessly. "I should have had to walk, and it's beginning to get dark. It's three miles, I think."

"Yes," said Bibbs. "It—it is beginning to get dark. I—I noticed that."

"I ought to tell you—I—" Mary began, confusedly. She bit her lip, sat silent a moment, then spoke with composure. "It must seem odd, my—"

"No, no!" Bibbs protested, earnestly. "Not in the—in the least."

"It does, though," said Mary. "I had not intended to come to the cemetery, Mr. Sheridan, but one of the men in charge at the house came and whispered to me that 'the family wished me to'—I think your sister sent him. So I came. But when we reached here I—oh, I felt that perhaps I—"

Bibbs nodded gravely. "Yes, yes," he murmured.

"I got out on the opposite side of the carriage," she continued. "I mean opposite from—from where all of you were. And I wandered off over in the other direction; and I didn't realize how little time—it takes. From where I was I couldn't see the carriages leaving—at least I didn't notice them. So when I got back, just now, you were the only one here. I didn't know the other people in the carriage I came in, and of course they didn't think to wait for me. That's why—"

"Yes," said Bibbs, "I—" And that seemed all he had to say just then.

Mary looked out through the dusty window. "I think we'd better be going home, if you please," she said.

"Yes," Bibbs agreed, not moving. "It will be dark before we get there."

She gave him a quick little glance. "I think you must be very tired, Mr. Sheridan; and I know you have reason to be," she said, gently. "If you'll let me, I'll—" And without explaining her purpose she opened the door on her side of the coupé and leaned out.

Bibbs stared in blank perplexity, not knowing what she meant to do.

"Driver!" she called, in her clear voice, loudly. "Driver! We'd like to start, please! Driver! Stop at the house just north of Mr. Sheridan's, please." The wheels began to move, and she leaned back beside Bibbs once more. "I noticed that he was asleep when we got in," she said. "I suppose they have a great deal of night work."

Bibbs drew a long breath and waited till he could command

his voice. "I've never been able to apologize quickly," he said, with his accustomed slowness, "because if I try to I stammer. My brother Roscoe whipped me once, when we were boys, for stepping on his slate-pencil. It took me so long to tell him it was an accident, he finished before I did."

Mary Vertrees had never heard anything quite like the drawling, gentle voice or the odd implication that his not noticing the motionless state of their vehicle was an "accident." She had formed a casual impression of him, not without sympathy, but at once she discovered that he was unlike any of her cursory and vague imaginings of him. And suddenly she saw a picture he had not intended to paint for sympathy: a sturdy boy hammering a smaller, sickly boy, and the sickly boy unresentful. Not that picture alone; others flashed before her. Instantaneously she had a glimpse of Bibbs's life and into his life. She had a queer feeling, new to her experience, of knowing him instantly. It startled her a little; and then, with some surprise, she realized that she was glad he had sat so long, after getting into the coupé, before he noticed that it had not started. What she did not realize, however, was that she had made no response to his apology, and they passed out of the cemetery gates, neither having spoken again.

Bibbs was so content with the silence he did not know that it was silence. The dusk, gathering in their small inclosure, was filled with a rich presence for him; and presently it was so dark that neither of the two could see the other, nor did even their garments touch. But neither had any sense of being alone. The wheels creaked steadily, rumbling presently on paved streets; there were the sounds, as from a distance, of the plod-plod of the horses; and sometimes the driver became audible, coughing asthmatically, or saying, "You, *Joe!*" with a spiritless flap of the whip upon an unresponsive back. Oblongs of light from the lamps at street-corners came swimming into the interior of the coupé and, thinning rapidly to lances, passed utterly, leaving greater darkness. And yet neither of these two last attendants at Jim Sheridan's funeral broke the silence.

It was Mary who perceived the strangeness of it—too late. Abruptly she realized that for an indefinite interval she had been thinking of her companion and not talking to him. "Mr. Sheridan," she began, not knowing what she was going to say, but impelled to say anything, as she realized the queerness of this drive—"Mr. Sheridan, I—"

The coupé stopped. "You, *Joe!*" said the driver, reproachfully, and climbed down and opened the door.

"What's the trouble?" Bibbs inquired.

"Lady said stop at first house north of Mr. Sheridan's, sir."

Mary was incredulous; she felt that it couldn't be true and that it mustn't be true that they had driven all the way without speaking.

"What?" Bibbs demanded.

"We're there, sir," said the driver, sympathetically. "Next house north of Mr. Sheridan's."

Bibbs descended to the curb. "Why, yes," he said. "Yes, you seem to be right." And while he stood staring at the dimly illuminated front windows of Mr. Vertrees's house Mary got out, unassisted.

"Let me help you," said Bibbs, stepping toward her mechanically; and she was several feet from the coupé when he spoke.

"Oh no," she murmured. "I think I can—" She meant that she could get out of the coupé without help, but, perceiving that she had already accomplished this feat, she decided not to complete the sentence.

"You, *Joe!*" cried the driver, angrily, climbing to his box. And he rumbled away at his team's best pace—a snail's.

"Thank you for bringing me home, Mr. Sheridan," said Mary, stiffly. She did not offer her hand. "Good night."

"Good night," Bibbs said in response, and, turning with her, walked beside her to the door. Mary made that a short walk;

she almost ran. Realization of the queerness of their drive was growing upon her, beginning to shock her; she stepped aside from the light that fell through the glass panels of the door and withheld her hand as it touched the old-fashioned bell-handle.

"I'm quite safe, thank you," she said, with a little emphasis. "Good night."

"Good night," said Bibbs, and went obediently. When he reached the street he looked back, but she had vanished within the house.

Moving slowly away, he caromed against two people who were turning out from the pavement to cross the street. They were Roscoe and his wife.

"Where are your eyes, Bibbs?" demanded Roscoe. "Sleep-walking, as usual?"

But Sibyl took the wanderer by the arm. "Come over to our house for a little while, Bibbs," she urged. "I want to—"

"No, I'd better—"

"Yes. I want you to. Your father's gone to bed, and they're all quiet over there—all worn out. Just come for a minute."

He yielded, and when they were in the house she repeated herself with real feeling: "'All worn out!' Well, if anybody is, *you* are, Bibbs! And I don't wonder; you've done every bit of the work of it. You mustn't get down sick again. I'm going to make you take a little brandy."

He let her have her own way, following her into the dining-room, and was grateful when she brought him a tiny glass filled from one of the decanters on the sideboard. Roscoe gloomily poured for himself a much heavier libation in a larger glass; and the two men sat, while Sibyl leaned against the sideboard, reviewing the episodes of the day and recalling the names of the donors of flowers and wreaths. She pressed Bibbs to remain longer when he rose to go, and then, as he persisted, she went with him to the front door. He opened it, and she said:

"Bibbs, you were coming out of the Vertreeses' house when we met you. How did you happen to be there?"

"I had only been to the door," he said. "Good night, Sibyl."

"Wait," she insisted. "We saw you coming out."

"I wasn't," he explained, moving to depart. "I'd just brought Miss Vertrees home."

"What?" she cried.

"Yes," he said, and stepped out upon the porch, "that was it. Good night, Sibyl."

"Wait!" she said, following him across the threshold. "How did that happen? I thought you were going to wait while those men filled the—the—" She paused, but moved nearer him insistently.

"I did wait. Miss Vertrees was there," he said, reluctantly. "She had walked away for a while and didn't notice that the carriages were leaving. When she came back the coupé waiting for me was the only one left."

Sibyl regarded him with dilating eyes. She spoke with a slow breathlessness. "And she drove home from Jim's funeral —with you!"

Without warning she burst into laughter, clapped her hand ineffectually over her mouth, and ran back uproariously into the house, hurling the door shut behind her.

CHAPTER THIRTEEN

Bibbs went home pondering. He did not understand why Sibyl had laughed. The laughter itself had been spontaneous and beyond suspicion, but it seemed to him that she had only affected the effort to suppress it and that she wished it to be significant. Significant of what? And why had she wished to impress upon him the fact of her overwhelming amusement? He found no answer, but she had succeeded in disturbing him, and he wished that he had not encountered her.

At home, uncles, aunts, and cousins from out of town were wandering about the house, several mournfully admiring the "Bay of Naples," and others occupied with the Moor and the plumbing, while they waited for trains. Edith and her mother had retired to some upper fastness, but Bibbs interviewed Jackson and had the various groups of relatives summoned to the dining-room for food. One great-uncle, old Gideon Sheridan from Boonville, could not be found, and Bibbs went in search of him. He ransacked the house, discovering the missing antique at last by accident. Passing his father's closed door on tiptoe, Bibbs heard a murmurous sound, and paused to listen. The sound proved to be a quavering and rickety voice, monotonously bleating.

"The Lo-ord givuth and the Lo-ord takuth away! We got to remember that; we got to remember that! I'm a-gittin' along, James; I'm a-gittin' along, and I've seen a-many of 'em go—two daughters and a son the Lord give me, and He has taken all away. For the Lo-ord givuth and the Lo-ord takuth away! Remember the words of Bildad the Shuhite,[1] James. Bildad the Shuhite says, 'He shall have neither son nor nephew among his people, nor any remaining in his dwellings.' Bildad the Shuhite—"

Bibbs opened the door softly. His father was lying upon the bed, in his underclothes, face downward, and Uncle Gideon sat near by, swinging backward and forward in a rocking-chair, stroking his long white beard and gazing at the ceiling as he talked. Bibbs beckoned him urgently, but Uncle Gideon paid no attention.

---

[1] A character in the drama of Job, one of the books of the Bible. Job was sorrowing for the loss of his children, as well as enduring other afflictions, when Bildad attempted to comfort him by the reflection that all his misfortunes were the result of the sins of his children and himself.

"Bildad the Shuhite spake and he says, 'If thy children have sinned against Him and He have cast them away—"

There was a muffled explosion beneath the floor, and the windows rattled. The figure lying face downward on the bed did not move, but Uncle Gideon leaped from his chair. "My God!" he cried. "What's that?"

There came a second explosion, and Uncle Gideon ran out into the hall. Bibbs went to the head of the great staircase, and, looking down, discovered the source of the disturbance. Gideon's grandson, a boy of fourteen, had brought his camera to the funeral and was taking "flash-lights" of the Moor. Uncle Gideon, reassured by Bibbs's explanation, would have returned to finish his quotation from Bildad the Shuhite, but Bibbs detained him, and after a little argument persuaded him to descend to the dining-room whither Bibbs followed, after closing the door of his father's room.

He kept his eye on Gideon after dinner, diplomatically preventing several attempts on the part of that comforter to reascend the stairs; and it was a relief to Bibbs when George announced that an automobile was waiting to convey the ancient man and his grandson to their train. They were the last to leave, and when they had gone Bibbs went sighing to his own room.

He stretched himself wearily upon the bed, but presently rose, went to the window, and looked for a long time at the darkened house where Mary Vertrees lived. Then he opened his trunk, took therefrom a small note-book half filled with fragmentary scribblings, and began to write:

Laughter after a funeral. In this reaction people will laugh at anything and at nothing. The band plays a dirge on the way to the cemetery, but when it turns back, and the mourning carriages are out of hearing, it strikes up, "Darktown is Out To-night." That is natural—but there are women whose laughter is like the whirring of whips. Why is it that certain kinds of laughter seem to spoil something hidden away from the laughers? If they do not know of it, and have never seen it, how can their laughter hurt it? Yet it does.

Beauty is not out of place among grave-stones. It is not out of place anywhere. But a woman who has been betrothed to a man would not look beautiful at his funeral. A woman might look beautiful, though, at the funeral of a man whom she had known and liked. And in that case, too, she would probably not want to talk if she drove home from the cemetery with his brother; nor would she want the brother to talk. Silence is usually either stupid or timid. But for a man who stammers if he tries to talk fast, and drawls so slowly, when he doesn't stammer, that nobody has time to listen to him, silence is advisable. Nevertheless, too much silence is open to suspicion. It may be reticence, or it may be a vacuum. It may be dignity, or it may be false teeth.

Sometimes an imperceptible odor will become perceptible in a small inclosure, such as a closed carriage. The ghost of gasolene rising from a lady's glove might be sweeter to the man riding beside her than all the scents of Arcady in spring. It depends on the lady—but there *are!*

Three miles may be three hundred miles, or it may be three feet. When it is three feet you have not time to say a great deal before you reach the end of it. Still, it may be that one should begin to speak.

No one could help wishing to stay in a world that holds some of the people that are in this world. There are some so wonderful you do not understand how the dead *could* die. How could they let themselves?

A falling building does not care who falls with it. It does not choose who shall be upon its roof and who shall not.

Silence *can* be golden? Yes. But perhaps if a woman of the world should find herself by accident sitting beside a man for the length of time it must necessarily take two slow old horses to jog three miles, she might expect that man to say something of some sort! Even if she thought him a feeble hypochondriac, even if she had heard from others that he was a disappointment to his own people, even if she had seen for herself that he was a useless and irritating encumbrance everywhere, she might expect him at least to speak

—she might expect him to open his mouth and try to make sounds, if he only barked. If he did not even try, but sat every step of the way as dumb as a frozen fish, she might *think* him a frozen fish. And she might be right. She might be right if she thought him about as pleasant a companion as—as Bildad the Shuhite!

Bibbs closed his note-book, replacing it in his trunk. Then, after a period of melancholy contemplation, he undressed, put on a dressing-gown and slippers, and went softly out into the hall—to his father's door. Upon the floor was a tray which Bibbs had sent George, earlier in the evening, to place upon a table in Sheridan's room—but the food was untouched. Bibbs stood listening outside the door for several minutes. There came no sound from within, and he went back to his own room and to bed.

In the morning he woke to a state of being hitherto unknown in his experience. Sometimes in the process of waking there is a little pause—sleep has gone, but coherent thought has not begun. It is a curious half-void, a glimpse of aphasia; and although the person experiencing it may not know for that instant his own name or age or sex, he may be acutely conscious of depression or elation. It is the moment, as we say, before we "remember"; and for the first time in Bibbs's life it came to him bringing a vague happiness. He woke to a sense of new riches; he had the feeling of a boy waking to a birthday. But when the next moment brought him his memory, he found nothing that could explain his exhilaration. On the contrary, under the circumstances it seemed grotesquely unwarranted. However, it was a brief visitation and was gone before he had finished dressing. It left a little trail, the pleased recollection of it and the puzzle of it, which remained unsolved. And, in fact, waking happily in the morning is not usually the result of a drive home from a funeral. No wonder the sequence evaded Bibbs Sheridan!

His father had gone when he came down-stairs. "Went on down to 's office, jes' same," Jackson informed him. "Came sat breakfas'-table, all by 'mself; eat nothin'. George bring nice breakfas', but he di'n' eat a thing. Yessuh, went on downtown, jes' same he yoosta do. Yessuh, I reckon putty much ev'y-thing goin' go on same as it yoosta do."

It struck Bibbs that Jackson was right. The day passed as other days had passed. Mrs. Sheridan and Edith were in black, and Mrs. Sheridan cried a little, now and then, but no other external difference was to be seen. Edith was quiet, but not noticeably depressed, and at lunch proved herself able to argue with her mother upon the propriety of receiving calls in the earliest stages of "mourning." Lunch was as usual— for Jim and his father had always lunched down-town—and the afternoon was as usual. Bibbs went for his drive, and his mother went with him, as she sometimes did when the weather was pleasant. Altogether, the usualness of things was rather startling to Bibbs.

During the drive Mrs. Sheridan talked fragmentarily of Jim's childhood. "But you wouldn't remember about that," she said, after narrating an episode. "You were too little. He was always a good boy, just like that. And he'd save whatever papa gave him, and put it in the bank. I reckon it 'll just about kill your father to put somebody in his place as president of the Realty Company, Bibbs. I know he can't move Roscoe over, he told me last week he'd already put as much on Roscoe as any one man could handle and not go crazy. Oh, it's a pity—" She stopped to wipe her eyes. "It's a pity you didn't run more with Jim, Bibbs, and kind o' pick up his ways. Think what it'd meant to papa now! You never did run with either Roscoe or Jim any, even before you got sick. Of course, you were younger; but it always *did* seem queer—and you three bein' brothers like that. I don't believe I ever saw you and Jim sit down together for a good talk in my life."

"Mother, I've been away so long," Bibbs returned, gently. "And since I came home I—"

"Oh, I ain't reproachin' you, Bibbs," she said. "Jim ain't

been home much of an evening since you got back—what with his work and callin' and goin' to the theater and places, and often not even at the house for dinner. Right the evening before he got hurt he had his dinner at some miser'ble rest'rant down by the Pump Works, he was so set on overseein' the night work and gettin' everything finished up right to the minute he told papa he would. I reckon you might 'a' put in more time with Jim if there'd been more opportunity, Bibbs. I expect you feel almost as if you scarcely really knew him right well."

"I suppose I really didn't, mother. He was busy, you see, and I hadn't much to say about the things that interested him, because I don't know much about them."

"It's a pity! Oh, it's a pity!" she moaned. "And you'll have to learn to know about 'em *now,* Bibbs! I haven't said much to you, because I felt it was all between your father and you, but I honestly do believe it will just kill him if he has to have any more trouble on top of all this! You mustn't *let* him, Bibbs—you mustn't! You don't know how he's grieved over you, and now he can't stand any more—he just can't! Whatever he says for you to do, you *do* it, Bibbs, you *do* it! I want you to promise me you will."

"I would if I could," he said, sorrowfully.

"No, no! Why can't you?" she cried, clutching his arm. "He wants you to go back to the machine-shop and—"

"And—'like it'!" said Bibbs.

"Yes, that's it—to go in a cheerful spirit. Dr. Gurney said it wouldn't hurt you if you went in a cheerful spirit—the doctor said that himself, Bibbs. So why can't you do it? Can't you do that much for your father? You ought to think what he's done for *you.* You got a beautiful house to live in; you got automobiles to ride in; you got fur coats and warm clothes; you been taken care of all your life. And you don't *know* how he worked for the money to give all these things to you! You don't *dream* what he had to go through and what he risked when we were startin' out in life; and you never *will* know! And now this blow has fallen on him out of a clear sky, and you make it out to be a hardship to do like he wants you to! And all on earth he asks is for you to go back to the work in a cheerful spirit, so it won't hurt you! That's all he asks. Look, Bibbs, we're gettin' back near home, but before we get there I want you to promise me that you'll do what he asks you to. Promise me!"

In her earnestness she cleared away her black veil that she might see him better, and it blew out on the smoky wind. He readjusted it for her before he spoke.

"I'll go back in as cheerful a spirit as I can, mother," he said.

"There!" she exclaimed, satisfied. "That's a good boy! That's all I wanted you to say."

"Don't give me any credit," he said, ruefully. "There isn't anything else for me to do."

"Now, don't begin talkin' *that* way!"

"No, no," he soothed her. "We'll have to begin to make the spirit a cheerful one. We may—" They were turning into their own driveway as he spoke, and he glanced at the old house next door. Mary Vertrees was visible in the twilight, standing upon the front steps, bareheaded, the door open behind her. She bowed gravely.

" 'We may'—what?" asked Mrs. Sheridan, with a slight impatience.

"What is it, mother?"

"You said, 'We may,' and didn't finish what you were sayin'."

"Did I?" said Bibbs, blankly. "Well, what *were* we saying?"

"Of all the queer boys!" she cried. "You always were. Always! You haven't forgot what you just promised me, have you?"

"No," he answered, as the car stopped. "No, the spirit will

be as cheerful as the flesh will let it, mother. It won't do to behave like—"

His voice was low, and in her movement to descend from the car she failed to hear his final words.

"Behave like who, Bibbs?"

"Nothing."

But she was fretful in her grief. "You said it wouldn't do to behave like *somebody*. Behave like *who?*"

"It was just nonsense," he explained, turning to go in. "An obscure person I don't think much of lately."

"Behave like *who?*" she repeated, and upon his yielding to her petulant insistence, she made up her mind that the only thing to do was to tell Dr. Gurney about it.

"Like Bildad the Shuhite!" was what Bibbs said.

CHAPTER FOURTEEN

THE outward usualness of things continued after dinner. It was Sheridan's custom to read the evening paper beside the fire in the library, while his wife, sitting near by, either sewed (from old habit) or allowed herself to be repeatedly baffled by one of the simpler forms of solitaire. To-night she did neither, but sat in her customary chair, gazing at the fire, while Sheridan let the unfolded paper rest upon his lap, though now and then he lifted it, as if to read, and let it fall back upon his knees again. Bibbs came in noiselessly and sat in a corner, doing nothing; and from a "reception-room" across the hall an indistinct vocal murmur became just audible at intervals. Once, when this murmur grew louder, under stress of some irrepressible merriment, Edith's voice could be heard—"Bobby, aren't you awful!" and Sheridan glanced across at his wife appealingly.

She rose at once and went into the "reception-room"; there

was a flurry of whispering, and the sound of tiptoeing in the hall—Edith and her suitor changing quarters to a more distant room. Mrs. Sheridan returned to her chair in the library.

"They won't bother you any more, papa," she said, in a comforting voice. "She told me at lunch he'd 'phoned he wanted to come up this evening, and I said I thought he'd better wait a few days, but she said she'd already told him he could." She paused, then added, rather guiltily: "I got kind of a notion maybe Roscoe don't like him as much as he used to. Maybe—maybe you better ask Roscoe, papa." And as Sheridan nodded solemnly, she concluded, in haste: "Don't say *I* said to. I might be wrong about it, anyway."

He nodded again, and they sat for some time in a silence which Mrs. Sheridan broke with a little sniff, having fallen into a reverie that brought tears. "That Miss Vertrees was a good girl," she said. "*She* was all right."

Her husband evidently had no difficulty in following her train of thought, for he nodded once more, affirmatively.

"Did you— How did you fix it about the—the Realty Company?" she faltered. "Did you—"

He rose heavily, helping himself to his feet by the arms of his chair. "I fixed it," he said, in a husky voice. "I moved Cantwell up, and put Johnston in Cantwell's place, and split up Johnston's work among four men with salaries high enough to take it." He went to her, put his hand upon her shoulder, and drew a long, audible, tremulous breath. "It's my bedtime, mamma; I'm goin' up." He dropped the hand from her shoulder and moved slowly away, but when he reached the door he stopped and spoke again, without turning to look at her. "The Realty Company 'll go right on just the same," he said. "It's like—it's like sand, mamma. It puts me in mind of chuldern playin' in a sand-pile. One of 'em sticks his finger in the sand and makes a hole, and another of 'em 'll pat the place with his hand, and all the little grains of sand run in and fill it up and settle against one another; and then, right away it's flat on top again, and you can't tell there ever was a hole there. The Realty Company 'll go on all right, mamma. There ain't anything anywhere, I recokon, that wouldn't go right on—just the same."

And he passed out slowly into the hall; then they heard his heavy tread upon the stairs.

Mrs. Sheridan, rising to follow him, turned a piteous face to her son. "It's so forlorn," she said, chokingly. "That's the first time he spoke since he came in the house this evening. I know it must 'a' hurt him to hear Edith laughin' with that Lamhorn. She'd oughtn't to let him come, right the very first evening this way; she'd oughtn't to done it! She just seems to lose her head over him, and it scares me. You heard what Sibyl said the other day, and—and you heard what—what—"

"What Edith said to Sibyl?" Bibbs finished the sentence for her.

"We *can't* have any trouble o' *that* kind!" she wailed. "Oh, it looks as if movin' up to this New House had brought us awful bad luck! It scares me!" She put both her hands over her face. "Oh, Bibbs, Bibbs! if you only wasn't so *queer!* If you could only been a kind of dependable son! I don't know what we're all comin' to!" And, weeping, she followed her husband.

Bibbs gazed for a while at the fire; then he rose abruptly, like a man who has come to a decision, and briskly sought the room—it was called "the smoking-room"—where Edith sat with Mr. Lamhorn. They looked up in no welcoming manner, at Bibbs's entrance, and moved their chairs to a less conspicuous adjacency.

"Good evening," said Bibbs, pleasantly; and he seated himself in a leather easy-chair near them.

"What is it?" asked Edith, plainly astonished.

"Nothing," he returned, smiling.

She frowned. "Did you want something?" she asked.

"Nothing in the world. Father and mother have gone upstairs; I sha'n't be going up for several hours, and there didn't seem to be anybody left for me to chat with except you and Mr. Lamhorn."

"'*Chat* with'!" she echoed, incredulously.

"I can talk about almost anything," said Bibbs with an air of genial politeness. "It doesn't matter to *me*. I don't know much about business—if that's what you happened to be talking about. But you aren't in business, are you, Mr. Lamhorn?"

"Not now," returned Lamhorn, shortly.

"I'm not, either," said Bibbs. "It was getting cloudier than usual, I noticed, just before dark, and there was wind from the southwest. Rain to-morrow, I shouldn't be surprised."

He seemed to feel that he had begun a conversation the support of which had now become the pleasurable duty of other parties; and he sat expectantly, looking first at his sister, then at Lamhorn, as if implying that it was their turn to speak. Edith returned his gaze with a mixture of astonishment and increasing anger, while Mr. Lamhorn was obviously disturbed, though Bibbs had been as considerate as possible in presenting the weather as a topic. Bibbs had perceived that Lamhorn had nothing in his mind at any time except "personalities"—he could talk about people and he could make love. Bibbs, wishing to be courteous, offered the weather.

Lamhorn refused it, and concluded from Bibbs's luxurious attitude in the leather chair that this half-crazy brother was a permanent fixture for the rest of the evening. There was no reason to hope that he would move, and Lamhorn found himself in danger of looking silly.

"I was just going," he said, rising.

"Oh *no!*" Edith cried, sharply.

"Yes. Good night! I think I—"

"Too bad," said Bibbs, genially, walking to the door with

the visitor, while Edith stood staring as the two disappeared in the hall. She heard Bibbs offering to "help" Lamhorn with his overcoat and the latter rather curtly declining assistance, these episodes of departure being followed by the closing of the outer door. She ran into the hall.

"What's the matter with you?" she cried, furiously. "What do you *mean?* How did you dare come in there when you knew—"

Her voice broke; she made a gesture of rage and despair, and ran up the stairs, sobbing. She fled to her mother's room, and when Bibbs came up, a few minutes later, Mrs. Sheridan met him at his door.

"Oh, Bibbs," she said, shaking her head woefully, "you'd oughtn't to distress your sister! She says you drove that young man right out of the house. You'd ought to been more considerate."

Bibbs smiled faintly, noting that Edith's door was open, with Edith's naïve shadow motionless across its threshold. "Yes," he said. "He doesn't appear to be much of a 'man's man.' He ran at just a glimpse of one."

Edith's shadow moved; her voice came quavering: "You call yourself one?"

"No, no," he answered. "I said, 'just a glimpse of one.' I didn't claim—" But her door slammed angrily; and he turned to his mother.

"There," he said, sighing. "That's almost the first time in my life I ever tried to be a man of action, mother, and I succeeded perfectly in what I tried to do. As a consequence I feel like a horse-thief!"

"You hurt her feelin's," she groaned. "You must 'a' gone at it too rough, Bibbs."

He looked upon her wanly. "That's my trouble, mother," he murmured. "I'm a plain, blunt fellow. I have rough ways, and I'm a rough man."

For once she perceived some meaning in his queerness.

"Hush your nonsense!" she said, good-naturedly, the astral of a troubled smile appearing. "You go to bed."

He kissed her and obeyed.

Edith gave him a cold greeting the next morning at the breakfast-table.

"You mustn't do that under a misapprehension," he warned her, when they were alone in the dining-room.

"Do what under a what?" she asked.

"Speak to me. I came into the smoking-room last night 'on purpose,' " he told her, gravely. "I have a prejudice against that young man."

She laughed. "I guess you think it means a great deal who you have prejudices against!" In mockery she adopted the manner of one who implores. "Bibbs, for pity's sake *promise* me, *don't* use *your* influence with papa against him!" And she laughed louder.

"Listen," he said, with peculiar earnestness. "I'll tell you now, because—because I've decided I'm one of the family." And then, as if the earnestness were too heavy for him to carry it further, he continued, in his usual tone, "I'm drunk with power, Edith."

"What do you want to tell me?" she demanded, brusquely.

"Lamhorn made love to Sibyl," he said.

Edith hooted. *"She* did to *him!* And because you overheard that spat between us the other day when I *the same as accused her of it, and said something like that to you afterward—"

"No," he said, gravely. "I *know.*"

"How?"

"I was there, one day a week ago, with Roscoe, and I heard Sibyl and Lamhorn—"

Edith screamed with laughter. "You were with *Roscoe*—and you heard Lamhorn making love to Sibyl!"

"No. I heard them quarreling."

"You're funnier than ever, Bibbs!" she cried. "You say he made love to her because you heard them quarreling!"

"That's it. If you want to know what's 'between' people, you can—by the way they quarrel."

"You'll kill me, Bibbs! What were they quarreling about?"

"Nothing. That's how I knew. People who quarrel over nothing!—it's always certain—"

Edith stopped laughing abruptly, but continued her mockery. "You ought to know. You've had so much experience, yourself!"

"I haven't any, Edith," he said. "My life has been about as exciting as an incubator chicken's. But I look out through the glass at things."

"Well, then," she said, "if you look out through the glass you must know what effect such stuff would have upon *me!*" She rose, visibly agitated. "What if it *was* true?" she demanded, bitterly. "What if it was true a hundred times over? You sit there with your silly face half ready to giggle and half ready to sniffle, and tell me stories like that, about Sibyl picking on Bobby Lamhorn and worrying him to death, and you think it matters to *me?* What if I already *knew* all about their 'quarreling'? What if I understood *why* she—" She broke off with a violent gesture, a sweep of her arm extended at full length, as if she hurled something to the ground. "Do you think a girl that really cared for a man would pay any attention to *that?* Or to *you,* Bibbs Sheridan!"

He looked at her steadily, and his gaze was as keen as it was steady. She met it with unwavering pride. Finally he nodded slowly, as if she had spoken and he meant to agree with what she said.

"Ah, yes," he said. "I won't come into the smoking-room again. I'm sorry, Edith. Nobody can make you see anything now. You'll never see until you see for yourself. The rest of us will do better to keep out of it—especially me!"

"That's sensible," she responded, curtly. "You're most surprising of all when you're sensible, Bibbs."

"Yes," he sighed. "I'm a dull dog. Shake hands and forgive me, Edith."

Thawing so far as to smile, she underwent this brief ceremony, and George appeared, summoning Bibbs to the library;
Dr. Gurney was waiting there, he announced. And Bibbs
gave his sister a shy but friendly touch upon the shoulder as
a complement to the handshaking, and left her.

Dr. Gurney was sitting by the log fire, alone in the room,
and he merely glanced over his shoulder when his patient
came in. He was not over fifty, in spite of Sheridan's habitual
"ole Doc Gurney." He was gray, however, almost as thin as
Bibbs, and nearly always he looked drowsy.

"Your father telephoned me yesterday afternoon, Bibbs,"
he said, not rising. "Wants me to 'look you over' again. Come
around here in front of me—between me and the fire. I want
to see if I can see through you."

"You mean you're too sleepy to move," returned Bibbs,
complying. "I think you'll notice that I'm getting worse."

"Taken on about twelve pounds," said Gurney. "Thirteen,
maybe."

"Twelve."

"Well, it won't do." The doctor rubbed his eyelids. "You're
so much better I'll have to use some machinery on you before
we can know just where you are. You come down to my
place this afternoon. Walk down—all the way. I suppose you
know why your father wants to know."

Bibbs nodded. "Machine-shop."

"Still hate it?"

Bibbs nodded again.

"Don't blame you!" the doctor grunted. "Yes, I expect it 'll
make a lump in your gizzard again. Well, what do you say?
Shall I tell him you've got the old lump there yet? You still
want to write, do you?"

"What's the use?" Bibbs said, smiling ruefully. "My kind
of writing!"

"Yes," the doctor agreed. "I suppose if you broke away and
lived on roots and berries until you began to 'attract the fa-

vorable attention of editors' you might be able to hope for an income of four or five hundred dollars a year by the time you're fifty."

"That's about it," Bibbs murmured.

"Of course I know what you want to do," said Gurney, drowsily. "You don't hate the machine-shop only; you hate the whole show—the noise and jar and dirt, the scramble—the whole bloomin' craze to 'get on.' You'd like to go somewhere in Algiers, or to Taormina, perhaps, and bask on a balcony, smelling flowers and writing sonnets. You'd grow fat on it and have a delicate little life all to yourself. Well, what do you say? I can lie like sixty, Bibbs! Shall I tell your father he'll lose another of his boys if you don't go to Sicily?"

"I don't want to go to Sicily," said Bibbs. "I want to stay right here."

The doctor's drowsiness disappeared for a moment, and he gave his patient a sharp glance. "It's a risk," he said. "I think we'll find you're so much better he'll send you back to the shop pretty quick. Something's got hold of you lately; you're not quite so lackadaisical as you used to be. But I warn you: I think the shop will knock you just as it did before, and perhaps even harder, Bibbs."

He rose, shook himself, and rubbed his eyelids.

"Well, when we go over you this afternoon what are we going to say about it?"

"Tell him I'm ready," said Bibbs, looking at the floor.

"Oh no," Gurney laughed. "Not quite yet; but you may be almost. We'll see. Don't forget I said to walk down."

And when the examination was concluded, that afternoon, the doctor informed Bibbs that the result was much too satisfactory to be pleasing. "Here's a new 'situation' for a one-act farce," he said, gloomily, to his next patient when Bibbs had gone. "Doctor tells a man he's well, and that's his death sentence, likely. Dam' funny world!"

Bibbs decided to walk home, though Gurney had not instructed him upon this point. In fact, Gurney seemed to have
no more instructions on any point, so discouraging was the
young man's improvement. It was a dingy afternoon, and the
smoke was evident not only to Bibbs's sight, but to his nostrils,
though most of the pedestrians were so saturated with the
smell that they could no longer detect it. Nearly all of them
walked hurriedly, too intent upon their destinations to be
more than half aware of the wayside; they wore the expressions
of people under a vague yet constant strain. They were all
lightly powdered, inside and out, with fine dust and grit from
the hard-paved streets, and they were unaware of that also.
They did not even notice that they saw the smoke, though the
thickened air was like a shrouding mist. And when Bibbs
passed the new "Sheridan Apartments," now almost completed, he observed that the marble of the vestibule was already
streaky with soot, like his gloves, which were new.

That recalled to him the faint odor of gasolene in the coupé
on the way from his brother's funeral, and this incited a train
of thought which continued till he reached the vicinity of his
home. His route was by a street parallel to that on which the
New House fronted, and in his preoccupation he walked a
block farther than he intended, so that, having crossed to his
own street, he approached the New House from the north,
and as he came to the corner of Mr. Vertrees's lot Mr. Vertrees's daughter emerged from the front door and walked
thoughtfully down the path to the old picket gate. She was
unconscious of the approach of the pedestrian from the north,
and did not see him until she had opened the gate and he was
almost beside her. Then she looked up, and as she saw him
she started visibly. And if this thing had happened to Robert
Lamhorn, he would have had a thought far beyond the
horizon of faint-hearted Bibbs's thoughts. Lamhorn, indeed,
would have spoken his thought. He would have said:

"You jumped because you were thinking of me!"

CHAPTER FIFTEEN

MARY was the picture of a lady flustered. She stood with one hand closing the gate behind her, and she had turned to go in the direction Bibbs was walking. There appeared to be nothing for it but that they should walk together, at least as far as the New House. But Bibbs had paused in his slow stride, and there elapsed an instant before either spoke or moved—it was no longer than that, and yet it sufficed for each to seem to say, by look and attitude, "Why, it's *you!*"

Then they both spoke at once, each hurriedly pronouncing the other's name as if about to deliver a message of importance. Then both came to a stop simultaneously, but Bibbs made a heroic effort, and as they began to walk on together he contrived to find his voice.

"I—I—hate a frozen fish myself," he said. "I think three miles was too long for you to put up with one."

"Good gracious!" she cried, turning to him a glowing face from which restraint and embarrassment had suddenly fled. "Mr. Sheridan, you're lovely to put it that way. But it's always the girl's place to say it's turning cooler! I ought to have been the one to show that we didn't know each other well enough not to say *something!* It was an imposition for me to have made you bring me home, and after I went into the house I decided I should have walked. Besides, it wasn't three miles to the car-line. I never thought of it!"

"No," said Bibbs, earnestly. "I didn't, either. I might have said something if I'd thought of anything. I'm talking now, though; I must remember that, and not worry about it later. I think I'm talking, though it doesn't sound intelligent even to me. I made up my mind that if I ever met you again I'd turn on my voice and keep it going, no matter what it said. I—"

She interrupted him with laughter, and Mary Vertrees's laugh was one which Bibbs's father had declared, after the house-warming, "a cripple would crawl five miles to hear." And at the merry lilting of it Bibbs's father's son took heart to forget some of his trepidation. "I'll be any kind of idiot," he said, "if you'll laugh at me some more. It won't be difficult for me."

She did; and Bibbs's cheeks showed a little actual color, which Mary perceived. It recalled to her, by contrast, her careless and irritated description of him to her mother just after she had seen him for the first time, "Rather tragic and altogether impossible." It seemed to her now that she must have been blind.

They had passed the New House without either of them showing—or possessing—any consciousness that it had been the destination of one of them.

"I'll keep on talking," Bibbs continued, cheerfully, "and you keep on laughing. I'm amounting to something in the world this afternoon. I'm making a noise, and that makes you make music. Don't be bothered by my bleating out such things as that. I'm really frightened, and that makes me bleat any-thing. I'm frightened about two things: I'm afraid of what I'll think of myself later if I don't keep talking—talking now, I mean—and I'm afraid of what I'll think of myself if I do. And besides these two things, I'm frightened, anyhow. I don't re-member talking as much as this more than once or twice in my life. I suppose it was always in me to do it, though, the first time I met any one who didn't know me well enough not to listen."

"But you're not really talking to me," said Mary. "You're just thinking aloud."

"No," he returned, gravely. "I'm not thinking at all; I'm only making vocal sounds because I believe it's more man-nerly. I seem to be the subject of what little meaning they possess, and I'd like to change it, but I don't know how. I haven't any experience in talking, and I don't know how to manage it."

"You needn't change the subject on my account, Mr. Sheridan," she said. "Not even if you really talked about yourself." She turned her face toward him as she spoke, and Bibbs caught his breath; he was pathetically amazed by the look she gave him. It was a glowing look, warmly friendly and understanding, and, what almost shocked him, it was an eagerly interested look. Bibbs was not accustomed to anything like that.

"I—you—I—I'm—" he stammered, and the faint color in his cheeks grew almost vivid.

She was still looking at him, and she saw the strange radiance that came into his face. There was something about him, too, that explained how "queer" many people might think him; but he did not seem "queer" to Mary Vertrees; he seemed the most quaintly natural person she had ever met.

He waited, and became coherent. "*You* say something now," he said. "I don't even belong in the chorus, and here I am, trying to sing the funny man's solo! You—"

"No," she interrupted. "I'd rather play your accompaniment."

"I'll stop and listen to it, then."

"Perhaps—" she began, but after pausing thoughtfully she made a gesture with her muff, indicating a large brick church which they were approaching. "Do you see that church, Mr. Sheridan?"

"I suppose I could," he answered in simple truthfulness, looking at her. "But I don't want to. Once, when I was ill, the nurse told me I'd better say anything that was on my mind, and I got the habit. The other reason I don't want to see the church is that I have a feeling it's where you're going, and where I'll be sent back."

She shook her head in cheery negation. "Not unless you want to be. Would you like to come with me?"

"Why—why—yes," he said. "Anywhere!" And again it was apparent that he spoke in simple truthfulness.

"Then come—if you care for organ music. The organist is an old friend of mine, and sometimes he plays for me. He's a dear old man. He had a degree from Bonn, and was a professor afterward, but he gave up everything for music. That's he, waiting in the doorway. He looks like Beethoven, doesn't he? I think he knows that, perhaps, and enjoys it a little. I hope so."

"Yes," said Bibbs, as they reached the church steps. "I think Beethoven would like it, too. It must be pleasant to look like other people."

"I haven't kept you?" Mary said to the organist.

"No, no," he answered, heartily. "I would not mind so only you should shooer come!"

"This is Mr. Sheridan, Dr. Kraft. He has come to listen with me."

The organist looked bluntly surprised. "Iss that *so?*" he exclaimed. "Well, I am glad if you wish him, and if he can stant my liddle playink. He iss musician himself, then, of course."

"No," said Bibbs, as the three entered the church together. "I—I played the—I tried to play—" Fortunately he checked himself; he had been about to offer the information that he had failed to master the jews'-harp in his boyhood. "No, I'm not a musician," he contented himself with saying.

"What?" Dr. Kraft's surprise increased. "Young man, you are fortunate! I play for Miss Vertrees; she comes always alone. You are the first. You are the first one *ever!*"

They had reached the head of the central aisle, and as the organist finished speaking Bibbs stopped short, turning to took at Mary Vertrees in a dazed way that was not of her perceiving; for, though she stopped as he did, her gaze followed the organist, who was walking away from them toward the front of the church, shaking his white Beethovian mane roguishly.

"It's false pretenses on my part," Bibbs said. "You mean to be kind to the sick, but I'm not an anvalid any more. I'm so well I'm going.back to work in a few days. I'd better leave before he begins to play, hadn't I?"

"No," said Mary, beginning to walk forward. "Not unless you don't like great music."

He followed her to a seat about half-way up the aisle while Dr. Kraft ascended to the organ. It was an enormous one, the procession of pipes ranging from long, starveling whistles to thundering fat guns; they covered all the rear wall of the church, and the organist's figure, reaching its high perch, looked like that of some Lilliputian magician ludicrously daring the attempt to control a monster certain to overwhelm him.

"This afternoon some Handel!" he turned to shout.

Mary nodded. "Will you like that?" she asked Bibbs.

"I don't know. I never heard any except 'Largo.' I don't know anything about music. I don't even know how to pretend I do. If I knew enough to pretend, I would."

"No," said Mary, looking at him and smiling faintly, "you wouldn't."

She turned away as a great sound began to swim and tremble in the air; the huge empty space of the church filled with it, and the two people listening filled with it; the universe seemed to fill and thrill with it. The two sat intensely still, the great sound all round about them, while the church grew dusky, and only the organist's lamp made a tiny star of light. His white head moved from side to side beneath it rhythmically, or lunged and recovered with the fierceness of a duelist thrusting, but he was magnificently the master of his giant, and it sang to his magic as he bade it.

Bibbs was swept away upon that mighty singing. Such a

thing was wholly unknown to him; there had been no music in his meager life. Unlike the tale, it was the Princess Bedrul-budour [1] who had brought him to the enchanted cave, and that—for Bibbs—was what made its magic dazing. It seemed to him a long, long time since he had been walking home drearily from Dr. Gurney's office; it seemed to him that he had set out upon a happy journey since then, and that he had reached another planet, where Mary Vertrees and he sat alone together listening to a vast choiring of invisible soldiers and holy angels. There were armies of voices about them singing praise and thanksgiving; and yet they were alone. It was incredible that the walls of the church were not the boundaries of the universe, to remain so for ever; incredible that there was a smoky street just yonder, where housemaids were bringing in evening papers from front steps and where children were taking their last spins on roller-skates before being haled indoors for dinner.

He had a curious sense of communication with his new friend. He knew it could not be so, and yet he felt as if all the time he spoke to her, saying: "You hear this strain? You hear that strain? You know the dream that these sounds bring to me?" And it seemed to him as though she answered continually: "I hear! I hear that strain, and I hear the new one that you are hearing now. I know the dream that these sounds bring to you. Yes, yes, I hear it all! We hear—together!"

And though the church grew so dim that all was mysterious shadow except the vague planes of the windows and the organist's light, with the white head moving beneath it, Bibbs had no consciousness that the girl sitting beside him had grown shadowy; he seemed to see her as plainly as ever in the darkness, though he did not look at her. And all the mighty chanting of the organ's multitudinous voices that afternoon seemed to Bibbs to be chorusing of her and interpreting

[1] The princess found in the story of the Wonderful Lamp, from *Arabian Nights*.

her, singing her thoughts and singing for him the world of humble gratitude that was in his heart because she was so kind to him. It all meant Mary.

CHAPTER SIXTEEN

B UT when she asked him what it meant, on their homeward way, he was silent. They had come a few paces from the church without speaking, walking slowly.

"I'll tell you what it meant to me," she said, as he did not immediately reply. "Almost any music of Handel's always means one thing above all others to me: courage! That's it. It makes cowardice or whining seem so infinitesimal—it makes *most* things in our hustling little lives seem infinitesimal."

"Yes," he said. "It seems odd, doesn't it, that people downtown are hurrying to trains and hanging to straps in trolleycars, weltering every way to get home and feed and sleep so they can get down-town to-morrow. And yet there isn't anything down there worth getting to. They're like servants drudging to keep the house going, and believing the drudgery itself is the great thing. They make so much noise and fuss and dirt they forget that the house was meant to live in. The housework has to be done, but the people who do it have been so overpaid that they're confused and worship the housework. They're overpaid, and yet, poor things! they haven't anything that a chicken can't have. Of course, when the world gets to paying its wages sensibly that will be different."

"Do you mean 'communism'?" she asked, and she made their slow pace a little slower—they had only three blocks to go.

"Whatever the word is, I only mean that things don't look very sensible now—especially to a man that wants to keep out of 'em and can't! 'Communism'? Well, at least any 'decent sport' would say it's fair for all the strong runners to start from the same mark and give the weak ones a fair distance ahead, so that all can run something like even on the stretch. And wouldn't it be pleasant, really, if they could all cross the winning-line together? Who really enjoys beating anybody—if he sees the beaten man's face? The only way we can enjoy getting ahead of other people nowadays is by forgetting what the other people feel. And that," he added, "is nothing of what the music meant to me. You see, if I keep talking about what it didn't mean I can keep from telling you what it did mean."

"Didn't it mean courage to you, too—a little?" she asked. "Triumph and praise were in it, and somehow those things mean courage to me."

"Yes, they were all there," Bibbs said. "I don't know the name of what he played, but I shouldn't think it would matter much. The man that makes the music must leave it to you what it can mean to you, and the name he puts to it can't make much difference—except to himself and people very much like him, I suppose."

"I suppose that's true, though I'd never thought of it like that."

"I imagine music must make feelings and paint pictures in the minds of the people who hear it," Bibbs went on, musingly, "according to their own natures as much as according to the music itself. The musician might compose something and play it, wanting you to think of the Holy Grail, and some people who heard it would think of a prayer-meeting, and some would think of how good they were themselves, and a boy might think of himself at the head of a solemn procession, carrying a banner and riding a white horse. And then, if there were some jubilant passages in the music, he'd think of a circus."

They had reached her gate, and she set her hand upon it, but did not open it. Bibbs felt that this was almost the kindest of her kindnesses—not to be prompt in leaving him.

"After all," she said, "you didn't tell me whether you liked it."

"No. I didn't need to."

"No, that's true, and I didn't need to ask. I knew. But you said you were trying to keep from telling me what it did mean."

"I can't keep from telling it any longer," he said. "The music meant to me—it meant the kindness of—of you."

"Kindness? How?"

"You thought I was a sort of lonely tramp—and sick—"

"No," she said, decidedly. "I thought perhaps you'd like to hear Dr. Kraft play. And you did."

"It's curious; sometimes it seemed to me that it was you who were playing."

Mary laughed. "I? I strum! Piano. A little Chopin—Grieg—Chaminade. You wouldn't listen!"

Bibbs drew a deep breath. "I'm frightened again," he said, in an unsteady voice. "I'm afraid you'll think I'm pushing, but—" He paused, and the words sank to a murmur.

"Oh, if you want *me* to play for you!" she said. "Yes, gladly. It will be merely absurd after what you heard this afternoon. I play like a hundred thousand other girls, and I like it. I'm glad when any one's willing to listen, and if you—" She stopped, checked by a sudden recollection, and laughed ruefully. "But my piano won't be here after tonight. I—I'm sending it away to-morrow. I'm afraid that if you'd like me to play to you you'd have to come this evening."

"You'll let me?" he cried.

"Certainly, if you care to."

"If *I* could play—" he said, wistfully, "if I could play like that old man in the church I could thank you."

"Ah, but you haven't heard me play. I *know* you liked this afternoon, but—"

"Yes," said Bibbs. "It was the greatest happiness I've ever known."

It was too dark to see his face, but his voice held such plain honesty, and he spoke with such complete unconsciousness of saying anything especially significant, that she knew it was the truth. For a moment she was nonplussed, then she opened the gate and went in. "You'll come after dinner, then?"

"Yes," he said, not moving. "Would you mind if I stood here until time to come in?"

She had reached the steps, and at that she turned, offering him the response of laughter and a gay gesture of her muff toward the lighted windows of the New House, as though bidding him to run home to his dinner.

That night, Bibbs sat writing in his note-book.

Music can come into a blank life and fill it. Everything that is beautiful is music, if you can listen.

There is no gracefulness like that of a graceful woman at a grand piano. There is a swimming loveliness of line that seems to merge with the running of the sound, and you seem, as you watch her, to see what you are hearing and to hear what you are seeing.

There are women who make you think of pine woods coming down to a sparkling sea. The air about such a woman is bracing, and when she is near you, you feel strong and ambitious; you forget that the world doesn't like you. You think that perhaps you are a great fellow, after all. Then you come away and feel like a boy who has fallen in love with his Sunday-school teacher. You'll be whipped for it—and ought to be.

There are women who make you think of Diana, crowned with the moon. But they do not have the "Greek profile." I do not believe Helen of Troy had a "Greek profile"; they would not have fought about her if her nose had been quite that long. The Greek nose is not the adorable nose. The adorable nose is about an eighth of an inch shorter.

Much of the music of Wagner, it appears, is not suitable to the piano. Wagner was a composer who could interpret into music such things as the primitive impulses of humanity—he could have made a machine-shop into music. But not if he had to work in it. Wagner was always dealing in immensities—a machine-shop would have put a majestic lump in so grand a gizzard as that.

There is a mystery about pianos, it seems. Sometimes they have to be "sent away." That is how some people speak of the penitentiary. "Sent away" is a euphemism for "sent to prison." But pianos are not sent to prison, and they are not sent to the tuner—the tuner is sent to them. Why are pianos "sent away"—and where?

Sometimes a glorious day shines into the most ordinary and useless life. Happiness and beauty come caroling out of the air into the gloomy house of that life as if some stray angel just happened to perch on the roof-tree, resting and singing. And the night after such a day is lustrous and splendid with the memory of it. Music and beauty and kindness—those are the three greatest things God can give us. To bring them all in one day to one who expected nothing—ah! the heart that received them should be as humble as it is thankful. But it is hard to be humble when one is so rich with new memories. It is impossible to be humble after a day of glory.

Yes—the adorable nose is more than an eighth of an inch shorter than the Greek nose. It is a full quarter of an inch shorter.

There are women who will be kinder to a sick tramp than to a conquering hero. But the sick tramp had better remember that's what he is. Take care, take care! Humble's the word!

CHAPTER SEVENTEEN

THAT "mystery about pianos" which troubled Bibbs had been a mystery to Mr. Vertrees, and it was being explained to him at about the time Bibbs scribbled the reference to it in his notes. Mary had gone up-stairs upon Bibbs's departure at ten o'clock, and Mr. and Mrs. Vertrees sat until after midnight in the library, talking. And in all that time they found not one cheerful topic, but became more depressed with everything and with every phase of everything that they discussed—no extraordinary state of affairs in a family which has always "held up its head," only to arrive in the end at a point where all it can do is to look on helplessly at the processes of its own financial dissolution. For that was the point which this despairing couple had reached—they could do nothing except look on and talk about it. They were only vaporing, and they knew it.

"She needn't to have done that about her piano," vapored Mr. Vertrees. "We could have managed somehow without it. At least she ought to have consulted me, and if she insisted I could have arranged the details with the—the dealer."

"She thought that it might be—annoying for you," Mrs. Vertrees explained. "Really, she planned for you not to know about it until they had removed—until after to-morrow, that is, but I decided to—to mention it. You see, she didn't even tell me about it until this morning. She has another idea, too, I'm afraid. It's—it's—"

"Well?" he urged, as she found it difficult to go on.

"Her other idea is—that is, it was—I think it can be avoided, of course—it was about her furs."

"No!" he exclaimed, quickly. "I won't have it! You must see to that. I'd rather not talk to her about it, but you mustn't let her."

"I'll try not," his wife promised. "Of course, they're very handsome."

"All the more reason for her to keep them!" he returned, irritably. "We're not *that* far gone, I think!"

"Perhaps not yet," Mrs. Vertrees said. "She seems to be troubled about the—the coal matter and—about Tilly. Of course the piano will take care of some things like those for a while and—"

"I don't like it. I gave her the piano to play on, not to—"

"You mustn't be distressed about it in *one* way," she said, comfortingly. "She arranged with the—with the purchaser that the men will come for it about half after five in the afternoon. The days are so short now it's really quite winter."

"Oh yes," he agreed, moodily. "So far as that goes people

have a right to move a piece of furniture without stirring up the neighbors, I suppose, even by daylight. I don't suppose *our* neighbors are paying much attention just now, though I hear Sheridan was back in his office early the morning after the funeral."

Mrs. Vertrees made a little sound of commiseration. "I don't believe that was because he wasn't suffering, though. I'm sure it was only because he felt his business was so important. Mary told me he seemed wrapped up in his son's succeeding; and that was what he bragged about most. He isn't vulgar in his boasting, I understand; he doesn't talk a great deal about his—his actual money—though there was something about blades of grass that I didn't comprehend. I think he meant something about his energy—but perhaps not. No, his bragging usually seemed to be not so much a personal vainglory as about his family and the greatness of this city."

" 'Greatness of this city'!" Mr. Vertrees echoed, with dull bitterness. "It's nothing but a coal-hole! I suppose it looks 'great' to the man who has the luck to make it work for him. I suppose it looks 'great' to any *young* man, too, starting out to make his fortune out of it. The fellows that get what they want out of it say it's 'great,' and everybody else gets the habit. But you have a different point of view if it's the city that got what it wanted out of you! Of course Sheridan says it's 'great.' "

Mrs. Vertrees seemed unaware of this unusual outburst. "I believe," she began, timidly, "he doesn't boast of—that is, I understand he has never seemed so interested in the—the other one."

Her husband's face was dark, but at that a heavier shadow fell upon it; he looked more haggard than before. " 'The other one,' " he repeated, averting his eyes. "You mean—you mean the third son—the one that was here this evening?"

"Yes, the—the youngest," she returned, her voice so feeble it was almost a whisper.

And then neither of them spoke for several long minutes. Nor did either look at the other during that silence.

At last Mr. Vertrees contrived to cough, but not convincingly. "What—ah—what was it Mary said about him out in the hall, when she came in this afternoon? I heard you asking her something about him, but she answered in such a low voice I didn't—ah—happen to catch it."

"She—she didn't say much. All she said was this: I asked her if she had enjoyed her walk with him, and she said, 'He's the most wistful creature I've ever known.' "

"Well?"

"That was all. He *is* wistful-looking; and so fragile—though he doesn't seem quite so much so lately. I was watching Mary from the window when she went out to-day, and he joined her, and if I hadn't known about him I'd have thought he had quite an interesting face."

"If you 'hadn't known about him'? Known what?"

"Oh, nothing, of course," she said, hurriedly. "Nothing definite, that is. Mary said decidedly, long ago, that he's not at all insane, as we thought at first. It's only—well, of course it *is* odd, their attitude about him. I suppose it's some nervous trouble that makes him—perhaps a little queer at times, so that he can't apply himself to anything—or perhaps does odd things. But, after all, of course, we only have an impression about it. We don't know—that is, positively. I—" She paused, then went on: "I didn't know just how to ask—that is—I didn't mention it to Mary. I didn't— I—" The poor lady floundered pitifully, concluding with a mumble. "So soon after—after the—the shock."

"I don't think I've caught more than a glimpse of him," said Mr. Vertrees. 'I wouldn't know him if I saw him, but your impression of him is—" He broke off suddenly, springing to his feet in agitation. "I can't imagine her—oh *no!*" he gasped. And he began to pace the floor. "A half-witted epileptic!"

"No, no!" she cried. "He may be all right. We—"

"Oh, it's horrible! I can't—" He threw himself back into his chair again, sweeping his hands across his face, then letting them fall limply at his sides.

Mrs. Vertrees was tremulous. "You mustn't give way so," she said, inspired for once almost to direct discourse. "Whatever Mary might think of doing, it wouldn't be on her own account; it would be on ours. But if *we* should—should consider it, that wouldn't be on *our* own account. It isn't because we think of ourselves."

"Oh God, no!" he groaned. "Not for us! We can go to the poorhouse, but Mary can't be a stenographer!"

Sighing, Mrs. Vertrees resumed her obliqueness. "Of course," she murmured, "it all seems very premature, speculating about such things, but I had a queer sort of feeling that she seemed quite interested in this—" She had almost said "in this one," but checked herself. "In this young man. It's natural, of course; she is always so strong and well, and he is—he seems to be, that is—rather appealing to the—the sympathies."

"Yes!" he agreed, bitterly. "Precisely. The sympathies!"

"Perhaps," she faltered—"perhaps you might feel easier if I could have a little talk with some one?"

"With whom?"

"I had thought of—not going about it too brusquely, of course, but perhaps just waiting for his name to be mentioned, if I happened to be talking with somebody that knew the family—and then I might find a chance to say that I was sorry to hear he'd been ill so much, and— Something of that kind perhaps?"

"You don't know anybody that knows the family."

"Yes. That is—well, in a way, of course, one *of* the family. That Mrs. Roscoe Sheridan is not a—that is, she's rather a pleasant-faced little woman, I think, and of course rather ordinary. I think she is interested about—that is, of course, she'd be anxious to be more intimate with Mary, naturally. She's always looking over here from her house; she was looking out

of the window this afternoon when Mary went out, I noticed
—though I don't think Mary saw her. I'm sure she wouldn't
think it out of place to—to be frank about matters. She called
the other day, and Mary must rather like her—she said that
evening that the call had done her good. Don't you think it
might be wise?"

"Wise? I don't know. I feel that the whole matter is impossible."

"Yes, so do I," she returned, promptly. "It isn't really a
thing we should be considering seriously, of course. Still—"

"I should say not! But possibly—"

Thus they skirmished up and down the field, but before
they turned the lights out and went up-stairs it was thoroughly
understood between them that Mrs. Vertrees should seek the
earliest opportunity to obtain definite information from Sibyl
Sheridan concerning the mental and physical status of Bibbs.
And if he were subject to attacks of lunacy, the unhappy pair
decided to prevent the sacrifice they supposed their daughter
intended to make of herself. Altogether, if there were spiteful
ghosts in the old house that night, eavesdropping upon the
woeful comedy, they must have died anew of laughter!

Mrs. Vertrees's opportunity occurred the very next afternoon. Darkness had fallen, and the piano movers had come.
They were carrying the piano down the front steps, and Mrs.
Vertrees was standing in the open doorway behind them, pre-
paring to withdraw, when she heard a sharp exclamation; and
Mrs. Roscoe Sheridan, bareheaded, emerged from the shadow
into the light of the doorway.

"Good gracious!" she cried. "It did give me a fright!"

"It's Mrs. Sheridan, isn't it?" Mrs. Vertrees was perplexed by
this informal appearance, but she reflected that it might be
providential. "Won't you come in?"

"No. Oh no, thank you!" Sibyl panted, pressing her hand
to her side. "You don't know what a fright you've given me!
And it was nothing but your piano!" She laughed shrilly.

"You know, since our tragedy coming so suddenly the other day, you have no idea how upset I've been—almost hysterical! And I just glanced out of the window, a minute or so ago, and saw your door wide open and black figures of men against the light, carrying something heavy, and I almost fainted. You see, it was just the way it looked when I saw them bringing my poor brother-in-law in, next door, only such a few short days ago. And I thought I'd seen your daughter start for a drive with Bibbs Sheridan in a car about three o'clock—and— They aren't back yet, are they?"

"No. Good heavens!"

"And the only thing I could think of was that something must have happened to them, and I just dashed over—and it was only your *piano!*" She broke into laughter again. "I suppose you're just sending it somewhere to be repaired, aren't you?"

"It's—it's being taken down-town," said Mrs. Vertrees. "Won't you come in and make me a little visit. I was *so* sorry, the other day, that I was—ah—" She stopped inconsequently, then repeated her invitation. "Won't you come in? I'd really—"

"Thank you, but I must be running back. My husband usually gets home about this time, and I make a little point of it always to be there."

"That's very sweet." Mrs. Vertrees descended the steps and walked toward the street with Sibyl. "It's quite balmy for so late in November, isn't it? Almost like a May evening."

"I'm afraid Miss Vertrees will miss her piano," said Sibyl, watching the instrument disappear into the big van at the curb. "She plays wonderfully, Mrs. Kittersby tells me."

"Yes, she plays very well. One of your relatives came to hear her yesterday, after dinner, and I think she played all evening for him."

"You mean Bibbs?" asked Sibyl.

"The—the youngest Mr. Sheridan. Yes. He's very musical, isn't he?"

"I never heard of it. But I shouldn't think it would matter much whether he was or not, if he could get Miss Vertrees to play to him. Does your daughter expect the piano back soon?"

"I—I believe not immediately. Mr. Sheridan came last evening to hear her play because she had arranged with the—that is, it was to be removed this afternoon. He seems almost well again."

"Yes." Sibyl nodded. "His father's going to try to start him to work."

"He seems very delicate," said Mrs. Vertrees. "I shouldn't think he would be able to stand a great deal, either physically or—" She paused and then added, glowing with the sense of her own adroitness—"or mentally."

"Oh, mentally Bibbs is all right," said Sibyl, in an odd voice.

"Entirely?" Mrs. Vertrees asked, breathlessly.

"Yes, entirely."

"But has he *always* been?" This question came with the same anxious eagerness.

"Certainly. He had a long siege of nervous dyspepsia, but he's over it."

"And you think—"

"Bibbs is all right. You needn't wor—" Sibyl choked, and pressed her handkerchief to her mouth. "Good night, Mrs. Vertrees," she said, hurriedly, as the head-lights of an automobile swung round the corner above, sending a brightening glare toward the edge of the pavement where the two ladies were standing.

"Won't you come in?" urged Mrs. Vertrees, cordially, hearing the sound of a cheerful voice out of the darkness beyond the approaching glare. "Do! There's Mary now, and she—"

But Sibyl was half-way across the street. "No, thanks," she called. "I hope she won't miss her piano!" And she ran into her own house and plunged headlong upon a leather divan in the hall, holding her handkerchief over her mouth.

The noise of her tumultuous entrance was evidently startling in the quiet house, for upon the bang of the door there followed the crash of a decanter, dropped upon the floor of the dining-room at the end of the hall; and, after a rumble of indistinct profanity, Roscoe came forth, holding a dripping napkin in his hand.

"What's your excitement?" he demanded. "What do you find to go into hysterics over? Another death in the family?"

"Oh, it's funny!" she gasped. "Those old frostbitten people! I guess *they're* getting their come-upance!" Lying prone, she elevated her feet in the air, clapping her heels together repeatedly, in an ecstasy.

"Come through, come through!" said her husband, crossly. "What you been up to?"

"Me?" she cried, dropping her feet and swinging around to face him. "Nothing. It's them! Those Vertreeses!" She wiped her eyes. "They've had to sell their piano!"

"Well, what of it?"

"That Mrs. Kittersby told me all about 'em a week ago," said Sibyl. "They've been hard up for a long time, and she says as long ago as last winter she knew that girl got a pair of walking-shoes re-soled and patched, because she got it done the same place Mrs. Kittersby's cook had *hers!* And the night of the house-warming I kind of got suspicious, myself. She didn't have one single piece of any kind of real jewelry, and you could see her dress was an old one done over. Men can't tell those things, and you all made a big fuss over her, but I thought she looked a sight, myself! Of course, *Edith* was crazy to have her, and—"

"Well, well?" he urged, impatiently.

"Well, I'm *telling* you! Mrs. Kittersby says they haven't got a *thing!* Just absolutely *nothing*—and they don't know anywhere to turn! The family's all died out but them, and all the relatives they got are very distant, and live East and scarcely know 'em. She says the whole town's been wondering what *would* become of 'em. The girl had plenty chances to marry up to a year or so ago, but she was so indifferent she scared the men off, and the ones that had wanted to went and married other girls. Gracious! they were lucky! Marry *her?* The man that found himself tied up to *that* girl—"

"Terrible funny, terrible funny!" said Roscoe, with sarcasm. "It's so funny I broke a cut-glass decanter and spilled a quart of—"

"Wait!" she begged. "You'll see. I was sitting by the window a little while ago, and I saw a big wagon drive up across the street and some men go into the house. It was too dark to make out much, and for a minute I got the idea they were moving out—the house has been foreclosed on, Mrs. Kittersby says. It seemed funny, too, because I knew that girl was out riding with Bibbs. Well, I thought I'd see, so I slipped over —and it was their *piano!* They'd sold it and were trying to sneak it out after dark, so nobody'd catch on!" Again she gave way to her enjoyment, but resumed, as her husband seemed about to interrupt the narrative, "Wait a minute, can't you? The old lady was superintending, and she gave it all away. I sized her up for one of those old churchy people that tell all kinds of lies except when it comes to so many words, and then they can't. She might just as well told me outright! Yes, they'd sold it; and I hope they'll pay some of their debts. They owe everybody, and last week a coal-dealer made an awful fuss at the door with Mr. Vertrees. Their cook told our up-stairs girl, and she said she didn't know *when* she'd seen any money, herself! Did you ever hear of such a case as that girl in your *life?*"

"What girl? Their cook?"

"That Vertrees girl! Don't you see they looked on our coming up into this neighborhood as their last chance? They were just going down and out, and here bobs up the green, rich Sheridan family! So they doll the girl up in her old things, made over, and send her out to get a Sheridan—she's *got* to get one! And she just goes in blind; and she tries it on first with *you*. You remember, she just plain *told* you she was going to mash you, and then she found out you were the married one, and turned right square around to Jim and carried him off his feet. Oh, Jim was landed—there's no doubt about *that!* But Jim was lucky; he didn't live to *stay* landed, and it's a good thing for him!" Sibyl's mirth had vanished, and she spoke with virulent rapidity. "Well, she couldn't get you, because you were married, and she couldn't get Jim, because Jim died. And there they were, dead broke! Do you know what she did? Do you know what she's *doing?*"

"No, I don't," said Roscoe, gruffly.

Sibyl's voice rose and culminated in a scream of renewed hilarity. *"Bibbs!* She waited in the graveyard, and drove home with him from *Jim's funeral!* Never spoke to him before! Jim wasn't *cold!"*

She rocked herself back and forth upon the divan.

"Bibbs!" she shrieked. "Bibbs! Roscoe, *think* of it! *Bibbs!"*

He stared unsympathetically, but her mirth was unabated for all that. "And yesterday," she continued, between paroxysms—"yesterday she came out of the house—just as he was passing. She must have been looking out—waiting the chance; I saw the old lady watching at the window! And she got him there last night—to *'play'* to him; the old lady gave that away! And to-day she made him take her out in a machine! And the cream of it is that they didn't even know whether he was *insane* or not—they thought maybe he was, but she went after him just the same! The old lady set herself to pump me about it to-day. *Bibbs!* Oh, my Lord! *Bibbs!"*

But Roscoe looked grim. "So it's funny to you, is it? It sounds kind of pitiful to me. I should think it would to a woman, too."

"Oh, it might," she returned, sobering. "It might, if those people weren't such frozen-faced smart Alecks. If they'd had the decency to come down off the perch a little I probably wouldn't think it was funny, but to see 'em sit up on their pedestal all the time they're eating dirt—well, I think it's funny! That girl sits up as if she was Queen Elizabeth, and expects people to wallow on the ground before her until they get near enough for her to give 'em a good kick with her old patched shoes—oh, she'd do *that,* all right!—and then she powders up and goes out to mash—*Bibbs Sheridan!*"

"Look here," said Roscoe, heavily; "I don't care about that one way or another. If you're through, I got something I want to talk to you about. I was going to, that day just before we heard about Jim."

At this Sibyl stiffened quickly; her eyes became intensely bright. "What is it?"

"Well," he began, frowning, "what I was going to say then—" He broke off, and, becoming conscious that he was still holding the wet napkin in his hand, threw it pettishly into a corner. "I never expected I'd have to say anything like this to anybody I *married;* but I was going to ask you what was the matter between you and Lamhorn."

Sibyl uttered a sharp monosyllable. "Well?"

"I felt the time had come for me to know about it," he went on. "You never told me anything—"

"You never asked," she interposed, curtly.

"Well, we'd got in a way of not talking much," said Roscoe. "It looks to me now as if we'd pretty much lost the run of each other the way a good many people do. I don't say it wasn't my fault. I was up early and down to work all day, and I'd come home tired at night, and want to go to bed soon as I'd got the paper read—unless there was some good musical show in town. Well, you seemed all right until here lately, the last month or so, I began to see something was wrong. I couldn't help seeing it."

"Wrong?" she said. "What like?"

"You changed; you didn't look the same. You were all

strung up and excited and fidgety; you got to looking peakid and run down. Now then, Lamhorn had been going with us a good while, but I noticed that not long ago you got to picking on him about every little thing he did; you got to quarreling with him when I was there and when I wasn't. I could see you'd been quarreling whenever I came in and he was here."

"Do you object to that?" asked Sibyl, breathing quickly.

"Yes—when it injures my wife's health!" he returned, with a quick lift of his eyes to hers. "You began to run down just about the time you began falling out with him." He stepped close to her. "See here, Sibyl, I'm going to know what it means."

"Oh, you *are?*" she snapped.

"You're trembling," he said, gravely.

"Yes. I'm angry enough to do more than tremble, you'll find. Go on!"

"That was all I was going to say the other day," he said. "I was going to ask you—"

"Yes, that was all you were going to say *the other day*. Yes. What else have you to say to-night?"

"To-night," he replied, with grim swiftness, "I want to know why you keep telephoning him you want to see him since he stopped coming here."

She made a long, low sound of comprehension before she said, "And what else did Edith want you to ask me?"

"I want to know what you say over the telephone to Lamhorn," he said, fiercely.

"Is that all Edith told you to ask me? You saw her when you stopped in there on your way home this evening, didn't you? Didn't she tell you then what I said over the telephone to Mr. Lamhorn?"

"No, she didn't!" he vociferated, his voice growing louder. "She said, 'You tell your wife to stop telephoning Robert Lam-

horn to come and see her, because he isn't going to do it!'
That's what she said! And I want to know what it means. I
intend—"

A maid appeared at the lower end of the hall. "Dinner is
ready," she said, and, giving the troubled pair one glance,
went demurely into the dining-room. Roscoe disregarded the
interruption.

"I intend to know exactly what has been going on," he
declared. "I mean to know just what—"

Sibyl jumped up, almost touching him, standing face to face
with him.

"Oh, you *do!*" she cried, shrilly. "You mean to know just
what's what, do you? You listen to your sister insinuating ugly
things about your wife, and then you come home making a
scene before the servants and humiliating me in their presence!
Do you suppose that Irish girl didn't hear every word you
said? You go in there and eat your dinner alone! Go on! Go
and eat your dinner alone—because *I* won't eat with you!"

And she broke away from the detaining grasp he sought to
fasten upon her, and dashed up the stairway, panting. He
heard the door of her room slam overhead, and the sharp click
of the key in the lock.

CHAPTER EIGHTEEN

At seven o'clock on the last morning of that month, Sheridan, passing through the upper hall on his way to descend the stairs for breakfast, found a couple of scribbled
sheets of note-paper lying on the floor. A window had been
open in Bibbs's room the evening before; he had left his note-
book on the sill—and the sheets were loose. The door was
open, and when Bibbs came in and closed it, he did not no-

tice that the two sheets had blown out into the hall. Sheridan
recognized the handwriting and put the sheets in his coat
pocket, intending to give them to George or Jackson for return to the owner, but he forgot and carried them down-town
with him. At noon he found himself alone in his office, and,
having a little leisure, remembered the bits of manuscript,
took them out, and glanced at them. A glance was enough to
reveal that they were not epistolary. Sheridan would not have
read a "private letter" that came into his possession in that
way, though in a "matter of business" he might have felt it his
duty to take advantage of an opportunity afforded in any
manner whatsoever. Having satisfied himself that Bibbs's
scribblings were only a sample of the kind of writing his son
preferred to the machine-shop, he decided, innocently enough,
that he would be justified in reading them.

It appears that a lady will nod pleasantly upon some windy
generalization of a companion, and will wear the most agreeable
expression of accepting it as the law, and then—days afterward,
when the thing is a mummy to its promulgator—she will inquire
out of a clear sky: *"Why* did you say that the people down-town
have nothing in life that a chicken hasn't? What did you mean?"
And she may say it in a manner that makes a sensible reply very
difficult—you will be so full of wonder that she remembered so
seriously.

Yet, what does the rooster lack? He has food and shelter; he is
warm in winter; his wives raise not one fine family for him, but
dozens. He has a clear sky over him; he breathes sweet air; he
walks in his April orchard under a roof of flowers. He must die,
violently perhaps, but quickly. Is Midas's [1] cancer a better way?
The rooster's wives and children must die. Are those of Midas im-

---

[1] According to a story in Greek mythology, Midas had showed a kindness
to the god Dionysus, who promised to grant any request that Midas might
make. Midas asked that all which he touched might turn to gold. He found,
however, that his new power carried with it some inconvenience, since even
his food was transformed.

mortal? His life is shorter than the life of Midas, but Midas's life is only a sixth as long as that of the Galapagos tortoise.[2]

The worthy money-worker takes his vacation so that he may refresh himself anew for the hard work of getting nothing that the rooster doesn't get. The office-building has an elevator, the rooster flies up to the bough. Midas has a machine to take him to his work; the rooster finds his worm underfoot. The "business man" feels a pressure sometimes, without knowing why, and sits late at wine after the day's labor; next morning he curses his head because it interferes with the work—he swears never to relieve that pressure again. The rooster has no pressure and no wine; this difference is in his favor.

The rooster is a dependent; he depends upon the farmer and the weather. Midas is a dependent; he depends upon the farmer and the weather. The rooster thinks only of the moment; Midas provides for to-morrow. What does he provide for to-morrow? Nothing that the rooster will not have without providing.

The rooster and the prosperous worker: they are born, they grub, they love; they grub and love grubbing; they grub and they die. Neither knows beauty; neither knows knowledge. And after all, when Midas dies and rooster dies, there is one thing Midas has had and rooster has not. Midas has had the excitement of accumulating what he has grubbed, and that has been his life and his love and his god. He cannot take that god with him when he dies. I wonder if the worthy gods are those we can take with us.

Midas must teach all to be as Midas; the young must be raised in his religion—

The manuscript ended there, and Sheridan was not anxious for more. He crumpled the sheets into a ball, depositing it (with vigor) in a waste-basket beside him; then, rising, he consulted a *Cyclopedia of Names,* which a book-agent had somehow sold to him years before; a volume now first put to use for the location of "Midas." Having read the legend, Sheridan walked up and down the spacious office, exhaling the breath of contempt. "Dam' fool!" he mumbled. But this was

[2] A giant turtle found in the Island of Galapagos, located in the Pacific Ocean on the equator.

no new thought, nor was the contrariness of Bibbs's notes a surprise to him; and presently he dismissed the matter from his mind.

He felt very lonely, and this was, daily, his hardest hour. For a long time he and Jim had lunched together habitually. Roscoe preferred a club luncheon, but Jim and his father almost always went to a small restaurant near the Sheridan Building, where they spent twenty minutes in the consumption of food, and twenty in talk, with cigars. Jim came for his father every day, at five minutes after twelve, and Sheridan was again in his office at five minutes before one. But now that Jim no longer came, Sheridan remained alone in his office; he had not gone out to lunch since Jim's death, nor did he have anything sent to him—he fasted until evening.

It was the time he missed Jim personally the most—the voice and eyes and handshake, all brisk and alert, all businesslike. But these things were not the keenest in Sheridan's grief; his sense of loss went far deeper. Roscoe was dependable, a steady old wheel-horse, and that was a great comfort; but it was in Jim that Sheridan had most happily perceived his own likeness. Jim was the one who would have been surest to keep the great property growing greater, year by year. Sheridan had fallen asleep, night after night, picturing what the growth would be under Jim. He had believed that Jim was absolutely certain to be one of the biggest men in the country. Well, it was all up to Roscoe now!

That reminded him of a question he had in mind to ask Roscoe. It was a question Sheridan considered of no present importance, but his wife had suggested it—though vaguely— and he had meant to speak to Roscoe about it. However, Roscoe had not come into his father's office for several days, and when Sheridan had seen his son at home there had been no opportunity.

He waited until the greater part of his day's work was over, toward four o'clock, and then went down to Roscoe's office, which was on a lower floor. He found several men waiting for business interviews in an outer room of the series Roscoe occupied; and he supposed that he would find his son busy with others, and that his question would have to be postponed, but when he entered the door marked "R. C. Sheridan. Private," Roscoe was there alone.

He was sitting with his back to the door, his feet on a window-sill, and he did not turn as his father opened the door.

"Some pretty good men out there waitin' to see you, my boy," said Sheridan. "What's the matter?"

"Nothing," Roscoe answered indistinctly, not moving.

"Well, I guess that's all right, too. I let 'em wait sometimes myself! I just wanted to ask you a question, but I expect it'll keep, if you're workin' something out in your mind."

Roscoe made no reply; and his father, who had turned to the door, paused with his hand on the knob, staring curiously at the motionless figure in the chair. Usually the son seemed pleased and eager when he came to the office. "You're all right, ain't you?" said Sheridan. "Not sick, are you?"

"No."

Sheridan was puzzled; then, abruptly, he decided to ask his question. "I wanted to talk to you about that young Lamhorn," he said. "I guess your mother thinks he's comin' to see Edith pretty often, and you known him longer 'n any of us, so—"

"I won't," said Roscoe, thickly—"I won't say a dam' thing about him!"

Sheridan uttered an exclamation and walked quickly to a position near the window where he could see his son's face. Roscoe's eyes were bloodshot and vacuous; his hair was disordered, his mouth was distorted, and he was deathly pale. The father stood aghast.

"By George!" he muttered. *"Roscoe!"*

"My name," said Roscoe. "Can' help that."

"*Roscoe!*" Blank astonishment was Sheridan's first sensation. Probably nothing in the world could have more amazed
him than to find Roscoe—the steady old wheel-horse—in this
condition. "How'd you *get* this way?" he demanded. "You
caught cold and took too much for it?"

For reply Roscoe laughed hoarsely. "Yeuh! Cold! I been
drinkun all time, lately. Firs' you notice it?"

"By George!" cried Sheridan. "I *thought* I'd smelt it on you
a good deal lately, but I wouldn't 'a' believed you'd take
more'n was good for you. Boh! To see you like a common
hog!"

Roscoe chuckled and threw out his right arm in a meaningless gesture. "Hog!" he repeated, chuckling.

"Yes, a hog!" said Sheridan, angrily. "In business hours! I
don't object to anybody's takin' a drink if he wants to, out o'
business hours; nor, if a man keeps his work right up to the
scratch, I wouldn't be the one to baste him if he got good an'
drunk once in two, three years, maybe. It ain't *my* way. I let it
alone, but I never believed in forcin' my way on a grown-up son
in moral matters. I guess I was wrong! You think them men
out there are waitin' to talk business with a drunkard? You
think you can come to your office and do business drunk? By
George! I wonder how often this has been happening and me not
on to it! I'll have a look over your books to-morrow, and I'll—"

Roscoe stumbled to his feet, laughing wildly, and stood
swaying, contriving to hold himself in position by clutching
the back of the heavy chair in which he had been sitting.

"Hoo—hoorah!" he cried. " 'S my principles, too. Be drunkard all you want to—outside business hours. Don' for Gossake
le'n'thing innerfere business hours! Business! Thassit! You're
right, father. Drink! Die! L'everything go to hell, but *don'*
let innerfere business!"

Sheridan had seized the telephone upon Roscoe's desk, and
was calling his own office, overhead. "Abercrombie? Come
down to my son Roscoe's suite and get rid of some gentlemen

that are waitin' there to see him in room two-fourteen. There's Maples and Schirmer and a couple o' fellows on the Kinsey business. Tell 'em something's come up *I* have to go over with Roscoe, and tell 'em to come back day after to-morrow at two. You needn't come in to let me know they're gone; we don't want to be disturbed. Tell Pauley to call my house and send Claus down here with a closed car. We may have to go out. Tell him to hustle, and call me at Roscoe's room as soon as the car gets here. 'T's all!"

Roscoe had laughed bitterly throughout this monologue. "Drunk in business hours! Thass awf'l! Mus'n' do such thing! Mus'n' get drunk, mus'n' gamble, mus'n' kill 'nybody—not in business hours! All right any other time. Kill 'nybody you want to—'s long 'tain't in business hours! Fine! Mus'n' have any trouble 't 'll innerfere business. Keep your trouble 't home. Don' bring it to th' office. Might innerfere business. Have funerals on Sunday—might innerfere business! Don' let your wife innerfere business! Keep all, all, *all* your trouble an' your meanness, an' your trad—your tradegy—keep 'em *all* for home use! If you got die, go on die 't home—don' die round th' office! Might innerfere business!"

Sheridan picked up a newspaper from Roscoe's desk, and sat down with his back to his son, affecting to read. Roscoe seemed to be unaware of his father's significant posture.

"You know wh' *I* think?" he went on. "I think Bibbs only one the fam'ly any 'telligence at all. Won' work, an' di'n' get married. Jim worked, an' he got killed. I worked, an' I got married. Look at me! Jus' look at me, I ask you. Fine 'dustriss young business man. Look whass happen' to me! Fine!" He lifted his hand from the sustaining chair in a deplorable gesture, and, immediately losing his balance, fell across the chair and caromed to the floor with a crash, remaining prostrate for several minutes, during which Sheridan did not relax his apparent attention to the newspaper. He did not even look round at the sound of Roscoe's fall.

Roscoe slowly climbed to an upright position, pulling him-self up by holding to the chair. He was slightly sobered out-wardly, having progressed in the prostrate interval to a state of befuddlement less volatile. He rubbed his dazed eyes with the back of his left hand.

"What—what you ask me while ago?" he said.

"Nothin'."

"Yes, you did. What—what was it?"

"Nothin'. You better sit down."

"You ask' me what I thought about Lamhorn. You did ask me that. Well, I won't tell you. I won't say dam' word 'bout him!"

The telephone-bell tinkled. Sheridan placed the receiver to his ear and said, "Right down." Then he got Roscoe's coat and hat from a closet and brought them to his son. "Get into this coat," he said. "You're goin' home."

"All ri'," Roscoe murmured, obediently.

They went out into the main hall by a side door, not pass-ing through the outer office; and Sheridan waited for an empty elevator, stopped it, and told the operator to take on no more passengers until they reached the ground floor. Roscoe walked out of the building and got into the automobile without lurching, and twenty minutes later walked into his own house in the same manner, neither he nor his father having spoken a word in the interval.

Sheridan did not go in with him; he went home, and to his own room without meeting any of his family. But as he passed Bibbs's door he heard from within the sound of a cheerful young voice humming jubilant fragments of song:

> *Who* looks a mustang in the eye? . . .
> With a leap from the ground
> To the saddle in a bound.
> And away—and away!
> Hi-yay!

It was the first time in Sheridan's life that he had ever detected any musical symptom whatever in Bibbs—he had never even heard him whistle—and it seemed the last touch of irony that the useless fool should be merry to-day.

To Sheridan it was Tom o' Bedlam [3] singing while the house burned; and he did not tarry to enjoy the melody, but went into his own room and locked the door.

CHAPTER NINETEEN

HE EMERGED only upon a second summons to dinner, two hours later, and came to the table so white and silent that his wife made her anxiety manifest and was but partially reassured by his explanation that his lunch had "disagreed" with him a little.

Presently, however, he spoke effectively. Bibbs, whose appetite had become hearty, was helping himself to a second breast of capon from white-jacket's salver. "Here's another difference between Midas and chicken," Sheridan remarked, grimly. "Midas can eat rooster, but rooster can't eat Midas. I reckon you overlooked that. Midas looks to me like he had the advantage there."

Bibbs retained enough presence of mind to transfer the capon breast to his plate without dropping it and to respond, "Yes—he crows over it."

Having returned his antagonist's fire in this fashion, he blushed—for he could blush distinctly now—and his mother looked upon him with pleasure, though the reference to Midas

[3] A harmless lunatic. The priory of St. Mary of Bethlehem in London, founded in 1247, was used as a hospital for the insane as early as 1402. The name became corrupted to Bedlam.

and roosters was of course jargon to her. "Did you ever see anybody improve the way that child has!" she exclaimed. "I declare, Bibbs, sometimes lately you look right handsome!"

"He's got to be such a gadabout," Edith giggled.

"I found something of his on the floor up-stairs this morning, before anybody was up," said Sheridan. "I reckon if people lose things in this house and expect to get 'em back, they better get up as soon as I do."

"What was it he lost?" asked Edith.

"He knows!" her father returned. "Seems to me like I forgot to bring it home with me. I looked it over—thought probably it was something pretty important, belongin' to a busy man like him." He affected to search his pockets. "What *did* I do with it, now? Oh yes! Seems to me like I remember leavin' it down at the office—in the waste-basket."

"Good place for it," Bibbs murmured, still red.

Sheridan gave him a grin. "Perhaps pretty soon you'll be gettin' up early enough to find things before *I* do!"

It was a threat, and Bibbs repeated the substance of it, later in the evening, to Mary Vertrees—they had come to know each other that well.

"My time's here at last," he said, as they sat together in the melancholy gas-light of the room which had been denuded of its piano. That removal had left an emptiness so distressing to Mr. and Mrs. Vertrees that neither of them had crossed the threshold since the dark day; but the gas-light, though from a single jet, shed no melancholy upon Bibbs, nor could any room seem bare that knew the glowing presence of Mary. He spoke lightly, not sadly.

"Yes, it's come. I've shirked and put off, but I can't shirk and put off any longer. It's really my part to go to him—at least it would save my face. He means what he says, and the time's come to serve my sentence. Hard labor for life, I think."

Mary shook her head. "I don't think so. He's too kind."

"You think my father's *kind?*" And Bibbs stared at her.

"Yes. I'm sure of it. I've felt that he has a great, brave heart. It's only that he has to be kind in his own way—because he can't understand any other way."

"Ah yes," said Bibbs. "If that's what you mean by 'kind'!"

She looked at him gravely, earnest concern in her friendly eyes. "It's going to be pretty hard for you, isn't it?"

"Oh—self-pity!" he returned, smiling. "This has been just the last flicker of revolt. Nobody minds work if he likes the kind of work. There'd be no loafers in the world if each man found the thing that he could do best; but the only work I happen to want to do is useless—so I have to give it up. To-morrow I'll be a day-laborer."

"What is it like—exactly?"

"I get up at six," he said. "I have a lunch-basket to carry with me, which is aristocratic and no advantage. The other workmen have tin buckets, and tin buckets are better. I leave the house at six-thirty, and I'm at work in my overalls at seven. I have an hour off at noon, and work again from one till five."

"But the work itself?"

"It wasn't muscularly exhausting—not at all. They couldn't give me a heavier job because I wasn't good enough."

"But what will you do? I want to know."

"When I left," said Bibbs, "I was 'on' what they call over there a 'clipping-machine,' in one of the 'by-products' departments, and that's what I'll be sent back to."

"But what is it?" she insisted.

Bibbs explained. "It's very simple and very easy. I feed long strips of zinc into a pair of steel jaws, and the jaws bite the zinc into little circles. All I have to do is to see that the strip goes into the jaws at a certain angle—and yet I was a very bad hand at it."

He had kept his voice cheerful as he spoke, but he had grown a shade paler, and there was a latent anguish deep in his eyes. He may have known it and wished her not to see it, for he turned away.

"You do that all day long?" she asked, and as he nodded, "It seems incredible!" she exclaimed. "*You* feeding a strip of zinc into a machine nine hours a day! No wonder—" She broke off, and then, after a keen glance at his face, she said: "I should think you *would* have been a 'bad hand at it'!"

He laughed ruefully. "I think it's the noise, though I'm ashamed to say it. You see, it's a very powerful machine, and there's a sort of rhythmical crashing—a crash every time the jaws bite off a circle."

"How often is that?"

"The thing should make about sixty-eight disks a minute— a little more than one a second."

"And you're close to it?"

"Oh, the workman has to sit in its lap," he said, turning to her more gaily. "The others don't mind. You see, it's something wrong with me. I have an idiotic way of flinching from the confounded thing—I flinch and duck a little every time the crash comes, and I couldn't get over it. I was a treat to the other workmen in that room; they'll be glad to see me back. They used to laugh at me all day long."

Mary's gaze was averted from Bibbs now; she sat with her elbow resting on the arm of the chair, her lifted hand pressed against her cheek. She was staring at the wall, and her eyes had a burning brightness in them.

"It doesn't seem possible any one could do that to you," she said, in a low voice. "No. He's not kind. He ought to be proud to help you to the leisure to write books; it should be his greatest privilege to have them published for you—"

"Can't you *see* him?" Bibbs interrupted, a faint ripple of hilarity in his voice. "If he could understand what you're saying—and if you can imagine his taking such a notion, he'd have had R. T. Bloss put up posters all over the country: 'Read B. Sheridan. Read the Poet with a Punch!' No. It's just as well he never got the— But what's the use? I've never written anything worth printing, and I never shall."

"You could!" she said.

"That's because you've never seen the poor little things I've tried to do."

"You wouldn't let me, but I *know* you could! Ah, it's a pity!"

"It isn't," said Bibbs, honestly. "I never could—but you're the kindest lady in this world, Miss Vertrees."

She gave him a flashing glance, and it was as kind as he said she was. "That sounds wrong," she said, impulsively. "I mean 'Miss Vertrees.' I've thought of you by your first name ever since I met you. Wouldn't you rather call me 'Mary'?"

Bibbs was dazzled; he drew a long, deep breath and did not speak.

"Wouldn't you?" she asked, without a trace of coquetry.

"If I *can!*" he said, in a low voice.

"Ah, that's very pretty!" she laughed. "You're such an honest person, it's pleasant to have you gallant sometimes, by way of variety." She became grave again immediately. "I hear myself laughing as if it were some one else. It sounds like laughter on the eve of a great calamity." She got up restlessly, crossed the room and leaned against the wall, facing him. "You've *got* to go back to that place?"

He nodded.

"And the other time you did it—"

"Just over it," said Bibbs. "Two years. But I don't mind the prospect of a repetition so much as—"

"So much as what?" she prompted, as he stopped.

Bibbs looked up at her shyly. "I want to say it, but—but I come to a dead balk when I try. I—"

"Go on. Say it, whatever it is," she bade him. "You wouldn't know how to say anything I shouldn't like."

"I doubt if you'd either like or dislike what I want to say," he returned, moving uncomfortably in his chair and looking at his feet—he seemed to feel awkward, thoroughly. "You see, all my life—until I met you—if I ever felt like saying anything, I wrote it instead. Saying things is a new trick for me, and this—well, it's just this: I used to feel as if I hadn't ever had any sort of a life at all. I'd never been of use to anything or anybody, and I'd never had anything, myself, except a kind of haphazard thinking. But now it's different—I'm still of no use to anybody, and I don't see any prospect of being useful, but I have had something for myself. I've had a beautiful and happy experience, and it makes my life seem to be—I mean I'm glad I've lived it! That's all; it's your letting me be near you sometimes, as you have, this strange, beautiful, happy little while!"

He did not once look up, and reached silence, at the end of what he had to say, with his eyes still awkwardly regarding his feet. She did not speak, but a soft rustling of her garments let him know that she had gone back to her chair again. The house was still; the shabby old room was so quiet that the sound of a creaking in the wall seemed sharp and loud.

And yet, when Mary spoke at last, her voice was barely audible. "If you think it has been—happy—to be friends with me—you'd want to—to make it last."

"Yes," said Bibbs, as faintly.

"You'd want to go on being my friend as long as we live, wouldn't you?"

"Yes," he gulped.

"But you make that kind of speech to me because you think it's over."

He tried to evade her. "Oh, a day-laborer can't come in his overalls—"

"No," she interrupted, with a sudden sharpness. "You said what you did because you think the shop's going to kill you."

"No, no!"

"Yes, you do think that!" She rose to her feet again and came and stood before him. "Or you think it's going to send you back to the sanitarium. Don't deny it, Bibbs. There! See how easily I call you that! You see I'm a friend, or I couldn't do it. Well, if you meant what you said—and you did mean it, I know it!—you're not going to go back to the sanitarium. The shop sha'n't hurt you. It sha'n't!"

And now Bibbs looked up. She stood before him, straight and tall, splendid in generous strength, her eyes shining and wet.

"If I mean *that* much to you," she cried, "they can't harm you! Go back to the shop—but come to me when your day's work is done. Let the machines crash their sixty-eight times a minute, but remember each crash that deafens you is that much nearer the evening and me!"

He stumbled to his feet. "You say—" he gasped.

"Every evening, dear Bibbs!"

He could only stare, bewildered.

"*Every* evening. I want you. They sha'n't hurt you again!" And she held out her hand to him; it was strong and warm in his tremulous clasp. "If I could, I'd go and feed the strips of zinc to the machine with you," she said. "But all day long I'll send my thoughts to you. You must keep remembering that your friend stands beside you. And when the work is done—won't the night make up for the day?"

Light seemed to glow from her; he was blinded by that radiance of kindness. But all he could say was, huskily, "To think you're there—with me—standing beside the old zinc-eater—"

And they laughed and looked at each other, and at last Bibbs found what it meant not to be alone in the world. He had a friend.

CHAPTER TWENTY

WHEN he came into the New House, a few minutes later, he found his father sitting alone by the library fire. Bibbs went in and stood before him.

"I'm cured, father," he said. "When do I go back to the shop? I'm ready."

The desolate and grim old man did not relax. "I was sittin' up to give you a last chance to say something like that. I reckon it's about time! I just wanted to see if you'd have manhood enough not to make me take you over there by the collar. Last night I made up my mind I'd give you just one more day. Well, you got to it before I did—pretty close to the eleventh hour! All right. Start in to-morrow. It's the first o' the month. Think you can get up in time?"

"Six o'clock," Bibbs responded, briskly. "And I want to tell you—I'm going in a 'cheerful spirit.' As you said, I'll go and I'll 'like it'!"

"That's *your* lookout!" his father grunted. "They'll put you back on the clippin'-machine. You get nine dollars a week."

"More than I'm worth, too," said Bibbs, cheerily. "That reminds me, I didn't mean *you* by 'Midas' in that nonsense I'd been writing. I meant—"

"Makes a hell of a lot o' difference what you meant!"

"I just wanted you to know. Good night, father."

"G'night!"

The sound of the young man's footsteps ascending the stairs became inaudible, and the house was quiet. But presently, as Sheridan sat staring angrily at the fire, the shuffling of a pair of slippers could be heard descending, and Mrs. Sheridan made her appearance, her oblique expression and the state of her toilette being those of a person who, after trying unsuccessfully to sleep on one side, has got up to look for burglars.

"Papa!" she exclaimed, drowsily. "Why'n't you go to bed? It must be goin' on 'leven o'clock!"

She yawned, and seated herself near him, stretching out her hands to the fire. "What's the matter?" she asked, sleep and anxiety striving sluggishly with each other in her voice. "I knew you were worried all dinner-time. You got something new on your mind besides Jim's bein' taken away like he was. What's worryin' you now, papa?"

"Nothin'."

She jeered feebly. "N' tell *me* that! You sat up to see Bibbs, didn't you?"

"He starts in at the shop again to-morrow morning," said Sheridan.

"Just the same as he did before?"

"Just pre-*cisely!*"

"How—how long you goin' to keep him at it, papa?" she asked, timidly.

"Until he *knows* something!" The unhappy man struck his palms together, then got to his feet and began to pace the room, as was his wont when he talked. "He'll go back to the machine he couldn't learn to tend properly in the six months he was there, and he'll stick to it till he *does* learn it! Do you suppose that lummix ever asked himself *why* I want him to learn it? No! And I ain't a-goin' to tell him, either! When he went there I had 'em set him on the simplest machine we got —and he stuck there! How much prospect would there be of his learnin' to run the whole business if he can't run the easiest machine in it? I sent him there to make him *thorough*. And what happened? He didn't *like* it! That boy's whole life, there's been a settin' up o' something mulish that's against everything I want him to do. I don't know what it is, but it's got to be worked out of him. Now, labor ain't any more a simple question than what it was when we were young. My idea is that, outside o' union troubles, the man that can manage workin'-men is the man that's been one himself. Well,

I set Bibbs to learn the men and to learn the business, and *he* set himself to balk on the first job! That's what he did, and the balk's lasted close on to three years. If he balks again I'm just done with him! Sometimes I feel like I was pretty near done with everything, anyhow!"

"I knew there was something else," said Mrs. Sheridan, blinking over a yawn. "You better let it go till to-morrow and get to bed now—'less you'll tell me?"

"Suppose something happened to Roscoe," he said. *"Then* what 'd I have to look forward to? *Then* what could I depend on to hold things together? A lummix! A lummix that hasn't learned how to push a strip o' zinc along a groove!"

"Roscoe?" she yawned. "You needn't worry about Roscoe, papa. He's the strongest child we had. I never did know anybody keep better health than he does. I don't believe he's even had a cold in five years. You better go up to bed, papa."

"Suppose something *did* happen to him, though. You don't know what it means, keepin' property together these days— just keepin' it *alive,* let alone makin' it grow the way *I* do. I've seen too many estates hacked away in chunks, big and little. I tell you when a man dies the wolves come out o' the woods, pack after pack, to see what they can tear off for themselves; and if that dead man's chuldern ain't on the job, night and day, everything he built 'll get carried off. Carried off? I've seen a big fortune behave like an ash-barrel in a cyclone— there wasn't even a dust-heap left to tell where it stood! I've seen it, time and time again. My Lord! when I think o' such things comin' to *me!* It don't seem like I deserved it—no man ever tried harder to raise his boys right than I have. I planned and planned and planned how to bring 'em up to be guards to drive the wolves off, and how to be builders to build, and build bigger. I tell you this business life is no fool's job nowadays—a man's got to have eyes in the back of his head. You hear talk, sometimes, 'd make you think the millennium had come—but right the next breath you'll hear somebody hollerin'

about 'the great unrest.' You *bet* there's a 'great unrest'!
There ain't any man alive smart enough to see what it's goin'
to do to us in the end, nor what day it's got set to bust loose,
but it's frothin' and bubblin' in the boiler. This country's been
fillin' up with it from all over the world for a good many
years, and the old camp-meetin' days are dead and done with.
Church ain't what it used to be. Nothin's what it used to be
—everything's turned up from the bottom, and the growth is
so big the roots stick out in the air. There's an awful ruction
goin' on, and you got to keep hoppin' if you're goin' to keep
your balance on the top of it. And the schemers! They run
like bugs on the bottom of a board—after any piece o' money
they hear is loose. Fool schemes and crooked schemes; the
fool ones are the most and the worst! You got to *fight* to keep
your money after you've made it. And the woods are full o'
mighty industrious men that's got only one motto: 'Get the
other fellow's money before he gets yours!' And when a man's
built as *I* have, when he's built good and strong, and made
good things grow and prosper—*those* are the fellows that lay
for the chance to slide in and sneak the benefit of it and put
their names to it! And what's the use my havin' ever been
born, if such a thing as that is goin' to happen? What's the
use my havin' worked my life and soul into my business, if
it's all goin' to be dispersed and scattered soon as I'm in the
ground?"

He strode up and down the long room, gesticulating—little
regarding the troubled and drowsy figure by the fireside. His
throat rumbled thunderously; the words came with stormy
bitterness. "You think this is a time for young men to be lyin'
on beds of ease? I tell you there never was such a time before;
there never was such opportunity. The sluggard is despoiled
while he sleeps—yes, by George! if a man lays down they'll
eat him before he wakes!—but the live man can build straight
up till he touches the sky! This is the business man's day; it
used to be the soldier's day and the statesman's day, but this is

ours! And it ain't a Sunday to go fishin'—it's turmoil! turmoil!—and you got to go out and live it and breathe it and
make it yourself, or you'll only be a dead man walkin' around
dreamin' you're alive. And that's what my son Bibbs has been
doin' all his life, and what he'd rather do now than go out and
do his part by me. And if anything happens to Roscoe—"

"Oh, do stop worryin' over such nonsense," Mrs. Sheridan
interrupted, irritated into sharp wakefulness for the moment.
"There isn't anything goin' to happen to Roscoe, and you're
just tormentin' yourself about nothin'. Aren't you *ever* goin' to
bed?"

Sheridan halted. "All right, mamma," he said, with a vast
sigh. "Let's go up." And he snapped off the electric light,
leaving only the rosy glow of the fire.

"Did you speak to Roscoe?" she yawned, rising lopsidedly
in her drowsiness. "Did you mention about what I told you
the other evening?"

"No. I will to-morrow."

But Roscoe did not come down-town the next day, nor the
next; nor did Sheridan see fit to enter his son's house. He
waited. Then, on the fourth day of the month, Roscoe walked
into his father's office at nine in the morning, when Sheridan
happened to be alone.

"They told me down-stairs you'd left word you wanted to
see me."

"Sit down," said Sheridan, rising.

Roscoe sat. His father walked close to him, sniffed suspici-
ously, and then walked away, smiling bitterly. "Boh!" he exclaimed. "Still at it!"

"Yes," said Roscoe. "I've had a couple of drinks this morning. What about it?"

"I reckon I better adopt some decent young man," his
father returned. "I'd bring Bibbs up here and put him in your
place if he was fit. I would!"

"Better do it," Roscoe assented, sullenly.

"When 'd you begin this thing?"

"I always did drink a little. Ever since I grew up, that is."

"Leave that talk out! You know what I mean."

"Well, I don't know as I ever had too much in office hours —until the other day."

Sheridan began cutting. "It's a lie. I've had Ray Wills up from your office. He didn't want to give you away, but I put the hooks into him, and he came through. You were drunk twice before and couldn't work. You been leavin' your office for drinks every few hours for the last three weeks. I been over your books. Your office is way behind. You haven't done any work, to count, in a month."

"All right," said Roscoe, drooping under the torture. "It's all true."

"What you goin' to do about it?"

Roscoe's head was sunk between his shoulders. "I can't stand very much talk about it, father," he said, pleadingly.

"No!" Sheridan cried. "Neither can I! What do you think it means to *me?*" He dropped into the chair at his big desk, groaning. "I can't stand to talk about it any more'n you can to listen, but I'm goin' to find out what's the matter with you, and I'm goin' to straighten you out!"

Roscoe shook his head helplessly.

"You can't straighten me out."

"See here!" said Sheridan. "Can you go back to your office and stay sober to-day, while I get my work done, or will I have to hire a couple o' huskies to follow you around and knock the whiskey out o' your hand if they see you tryin' to take it?"

"You needn't worry about that," said Roscoe, looking up with a faint resentment. "I'm not drinking because I've got a thirst."

"Well, what have you got?"

"Nothing. Nothing you can do anything about. Nothing, I tell you."

"We'll see about that!" said Sheridan, harshly. "Now I can't fool with you to-day, and you get up out o' that chair and get out o' my office. You bring your wife to dinner to-morrow. You didn't come last Sunday—but you come to-morrow. I'll talk this out with you when the women-folks are workin' the phonograph, after dinner. Can you keep sober till then? You better be sure, because I'm goin' to send Abercrombie down to your office every little while, and he'll let me know."

Roscoe paused at the door. "You told Abercrombie about it?" he asked.

"*Told* him!" And Sheridan laughed hideously. "Do you suppose there's an elevator-boy in the whole dam' building that ain't on to you?"

Roscoe settled his hat down over his eyes and went out.

CHAPTER TWENTY-ONE

"*Who* looks a mustang in the eye?
Changety, chang, chang! Bash! Crash! *Bang!*"

So sang Bibbs, his musical gaieties inaudible to his fellow-workmen because of the noise of the machinery. He had discovered long ago that the uproar was rhythmical, and it had been intolerable; but now, on the afternoon of the fourth day of his return, he was accompanying the swing and clash of the metals with jubilant vaquero fragments, mingling improvisations of his own among them, and mocking the zinc-eater's crash with vocal imitations:

Fearless and bold,
Chang! Bash! Behold!

> With a leap from the ground
> To the saddle in a bound,
>   And away—and away!
>   Hi-*yay!*
> *Who* looks a chang, chang, bash, crash, bang!
> *Who* cares a dash how you bash and you crash?
>   *Night's* on the way
>   *Each* time I say,
>   Hi-*yay!*
> Crash, chang! Bash, chang! Chang, bang, *bang!*

The long room was ceaselessly thundering with metallic sound; the air was thick with the smell of oil; the floor trembled perpetually; everything was implacably in motion—nowhere was there a rest for the dizzied eye. The first time he had entered the place Bibbs had become dizzy instantly, and six months of it had only added increasing nausea to faintness. But he felt neither now. *"All day long I'll send my thoughts to you. You must keep remembering that your friend stands beside you."* He saw her there beside him, and the greasy, roaring place became suffused with radiance. The poet was happy in his machine-shop; he was still a poet there. And he fed his old zinc-eater, and sang:

> Away—and away!
>   Hi-*yay!*
> Crash, bash, crash, bash, *chang!*
>   Wild are his eyes,
>   Fiercely he dies!
>   Hi-*yay!*
> Crash, bash, bang! Bash, *chang!*
>   Ready to fling
>   Our gloves in the ring—

He was unaware of a sensation that passed along the lines of workmen. Their great master had come among them, and they grinned to see him standing with Dr. Gurney behind the

unconscious Bibbs. Sheridan nodded to those nearest him—
he had personal acquaintance with nearly all of them—but he
kept his attention upon his son. Bibbs worked steadily, never
turning from his machine. Now and then he varied his musical programme with remarks addressed to the zinc-eater.

"Go on, you old crash-basher! Chew it up! It's good for you,
if you don't try to bolt your vittles. Fletcherize, you pig!
That's right—*you'll* never get a lump in your gizzard. Want
some more? Here's a nice, shiny one."

The words were indistinguishable, but Sheridan inclined
his head to Gurney's ear and shouted fiercely: "Talkin' to
himself! By George!"

Gurney laughed reassuringly, and shook his head.

Bibbs returned to song:

> Chang! Chang, bash, chang! It's *I!*
> *Who* looks a mustang in the eye?
> Fearless and bo—

His father grasped him by the arm. "Here!" he shouted.
"Let *me* show you how to run a strip through there. The
foreman says you're some better'n you used to be, but that's
no way to handle— Get out the way and let me show you
once."

"Better be careful," Bibbs warned him, stepping to one
side.

"Careful? Boh!" Sheridan seized a strip of zinc from the
box. "What you talkin' to yourself about? Tryin' to make
yourself think you're so abused you're goin' wrong in the
head?"

"'Abused'? No!" shouted Bibbs. "I was *singing*—because I
'like it'! I told you I'd come back and 'like it.'"

Sheridan may not have understood. At all events, he made
no reply, but began to run the strip of zinc through the
machine. He did it awkwardly—and with bad results.

"Here!" he shouted. "This is the way. Watch how *I* do it. There's nothin' to it, if you put your mind on it." By his own showing then his mind was not upon it. He continued to talk. "All you got to look out for is to keep it pressed over to—"

"Don't run your hand up with it," Bibbs vociferated, leaning toward him.

"Run nothin'! You *got* to—"

"Look out!" shouted Bibbs and Gurney together, and they both sprang forward. But Sheridan's right hand had followed the strip too far, and the zinc-eater had bitten off the tips of the first and second fingers. He swore vehemently, and wrung his hand, sending a shower of red drops over himself and Bibbs, but Gurney grasped his wrist, and said, sharply:

"Come out of here. Come over to the lavatory in the office. Bibbs, fetch my bag. It's in my machine, outside."

And when Bibbs brought the bag to the washroom he found the doctor still grasping Sheridan's wrist, holding the injured hand over a basin. Sheridan had lost color, and temper, too. He glared over his shoulder at his son as the latter handed the bag to Gurney.

"You go on back to your work," he said. "I've had worse snips than that from a pencil-sharpener."

"Oh no, you haven't!" said Gurney.

"I have, too!" Sheridan retorted, angrily. "Bibbs, you go on back to your work. There's no reason to stand around here watchin' ole Doc Gurney tryin' to keep himself awake workin' on a scratch that only needs a little court-plaster. I slipped, or it wouldn't happened. You get back on your job."

"All right," said Bibbs.

"*Here!*" Sheridan bellowed, as his son was passing out of the door. "You watch out when you're runnin' that machine! You hear what I say? I slipped, or I wouldn't got scratched, but you—*you're* liable to get your whole hand cut off! You keep your eyes open!"

"Yes, sir." And Bibbs returned to the zinc-eater thoughtfully.

Half an hour later, Gurney touched him on the shoulder and beckoned him outside, where conversation was possible. "I sent him home, Bibbs. He'll have to be careful of that hand. Go get your overalls off. I'll take you for a drive and leave you at home."

"Can't," said Bibbs. "Got to stick to my job till the whistle blows."

"No, you don't," the doctor returned, smothering a yawn. "He wants me to take you down to my office and give you an overhauling to see how much harm these four days on the machine have done you. I guess you folks have got that old man pretty thoroughly upset, between you, up at your house! But I don't need to go over you. I can see with my eyes half shut—"

"Yes," Bibbs interrupted, "that's what they are."

"I say I can see you're starting out, at least, in good shape. What's made the difference?"

"I like the machine," said Bibbs. "I've made a friend of it. I serenade it and talk to it, and then it talks back to me."

"Indeed, indeed? What does it say?"

"What I want to hear."

"Well, well!" The doctor stretched himself and stamped his foot repeatedly. "Better come along and take a drive with me. You can take the time off that he allowed for the examination, and—"

"Not at all," said Bibbs. "I'm going to stand by my old zinc-eater till five o'clock. I tell you I *like* it!"

"Then I suppose that's the end of your wanting to write."

"I don't know about that," Bibbs said, thoughtfully; "but the zinc-eater doesn't interfere with my thinking, at least. It's better than being in business; I'm sure of that. I don't want anything to change. I'd be content to lead just the life I'm leading now to the end of my days."

"You do beat the devil!" exclaimed Gurney. "Your father's right when he tells me you're a mystery. Perhaps the Almighty knew what He was doing when He made you, but it takes a lot of faith to believe it! Well, I'm off. Go on back to your murdering old machine." He climbed into his car, which he operated himself, but he refrained from setting it immediately in motion. "Well, I rubbed it in on the old man that you had warned him not to slide his hand along too far, and that he got hurt because he didn't pay attention to your warning, and because he was trying to show you how to do something you were already doing a great deal better than he could. You tell him I'll be around to look at it and change the dressing to-morrow morning. Good-by."

But when he paid the promised visit, the next morning, he did more than change the dressing upon the damaged hand. The injury was severe of its kind, and Gurney spent a long time over it, though Sheridan was rebellious and scornful, being brought to a degree of tractability only by means of horrible threats and talk of amputation. However, he appeared at the dinner-table with his hand supported in a sling, which he seemed to regard as an indignity, while the natural inquiries upon the subject evidently struck him as deliberate insults. Mrs. Sheridan, having been unable to contain her solicitude several times during the day, and having been checked each time in a manner that blanched her cheek, hastened to warn Roscoe and Sibyl, upon their arrival at five, to omit any reference to the injury and to avoid even looking at the sling if they possibly could.

The Sheridans dined on Sundays at five. Sibyl had taken pains not to arrive either before or after the hand was precisely on the hour; and the members of the family were all seated at the table within two minutes after she and Roscoe had entered the house.

It was a glum gathering, overhung with portents. The air seemed charged, awaiting any tiny ignition to explode; and

Mrs. Sheridan's expression, as she sat with her eyes fixed almost continually upon her husband, was that of a person engaged in prayer. Edith was pale and intent. Roscoe looked ill; Sibyl looked ill; and Sheridan looked both ill and explosive. Bibbs had more color than any of these, and there was a strange brightness, like a light, upon his face. It was curious to see anything so happy in the tense gloom of that household.

Edith ate little, but gazed nearly all the time at her plate. She never once looked at Sibyl, though Sibyl now and then gave her a quick glance, heavily charged, and then looked away. Roscoe ate nothing, and, like Edith, kept his eyes upon his plate and made believe to occupy himself with the viands thereon, loading his fork frequently, but not lifting it to his mouth. He did not once look at his father, though his father gazed heavily at him most of the time. And between Edith and Sibyl, and between Roscoe and his father, some bitter wireless communication seemed continually to be taking place throughout the long silences prevailing during this enlivening ceremony of Sabbath refection.

"Didn't you go to church this morning, Bibbs?" his mother asked, in the effort to break up one of those ghastly intervals.

"What did you say, mother?"

"Didn't you go to church this morning?"

"I think so," he answered, as from a roseate trance.

"You *think* so! Don't you know?"

"Oh yes. Yes, I went to church!"

"Which one?"

"Just down the street. It's brick."

"What was the sermon about?"

"What, mother?"

"Can't you hear me?" she cried. "I asked you what the sermon was about?"

He roused himself. "I think it was about—" He frowned, seeming to concentrate his will to recollect. "I think it was about something in the Bible."

White-jacket George was glad of an opportunity to leave the room and lean upon Mist' Jackson's shoulder in the pantry. "He don't know they *was* any suhmon!" he concluded, having narrated the dining-room dialogue. "All he know is he was with 'at lady lives nex' do'!" George was right.

"Did you go to church all by yourself, Bibbs?" Sibyl asked.

"No," he answered. "No, I didn't go alone."

"Oh?" Sibyl gave the ejaculation an upward twist, as of mocking inquiry, and followed it by another, expressive of hilarious comprehension. *"Oh!"*

Bibbs looked at her studiously, but she spoke no further. And that completed the conversation at the lugubrious feast.

Coffee came finally, was disposed of quickly, and the party dispersed to other parts of the house. Bibbs followed his father and Roscoe into the library, but was not well received.

"You go and listen to the phonograph with the women-folks," Sheridan commanded.

Bibbs retreated. "Sometimes you do seem to be a hard sort of man!" he said.

However, he went obediently into the gilt-and-brocade room to which his mother and his sister and his sister-in-law had helplessly withdrawn, according to their Sabbatical custom. Edith sat in a corner, tapping her feet together and looking at them; Sibyl sat in the center of the room; examining a brooch which she had detached from her throat; and Mrs. Sheridan was looking over a collection of records consisting exclusively of Caruso and rag-time. She selected one of the latter, remarking that she thought it "right pretty," and followed it with one of the former and the same remark.

As the second reached its conclusion, George appeared in the broad doorway, seeming to have an errand there, but he did not speak. Instead, he favored Edith with a benevolent smile, and she immediately left the room, George stepping aside for her to precede him, and then disappearing after her in the hall with an air of successful diplomacy. He made it perfectly clear that Edith had given him secret instructions and that it had been his pride and pleasure to fulfil them to the letter.

Sibyl stiffened in her chair; her lips parted, and she watched with curious eyes the vanishing back of the white jacket.

"What's that?" she asked, in a low voice, but sharply.

"Here's another right pretty record," said Mrs. Sheridan, affecting—with patent nervousness—not to hear. And she unloosed the music.

Sibyl bit her lip and began to tap her chin with the brooch. After a little while she turned to Bibbs, who reposed at half-length in a gold chair, with his eyes closed.

"Where did Edith go?" she asked, curiously.

"Edith?" he repeated, opening his eyes blankly. "Is she gone?"

Sibyl got up and stood in the doorway. She leaned against the casing, still tapping her chin with the brooch. Her eyes were dilating; she was suddenly at high tension, and her expression had become one of sharp excitement. She listened intently.

When the record was spun out she could hear Sheridan rumbling in the library, during the ensuing silence, and Roscoe's voice, querulous and husky: "I won't say anything at all. I tell you, you might just as well let me alone!"

But there were other sounds: a rustling and murmur, whispering, low protesting cadences in a male voice. And as Mrs. Sheridan started another record, a sudden, vital resolve leaped like fire in the eyes of Sibyl. She walked down the hall and straight into the smoking-room.

Lamhorn and Edith both sprang to their feet, separating. Edith became instantly deathly white with a rage that set her shaking from head to foot, and Lamhorn stuttered as he tried to speak.

But Edith's shaking was not so violent as Sibyl's, nor was her face so white. At sight of them and of their embrace, all possible consequences became nothing to Sibyl. She courtesied, holding up her skirts and contorting her lips to the semblance of a smile.

"Sit just as you were—both of you!" she said. And then to Edith: "Did you tell my husband I had been telephoning to Lamhorn?"

"You march out of here!" said Edith, fiercely. "March straight out of here!"

Sibyl leveled a forefinger at Lamhorn.

"Did you tell her I'd been telephoning you I wanted you to come?"

"Oh, good God!" Lamhorn said. "Hush!"

"You knew she'd tell my husband, *didn't* you?" she cried. "You knew that!"

"Hush!" he begged, panic-stricken.

"That was a *manly* thing to do! Oh, it was like a gentleman! You wouldn't come—you wouldn't even come for five minutes to hear what I had to say! You were *tired* of what I had to say! You'd heard it all a thousand times before, and you wouldn't come! No! No! *No!"* she stormed. "You wouldn't even come for five minutes, but you could tell that little cat! And *she* told my husband! You're a *man!"*

Edith saw in a flash that the consequences of battle would be ruinous to Sibyl, and the furious girl needed no further temptation to give way to her feelings. "Get out of this house!" she shrieked. "This is my father's house. Don't you dare speak to Robert like that!"

"No! No! I mustn't *speak—"*

"Don't you *dare!"*

Edith and Sibyl began to scream insults at each other simultaneously, fronting each other, their furious faces close. Their voices shrilled and rose and cracked—they screeched. They could be heard over the noise of the phonograph, which was playing a brass-band selection. They could be heard all over the house. They were heard in the kitchen; they could have been heard in the cellar. Neither of them cared for that.

"You told my husband!" screamed Sibyl, bringing her face still closer to Edith's. "You told my husband! This man put *that* in your hands to strike me with! *He* did!"

"I'll tell your husband again! I'll tell him everything I know! It's *time* your husband—"

They were swept asunder by a bandaged hand. "Do you want the neighbors in?" Sheridan thundered.

There fell a shocking silence. Frenzied Sibyl saw her husband and his mother in the doorway, and she understood what she had done. She moved slowly toward the door; then suddenly she began to run. She ran into the hall, and through it, and out of the house. Roscoe followed her heavily, his eyes on the ground.

"Now then!" said Sheridan to Lamhorn.

The words were indefinite, but the voice was not. Neither was the vicious gesture of the bandaged hand, which concluded its orbit in the direction of the door in a manner sufficient for the swift dispersal of George and Jackson and several female servants who hovered behind Mrs. Sheridan. They fled lightly.

"Papa, papa!" wailed Mrs. Sheridan. "Look at your hand! You'd oughtn't to been so rough with Edie; you hurt your hand on her shoulder. Look!"

There was, in fact, a spreading red stain upon the bandages at the tips of the fingers, and Sheridan put his hand back in the sling. "Now then!" he repeated. "You goin' to leave my house?"

"He will *not!*" sobbed Edith. "Don't you *dare* order him out!"

"Don't you bother, dear," said Lamhorn, quietly. "He doesn't understand. *You* mustn't be troubled." Pallor was becoming to him; he looked very handsome, and as he left the room he seemed in the girl's distraught eyes a persecuted noble, indifferent to the rabble yawping insult at his heels—the rabble being enacted by her father.

"Don't come back, either!" said Sheridan, realistic in this impersonation. "Keep off the premises!" he called savagely into the hall. "This family's through with you!"

"It is *not!*" Edith cried, breaking from her mother. "You'll *see* about that! You'll find out! You'll find out what'll happen! What's *he* done? I guess if *I* can stand it, it's none of *your* business, is it? What's *he* done, I'd like to know? You don't know anything about it. Don't you s'pose he told *me?* She was crazy about him soon as he began going there, and he flirted with her a little. That's everything he did, and it was before he met *me!* After that he wouldn't, and it wasn't anything, anyway—he never was serious a minute about it. *She* wanted it to be serious, and she was bound she wouldn't give him up. He told her long ago he cared about me, but she kept persecuting him and—"

"Yes," said Sheridan, sternly; "that's *his* side of it! That'll do! He doesn't come in this house again!"

"You look out!" Edith cried.

"Yes, I'll look out! I'd 'a' told you to-day he wasn't to be allowed on the premises, but I had other things on my mind. I had Abercrombie look up this young man privately, and he's no 'count. He's no 'count on earth! He's no good! He's *nothin'!* But it wouldn't matter if he was George Washington, after what's happened and what I've heard tonight!"

"But, papa," Mrs. Sheridan began, "if Edie says it was all Sibyl's fault, makin' up to him, and he never encouraged her much, nor—"

"'S enough!" he roared. "He keeps off these premises! And if any of you so much as ever speak his name to me again—"

But Edith screamed, clapping her hands over her ears to shut out the sound of his voice, and ran up-stairs, sobbing loudly, followed by her mother. However, Mrs. Sheridan descended a few minutes later and joined her husband in the library. Bibbs, still sitting in his gold chair, saw her pass, roused himself from reverie, and strolled in after her.

"She locked her door," said Mrs. Sheridan, shaking her head woefully. "She wouldn't even answer me. They wasn't a sound from her room."

"Well," said her husband, "she can settle her mind to it. She never speaks to that fellow again, and if he tries to telephone her to-morrow— Here! You tell the help if he calls up to ring off and say it's my orders. No, you needn't. I'll tell 'em myself."

"Better not," said Bibbs, gently.

His father glared at him.

"It's no good," said Bibbs. "Mother, when you were in love with father—"

"My goodness!" she cried. "You ain't a-goin' to compare your father to that—"

"Edith feels about him just what you did about father," said Bibbs. "And if your father had told you—"

"I won't *listen* to such silly talk!" she declared, angrily.

"So you're handin' out your advice, are you, Bibbs?" said Sheridan. "What is it?"

"Let her see him all she wants."

"You're a—" Sheridan gave it up. "I don't know what to call you!"

"Let her see him all she wants," Bibbs repeated, thoughtfully. "You're up against something too strong for you. If Edith were a weakling you'd have a chance this way, but she isn't. She's got a lot of your determination, father, and with what's going on inside of her she'll beat you. You can't keep her from seeing him, as long as she feels about him the way she does now. You can't make her think less of him, either. Nobody can. Your only chance is that she'll do it for herself, and if you give her time and go easy she probably will. Marriage would do it for her quickest, but that's just what you don't want, and as you *don't* want it, you'd better—"

"I can't stand any more!" Sheridan burst out. "If it's come to *Bibbs* advisin' me how to run this house I better resign. Mamma, where's that nigger George? Maybe *he's* got some plan how I better manage my family. Bibbs, for God's sake go and lay down! 'Let her see him all she wants'! Oh, Lord! here's wisdom; here's—"

"Bibbs," said Mrs. Sheridan, "if you haven't got anything to do, you might step over and take Sibyl's wraps home—she left 'em in the hall. I don't think you seem to quiet your poor father very much just now."

"All right." And Bibbs bore Sibyl's wraps across the street and delivered them to Roscoe, who met him at the door. Bibbs said only, "Forgot these," and, "Good night, Roscoe," cordially and cheerfully, and returned to the New House. His mother and father were still talking in the library, but with discretion he passed rapidly on and upward to his own room, and there he proceeded to write in his note-book.

CHAPTER TWENTY-TWO

THERE seems to be another curious thing about Love [Bibbs wrote]. Love is blind while it lives and only opens its eyes and becomes very wide awake when it dies. Let it alone until then.

You cannot reason with love or with any other passion. The wise will not wish for love—nor for ambition. These are passions and bring others in their train—hatreds and jealousies—all blind. Friendship and a quiet heart for the wise.

What a turbulence is love! It is dangerous for a blind thing to be turbulent; there are precipices in life. One would not cross a mountain-pass with a thick cloth over his eyes. Lovers do. Friendship walks gently and with open eyes.

To walk to church with a friend! To sit beside her there! To rise when she rises, and to touch with one's thumb and fingers the other half of the hymn-book that she holds! What lover, with his fierce ways, could know this transcendent happiness?

Friendship brings everything that heaven could bring. There is no labor that cannot become a living rapture if you know that a friend is thinking of you as you labor. So you sing at your work. For the work is part of the thoughts of your friend; so you love it!

Love is demanding and claiming and insistent. Friendship is all kindness—it makes the world glorious with kindness. What color you see when you walk with a friend! You see that the gray sky is brilliant and shimmering; you see that the smoke has warm browns and is marvelously sculptured—the air becomes iridescent. You see the gold in brown hair. Light floods everything.

When you walk to church with a friend you know that life can give you nothing richer. You pray that there will be no change in anything for ever.

What an adorable thing it is to discover a little foible in your friend, a bit of vanity that gives you one thing more about her to adore! On a cold morning she will perhaps walk to church with you without her furs, and she will blush and return an evasive answer when you ask her why she does not wear them. You will say no more, because you understand. She looks beautiful in her furs; you love their darkness against her cheek; but you comprehend that they conceal the loveliness of her throat and the fine line of her chin, and that she also has comprehended this, and, wishing to look still more bewitching, discards her furs at the risk of taking cold. So you hold your peace, and try to look as if you had not thought it out.

This theory is satisfactory except that it does not account for the absence of the muff. Ah, well, there must always be a mystery somewhere! Mystery is a part of enchantment.

Manual labor is best. Your heart can sing and your mind can dream while your hands are working. You could not have a singing heart and a dreaming mind all day if you had to scheme out dollars, or if you had to add columns of figures. Those things take your attention. You cannot be thinking of your friend while you write letters beginning, "Yours of the 17th inst. rec'd and contents duly noted." But to work with your hands all day, thinking and singing, and then, after nightfall, to hear the ineffable kindness of your friend's greeting—always there—for you! Who would wake from such a dream as this?

Dawn and the sea—music in moonlit gardens—nightingales serenading through almond-groves in bloom—what could bring such things into the city's turmoil? Yet they are here, and roses blossom in the soot. That is what it means not to be alone! That is what a friend gives you!

Having thus demonstrated that he was about twenty-five and had formed a somewhat indefinite definition of friendship, but one entirely his own (and perhaps Mary's) Bibbs went to bed, and was the only Sheridan to sleep soundly through the night and to wake at dawn with a light heart.

His cheerfulness was vaguely diminished by the troublous state of affairs in his family. He had recognized his condition when he wrote, "Who would wake from such a dream as this?" Bibbs was a sympathetic person, easily touched, but he was indeed living in a dream, and all things outside of it were veiled and remote—for that is the way of youth in a dream. And Bibbs, who had never before been of any age, either old or young, had come to his youth at last.

He went whistling from the house before even his father had come down-stairs. There was a fog outdoors, saturated with a fine powder of soot, and though Bibbs noticed absently the dim shape of an automobile at the curb before Roscoe's house, he did not recognize it as Dr. Gurney's, but went cheerily on his way through the dingy mist. And when he was once more installed beside his faithful zinc-eater he whistled and sang to it, as other workmen did to their own machines sometimes, when things went well. His comrades in the shop glanced at him amusedly now and then. They liked him, and he ate his lunch at noon with a group of Socialists who approved of his ideas and talked of electing him to their association.

The short days of the year had come, and it was dark before the whistles blew. When the signal came, Bibbs went to the office, where he divested himself of his overalls—his single divergence from the routine of his fellow-workmen—and after that he used soap and water copiously. This was his transformation scene: he passed into the office a rather frail young working-man noticeably begrimed, and passed out of it to the pavement a cheerfully preoccupied sample of gentry, fastidious to the point of elegance.

The sidewalk was crowded with the bearers of dinner-pails, men and boys and women and girls from the work-rooms that closed at five. Many hurried and some loitered; they went both east and west, jostling one another, and Bibbs, turning his face homeward, was forced to go slowly.

Coming toward him, as slowly, through the crowd, a tall girl caught sight of his long, thin figure and stood still until he had almost passed her, for in the thick crowd and the thicker gloom he did not recognize her, though his shoulder actually touched hers. He would have gone by, but she laughed delightedly; and he stopped short, startled. Two boys, one chasing the other, swept between them, and Bibbs stood still, peering about him in deep perplexity. She leaned toward him.

"I knew *you!*" she said.

"Good heavens!" cried Bibbs. "I thought it was your voice coming out of a star!"

"There's only smoke overhead," said Mary, and laughed again. "There aren't any stars."

"Oh yes, there were—when you laughed!"

She took his arm, and they went on. "I've come to walk home with you, Bibbs. I wanted to."

"But were you here in the—"

"In the dark? Yes! Waiting? Yes!"

Bibbs was radiant; he felt suffocated with happiness. He began to scold her.

"But it's not safe, and I'm not worth it. You shouldn't have— You ought to know better. What did—"

"I only waited about twelve seconds," she laughed. "I'd just got here."

"But to come all this way and to this part of town in the dark, you—"

"I was in this part of town already," she said. "At least, I was only seven or eight blocks away, and it was dark when I came out, and I'd have had to go home alone—and I preferred going home with you."

"It's pretty beautiful for me," said Bibbs, with a deep breath. "You'll never know what it was to hear your laugh in the darkness—and then to—to see you standing there! Oh, it was like—it was like— How can I *tell* you what it was like?" They had passed beyond the crowd now, and a crossing-lamp shone upon them, which revealed the fact that again she was without her furs. Here was a puzzle. Why did that adorable little vanity of hers bring her out without them in the *dark*? But of course she had gone out long before dark. For undefinable reasons this explanation was not quite satisfactory; however, allowing it to stand, his solicitude for her took another turn. "I think you ought to have a car," he said, "especially when you want to be out after dark. You need one in winter, anyhow. Have you ever asked your father for one?"

"No," said Mary. "I don't think I'd care for one particularly."

"I wish you would." Bibbs's tone was earnest and troubled. "I think in winter you—"

"No, no," she interrupted, lightly. "I don't need—"

"But my mother tried to insist on sending one over here every afternoon for me. I wouldn't let her, because I like the walk, but a girl—"

"A girl likes to walk, too," said Mary. "Let me tell you where I've been this afternoon and how I happened to be near enough to make you take me home. I've been to see a little old man who makes pictures of the smoke. He has a sort of warehouse for a studio, and he lives there with his mother and his wife and their seven children, and he's gloriously happy. I'd seen one of his pictures at an exhibition, and I wanted to see more of them, so he showed them to me. He has almost everything he ever painted; I don't suppose he's sold more than four or five pictures in his life. He gives drawing-lessons to keep alive."

"How do you mean he paints the smoke?" Bibbs asked.

"Literally. He paints from his studio window and from the street—anywhere. He just paints what's around him—and it's beautiful."

"The smoke?"

"Wonderful! He sees the sky through it, somehow. He does the ugly roofs of cheap houses through a haze of smoke, and he does smoky sunsets and smoky sunrises, and he has other things with the heavy, solid, slow columns of smoke going far out and growing more ethereal and mixing with the hazy light in the distance; and he has others with the broken sky-line of down-town, all misted with the smoke and with puffs and jets of vapor that have colors like an orchard in mid-April. I'm going to take you there some Sunday afternoon, Bibbs."

"You're showing me the town," he said. "I didn't know what was in it at all."

"There are workers in beauty here," she told him, gently. "There are other painters more prosperous than my friend. There are all sorts of things."

"I didn't know."

"No. Since the town began growing so great that it called itself 'greater,' one could live here all one's life and know only the side of it that shows."

"The beauty-workers seem buried very deep," said Bibbs. "And I imagine that your friend who makes the smoke beautiful must be buried deepest of all. My father loves the smoke, but I can't imagine his buying one of your friend's pictures. He'd buy the 'Bay of Naples,' but he wouldn't get one of those. He'd think smoke in a picture was horrible—unless he could use it for an advertisement."

"Yes," she said, thoughtfully. "And really he's the town. They *are* buried pretty deep, it seems, sometimes, Bibbs."

"And yet it's all wonderful," he said. "It's wonderful to me."

"You mean the town is wonderful to you?"

"Yes, because everything is, since you called me your friend. The city is only a rumble on the horizon for me. It can't come any closer than the horizon so long as you let me see you standing by my old zinc-eater all day long, helping me. Mary—" He stopped with a gasp. "That's the first time I've called you 'Mary'!"

"Yes." She laughed, a little tremulously. "Though I wanted you to!"

"I said it without thinking. It must be because you came there to walk home with me. That must be it."

"Women like to have things said," Mary informed him, her tremulous laughter continuing. "Were you glad I came for you?"

"No—not 'glad.' I felt as if I were being carried straight up and up and up—over the clouds. I feel like that still. I think I'm that way most of the time. I wonder what I was like before I knew you. The person I was then seems to have been somebody else, not Bibbs Sheridan at all. It seems long, long ago. I was gloomy and sickly—somebody else—somebody I don't understand now, a coward afraid of shadows—afraid of things that didn't exist—afraid of my old zinc-eater! And now I'm only afraid of what might change anything."

She was silent a moment, and then, "You're happy, Bibbs?" she asked.

"Ah, don't you see?" he cried. "I want it to last for a thousand, thousand years, just as it is! You've made me so rich,

I'm a miser. I wouldn't have one thing different—nothing, nothing!"

"Dear Bibbs!" she said, and laughed happily.

CHAPTER TWENTY-THREE

Bibbs continued to live in the shelter of his dream. He had told Edith, after his ineffective effort to be useful in her affairs, that he had decided that he was "a member of the family"; but he appeared to have relapsed to the retired list after that one attempt at participancy—he was far enough detached from membership now. These were turbulent days in the New House, but Bibbs had no part whatever in the turbulence—he seemed an absent-minded stranger, present by accident and not wholly aware that he was present. He would sit, faintly smiling over pleasant imaginings and dear reminiscences of his own, while battle raged between Edith and her father, or while Sheridan unloosed jeremiads upon the sullen Roscoe, who drank heavily to endure them. The happy dreamer wandered into storm-areas like a somnambulist, and wandered out again unawakened. He was sorry for his father and for Roscoe, and for Edith and for Sibyl, but their sufferings and outcries seemed far away.

Sibyl was under Gurney's care. Roscoe had sent for him on Sunday night, not long after Bibbs returned the abandoned wraps; and during the first days of Sibyl's illness the doctor found it necessary to be with her frequently, and to install a muscular nurse. And whether he would or no, Gurney received from his hysterical patient a variety of pungent information which would have staggered anybody but a family physician. Among other things he was given to comprehend the change in Bibbs, and why the zinc-eater was not putting a lump in its operator's gizzard as of yore.

Sibyl was not delirious—she was a thin little ego writhing and shrieking in pain. Life had hurt her, and had driven her into hurting herself; her condition was only the adult's terrible exaggeration of that of a child after a bad bruise—there must be screaming and telling mother all about the hurt and how it happened. Sibyl babbled herself hoarse when Gurney withheld morphine. She went from the beginning to the end in a breath. No protest stopped her; nothing stopped her.

"You ought to let me die!" she wailed. "It's cruel not to let me die! What harm have I ever done to anybody that you want to keep me alive? Just look at my life! I only married Roscoe to get away from home, and look what that got me into!—look where I am now! He brought me to this town, and what did I have in my life but his *family*? And they didn't even know the right crowd! If they had, it might have been *something!* I had nothing—nothing—nothing in the world! I wanted to have a good time—and how could I? Where's any good time among these Sheridans? They never even had wine on the table! I thought I was marrying into a rich family where I'd meet attractive people I'd read about, and travel, and go to dances—and, oh, my Lord! all I got was these Sheridans! I did the best I could; I did, indeed! Oh, I *did!* I just tried to live. Every woman's got a right to live, some time in her life, I guess! Things were just beginning to look brighter—we'd moved up here, and that frozen crowd across the street were after Jim for their daughter, and they'd have started us with the right people—and then I saw how Edith was getting him away from me. She did it, too! She got him! A girl with money can do that to a married woman—yes, she can, every time! And what could I do? What can any woman do in my fix? I couldn't do *anything* but try to stand it—and I couldn't stand it! I went to that icicle—that Vertrees girl—and she could have helped me a little, and it wouldn't have hurt her. It wouldn't have done her any harm to help me *that* little!

She treated me as if I'd been dirt that she wouldn't even take the trouble to sweep out of her house! Let her *wait!*" Sibyl's voice, hoarse from babbling, became no more than a husky whisper, though she strove to make it louder. She struggled half upright, and the nurse restrained her. "I'd get up out of this bed to show her she can't do such things to me! I was absolutely ladylike, and she walked out and left me there alone! She'll *see!* She started after Bibbs before Jim's casket was fairly underground, and she thinks she's landed that poor loon—but she'll see! She'll see! If I'm ever able to walk across the street again I'll show her how to treat a woman in trouble that comes to her for help! It wouldn't have hurt her any— it wouldn't—it wouldn't. And Edith needn't have told what she told Roscoe—it wouldn't have hurt her to let me alone. And *he* told her I bored him—telephoning him I wanted to see him. He needn't have done it! He needn't—needn't—" Her voice grew fainter, for that while, with exhaustion, though she would go over it all again as soon as her strength returned. She lay panting. Then, seeing her husband standing disheveled in the doorway, "Don't come in, Roscoe," she murmured. "I don't want to see you." And as he turned away she added, "I'm kind of sorry for you, Roscoe."

Her antagonist, Edith, was not more coherent in her own wailings, and she had the advantage of a mother for listener. She had also the disadvantage of a mother for duenna, and Mrs. Sheridan, under her husband's sharp tutelage, proved an effective one. Edith was reduced to telephoning Lamhorn from shops whenever she could juggle her mother into a momentary distraction over a counter.

Edith was incomparably more in love than before Lamhorn's expulsion. Her whole being was nothing but the determination to hurdle everything that separated her from him. She was in a state that could be altered by only the lightest and most delicate diplomacy of suggestion, but Sheridan, like legions of other parents, intensified her passion and fed it hourly fuel by opposing to it an intolerable force. He swore she should cool, and thus set her on fire.

Edith planned neatly. She fought hard, every other evening, with her father, and kept her bed betweentimes to let him see what his violence had done to her. Then, when the mere sight of her set him to breathing fast, she said pitiably that she might bear her trouble better if she went away; it was impossible to be in the same town with Lamhorn and not think always of him. Perhaps in New York she might forget a little. She had written to a school friend, established quietly with an aunt in apartments—and a month or so of theaters and restaurants might bring peace. Sheridan shouted with relief; he gave her a copious cheque, and she left upon a Monday morning, wearing violets with her mourning and having kissed everybody good-by except Sibyl and Bibbs. She might have kissed Bibbs, but he failed to realize that the day of her departure had arrived, and was surprised, on returning from his zinc-eater, that evening, to find her gone. "I suppose they'll be married there," he said, casually.

Sheridan, seated, warming his stockinged feet at the fire, jumped up, fuming. "Either you go out o' here, or I will, Bibbs!" he snorted. "I don't want to be in the same room with the particular kind of idiot you are! She's through with that riff-raff; all she needed was to be kept away from him a few weeks, and I *kept* her away, and it did the business. For Heaven's sake, go on out o' here!"

Bibbs obeyed the gesture of a hand still bandaged. And the black silk sling was still round Sheridan's neck, but no word of Gurney's and no excruciating twinge of pain could keep Sheridan's hand in the sling. The wounds, slight enough originally, had become infected the first time he had dislodged the bandages, and healing was long delayed. Sheridan had the habit of gesture; he could not "take time to remember," he said, that he must be careful, and he had also a curious indignation with his hurt; he refused to pay it the compliment of admitting its existence.

The Saturday following Edith's departure Gurney came to the Sheridan Building to dress the wounds and to have a talk with Sheridan which the doctor felt had become necessary. But he was a little before the appointed time and was obliged to wait a few minutes in an anteroom—there was a directors' meeting of some sort in Sheridan's office. The door was slightly ajar, leaking cigar-smoke and oratory, the latter all Sheridan's and Gurney listened.

"No, sir; no, sir; no, sir!" he heard the big voice rumbling, and then, breaking into thunder, "I tell you NO! Some o' you men make me sick! You'd lose your confidence in Almighty God if a doodle-bug flipped his hind leg at you! You say money's tight all over the country. Well, what if it is? There's no reason for it to be tight, and it's not goin' to keep *our* money tight! You're always runnin' to the woodshed to hide your nickels in a crack because some fool newspaper says the market's a little skeery! You listen to every street-corner croaker and then come and set here and try to scare *me* out of a big thing! We're *in* on this—understand? I tell you there never *was* better times. These are good times and big times, and I won't stand for any other kind o' talk. This country's on its feet as it never was before, and this city's on its feet and goin' to stay there!" And Gurney heard a series of whacks and thumps upon the desk. "'Bad times'!" Sheridan vociferated, with accompanying thumps. "Rabbit talk! These times are glorious, I tell you! We're in the promised land, and we're goin' to *stay* there! That's all, gentlemen. The loan goes!"

The directors came forth, flushed and murmurous, and Gurney hastened in. His guess was correct: Sheridan had been thumping the desk with his right hand. The physician scolded wearily, making good the fresh damage as best he might; and then he said what he had to say on the subject of Roscoe and Sibyl, his opinion meeting, as he expected, a warmly hostile reception. But the result of this conversation was that by telephonic command Roscoe awaited his father, an hour later, in the library at the New House.

"Gurney says your wife's able to travel," Sheridan said brusquely, as he came in.

"Yes." Roscoe occupied a deep chair and sat in the dejected attitude which had become his habit. "Yes, she is."

"Edith had to leave town, and so Sybil thinks she'll have to, too!"

"Oh, I wouldn't put it that way," Roscoe protested, drearily.

"No, I hear *you* wouldn't!" There was a bitter gibe in the father's voice, and he added: "It's a good thing she's goin' abroad—if she'll stay there. I shouldn't think any of us want her here any more—you least of all!"

"It's no use your talking that way," said Roscoe. "You won't do any good."

"Well, when you comin' back to your office?" Sheridan used a brisker, kinder tone. "Three weeks since you showed up there at all. When you goin' to be ready to cut out whiskey and all the rest o' the foolishness and start in again? You ought to be able to make up for a lot o' lost time and a lot o' spilt milk when that woman takes herself out o' the way and lets you and all the rest of us alone."

"It's no use, father, I tell you. I know what Gurney was going to say to you. I'm not going back to the office. I'm *done!*"

"Wait a minute before you talk that way!" Sheridan began his sentry-go up and down the room. "I suppose you know it's taken two pretty good men about sixteen hours a day to set things straight and get 'em runnin' right again, down in your office?"

"They must be good men." Roscoe nodded indifferently. "I thought I was doing about eight men's work. I'm glad you found two that could handle it."

"Look here! If I worked you it was for your own good. There are plenty men drive harder 'n *I* do, and—"

"Yes. There are some that break down all the other men that work with 'em. They either die, or go crazy, or have to quit, and are no use the rest of their lives. The last's my case, I guess—'complicated by domestic difficulties'!"

"You set there and tell me you give up?" Sheridan's voice shook, and so did the gesticulating hand which he extended appealingly toward the despondent figure. "Don't do it, Roscoe! Don't say it! Say you'll come down there again and be a man! This woman ain't goin' to trouble you any more. The work ain't goin' to hurt you if you haven't got her to worry you, and you can get shut o' this nasty whiskey-guzzlin'; it ain't fastened on you yet. Don't say—"

"It's no use on earth," Roscoe mumbled. "No use on earth."

"Look here! If you want another month's vacation—"

"I know Gurney told you, so what's the use talking about 'vacations'?"

"Gurney!" Sheridan vociferated the name savagely. "It's Gurney, Gurney, Gurney! Always Gurney! I don't know what the world's comin' to with everybody runnin' around squealin', 'The doctor says this,' and, 'The doctor says that'! It makes me sick! How's this country expect to get its Work done if Gurney and all the other old nanny-goats keep up this blattin'— 'Oh, oh! Don't lift that stick o' wood; you'll ruin your *nerves!*' So he says you got 'nervous exhaustion induced by overwork and emotional strain.' They always got to stick the Work in if they see a chance! I reckon you did have the 'emotional strain,' and that's all's the matter with you. You'll be over it soon's this woman's gone, and Work's the very thing to make you quit frettin' about her."

"Did Gurney tell you I was fit to work?"

"Shut up!" Sheridan bellowed. "I'm so sick o' that man's name I feel like shootin' anybody that says it to me!" He fumed and chafed, swearing indistinctly, then came and stood before his son. "Look here; do you think you're doin' the square thing by me? Do you? How much you worth?"

"I've got between seven and eight thousand a year clear, of my own, outside the salary. That much is mine whether I work or not."

"It is? You could 'a' pulled it out without me, I suppose you think, at your age?"

"No. But it's mine, and it's enough."

"My Lord! It's about what a Congressman gets, and you want to quit there! I suppose you think you'll get the rest when *I* kick the bucket, and all you have to do is lay back and wait! You let me tell you right here, you'll never see one cent of it. You go out o' business now, and what would you know about handlin' it five or ten or twenty years from now? Because I intend to *stay* here a little while yet, my boy! They'd either get it away from you or you'd sell for a nickel and let it be split up and—" He whirled about, marched to the other end of the room, and stood silent a moment. Then he said, solemnly: "Listen. If you go out now, you leave me in the lurch, with nothin' on God's green earth to depend on but your brother—and you know what he is. I've depended on you for it *all* since Jim died. Now you've listened to that dam' doctor, and he says maybe you won't ever be as good a man as you were, and that certainly you won't be for a year or so— probably more. Now, that's all a lie. Men don't break down that way at your age. Look at *me!* And *I* tell you, you can shake this thing off. All you need is a little *get*-up and a little gumption. Men don't go away for *years* and then come back into *moving* businesses like ours—they lose the strings. And if you could, I won't let you—if you lay down on me now, I won't —and that's because if you lay down you prove you ain't the man I thought you were." He cleared his throat and finished quietly: "Roscoe, will you take a month's vacation and come back and go to it?"

"No," said Roscoe, listlessly. "I'm through."

"All right," said Sheridan. He picked up the evening paper

from a table, went to a chair by the fire and sat down, his back to his son. "Good-by."

Roscoe rose, his head hanging, but there was a dull relief in his eyes. "Best I can do," he muttered, seeming about to depart, yet lingering. "I figure it out a good deal like this," he said. "I didn't *know* my job was any strain, and I managed all right, but from what Gur—from what I hear, I was just up to the limit of my nerves from overwork, and the—the trouble at home was the extra strain that's fixed me the way I am. I tried to brace, so I could stand the work and the trouble too, on whiskey—and that put the finish to me! I—I'm not hitting it as hard as I was for a while, and I reckon pretty soon, if I can get to feeling a little more energy, I better try to quit entirely —I don't know. I'm all in—and the doctor says so. I thought I was running along fine up to a few months ago, but all the time I was ready to bust, and didn't know it. Now, then, I don't want you to blame Sibyl, and if I were you I wouldn't speak of her as 'that woman,' because she's your daughter-in-law and going to stay that way. She didn't do anything wicked. It was a shock to me, and I don't deny it, to find what she had done—encouraging that fellow to hang around her after he began trying to flirt with her, and losing her head over him the way she did. I don't deny it was a shock and that it 'll always be a hurt inside of me I'll never get over. But it was my fault; I didn't understand a woman's nature." Poor Roscoe spoke in the most profound and desolate earnest. "A woman craves society, and gaiety, and meeting attractive people, and traveling. Well, I can't give her the other things, but I can give her the traveling—real traveling, not just going to Atlantic City or New Orleans, the way she has, two, three times. A woman has to have something in her life besides a business man. And that's *all* I was. I never understood till I heard her talking when she was so sick, and I believe if you'd heard her then you wouldn't speak so hard-heartedly about her; I believe you might have forgiven her like I have. That's all. I never cared anything for any girl but her in my life, but I was so busy with business I put it ahead of her. I never *thought* about her, I was so busy thinking business. Well, this is where it's brought us to—and now when you talk about 'business' to me I feel the way you do when anybody talks about Gurney to you. The word 'business' makes me dizzy—it makes me honestly sick at the stomach. I believe if I had to go down-town and step inside that office door I'd fall down on the floor, deathly sick. You talk about a 'month's vacation'—and I get just as sick. I'm rattled—I can't plan—I haven't got any plans—can't make any, except to take my girl and get just as far away from that office as I can—and stay. We're going to Japan first, and if we—"

His father rustled the paper. "I said good-by, Roscoe."

"Good-by," said Roscoe, listlessly.

CHAPTER TWENTY-FOUR

SHERIDAN waited until he heard the sound of the outer door closing; then he rose and pushed a tiny disk set in the wall. Jackson appeared.

"Has Bibbs got home from work?"

"Mist' Bibbs? No, suh."

"Tell him I want to see him, soon as he comes."

"Yessuh."

Sheridan returned to his chair and fixed his attention fiercely upon the newspaper. He found it difficult to pursue the items beyond their explanatory rubrics—there was nothing unusual or startling to concentrate his attention:

"Motorman Puts Blame on Brakes. Three Killed when Car Slides." "Burglars Make Big Haul." "Board Works Approve Big Car-line Extension." "Hold-up Men Injure Two. Man

Found in Alley, Skull Fractured." "Sickening Story Told in Divorce Court." "Plan New Eighteen-story Structure." "School-girl Meets Death under Automobile." "Negro Cuts Three. One Dead." "Life Crushed Out. Third Elevator Accident in Same Building Causes Action by Coroner." "Declare Militia will be Menace. Polish Societies Protest to Governor in Church Rioting Case." "Short $3,500 in Accounts, Trusted Man Kills Self with Drug." "Found Frozen. Family Without Food or Fuel. Baby Dead when Parents Return Home from Seeking Work." "Minister Returned from Trip Abroad Lectures on Big Future of Our City. Sees Big Improvement during Short Absence. Says No European City Holds Candle." (Sheridan nodded approvingly here.)

Bibbs came through the hall whistling, and entered the room briskly. "Well, father, did you want me?"

"Yes. Sit down." Sheridan got up, and Bibbs took a seat by the fire, holding out his hands to the crackling blaze, for it was cold outdoors.

"I came within seven of the shop record to-day," he said. "I handled more strips than any other workman has any day this month. The nearest to me is sixteen behind."

"There!" exclaimed his father, greatly pleased. "What'd I tell you? I'd like to hear Gurney hint again that I wasn't right in sending you there—I would just like to hear him! And you —ain't you ashamed of makin' such a fuss about it? Ain't you?"

"I didn't go at it in the right spirit the other time," Bibbs said, smiling brightly, his face ruddy in the cheerful firelight. "I didn't know the difference it meant to like a thing."

"Well, I guess I've pretty thoroughly vindicated my judgment. I guess I *have!* I said the shop 'd be good for you, and it was. I said it wouldn't hurt you, and it hasn't. It's been just exactly what I said it would be. Ain't that so?"

"Looks like it!" Bibbs agreed, gaily.

"Well, I'd like to know any place I been wrong, first and

last! Instead o' hurtin' you, it's been the makin' of you—physically. You're a good inch taller'n what I am, and you'd be a bigger man than what I am if you'd get some flesh on your bones; and you *are* gettin' a little. Physically, it's started you out to be the huskiest one o' the whole family. Now, then, mentally—that's different. I don't say it unkindly, Bibbs, but you got to do something for yourself mentally, just like what's begun physically. And I'm goin' to help you."

Sheridan decided to sit down again. He brought his chair close to his son's, and, leaning over, tapped Bibbs's knee confidentially. "I got plans for you, Bibbs," he said.

Bibbs instantly looked thoroughly alarmed. He drew back. "I—I'm all right now, father."

"Listen." Sheridan settled himself in his chair, and spoke in the tone of a reasonable man reasoning. "Listen here, Bibbs. I had another blow to-day, and it was a hard one and right in the face, though I *have* been expectin' it some little time back. Well, it's got to be met. Now I'll be frank with you. As I said a minute ago, mentally I couldn't ever called you exactly strong. You been a little weak both ways, most of your life. Not but what I think you *got* a mentality, if you'd learn to use it. You got will-power, I'll say that for you. I never knew boy or man that could be stubborner—never one in my life! Now, then, you've showed you could learn to run that machine best of any man in the shop, in no time at all. That looks to me like you could learn to do other things. I don't deny but what it's an encouragin' sign. I don't deny that, at all. Well, that helps me to think the case ain't so hopeless as it looks. You're all I got to meet this blow with, but maybe you ain't as poor material as I thought. Your tellin' me about comin' within seven strips of the shop's record to-day looks to me like encouragin' information brought in at just about the right time. Now, then, I'm goin' to give you a raise. I wanted to send you straight on up through the shops—a year or two, maybe—but I can't do it. I lost Jim, and now I've lost Roscoe.

He's quit. He's laid down on me. If he ever comes back at all, he'll be a long time pickin' up the strings, and, anyway, he ain't the man I thought he was. I can't count on him. I got to have *somebody* I *know* I can count on. And I'm down to this: you're my last chance. Bibbs, I got to learn you to use what brains you got and see if we can't develop 'em a little. Who knows? And I'm goin' to put my time in on it. I'm goin' to take you right down-town with *me,* and I won't be hard on you if you're a little slow at first. And I'm goin' to do the big thing for you. I'm goin' to make you feel you got to do the big thing for me, in return. I've vindicated my policy with you about the shop, and now I'm goin' to turn right around and swing you 'way over ahead of where the other boys started, and I'm goin' to make an appeal to your ambition that 'll make you dizzy!" He tapped his son on the knee again. "Bibbs, I'm goin' to start you off this way: I'm goin' to make you a director in the Pump Works Company; I'm goin' to make you vice-president of the Realty Company and a vice-president of the Trust Company!"

Bibbs jumped to his feet, blanched. "Oh no!" he cried.

Sheridan took his dismay to be the excitement of sudden joy. "Yes, sir! And there's some pretty fat little salaries goes with those vice-presidencies, and a pinch o' stock in the Pump Company with the directorship. You thought I was pretty mean about the shop—oh, I know you did!—but you see the old man can play it both ways. And so right now, the minute you've begun to make good the way I wanted you to, I deal from the new deck. And I'll keep on handin' it out bigger and bigger every time you show me you're big enough to play the hand I deal you. I'm startin' you with a pretty big one, my boy!"

"But I don't—I don't—I don't want it!" Bibbs stammered.

"What 'd you say?" Sheridan thought he had not heard aright.

"I don't want it, father. I thank you—I do thank you—"

Sheridan looked perplexed. "What's the matter with you? Didn't you understand what I was tellin' you?"

"Yes."

"You sure? I reckon you didn't. I offered—"

"I know, I know! But I can't take it."

"What's the matter with you?" Sheridan was half amazed, half suspicious. "Your head feel funny?"

"I've never been quite so sane in my life," said Bibbs, "as I have lately. And I've got just what I want. I'm living exactly the right life. I'm earning my daily bread, and I'm happy in doing it. My wages are enough. I don't want any more money, and I don't deserve any—"

"Damnation!" Sheridan sprang up. "You've turned Socialist! You been listening to those fellows down there, and you—"

"No, sir. I think there's a great deal in what they say, but that isn't it."

Sheridan tried to restrain his growing fury, and succeeded partially. "Then what is it? What's the matter?"

"Nothing," his son returned, nervously. "Nothing—except that I'm content. I don't want to change anything."

"Why not?"

Bibbs had the incredible folly to try to explain. "I'll tell you, father, if I can. I know it may be hard to understand—"

"Yes, I think it may be," said Sheridan, grimly. "What you say usually is a *little* that way. Go on!"

Perturbed and distressed, Bibbs rose instinctively; he felt himself at every possible disadvantage. He was a sleeper clinging to a dream—a rough hand stretched to shake him and waken him. He went to a table and made vague drawings upon it with a finger, and as he spoke he kept his eyes lowered. "You weren't altogether right about the shop—that is, in one way you weren't, father." He glanced up apprehensively. Sheridan stood facing him, expressionless, and made no attempt to interrupt. "That's difficult to explain," Bibbs continued, lowering his eyes again, to follow the tracings of his finger. "I—I.believe the shop might have done for me this time if I hadn't—if something hadn't helped me to—oh, not only to bear it, but to be happy in it. Well, I *am* happy in it. I want to go on just as I am. And of all things on earth that I don't want, I don't want to live a business life—I don't want to be drawn into it. I don't think it *is* living—and now I *am* living. I have the healthful toil—and I can think. In business as important as yours I couldn't think anything but business. I don't —I don't think making money is worth while."

"Go on," said Sheridan, curtly, as Bibbs paused timidly.

"It hasn't seemed to get anywhere, that *I* can see," said Bibbs. "You think this city is rich and powerful—but what's the use of its being rich and powerful? They don't teach the children any more in the schools because the city is rich and powerful. They teach them more than they used to because some people —not rich and powerful people—have thought the thoughts to teach the children. And yet when you've been reading the paper I've heard you objecting to the children being taught anything except what would help them to make money. You said it was wasting the taxes. You want them taught to make a living, but not to live. When I was a little boy this wasn't an ugly town; now it's hideous. What's the use of being big just to be hideous? I mean I don't think all this has meant really going ahead—it's just been getting bigger and dirtier and noisier. Wasn't the whole country happier and in many ways wiser when it was smaller and cleaner and quieter and kinder? I know you think I'm an utter fool, father, but, after all, though, aren't business and politics just the housekeeping part of life? And wouldn't you despise a woman that not only made her housekeeping her ambition, but did it so noisily and dirtily that the whole neighborhood was in a continual turmoil over it? And suppose she talked and thought about her housekeeping all the time, and was always having additions built to her house when she couldn't keep clean what she already had; and suppose, with it all, she made the house altogether unpeaceful and unlivable—"

"Just one minute!" Sheridan interrupted, adding, with terrible courtesy, "If you will permit me? Have you ever been right about anything?"

"I don't quite—"

"I ask the simple question: Have you ever been right about anything whatever in the course of your life? Have you ever been right upon any subject or question you've thought about and talked about? Can you mention one single time when you were proved to be right?"

He was flourishing the bandaged hand as he spoke, but Bibbs said only, "If I've always been wrong before, surely there's more chance that I'm right about this. It seems reasonable to suppose something would be due to bring up my average."

"Yes, I thought you wouldn't see the point. And there's another you probably couldn't see, but I'll take the liberty to mention it. You been balkin' all your life. Pretty much everything I ever wanted you to do, you'd let out *some* kind of a holler, like you are now—and yet I can't seem to remember once when you didn't have to lay down and do what I said. But go on with your remarks about our city and the business of this country. Go on!"

"I don't want to be part of it," said Bibbs, with unwonted decision. "I want to keep to myself, and I'm doing it now. I couldn't, if I went down there with you. I'd be swallowed into it. I don't care for money enough to—"

"No," his father interrupted, still dangerously quiet. "You've never had to earn a living. Anybody could tell that by what you say. Now, let me remind you: you're sleepin' in a pretty good bed; you're eatin' pretty fair food; you're wearin' pretty fine clothes. Just suppose one o' these noisy housekeepers—

me, for instance—decided to let you do your own house-keepin'. May I ask what your proposition would be?"

"I'm earning nine dollars a week," said Bibbs, sturdily. "It's enough. I shouldn't mind at all."

"Who's payin' you that nine dollars a week?"

"My work!" Bibbs answered. "And I've done so well on that clipping-machine I believe I could work up to fifteen or even twenty a week at another job. I could be a fair plumber in a few months, I'm sure. I'd rather have a trade than be in business—I should, infinitely!"

"You better set about learnin' one pretty dam' quick!" But Sheridan struggled with his temper and again was partially successful in controlling it. "You better learn a trade over Sunday, because you're either goin' down with me to my of-fice Monday morning—or—you can go to plumbing!"

"All right," said Bibbs, gently. "I can get along."

Sheridan raised his hands sardonically, as in prayer. "O God," he said, "this boy was crazy enough before he began to earn nine dollars a week, and now his money's gone to his head! Can't You do nothin' for him?" Then he flung his hands apart, palms outward, in a furious gesture of dismissal. "Get out o' this room! You got a skull that's thicker'n a whale's thigh-bone, but it's cracked spang all the way across! You hated the machine-shop so bad when I sent you there, you went and stayed sick for over two years—and now, when I offer to take you out of it and give you the mint, you holler for the shop like a calf for its mammy! You're cracked! Oh, but I got a fine layout here! One son died, one quit, and one's a loon! The loon's all I got left! H. P. Ellersly's wife had a crazy brother, and they undertook to keep him at the house. First morning he was there he walked straight through a ten-dollar plate-glass window out into the yard. He says, 'Oh, look at the pretty dandelion!' That's what you're doin'! You want to spend your life sayin', 'Oh, look at the pretty dandelion!' and you don't care a tinker's dam' what you bust! Well, mister, loon or no loon, cracked and crazy or whatever you are, I'll take you with me Monday morning, and I'll work you and learn you—yes, and I'll lam you, if I got to—until I've made something out of you that's fit to be called a business man! I'll keep at you while I'm able to stand, and if I have to lay down to die I'll be whisperin' at you till they get the embalmin'-fluid into me! Now go on, and don't let me hear from you again till you can come and tell me you've waked up, you poor pitiful, dandelion-pickin' *sleep-walker!*"

Bibbs gave him a queer look. There was something like reproach in it, for once; but there was more than that—he seemed to be startled by his father's last word.

CHAPTER TWENTY-FIVE

THERE was sleet that evening, with a whooping wind, but neither this storm nor that other which so imminently threatened him held place in the consciousness of Bibbs Sheridan when he came once more to the presence of Mary. All was right in his world as he sat with her, reading Maurice Maeterlinck's *Alladine and Palomides*. The sorrowful light of the gas-jet might have been May morning sunshine flashing amber and rose through the glowing windows of the Sainte-Chapelle,[1] it was so bright for Bibbs. And while the zinc-eater held out to bring him such golden nights as these, all the king's horses and all the king's men might not serve to break the spell.

---

[1] A small Gothic church in Paris, now attached to the Palais de Justice. It was built in 1248 by St. Louis of France. It is celebrated for the exceptional beauty of its stained-glass windows, especially the magnificent rose window at one end.

Bibbs read slowly, but in a reasonable manner, as if he were talking; and Mary, looking at him steadily from beneath her curved fingers, appeared to discover no fault. It had grown to be her habit to look at him whenever there was an opportunity. It may be said, in truth, that while they were together, and it was light, she looked at him all the time.

When he came to the end of *Alladine and Palomides* they were silent a little while, considering together; then he turned back the pages and said:

"There's something I want to read over. This:

You would think I threw a window open on the dawn. . . . She has a soul that can be seen around her—that takes you in its arms like an ailing child and without saying anything to you consoles you for everything. . . . I shall never understand it all. I do not know how it can all be, but my knees bend in spite of me when I speak of it. . . .

He stopped and looked at her.

"You boy!" said Mary, not very clearly.

"Oh yes," he returned. "But it's true—especially my knees!"

"You boy!" she murmured again, blushing charmingly. "You might read another line over. The first time I ever saw you, Bibbs, you were looking into a mirror. Do it again. But you needn't read it—I can give it to you: 'A little Greek slave that came from the heart of Arcady!'"

"*I!* I'm one of the hands at the Pump Works—and going to stay one, unless I have to decide to study plumbing."

"No." She shook her head. "You love and want what's beautiful and delicate and serene; it's really art that you want in your life, and have always wanted. You seemed to me, from the first, the most wistful person I had ever known, and that's what you were wistful for."

Bibbs looked doubtful and more wistful than ever; but after a moment or two the matter seemed to clarify itself to him. "Why, no," he said; "I wanted something else more than that. I wanted you."

"And here I am!" she laughed, completely understanding. "I think we're like those two in *The Cloister and the Hearth*. I'm just the rough Burgundian cross-bow man, Denys, who followed that gentle Gerard and told everybody that the devil was dead."

"He isn't, though," said Bibbs, as a hoarse little bell in the next room began a series of snappings which proved to be ten, upon count. "He gets into the clock whenever I'm with you." And, sighing deeply, he rose to go.

"You're always very prompt about leaving me."

"I—I try to be," he said. "It isn't easy to be careful not to risk everything by giving myself a little more at a time. If I ever saw you look tired—"

"Have you ever?"

"Not yet. You always look—you always look—"

"How?"

"Care-free. That's it. Except when you feel sorry for me about something, you always have that splendid look. It puts courage into people to see it. If I had a struggle to face I'd keep remembering that look—and I'd never give up! It's a brave look, too, as though gaiety might be a kind of gallantry on your part, and yet I don't quite understand why it should be, either." He smiled quizzically, looking down upon her. "Mary, you haven't a 'secret sorrow,' have you?"

For answer she only laughed.

"No," he said; "I can't imagine you with a care in the world. I think that's why you were so kind to me—you have nothing but happiness in your own life, and so you could spare time to make my troubles turn to happiness, too. But there's one little time in the twenty-four hours when I'm not happy. It's now, when I have to say good night. I feel dismal every time it comes—and then, when I've left the house, there's a bad little blankness, a black void, as though I were temporarily dead; and it lasts until I get it established in my mind that I'm really beginning another day that's to end with *you* again.

Then I cheer up. But now's the bad time—and I must go through it, and so—good night." And he added with a pungent vehemence of which he was little aware, "I hate it!"

"Do you?" she said, rising to go to the door with him. But he stood motionless, gazing at her wonderingly.

"Mary! Your eyes are so—" He stopped.

"Yes?" But she looked quickly away.

"I don't know," he said. "I thought just then—"

"What did you think?"

"I don't know—it seemed to me that there was something I ought to understand—and didn't."

She laughed and met his wondering gaze again frankly. "My eyes are pleased," she said. "I'm glad that you miss me a little after you go."

"But to-morrow's coming faster than other days if you'll let it," he said.

She inclined her head. "Yes. I'll—'let it'!"

"Going to church," said Bibbs. "It *is* going to church when I go with you!"

She went to the front door with him; she always went that far. They had formed a little code of leave-taking, by habit, neither of them ever speaking of it; but it was always the same. She always stood in the doorway until he reached the sidewalk, and there he always turned and looked back, and she waved her hand to him. Then he went on, halfway to the New House, and looked back again, and Mary was not in the doorway, but the door was open and the light shone. It was as if she meant to tell him that she would never shut him out; he could always see that friendly light of the open doorway— as if it were open for him to come back, if he would. He could see it until a wing of the New House came between, when he went up the path. The open doorway seemed to him the beautiful symbol of her friendship—of her thought of him; a symbol of herself and of her ineffable kindness.

And she kept the door open—even to-night, though the

sleet and fine snow swept in upon her bare throat and arms, and her brown hair was strewn with tiny white stars. His heart leaped as he turned and saw that she was there, waving her hand to him, as if she did not know that the storm touched her. When he had gone on, Mary did as she always did—she went into an unlit room across the hall from that in which they had spent the evening, and, looking from the window, watched him until he was out of sight. The storm made that difficult to-night, but she caught a glimpse of him under the street-lamp that stood between the two houses, and saw that he turned to look back again. Then, and not before, she looked at the upper windows of Roscoe's house across the street. They were dark. Mary waited, but after a little while she closed the front door and returned to her window. A moment later two of the upper windows of Roscoe's house flashed into light and a hand lowered the shade of one of them. Mary felt the cold then—it was the third night she had seen those windows lighted and that shade lowered, just after Bibbs had gone.

But Bibbs had no glance to spare for Roscoe's windows. He stopped for his last look back at the open door, and, with a thin mantle of white already upon his shoulders, made his way, gasping in the wind, to the lee of the sheltering wing of the New House.

A stricken George, muttering hoarsely, admitted him, and Bibbs became aware of a paroxysm within the house. Terrible sounds came from the library: Sheridan cursing as never before; his wife sobbing, her voice rising to an agonized squeal of protest upon each of a series of muffled detonations—the outrageous thumping of a bandaged hand upon wood; then Gurney, sharply imperious, "Keep your hand in that sling! Keep your hand in that sling, I say!"

"*Look!*" George gasped, delighted to play herald for so important a tragedy; and he renewed upon his face the ghastly expression with which he had first beheld the ruins his calamitous gesture laid before the eyes of Bibbs. "Look at 'at lamidal statue!"

Gazing down the hall, Bibbs saw heroic wreckage, seemingly Byzantine—painted colossal fragments of a shattered torso, appallingly human; and gilded and silvered heaps of magnificence strewn among ruinous palms like the spoil of a barbarians' battle. There had been a massacre in the oasis—the Moor had been hurled headlong from his pedestal.

"He hit 'at ole lamidal statue," said George. *"Pow!"*

"My father?"

*"Yes*suh! *Pow!* he hit 'er! An' you' ma run tell me git doctuh quick 's I kin telefoam—she sho' you' pa goin' bus' a blood-vessel. He ain't takin' on 'tall *now*. He ain't nothin' 'tall to what he was 'while ago. You done miss' it, Mist' Bibbs. Doctuh got him all quiet' down, to what he was. *Pow!* he hit 'er! Yessuh!" He took Bibbs's coat and proffered a crumpled telegraph form. "Here what come," he said. "I pick 'er up when he done stompin' on 'er. You read 'er, Mist' Bibbs—you' ma tell me tuhn 'er ovuh to you soon's you come in."

Bibbs read the telegram quickly. It was from New York and addressed to Mrs. Sheridan.

Sure you will all approve step have taken as was so wretched my health would probably suffered severely Robert and I were married this afternoon thought best have quiet wedding absolutely sure you will understand wisdom of step when you know Robert better am happiest woman in world are leaving for Florida will wire address when settled will remain till spring love to all father will like him too when knows him like I do he is just ideal.

EDITH LAMHORN.

CHAPTER TWENTY-SIX

GEORGE departed, and Bibbs was left gazing upon chaos
and listening to thunder. He could not reach the stairway without passing the open doors of the library, and he
was convinced that the mere glimpse of him, just then, would
prove nothing less than insufferable for his father. For that
reason he was about to make his escape into the gold-and-
brocade room, intending to keep out of sight, when he heard
Sheridan vociferously demanding his presence.

"Tell him to come in here! He's out there. I heard George
just let him in. Now you'll *see!*" And tear-stained Mrs. Sheridan, looking out into the hall, beckoned to her son.

Bibbs went as far as the doorway. Gurney sat winding a
strip of white cotton, his black bag open upon a chair near
by; and Sheridan was striding up and down, his hand so
heavily wrapped in fresh bandages that he seemed to be
wearing a small boxing-glove. His eyes were bloodshot; his
forehead was heavily bedewed; one side of his collar had
broken loose, and there were blood-stains upon his right cuff.

"*There's* our little sunshine!" he cried, as Bibbs appeared.
"*There's* the hope o' the family—my lifelong pride and joy! I
want—"

"Keep your hand in that sling," said Gurney, sharply.

Sheridan turned upon him, uttering a sound like a howl.
"For God's sake, sing another tune!" he cried. "You said you
'came as a doctor but stay as a friend,' and in that capacity you
undertake to sit up and criticize *me*—"

"Oh, talk sense," said the doctor, and yawned intentionally.
"What do you want Bibbs to say?"

"You were sittin' up there tellin' me I got 'hysterical'—
'hysterical,' oh Lord! You sat up there and told me I got
'hysterical' over nothin'! You sat up there tellin' me I didn't

have as heavy burdens as many another man you knew. I just want you to hear *this*. Now listen!" He swung toward the quiet figure waiting in the doorway. "Bibbs, will you come down-town with me Monday morning and let me start you with two vice-presidencies, a directorship, stock, and salaries? I ask you."

"No, father," said Bibbs, gently.

Sheridan looked at Gurney and then faced his son once more.

"Bibbs, you want to stay in the shop, do you, at nine dollars a week, instead of takin' up my offer?"

"Yes, sir."

"And I'd like the doctor to hear: What 'll you do if I decide you're too high-priced a workin'-man either to live in my house or work in my shop?"

"Find other work," said Bibbs.

"There! You hear him for yourself!" Sheridan cried. "You hear what—"

"Keep your hand in that sling! Yes, I hear him."

Sheridan leaned over Gurney and shouted, in a voice that cracked and broke, piping into falsetto. "He thinks of bein' a *plumber!* He wants to be a *plumber!* He told me he couldn't *think* if he went into business—he wants to be a plumber so he can *think!*"

He fell back a step, wiping his forehead with the back of his left hand. "There! That's my son! That's the only son I got now! That's my chance to live," he cried, with a bitterness that seemed to leave ashes in his throat. "That's my one chance to live—that thing you see in the doorway yonder!"

Dr. Gurney thoughtfully regarded the bandage strip he had been winding, and tossed it into the open bag. "What's the matter with giving Bibbs a chance to live?" he said, coolly. "I would if I were you. You've had *two* that went into business."

Sheridan's mouth moved grotesquely before he could speak. "Joe Gurney," he said, when he could command himself so far, "are you accusin' me of the responsibility for the death of my son James?"

"I accuse you of nothing," said the doctor. "But just once I'd like to have it out with you on the question of Bibbs—and while he's here, too." He got up, walked to the fire, and stood warming his hands behind his back and smiling. "Look here, old fellow, let's be reasonable," he said. "You were bound Bibbs should go to the shop again, and I gave you and him, both, to understand pretty plainly that if he went it was at the risk of his life. Well, what did he do? He said he wanted to go. And he did go, and he's made good there. Now, see: Isn't that enough? Can't you let him off now? He wants to write, and how do you know that he couldn't do it if you gave him a chance? How do you know he hasn't some message—something to say that might make the world just a little bit happier or wiser? He *might*—in time—it's a possibility not to be denied. Now he can't deliver any message if he goes down there with you, and he won't *have* any to deliver. I don't say going down with you is likely to injure his health, as I thought the shop would, and as the shop did, the first time. I'm not speaking as doctor now, anyhow. But I tell you one thing I know: if you take him down there you'll kill something that I feel is in him, and it's finer, I think, than his physical body, and you'll kill it deader than a door-nail! And so why not let it live? You've about come to the end of your string, old fellow. Why not stop this perpetual devilish fighting and give Bibbs his chance?"

Sheridan stood looking at him fixedly. "What 'fighting?'"

"Yours—with nature." Gurney sustained the daunting gaze of his fierce antagonist equably. "You don't seem to understand that you've been struggling against actual law."

"What law?"

"Natural law," said Gurney. "What do you think beat you

with Edith? Did Edith, herself, beat you? Didn't she obey
without question something powerful that was against you?
Edith wasn't against you, and you weren't against *her,* but
you set yourself against the power that had her in its grip, and
it shot out a spurt of flame—and won in a walk! What's
taken Roscoe from you? Timbers bear just so much strain, old
man; but *you* wanted to send the load across the broken
bridge, and you thought you could bully or coax the cracked
thing into standing. Well, you couldn't! Now here's Bibbs.
There are thousands of men fit for the life you want him
to lead—and so is he. It wouldn't take half of Bibbs's brains
to be twice as good a business man as Jim and Roscoe put together."

"What!" Sheridan goggled at him like a zany.

"Your son Bibbs," said the doctor, composedly, "Bibbs Sheridan has the kind and quantity of 'gray matter' that will make
him a success in anything—if he ever wakes up! Personally I
should prefer him to remain asleep. I like him that way. But
the thousands of men fit for the life you want him to lead
aren't fit to do much with the life he *ought* to lead. Blindly,
he's been fighting for the chance to lead it—he's obeying something that begs to stay alive within him; and, blindly, he
knows you'll crush it out. You've set your will to do it. Let
me tell you something more. You don't know what you've become since Jim's going thwarted you—and that's what was
uppermost, a bafflement stronger than your normal grief.
You're half mad with a consuming fury against the very self
of the law—for it was the very self of the law that took Jim
from you. That was a law concerning the cohesion of mole-
cules. The very self of the law took Roscoe from you and
gave Edith the certainty of beating you; and the very self of
the law makes Bibbs deny you to-night. The *law* beats you.
Haven't you been whipped enough? But you want to whip
the law—you've set yourself against it, to bend it to your own
ends, to wield it and twist it—"

The voice broke from Sheridan's heaving chest in a shout. "Yes! And by God, I will!"

"So Ajax defied the lightning," said Gurney.

"I've heard that dam'-fool story, too," Sheridan retorted, fiercely. "That's for chuldern and niggers. It ain't twentieth century, let me tell you! 'Defied the lightning,' did he, the jackass! If he'd been half a man he'd 'a' got away with it. *We* don't go showin' off defyin' the lightning—we hitch it up and make it work for us like a black steer! A man nowadays would just as soon think o' defyin' a wood-shed!"

"Well, what about Bibbs?" said Gurney. "Will you be a really big man now and—"

"Gurney, you know a lot about bigness!" Sheridan began to walk to and fro again, and the doctor returned gloomily to his chair. He had shot his bolt the moment he judged its chance to strike center was best, but the target seemed unaware of the marksman.

"I'm tryin' to make a big man out o' that poor truck yonder," Sheridan went on, "and you step in, beggin' me to let him be Lord knows what—*I* don't! I suppose you figure it out that now I got a *son-in-law,* I mightn't need a son! Yes, I got a son-in-law now—a spender!"

"Oh, put your hand back!" said Gurney, wearily.

There was a bronze inkstand upon the table. Sheridan put his right hand in the sling, but with his left he swept the inkstand from the table and half-way across the room—a comet with a destroying black tail. Mrs. Sheridan shrieked and sprang toward it.

"Let it lay!" he shouted, fiercely. "Let it lay!" And, weeping, she obeyed. "Yes, sir," he went on, in a voice the more ominous for the sudden hush he put upon it. "I got a spender for a son-in-law! It's wonderful where property goes, sometimes. There was ole man Tracy—you remember him, Doc—J. R. Tracy, solid banker. He went into the bank as messenger, seventeen years old; he was president at forty-three, and he built that bank with his life for forty years more. He was down there from nine in the morning until four in the afternoon the day before he died—over eighty! Gilt edge, that bank? It was diamond edge! He used to eat a bag o' peanuts and an apple for lunch; but he wasn't stingy—he was just livin' in his business. He didn't care for pie or automobiles—he had his bank. It was an institution, and it come pretty near bein' the beatin' heart o' this town in its time. Well, that ole man used to pass one o' these here turned-up-nose and turned-up-pants cigarette boys on the streets. Never spoke to him, Tracy didn't. Speak to him? God! he wouldn't 'a' coughed on him! He wouldn't 'a' let him clean the cuspidors at the bank! Why, if he'd 'a' just seen him standin' in *front* the bank he'd 'a' had him run off the street. And yet all Tracy was doin' every day of his life was workin' for that cigarette boy! Tracy thought it was for the bank; he thought he was givin' his life and his life-blood and the blood of his brain for the bank, but he wasn't. It was every bit—from the time he went in at seventeen till he died in harness at eighty-three—it was every last lick of it just slavin' for that turned-up-nose, turned-up-pants cigarette boy. *And Tracy didn't even know his name!* He died, not ever havin' heard it, though he chased him off the front steps of his house once. The day after Tracy died his old-maid daughter married the cigarette—and there *ain't* any Tracy bank any more! And now"—his voice rose again—"and now *I* got a cigarette son-in-law!"

Gurney pointed to the flourishing right hand without speaking, and Sheridan once more returned it to the sling.

"My son-in-law likes Florida this winter," Sheridan went on. "That's good, and my son-in-law better enjoy it, because I don't think he'll be there next winter. They got twelve-thousand dollars to spend, and I hear it can be done in Florida by rich sons-in-law. When Roscoe's woman got me to spend that much on a porch for their new house, Edith wouldn't give me a minute's rest till I turned over the same to her. And she's got it, besides what I gave her to go East on. It 'll be gone long before this time next year, and when she comes home and leaves the cigarette behind—for good—she'll get some more. *My* name ain't Tracy, and there ain't goin' to be any Tracy business in the Sheridan family. And there ain't goin' to be any college foundin' and endowin' and trusteein', nor God-knows-what to keep my property alive when I'm gone! Edith 'll be back, and she'll get a girl's share when she's through with that cigarette, but—"

"By the way," interposed Gurney, "didn't Mrs. Sheridan tell me that Bibbs warned you Edith would marry Lamhorn in New York?"

Sheridan went completely to pieces: he swore, while his wife screamed and stopped her ears. And as he swore he pounded the table with his wounded hand, and when the doctor, after storming at him ineffectively, sprang to catch and protect that hand, Sheridan wrenched it away, tearing the bandage. He hammered the table till it leaped.

"Fool!" he panted, choking. "If he's shown gumption enough to guess right the first time in his life, it's enough for me to begin learnin' him on!" And, struggling with the doctor, he leaned toward Bibbs, thrusting forward his convulsed face, which was deathly pale. "My name ain't Tracy, I tell you!" he screamed, hoarsely. "You give in, you stubborn fool! I've had my way with you before, and I'll have my way with you now!"

Bibbs's face was as white as his father's, but he kept remembering that "splendid look" of Mary's which he had told her would give him courage in a struggle, so that he would "never give up."

"No. You can't have your way," he said. And then, obeying a significant motion of Gurney's head, he went out quickly, leaving them struggling.

CHAPTER TWENTY-SEVEN

Mrs. sheridan, in a wrapper, noiselessly opened the door of her husband's room at daybreak the next morning, and peered within the darkened chamber. At the "old" house they had shared a room, but the architect had chosen to separate them at the New, and they had not known how to formulate an objection, although to both of them something seemed vaguely reprehensible in the new arrangement.

Sheridan did not stir, and she was withdrawing her head from the aperture when he spoke.

"Oh, I'm *awake!* Come in, if you want to, and shut the door."

She came and sat by the bed. "I woke up thinkin' about it," she explained. "And the more I thought about it the surer I got I must be right, and I knew you'd be tormentin' yourself if you was awake, so—well, you got plenty other troubles, but I'm just sure you ain't goin' to have the worry with Bibbs it looks like."

"You *bet* I ain't!" he grunted.

"Look how biddable he was about goin' back to the Works," she continued. "He's a right good-hearted boy, really, and sometimes I honestly have to say he seems right smart, too. Now and then he'll say something sounds right bright. 'Course, most always it doesn't, and a good deal of the time, when he says things, why, I have to feel glad we haven't got company, because they'd think he didn't have any gumption at all. Yet, look at the way he did when Jim—when Jim got hurt. He took right hold o' things. 'Course he'd been sick himself so much and all—and the rest of us never had, much, and we were kind o' green about what to do in that kind o' trouble—still, he did take hold, and everything went off all right; you'll have to say that much, papa. And Dr. Gurney says he's got brains, and you can't deny but what the doctor's right considerable of a man. He acts sleepy, but that's only because he's got such a large practice—he's a pretty wide-awake kind of a man some ways. Well, what he says last night about Bibbs himself bein' asleep, and how much he'd amount to if he ever woke up—that's what I got to thinkin' about. You heard him, papa: he says, 'Bibbs 'll be a bigger business man than what Jim and Roscoe was put together—if he ever wakes up,' he says. Wasn't that exactly what he says?"

"I suppose so," said Sheridan, without exhibiting any interest. "Gurney's crazier 'n Bibbs, but if he wasn't—if what he says was true—what of it?"

"Listen, papa. Just suppose Bibbs took it into his mind to get married. You know where he goes all the time—"

"Oh, Lord, yes!" Sheridan turned over in the bed, his face to the wall, leaving visible of himself only the thick grizzle of his hair. "You better go back to sleep. He runs over there—every minute she'll let him, I suppose. Go back to bed. There's nothin' in it."

"*Why* ain't there?" she urged. "I know better—there is, too! You wait and see. There's just one thing in the world that'll wake the sleepiest young man alive up—yes, and make him *jump* up—and I don't care who he is or how sound asleep it looks like he is. That's when he takes it into his head to pick out some girl and settle down and have a home and chuldern of his own. *Then,* I guess, he'll go out after the money! You'll see. I've known dozens o' cases, and so 've you—moony, no-'count young men, all notions and talk, goin' to be ministers, maybe, or something; and there's just this one thing takes it out of 'em and brings 'em right down to business. Well, I never could make out just what it is Bibbs wants to be, really; doesn't seem he wants to be a minister exactly—he's so far-away you can't tell, and he never *says*—but I know this is goin' to get him right down to common sense. Now, I don't say that Bibbs has got the idea in his head yet—'r else he wouldn't be talkin' that fool-talk about nine dollars a week bein' good enough for him to live on. But it's *comin'*, papa, and he'll *jump* for whatever you want to hand him out. He will! And I can tell you this much, too: he'll want all the salary and stock he can get hold of, and he'll hustle to keep gettin' more. That girl's the kind that a young husband just goes crazy to give things to! She's pretty and fine-lookin', and things look nice on her, and I guess she'd like to have 'em about as well as the next. And I guess she isn't gettin' many these days, either, and she'll be pretty ready for the change. I saw her with her sleeves rolled up at the kitchen window the other day, and Jackson told me yesterday their cook left two weeks ago, and they haven't tried to hire another one. He says her and her mother been doin' the housework a good while, and now they're doin' the cookin', too. 'Course Bibbs wouldn't know that unless she's told him, and I reckon she wouldn't; she's kind o' stiffish-lookin', and Bibbs is too up in the clouds to notice anything like that for himself. They've never asked him to a meal in the house, but he wouldn't notice that, either —he's kind of innocent. Now I was thinkin'—you know, I don't suppose we've hardly mentioned the girl's name at table since Jim went, but it seems to me maybe if—"

Sheridan flung out his arms, uttering a sound half-groan, half-yawn. "You're barkin' up the wrong tree! Go on back to bed, mamma!"

"Why am I?" she demanded, crossly. "Why am I barkin' up the wrong tree?"

"Because you are. There's nothin' in it."

"I'll bet you," she said, rising—"I'll bet you he goes to church with her this morning. What you want to bet?"

"Go back to bed," he commanded. "I *know* what I'm talkin' about; there's nothin' in it, I tell you."

She shook her head perplexedly. "You think because—because Jim was runnin' so much with her it wouldn't look right?"

"No. Nothin' to do with it."

"Then—do you know something about it that you ain't told me?"

"Yes, I do," he grunted. "Now go on. Maybe I can get a little sleep. I ain't had any yet!"

"Well—" She went to the door, her expression downcast. "I thought maybe—but—" She coughed prefatorily. "Oh, papa, something else I wanted to tell you. I was talkin' to Roscoe over the 'phone last night when the telegram came, so I forgot to tell you, but—well, Sibyl wants to come over this afternoon. Roscoe says she has something she wants to say to us. It'll be the first time she's been out since she was able to sit up—and I reckon she wants to tell us she's sorry for what happened. They expect to get off by the end o' the week, and I reckon she wants to feel she's done what she could to kind o' make up. Anyway, that's what he said. I 'phoned him again about Edith, and he said it wouldn't disturb Sibyl, because she'd been expectin' it; she was sure all along it was goin' to happen; and, besides, I guess she's got all that foolishness pretty much out of her, bein' so sick. But what I thought was, no use bein' rough with her, papa—I expect she's suffered a good deal—and I don't think we'd ought to be, on Roscoe's account. You'll—you'll be kind o' polite to her, won't you, papa?"

He mumbled something which was smothered under the coverlet he had pulled over his head.

"What?" she said, timidly. "I was just sayin' I hoped you'd treat Sibyl all right when she comes, this afternoon. You will, won't you, papa?"

He threw the coverlet off furiously. "I presume so!" he roared.

She departed guiltily.

But if he had accepted her proffered wager that Bibbs would go to church with Mary Vertrees that morning, Mrs. Sheridan would have lost. Nevertheless, Bibbs and Mary did certainly set out from Mr. Vertrees's house with the purpose of going to church. That was their intention, and they had no other. They meant to go to church.

But it happened that they were attentively preoccupied in a conversation as they came to the church; and though Mary was looking to the right and Bibbs was looking to the left, Bibbs's leftward glance converged with Mary's rightward glance, and neither was looking far beyond the other at this time. It also happened that, though they were a little jostled among groups of people in the vicinity of the church, they passed this somewhat prominent edifice without being aware of their proximity to it, and they had gone an incredible number of blocks beyond it before they discovered their error. However, feeling that they might be embarrassingly late if they returned, they decided that a walk would make them as good. It was a windless winter morning, with an inch of crisp snow over the ground. So they walked, and for the most part they were silent, but on their way home, after they had turned back at noon, they began to be talkative again.

"Mary," said Bibbs, after a time, "am I a sleep-walker?"

She laughed a little, then looked grave. "Does your father say you are?"

"Yes—when he's in a mood to flatter me. Other times, other names. He has quite a list."

"You mustn't mind," she said, gently. "He's been getting some pretty severe shocks. What you've told me makes me pretty sorry for him, Bibbs. I've always been sure he's very big."

"Yes. Big and—blind. He's like a Hercules [1] without eyes and without any consciousness except that of his strength and of his purpose to grow stronger. Stronger for what? For nothing."

"Are you sure, Bibbs? It *can't* be for nothing; it must be stronger for something, even though he doesn't know what it

[1] One of the Greek gods, the incarnation of manly strength and a doer of superhuman deeds.

is. Perhaps what he and his kind are struggling for is something so great they *couldn't* see it—so great none of us could see it."

"No, he's just like some blind, unconscious thing heaving underground—"

"Till he breaks through and leaps out into the daylight," she finished for him, cheerily.

"Into the smoke," said Bibbs. "Look at the powder of coal-dust already dirtying the decent snow, even though it's Sunday. That's from the little pigs; the big ones aren't so bad, on Sunday! There's a fleck of soot on your cheek. Some pig sent it out into the air; he might as well have thrown it on you. It would have been braver, for then he'd have taken his chance of my whipping him for it if I could."

"*Is* there soot on my cheek, Bibbs, or were you only saying so rhetorically? *Is* there?"

"Is there? There *are* soot on your cheeks, Mary—a fleck on each. One landed since I mentioned the first."

She halted immediately, giving him her handkerchief, and he succeeded in transferring most of the black from her face to the cambric. They were entirely matter-of-course about it.

An elderly couple, it chanced, had been walking behind Bibbs and Mary for the last block or so, and passed ahead during the removal of the soot. "There!" said the elderly wife. "You're always wrong when you begin guessing about strangers. Those two young people aren't honeymooners at all—they've been married for years. A blind man could see that."

"I wish I did know who threw that soot on you," said Bibbs, looking up at the neighboring chimneys, as they went on. "They arrest children for throwing snowballs at the street-cars, but—"

"But they don't arrest the street-cars for shaking all the pic-

tures in the houses crooked every time they go by. Nor for
the uproar they make. I wonder what's the cost in nerves for
the noise of the city each year. Yes, we pay the price for living
in a 'growing town,' whether we have money to pay or none."

"Who is it gets the pay?" said Bibbs.

"Not I!" she laughed.

"Nobody gets it. There isn't any pay; there's only money.
And only some of the men downtown get much of that.
That's what my father wants me to get."

"Yes," she said, smiling to him, and nodding. "And you
don't want it, and you don't need it."

"But you don't think I'm a sleep-walker, Mary?" He had
told her of his father's new plans for him, though he had not
described the vigor and picturesqueness of their setting forth.
"You think I'm right?"

"A thousand times!" she cried. "There aren't so many happy
people in this world, I think—and you say you've found what
makes you happy. If it's a dream—keep it!"

"The thought of going down there—into the money shuffle
—I hate it as I never hated the shop!" he said. "I hate it! And
the city itself, the city that the money shuffle has made—just
look at it! Look at it in winter. The snow's tried hard to
make the ugliness bearable, but the ugliness is winning; it's
making the snow hideous; the snow's getting dirty on top,
and it's foul underneath with the dirt and disease of the un-
clean street. And the dirt and the ugliness and the rush and
the noise aren't the worst of it; it's what the dirt and ugliness
and rush and noise *mean*—that's the worst! The outward
things are insufferable, but they're only the expression of a
spirit—a blind embryo of a spirit, not yet a soul—oh, just
greed! And this 'go ahead' nonsense! Oughtn't it all to be a
fellowship? I shouldn't want to get ahead if I could—I'd want
to help the other fellow to keep up with me."

"I read something the other day and remembered it for

you," said Mary. "It was something Burne-Jones [2] said of a picture he was going to paint: 'In the first picture I shall make a man walking in the street of a great city, full of all kinds of happy life: children, and lovers walking, and ladies leaning from windows all down great lengths of street leading to the city walls; and there the gates are wide open, letting in a space of green field and cornfield in harvest; and all round his head a great rain of swirling autumn leaves blowing from a little walled graveyard.'"

"And if I painted," Bibbs returned, "I'd paint a lady walking in the street of a great city, full of all kinds of uproarious and futile life—children being taught only how to make money, and lovers hurrying to get richer, and ladies who'd given up trying to wash their windows clean, and the gates of the city wide open, letting in slums and slaughter-houses and freight-yards, and all round this lady's head a great rain of swirling soot—" He paused, adding, thoughtfully: "And yet I believe I'm glad that soot got on your cheek. It was just as if I were your brother—the way you gave me your handkerchief to rub it off for you. Still, Edith never—"

"Didn't she?" said Mary, as he paused again.

"No. And I—" He contented himself with shaking his head instead of offering more definite information. Then he realized that they were passing the New House, and he sighed profoundly. "Mary, our walk's almost over."

She looked as blank. "So it is, Bibbs."

They said no more until they came to her gate. As they drifted slowly to a stop, the door of Roscoe's house opened, and Roscoe came out with Sibyl, who was startlingly pale. She seemed little enfeebled by her illness, however, walking rather quickly at her husband's side and not taking his arm. The two crossed the street without appearing to see Mary and her

<hr />

[2] An English painter (1833–1898) well known for decorative design. Windows executed from his designs are to be found all over England and in churches abroad.

companion, and, entering the New House, were lost to sight. Mary gazed after them gravely, but Bibbs, looking at Mary, did not see them.

"Mary," he said, "you seem very serious. Is anything bothering you?"

"No, Bibbs." And she gave him a bright, quick look that made him instantly unreasonably happy.

"I know you want to go in—" he began.

"No. I don't want to."

"I mustn't keep you standing here, and I mustn't go in with you—but—I just wanted to say—I've seemed very stupid to myself this morning, grumbling about soot and all that—while all the time I—Mary, I think it's been the very happiest of all the hours you've given me. I do. And—I don't know just why—but it's seemed to me that it was one I'd always remember. And you," he added, falteringly, "you look so—so beautiful to-day!"

"It must have been the soot on my cheek, Bibbs."

"Mary, will you tell me something?" he asked.

"I think I will."

"It's something I've had a lot of theories about, but none of them ever just fits. You used to wear furs in the fall, but now it's so much colder, you don't—you never wear them at all any more. Why don't you?"

Her eyes fell for a moment, and she grew red. Then she looked up gaily. "Bibbs, if I tell you the answer will you promise not to ask any more questions?"

"Yes. Why did you stop wearing them?"

"Because I found I'd be warmer without them!" She caught his hand quickly in her own for an instant, laughed into his eyes, and ran into the house.

CHAPTER TWENTY-EIGHT

IT IS the consoling attribute of unused books that their decorative warmth will so often make even a ready-made library the actual "living-room" of a family to whom the shelved volumes are indeed sealed. Thus it was with Sheridan, who read nothing except newspapers, business letters, and figures; who looked upon books as he looked upon bric-à-brac or crocheting—when he was at home, and not abed or eating, he was in the library.

He stood in the many-colored light of the stained-glass window at the far end of the long room, when Roscoe and his wife came in, and he exhaled a solemnity. His deference to the Sabbath was manifest, as always, in the length of his coat and the closeness of his Saturday-night shave; and his expression, to match this religious pomp, was more than Sabbatical, but the most dismaying of his demonstrations was his keeping his hand in his sling.

Sibyl advanced to the middle of the room and halted there, not looking at him, but down at her muff, in which, it could be seen, her hands were nervously moving. Roscoe went to a chair in another part of the room. There was a deadly silence.

But Sibyl found a shaky voice, after an interval of gulping, though she was unable to lift her eyes, and the darkling lids continued to veil them. She spoke hurriedly, like an ungifted child reciting something committed to memory, but her sincerity was none the less evident for that.

"Father Sheridan, you and mother Sheridan have always been so kind to me, and I would hate to have you think I don't appreciate it, from the way I acted. I've come to tell you I am sorry for the way I did that night, and to say I know as well as anybody the way I behaved, and it will never happen again, because it's been a pretty hard lesson; and when we come back, some day, I hope you'll see that you've got a daughter-in-law you never need to be ashamed of again. I want to ask you to excuse me for the way I did, and I can say I haven't any feelings toward Edith now, but only wish her happiness and good in her new life. I thank you for all your kindness to me, and I know I made a poor return for it, but if you can overlook the way I behaved I know I would feel a good deal happier—and I know Roscoe would, too. I wish to promise not to be as foolish in the future, and the same error would never occur again to make us all so unhappy, if you can be charitable enough to excuse it this time."

He looked steadily at her without replying, and she stood before him, never lifting her eyes; motionless, save where the moving fur proved the agitation of her hands within the muff.

"All right," he said, at last.

She looked up then with vast relief, though there was a revelation of heavy tears when the eyelids lifted.

"Thank you," she said. "There's something else—about something different—I want to say to you, but I want mother Sheridan to hear it, too."

"She's up-stairs in her room," said Sheridan. "Roscoe—"

Sibyl interrupted. She had just seen Bibbs pass through the hall and begin to ascend the stairs; and in a flash she instinctively perceived the chance for precisely the effect she wanted.

"No, let me go," she said. "I want to speak to her a minute first, anyway."

And she went away quickly, gaining the top of the stairs in time to see Bibbs enter his room and close the door. Sibyl knew that Bibbs, in his room, had overheard her quarrel with Edith in the hall outside; for bitter Edith, thinking the more to shame her, had subsequently informed her of the circumstance. Sibyl had just remembered this, and with the recollection there had flashed the thought—out of her own experience—that people are often much more deeply impressed by words they overhear than by words directly addressed to them. Sibyl intended to make it impossible for Bibbs not to overhear. She did not hesitate—her heart was hot with the old sore, and she believed wholly in the justice of her cause and in the truth of what she was going to say. Fate was virtuous at times; it had delivered into her hands the girl who had affronted her.

Mrs. Sheridan was in her own room. The approach of Sibyl and Roscoe had driven her from the library, for she had miscalculated her husband's mood, and she felt that if he used his injured hand as a mark of emphasis again, in her presence, she would (as she thought of it) "have a fit right there." She heard Sibyl's step, and pretended to be putting a touch to her hair before a mirror.

"I was just coming down," she said, as the door opened.

"Yes, he wants you to," said Sibyl. "It's all right, mother Sheridan. He's forgiven me."

Mrs. Sheridan sniffed instantly; tears appeared. She kissed her daughter-in-law's cheek; then, in silence, regarded the mirror afresh, wiped her eyes, and applied powder.

"And I hope Edith will be happy," Sibyl added, inciting more applications of Mrs. Sheridan's handkerchief and powder.

"Yes, yes," murmured the good woman. "We mustn't make the worst of things."

"Well, there was something else I had to say, and he wants you to hear it, too," said Sibyl. "We better go down, mother Sheridan."

She led the way, Mrs. Sheridan following obediently, but, when they came to a spot close by Bibbs's door, Sibyl stopped. "I want to tell you about it first," she said, abruptly. "It isn't a secret, of course, in any way; it's something the whole family has to know, and the sooner the whole family knows it the better. It's something it wouldn't be *right* for us *all* not to understand, and of course father Sheridan most of all. But

I want to just kind of go over it first with you; it 'll kind of help me to see I got it all straight. I haven't got any reason for saying it except the good of the family, and it's nothing to me, one way or the other, of course, except for that. I oughtn't to 've behaved the way I did that night, and it seems to me if there's anything I can do to help the family, I ought to, because it would help show I felt the right way. Well, what I want to do is to tell this so's to keep the family from being made a fool of. I don't want to see the family just made use of and twisted around her finger by somebody that's got no more heart than so much ice, and just as sure to bring troubles in the long run as—as Edith's mistake is. Well, then, this is the way it is. I'll just tell you how it looks to me and see if it don't strike you the same way."

Within the room, Bibbs, much annoyed, tapped his ear with his pencil. He wished they wouldn't stand talking near his door when he was trying to write. He had just taken from his trunk the manuscript of a poem begun the preceding Sunday afternoon, and he had some ideas he wanted to fix upon paper before they maliciously seized the first opportunity to vanish, for they were but gossamer. Bibbs was pleased with the beginnings of his poem, and if he could carry it through he meant to dare greatly with it—he would venture it upon an editor. For he had his plan of life now: his day would be of manual labor and thinking—he could think of his friend and he could think in cadences for poems, to the crashing of the strong machines—and if his father turned him out of home and out of the Works, he would work elsewhere and live elsewhere. His father had the right, and it mattered very little to Bibbs—he faced the prospect of a working-man's lodging-house without trepidation. He could find a washstand to write upon, he thought; and every evening when he left Mary he would write a little; and he would write on holidays and on Sundays,—on Sundays in the afternoon. In a lodging-house, at least he wouldn't be interrupted by his sister-in-law's choosing the immediate vicinity of his door for conversations evidently important to herself, but merely disturbing to him. He frowned plaintively, wishing he could think of some polite way of asking her to go away. But, as she went on, he started violently, dropping manuscript and pencil upon the floor.

"I don't know whether you heard it, mother Sheridan," she said, "but this old Vertrees house, next door, has been sold on foreclosure, and all *they* got out of it was an agreement that lets 'em live there a little longer. Roscoe told me, and he says he heard Mr. Vertrees has been up and down the streets more 'n two years, tryin' to get a job he could call a 'position,' and couldn't land it. You heard anything about it, mother Sheridan?"

"Well, I *did* know they been doin' their own housework a good while back," said Mrs. Sheridan. "And now they're doin' the cookin', too."

Sibyl sent forth a little titter with a sharp edge. "I hope they find something to cook! She sold her piano mighty quick after Jim died!"

Bibbs jumped up. He was trembling from head to foot and he was dizzy—of all the real things he could never have dreamed in his dream the last would have been what he heard now. He felt that something incredible was happening, and that he was powerless to stop it. It seemed to him that heavy blows were falling upon his head and upon Mary's; it seemed to him that he and Mary were being struck and beaten physically—and that something hideous impended. He wanted to shout to Sibyl to be silent, but he could not; he could only stand, swallowing and trembling.

"What I think the whole family ought to understand is just this," said Sibyl, sharply. "Those people were so hard up that this Miss Vertrees started after Bibbs before they knew whether he was *insane* or not! They'd got a notion he might be, from his being in a sanitarium, and Mrs. Vertrees *asked* me if he was insane, the very first day Bibbs took the daughter out auto-riding!" She paused a moment, looking at Mrs. Sheridan, but listening intently. There was no sound from within the room.

"No!" exclaimed Mrs. Sheridan.

"It's the truth," Sibyl declared, loudly. "Oh, of course we were all crazy about that girl at first. We were pretty green when we moved up here, and we thought she'd get us *in* —but it didn't take *me* long to read her! Her family were down and out when it came to money—and they had to go after it, one way or another, *somehow!* So she started for Roscoe; but she found out pretty quick he was married, and she turned right around to Jim—and she landed him! There's no doubt about it, she had Jim, and if he'd lived you'd had another daughter-in-law before this, as sure as I stand here telling you the God's truth about it! Well—when Jim was left in the cemetery she was waiting out there to drive home with Bibbs! Jim wasn't *cold*—and she didn't know whether Bibbs was insane or not, but he was the only one of the rich Sheridan boys left. She had to get him."

The texture of what was the truth made an even fabric with what was not, in Sibyl's mind; she believed every word that she uttered, and she spoke with the rapidity and ve-hemence of fierce conviction.

"What I feel about it is," she said, "it oughtn't to be al-lowed to go on. It's too mean! I like poor Bibbs, and I don't want to see him made such a fool of, and I don't want to see the family made such a fool of! I like poor Bibbs, but if he'd only stop to think a minute himself he'd have to realize he isn't the kind of a man *any* girl would be apt to fall in love with. He's better-looking lately, maybe, but you know how he *was*—just kind of a long white rag in good clothes. And girls like men with some *go* to 'em—*some* sort of dashing-ness, anyhow! Nobody ever looked at poor Bibbs before, and neither'd she—no, *sir!* not till she'd tried both Roscoe and

Jim first! It was only when her and her family got desperate that she—"

Bibbs—whiter than when he came from the sanitarium—opened the door. He stepped across its threshold and stood looking at her. Both women screamed.

"Oh, good heavens!" cried Sibyl. "Were you in *there?* Oh, I wouldn't—" She seized Mrs. Sheridan's arm, pulling her toward the stairway. "Come on, mother Sheridan!" she urged, and as the befuddled and confused lady obeyed, Sibyl left a trail of noisy exclamations: "Good gracious! Oh, I wouldn't— Too bad! I didn't *dream* he was there! I wouldn't hurt his feelings! Not for the world! Of course he had to know *some* time! But, good heavens—"

She heard his door close as she and Mrs. Sheridan reached the top of the stairs, and she glanced over her shoulder quickly, but Bibbs was not following; he had gone back into his room.

"He—he looked—oh, terrible bad!" stammered Mrs. Sheridan. "I—I wish—"

"Still, it's a good deal better he knows about it," said Sibyl. "I shouldn't wonder it might turn out the very best thing could happened. Come on!"

And completing their descent to the library, the two made their appearance to Roscoe and his father. Sibyl at once gave a full and truthful account of what had taken place, repeating her own remarks, and omitting only the fact that it was through her design that Bibbs had overheard them.

"But as I told mother Sheridan," she said, in conclusion, "it might turn out for the very best that he did hear—just that way. Don't you think so, father Sheridan?"

He merely grunted in reply, and sat rubbing the thick hair on the top of his head with his left hand and looking at the fire. He had given no sign of being impressed in any manner by her exposure of Mary Vertrees's character; but his impas-

sivity did not dismay Sibyl—it was Bibbs whom she desired
to impress, and she was content in that matter.

"I'm sure it was all for the best," she said. "It's over now,
and he knows what she is. In one way I think it was lucky,
because, just hearing a thing that way, a person can tell it's
so—and he knows *I* haven't got any ax to grind except his
own good and the good of the family."

Mrs. Sheridan went nervously to the door and stood there,
looking toward the stairway. "I wish—I wish I knew what
he was doin'," she said. "He did look terrible bad. It was like
something had been done to him that was—I don't know
what. I never saw anybody look like he did. He looked—so
queer. It was like you'd—" She called down the hall,
"George!"

"Yes'm?"

"Were you up in Mr. Bibbs's room just now?"

"Yes'm. He ring bell; tole me make him fiah in his grate.
I done buil' him nice fiah. I reckon he ain' feelin' so well.
Yes'm." He departed.

"What do you expect he wants a fire for?" she asked, turning toward her husband "The house is warm as can be. I
do wish I—"

"Oh, quit frettin'!" said Sheridan.

"Well, I—I kind o' wish you hadn't said anything, Sibyl.
I know you meant it for the best and all, but I don't believe
it would been so much harm if—"

"Mother Sheridan, you don't mean you *want* that kind of
a girl in the family? Why, she—"

"I don't know, I don't know," the troubled woman qua-
vered. "If he liked her it seems kind of a pity to spoil it. He's
so queer, and he hasn't ever taken much enjoyment. And
besides, I believe the way it was, there was more chance of
him bein' willin' to do what papa wants him to. If she wants
to marry him—"

Sheridan interrupted her with a hooting laugh. "She don't!" he said. "You're barkin' up the wrong tree, Sibyl. She ain't that kind of a girl."

"But, father Sheridan, didn't she—"

He cut her short "That's enough. You may mean all right, but you guess wrong. So do you, mamma."

Sibyl cried out, "Oh! But just *look* how she ran after Jim—"

"She did not," he said, curtly. "She wouldn't take Jim. She turned him down cold."

"But that's impossi—"

"It's not. I *know* she did."

Sibyl looked flatly incredulous.

"And *you* needn't worry," he said, turning to his wife. "This won't have any effect on your idea, because there wasn't any sense to it, anyhow. D' you think she'd be very likely to take Bibbs—after she wouldn't take *Jim?* She's a good-hearted girl, and she lets Bibbs come to see her, but if she'd ever given him one sign of encouragement the way you women think, he wouldn't of acted the stubborn fool he has —he'd 'a' been at me long ago, beggin' me for some kind of a job he could support a wife on. There's nothin' in it—and I've got the same old fight with him on my hands I've had all his life—and the Lord knows what he won't do to balk me! What's happened now 'll probably only make him twice as stubborn, but—"

"'*Sh!*" Mrs. Sheridan, still in the doorway, lifted her hand. "That's his step—he's comin' down-stairs." She shrank away from the door as if she feared to have Bibbs see her. "I—I wonder—" she said, almost in a whisper—"I wonder what he's goin'—to do."

Her timorousness had its effect upon the others. Sheridan rose, frowning, but remained standing beside his chair; and Roscoe moved toward Sibyl, who stared uneasily at the open doorway. They listened as the slow steps descended the stairs and came toward the library.

Bibbs stopped upon the threshold, and with sick and haggard eyes looked slowly from one to the other until at last his gaze rested upon his father. Then he came and stood before him.

"I'm sorry you've had so much trouble with me," he said, gently. "You won't, any more. I'll take the job you offered me."

Sheridan did not speak—he stared, astounded and incredulous; and Bibbs had left the room before any of its occupants uttered a sound, though he went as slowly as he came. Mrs. Sheridan was the first to move. She went nervously back to the doorway, and then out into the hall. Bibbs had gone from the house.

Bibbs's mother had a feeling about him then that she had never known before; it was indefinite and vague, but very poignant—something in her mourned for him uncomprehendingly. She felt that an awful thing had been done to him, though she did not know what it was. She went up to his room.

The fire George had built for him was almost smothered under thick, charred ashes of paper. The lid of his trunk stood open, and the large upper tray, which she remembered to have seen full of papers and note-books, was empty. And somehow she understood that Bibbs had given up the mysterious vocation he had hoped to follow—and that he had given it up for ever. She thought it was the wisest thing he could have done—and yet, for an unknown reason, she sat upon the bed and wept a little before she went down-stairs.

So Sheridan had his way with Bibbs, all through.

CHAPTER TWENTY-NINE

As BIBBS came out of the New House, a Sunday trio was in course of passage upon the sidewalk: an ample young woman, placid of face; a black-clad, thin young man, whose expression was one of habitual anxiety, habitual wariness and habitual eagerness. He propelled a perambulator containing the third—and all three were newly cleaned, Sundayfied, and made fit to dine with the wife's relatives.

"How'd you like for me to be *that* young fella, mamma?" the husband whispered. "He's one of the sons, and there ain't but two left now."

The wife stared curiously at Bibbs. "Well, I don't know," she returned. "He looks to me like he had his own troubles."

"I expect he has, like anybody else," said the young husband, "but I guess we could stand a good deal if we had his money."

"Well, maybe, if you keep on the way you been, baby 'll be as well fixed as the Sheridans. You can't tell." She glanced back at Bibbs, who had turned north. "He walks kind of slow and stooped over, like."

"So much money in his pockets it makes him sag, I guess," said the young husband, with bitter admiration.

Mary, happening to glance from a window, saw Bibbs coming, and she started, clasping her hands together in a sudden alarm. She met him at the door.

"Bibbs!" she cried. "What is the matter? I saw something was terribly wrong when I— You look—" She paused, and he came in, not lifting his eyes to hers. Always when he crossed that threshold he had come with his head up and his wistful gaze seeking hers. "Ah, poor boy!" she said, with a gesture of understanding and pity. "I know what it is!"

He followed her into the room where they always sat, and sank into a chair.

"You needn't tell me," she said. "They've made you give up. Your father's won—you're going to do what he wants. You've given up."

Still without looking at her, he inclined his head in affirmation.

She gave a little cry of compassion, and came and sat near him. "Bibbs," she said, "I can be glad of one thing, though it's selfish. I can be glad you came straight to me. It's more to me than even if you'd come because you were happy." She did not speak again for a little while; then she said: "Bibbs—dear—could you tell me about it? Do you want to?"

Still he did not look up, but in a voice, shaken and husky he asked her a question so grotesque that at first she thought she had misunderstood his words.

"Mary," he said, "could you marry me?"

"What did you say, Bibbs?" she asked, quietly.

His tone and attitude did not change. "Will you marry me?"

Both of her hands leaped to her cheeks—she grew red and then white. She rose slowly and moved backward from him, staring at him, at first incredulously, then with an intense perplexity more and more luminous in her wide eyes; it was like a spoken question. The room filled with strangeness in the long silence—the two were so strange to each other. At last she said:

"What made you say that?"

He did not answer.

"Bibbs, look at me!" Her voice was loud and clear. "What made you say that? Look at me!"

He could not look at her, and he could not speak.

"What was it that made you?" she said. "I want you to tell me."

She went closer to him, her eyes ever brighter and wider with that intensity of wonder. "You've given up—to your father," she said, slowly, "and then you came to ask me—" She broke off. "Bibbs, do you want me to marry you?"

"Yes," he said, just audibly.

"No!" she cried. "You do not. Then what made you ask me? What is it that's happened?"

"Nothing."

"Wait," she said. "Let me think. It's something that happened since our walk this morning—yes, since you left me at noon. Something happened that—" She stopped abruptly, with a tremulous murmur of amazement and dawning comprehension. She remembered that Sibyl had gone to the New House.

Bibbs swallowed painfully and contrived to say, "I do—I do want you to—marry me, if—if—you could."

She looked at him, and slowly shook her head. "Bibbs, do you—" Her voice was as unsteady as his—little more than a whisper. "Do you think I'm—in love with you?"

"No," he said.

Somewhere in the still air of the room there was a whispered word; it did not seem to come from Mary's parted lips, but he was aware of it. "Why?"

"I've had nothing but dreams," Bibbs said, desolately, "but they weren't like that. Sibyl said no girl could care about me." He smiled faintly, though still he did not look at Mary. "And when I first came home Edith told me Sibyl was so anxious to marry that she'd have married *me*. She meant it to express Sibyl's extremity, you see. But I hardly needed either of them to tell me. I hadn't thought of myself as—well, not as particularly captivating!"

Oddly enough, Mary's pallor changed to an angry flush. "Those two!" she exclaimed, sharply; and then, with thoroughgoing contempt: "Lamhorn! That's like them!" She turned away, went to the bare little black mantel, and stood leaning upon it. Presently she asked: *"When* did Mrs. Roscoe Sheridan say that 'no girl' could care about you?"

"To-day."

Mary drew a deep breath. "I think I'm beginning to understand—a little." She bit her lip; there was anger in good truth in her eyes and in her voice. "Answer me once more," she said. "Bibbs, do you know now why I stopped wearing my furs?"

"Yes."

"I thought so! Your sister-in-law told you, didn't she?"

"I— I heard her say—"

"I think I know what happened, now." Mary's breath came fast and her voice shook, but she spoke rapidly. "You 'heard her say' more than that. You 'heard her say' that we were bitterly poor, and on that account I tried first to marry your brother—and then—" But now she faltered, and it was only after a convulsive effort that she was able to go on. "And then —that I tried to marry—you! You 'heard her say' that—and you believe that I don't care for you and that 'no girl' could care for you—but you think I am in such an 'extremity,' as Sibyl was—that you— And so, not wanting me, and believing that I could not want you—except for my 'extremity'—you took your father's offer and then came to ask me—to marry you! What had *I* shown you of myself that could make you—"

Suddenly she sank down, kneeling, with her face buried in her arms upon the lap of a chair, tears overwhelming her.

"Mary, Mary!" he cried, helplessly. "Oh *no*—you—you don't understand."

"I do, though!" she sobbed. "I do!"

He came and stood beside her. "You kill me!" he said. "I can't make it plain. From the first of your loveliness to me, I was all self. It was always you that gave and I that took. I was the dependent—I did nothing but lean on you. We always talked of me, not of you. It was all about my idiotic distresses and troubles. I thought of you as a kind of wonderful being that had no mortal or human suffering except by sympathy. You seemed to lean down—out of a rosy cloud—to be kind to me. I never dreamed *I* could do anything for *you!* I never dreamed you could need anything to be done for you by anybody. And to-day I heard that—that you—"

"You heard that I needed to marry—some one—anybody—with money," she sobbed. "And you thought we were so—so desperate—you believed that I had—"

"No!" he said, quickly. "I didn't believe you'd done one kind thing for me—for that. No, no, no! I knew you'd *never* thought of me except generously—to give. I said I couldn't make it plain!" he cried, despairingly.

"Wait!" She lifted her head and extended her hands to him unconsciously, like a child. "Help me up, Bibbs." Then, when she was once more upon her feet, she wiped her eyes and smiled upon him ruefully and faintly, but reassuringly, as if to tell him, in that way, that she knew he had not meant to hurt her. And that smile of hers, so lamentable but so faithfully friendly, misted his own eyes, for his shamefacedness lowered them no more.

"Let me tell you what you want to tell me," she said. "You can't, because you can't put it into words—they are too humiliating for me and you're too gentle to say them. Tell me, though, isn't it true? You didn't believe that I'd tried to make you fall in love with me—"

"Never! Never for an instant!"

"You didn't believe I'd tried to make you want to marry me—"

"No, no, no!"

"I believe it, Bibbs. You thought that I was fond of you; you knew I cared for you—but you didn't think I might be—in love with you. But you thought that I might marry you without being in love with you because you did believe I had tried to marry your brother, and—"

"Mary, I only knew—for the first time—that you—that you were—"

"Were desperately poor," she said. "You can't even say that! Bibbs, it was true: I did try to make Jim want to marry me. I did!" And she sank down into the chair, weeping bitterly again. Bibbs was agonized.

"Mary," he groaned, "I didn't know you *could* cry!"

"Listen," she said. "Listen till I get through—I want you to understand. We were poor, and we weren't fitted to be. We never had been, and we didn't know what to do. We'd been almost rich, there was plenty, but my father wanted to take advantage of the growth of the town; he wanted to be richer, but instead—well, just about the time your father finished building next door we found we hadn't anything. People say that, sometimes, meaning that they haven't anything in comparison with other people of their own kind, but we really hadn't anything—we hadn't anything at all, Bibbs! And we couldn't *do* anything. You might wonder why I didn't 'try to be a stenographer'—and I wonder myself why, when a family loses its money, people always say the daughters 'ought to go and be stenographers.' It's curious! —as if a wave of the hand made you into a stenographer. No, I'd been raised to be either married comfortably or a well-to-do old maid, if I chose not to marry. The poverty came on slowly, Bibbs, but at last it was all there—and I didn't know how to be a stenographer. I didn't know how to be anything except a well-to-do old maid or somebody's wife —and I couldn't be a well-to-do old maid. Then, Bibbs, I did what I'd been raised to know how to do. I went out to be fascinating and be married. I did it openly, at least, and with a kind of decent honesty. I told your brother I had meant to fascinate him and that I was not in love with him, but I let him think that perhaps I meant to marry him. I think I did mean to marry him. I had never cared for anybody, and I thought it might be there really *wasn't* anything more than a kind of excited fondness. I can't be sure, but I think that though I did mean to marry him I never should have done it, because that sort of a marriage is—it's sacrilege—something would have stopped me. Something did stop me; it was your sister-in-law, Sibyl. She meant no harm—but she was horrible, and she put what I was doing into such horrible words—and they were the truth—oh! I *saw* myself! She was proposing a miserable compact with me—and I couldn't breathe the air of the same room with her, though I'd so cheapened myself she had a right to assume that I *would*. But I couldn't! I left her, and I wrote to your brother—just a quick scrawl. I told him just what I'd done; I asked his pardon, and I said I would not marry him. I posted the letter, but he never got it. That was the afternoon he was killed. That's all, Bibbs. Now you know what I did—and you know—*me!*" She pressed her clenched hands tightly against her eyes, leaning far forward, her head bowed before him.

Bibbs had forgotten himself long ago; his heart broke for her. "Couldn't you— Isn't there— Won't you—" he stammered. "Mary, I'm going with father. Isn't there some way you could use the money without—without—"

She gave a choked little laugh.

"You gave me something to live for," he said. "You kept me alive, I think—and I've hurt you like this!"

"Not you—oh no!"

"You could forgive me, Mary?"

"Oh, a thousand times!" Her right hand went out in a faltering gesture, and just touched his own for an instant. "But there's nothing to forgive."

"And you can't—you can't—"

"Can't what, Bibbs?"

"You couldn't—"

"Marry you?" she said for him.

"Yes."

"No, no, no!" She sprang up, facing him, and, without

knowing what she did, she set her hands upon his breast, pushing him back from her a little. "I can't, I can't! Don't you *see?*"

"Mary—"

"No, no! And you must go now, Bibbs; I can't bear any more—please—"

"*Mary—*"

"Never, never, never!" she cried, in a passion of tears. "You mustn't come any more. I can't see you, dear! Never, never, never!"

Somehow, in helpless, stumbling obedience to her beseeching gesture, he got himself to the door and out of the house.

CHAPTER THIRTY

SIBYL and Roscoe were upon the point of leaving when Bibbs returned to the New House. He went straight to Sibyl and spoke to her quietly, but so that the others might hear.

"When you said that if I'd stop to think, I'd realize that no one would be apt to care enough about me to marry me, you were right," he said. "I thought perhaps you weren't, and so I asked Miss Vertrees to marry me. It proved what you said of me, and disproved what you said of her. She refused."

And, having thus spoken, he quitted the room as straightforwardly as he had entered it.

"He's *so* queer!" Mrs. Sheridan gasped. "Who on earth would thought of his doin' *that?*"

"I told you," said her husband, grimly.

"You didn't tell us he'd go over there and—"

"I told you she wouldn't have him. I told you she wouldn't have *Jim*, didn't I?"

Sibyl was altogether taken aback. "Do you suppose it's true? Do you suppose she *wouldn't?*"

"He didn't look exactly like a young man that had just got things fixed up fine with his girl," said Sheridan. "Not to me he didn't!"

"But why would—"

"I told you," he interrupted, angrily, "she ain't that kind of a girl! If you got to have proof, well, I'll tell you and get it over with, though I'd pretty near just as soon not have to talk a whole lot about my dead boy's private affairs. She wrote to Jim she couldn't take him, and it was a good, straight letter, too. It came to Jim's office; he never saw it. She wrote it the afternoon he was hurt."

"I remember I saw her put a letter in the mail-box that afternoon," said Roscoe. "Don't you remember, Sibyl? I told you about it—I was waiting for you while you were in there so long talking to her mother. It was just before we saw that something was wrong over here, and Edith came and called me."

Sibyl shook her head, but she remembered. And she was not cast down, for, although some remnants of perplexity were left in her eyes, they were dimmed by an increasing glow of triumph; and she departed—after some further fragmentary discourse—visibly elated. After all, the guilty had not been exalted; and she perceived vaguely, but none the less surely, that her injury had been copiously avenged. She bestowed a contented glance upon the old house with the cupola, as she and Roscoe crossed the street.

When they had gone, Mrs. Sheridan indulged in reverie, but after a while she said, uneasily, "Papa, you think it would be any use to tell Bibbs about that letter?"

"I don't know," he answered, walking moodily to the window. "I been thinkin' about it." He came to a decision. "I reckon I will." And he went up to Bibbs's room.

"Well, you goin' back on what you said?" he inquired, brusquely, as he opened the door. "You goin' to take it back and lay down on me again?"

"No," said Bibbs.

"Well, perhaps I didn't have any call to accuse you of that. I don't know as you ever did go back on anything you said, exactly, though the Lord knows you've laid down on me enough. You certainly have!" Sheridan was baffled. This was not what he wished to say, but his words were unmanageable; he found himself unable to control them, and his querulous abuse went on in spite of him. "I can't say I expect much of you—not from the way you always been, up to now —unless you turn over a new leaf, and I don't see any encouragement to think you're goin' to do *that!* If you go down there and show a spark o' real *git*-up, I reckon the whole office 'll fall in a faint. But if you're ever goin' to show any, you better begin right at the beginning and begin to show it to-morrow."

"Yes—I'll try."

"You better, if it's in you!" Sheridan was sheerly nonplussed. He had always been able to say whatever he wished to say, but his tongue seemed bewitched. He had come to tell Bibbs about Mary's letter, and to his own angry astonishment he found it impossible to do anything except to scold like a drudge-driver. "You better come down there with your mind made up to hustle harder than the hardest workin'-man that's under you, or you'll not get on very good with me, I tell you! The way to get ahead—and you better set it down in your books—the way to get ahead is to do ten times the work of the hardest worker that works *for* you. But you don't know what work is, yet. All you've ever done was just stand around and feed a machine a child could handle, and then come home and take a bath and go callin'. I tell you you're up against a mighty different proposition now, and if you're worth your salt—and you never showed any signs of it yet— not any signs that stuck out enough to bang somebody on the head and make 'em sit up and take notice—well, I want to say, right here and now—and you better listen, because I want to say just what I *do* say. I say—"

He meandered to a full stop. His mouth hung open, and his mind was a hopeless blank.

Bibbs looked up patiently—an old, old look. "Yes, father; I'm listening."

"That's all," said Sheridan, frowning heavily. "That's all I came to say, and you better see 't you remember it!"

He shook his head warningly, and went out, closing the door behind him with a crash. However, no sound of footsteps indicated his departure. He stopped just outside the door, and stood there a minute or more. Then abruptly he turned the knob and exhibited to his son a forehead liberally covered with perspiration.

"Look here," he said, crossly. "That girl over yonder wrote Jim a letter—"

"I know," said Bibbs. "She told me."

"Well, I thought you needn't feel so much upset about it—" The door closed on his voice as he withdrew, but the conclusion of the sentence was nevertheless audible—"if you knew she wouldn't have Jim, either."

And he stamped his way down-stairs to tell his wife to quit her frettin' and not bother him with any more fool's errands. She was about to inquire what Bibbs "said," but after a second thought she decided not to speak at all. She merely murmured a wordless assent, and verbal communication was given over between them for the rest of that afternoon.

Bibbs and his father were gone when Mrs. Sheridan woke, the next morning, and she had a dreary day. She missed Edith woefully, and she worried about what might be taking place in the Sheridan Building. She felt that everything depended on how Bibbs "took hold," and upon her husband's return in the evening she seized upon the first opportunity to ask him how things had gone. He was noncommittal. What could anybody tell by the first day? He'd seen plenty go at things well enough right at the start and then blow up. Pretty near anybody could show up fair the first day or so. There was a big job ahead. This material, such as it was—Bibbs, in fact—had to be broken in to handling the work Roscoe had done; and then, at least as an overseer, he must take Jim's position in the Realty Company as well. He told her to ask him again in a month.

But during the course of dinner she gathered from some disjointed remarks of his that he and Bibbs had lunched together at the small restaurant where it had been Sheridan's custom to lunch with Jim, and she took this to be an encouraging sign. Bibbs went to his room as soon as they left the table, and her husband was not communicative after reading his paper.

She became an anxious spectator of Bibbs's progress as a man of business, although it was a progress she could glimpse but dimly and only in the evening, through his remarks and his father's at dinner. Usually Bibbs was silent, except when directly addressed, but on the first evening of the third week of his new career he offered an opinion which had apparently been the subject of previous argument.

"I'd like you to understand just what I meant about those storage-rooms, father," he said, as Jackson placed his coffee before him. "Abercrombie agreed with me, but you wouldn't listen to him."

"You can talk, if you want to, and I'll listen," Sheridan returned, "but you can't show me that Jim ever took up with a bad thing. The roof fell because it hadn't had time to settle and on account of weather conditions. I want that building put just the way Jim planned it."

"You can't have it," said Bibbs. "You can't, because Jim planned for the building to stand up, and it won't do it. The other one—the one that didn't fall—is so shot with cracks we haven't dared use it for storage. It won't stand weight. There's only one thing to do: get both buildings down as quickly as we can, and build over. Brick's the best and cheapest in the long run for that type."

Sheridan looked sarcastic. "Fine! What we goin' to do for storage-rooms while we're waitin' for those few bricks to be laid?"

"Rent," Bibbs returned, promptly. "We'll lose money if we don't rent, anyhow—they were waiting so long for you to give the warehouse matter your attention after the roof fell. You don't know what an amount of stuff they've got piled up on us over there. We'd have to rent until we could patch up those process perils—and the Krivitch Manufacturing Company's plant is empty, right across the street. I took an option on it for us this morning."

Sheridan's expression was queer. "Look here!" he said, sharply. "Did you go and do that without consulting me?"

"It didn't cost anything," said Bibbs. "It's only until to-morrow afternoon at two o'clock. I undertook to convince you before then."

"Oh, you did?" Sheridan's tone was sardonic. "Well, just suppose you couldn't convince me."

"I can, though—and I intend to," said Bibbs, quietly. "I don't think you understand the condition of those buildings you want patched up."

"Now, see here," said Sheridan, with slow emphasis; "suppose I had my mind set about this. *Jim* thought they'd stand, and suppose it was—well, kind of a matter of sentiment with me to prove he was right."

Bibbs looked at him compassionately. "I'm sorry if you have a sentiment about it, father," he said. "But whether you have or not can't make a difference. You'll get other people hurt if you trust that process, and that won't do. And if you want a monument to Jim, at least you want one that will stand. Besides, I don't think you can reasonably defend sentiment in this particular kind of affair."

"Oh, you don't?"

"No, but I'm sorry you didn't tell me you felt it."

Sheridan was puzzled by his son's tone. "Why are you 'sorry'?" he asked, curiously.

"Because I had the building inspector up there, this noon," said Bibbs, "and I had him condemn both those buildings."

"What?"

"He'd been afraid to do it before, until he heard from us—afraid you'd see he lost his job. But he can't un-condemn them—they've got to come down now."

Sheridan gave him a long and piercing stare from beneath lowered brows. Finally he said, "How long did they give you on that option to convince me?"

"Until two o'clock to-morrow afternoon."

"All right," said Sheridan, not relaxing. "I'm convinced."

Bibbs jumped up. "I thought you would be. I'll telephone the Krivitch agent. He gave me the option until to-morrow, but I told him I'd settle it this evening."

Sheridan gazed after him as he left the room, and then, though his expression did not alter in the slightest, a sound came from him that startled his wife. It had been a long time since she had heard anything resembling a chuckle from him, and this sound—although it was grim and dry—bore that resemblance.

She brightened eagerly. "Looks like he was startin' right well, don't it, papa?"

"Startin'? Lord! He got me on the hip! Why, *he* knew what I wanted—that's why he had the inspector up there, so 't he'd have me beat before we even started to talk about it. And did you hear him? 'Can't reasonably defend *sentiment!*' And the way he says 'Us': 'Took an option for Us'! 'Stuff piled up on Us'!"

There was always an alloy for Mrs. Sheridan. "I don't just like the way he looks, though, papa."

"Oh, there's got to be something! Only one chick left at home, so you start to frettin' about *it!*"

"No. He's changed. There's kind of a settish look to his face, and—"

"I guess that's the common sense comin' out on him, then," said Sheridan. "You'll see symptoms like that in a good many business men, I expect."

"Well, and he don't have as good color as he was gettin' before. And he'd begun to fill out some, but—"

Sheridan gave forth another dry chuckle, and, going round the table to her, patted her upon the shoulder with his left hand, his right being still heavily bandaged, though he no longer wore a sling. "That's the way it is with you, mamma —got to take your frettin' out one way if you don't another!"

"No. He don't look well. It ain't exactly the way he looked when he begun to get sick that time, but he kind o' seems to be losin', some way."

"Yes, he may 'a' lost something," said Sheridan. "I expect he's lost a whole lot o' foolishness besides his God-forsaken notions about writin' poetry and—"

"No," his wife persisted. "I mean he looks right peakid. And yesterday, when he was settin' with us, he kept lookin' out the window. He wasn't readin'."

"Well, why shouldn't he look out the window?"

"He was lookin' over there. He never read a word all afternoon, I don't believe."

"Look here!" said Sheridan. "Bibbs might 'a' kept goin' on over there the rest of his life, moonin' on and on, but what he heard Sibyl say did one big thing, anyway. It woke him up out of his trance. Well, he had to go and bust clean out with a bang; and that stopped his goin' over there, and it stopped his poetry, but I reckon he's begun to get pretty fair pay for what he lost. I guess a good many young men have had to get over worries like this; they got to lose *something* if they're goin' to keep ahead o' the procession nowadays—and it kind o' looks to me, mamma, like Bibbs might keep quite a considerable long way ahead. Why, a year from now I'll bet you

he won't know there ever *was* such a thing as poetry! And
ain't he funny? He wanted to stick to the shop so's he could
'think'! What he meant was, think about something useless.
Well, I guess he's keepin' his mind pretty occupied the other
way these days. Yes, sir, it took a pretty fair-sized shock to get
him out of his trance, but it certainly did the business." He
patted his wife's shoulder again, and then, without any
prefatory symptoms, broke into a boisterous laugh.

"Honest, mamma, he works like a gorilla!"

CHAPTER THIRTY-ONE

AND so Bibbs sat in the porch of the temple with the money-
changers. But no One came to scourge him forth, for this
was the temple of Bigness, and the changing of money was
holy worship and true religion. The priests wore that "settish"
look Bibbs's mother had seen beginning to develop about his
mouth and eyes—a wary look which she could not define,
but it comes with service at the temple; and it was the more
marked upon Bibbs for his sharp awakening to the necessities
of that service.

He did as little "useless" thinking as possible, giving himself
no time for it. He worked continuously, keeping his thoughts
still on his work when he came home at night; and he talked
of nothing whatever except his work. But he did not sing at
it. He was often in the streets, and people were not allowed
to sing in the streets. They might make any manner of hideous uproar—they could shake buildings; they could out-thun-
der the thunder, deafen the deaf, and kill the sick with noise;
or they could walk the streets or drive through them bawling,
squawking, or screeching, as they chose, if the noise was trace-
ably connected with business; though street musicians were
not tolerated, being considered a nuisance and an interference.

A man or woman who went singing for pleasure through the streets—like a crazy Neapolitan—would have been stopped, and belike locked up; for Freedom does not mean that a citizen is allowed to do every outrageous thing that comes into his head. The streets were dangerous enough, in all conscience, without any singing! and the Motor Federation issued public warnings declaring that the pedestrian's life was in his own hands, and giving directions how to proceed with the least peril. However, Bibbs Sheridan had no desire to sing in the streets, or anywhere. He had gone to his work with an energy that, for the start, at least, was bitter, and there was no song left in him.

He began to know his active fellow-citizens. Here and there among them he found a leisurely, kind soul, a relic of the old period of neighborliness, "pioneer stock," usually; and there were men—particularly among the merchants and manufacturers—"so honest they leaned backward"; reputations sometimes attested by stories of heroic sacrifices to honor; nor were there lacking some instances of generosity even nobler. Here and there, too, were book-men, in their little leisure; and, among the Germans, music-men. And these, with the others, worshiped Bigness and the growth, each man serving for his own sake and for what he could get out of it, but all united in their faith in the beneficence and glory of their god.

To almost all alike that service stood as the most important thing in life, except on occasion of some such vital, brief interregnum as the dangerous illness of a wife or child. In the way of "relaxation" some of the servers took golf; some took fishing; some took "shows"—a mixture of infantile and Negroid humor, stockings, and tin music; some took an occasional debauch; some took trips; some took cards; and some took nothing. The high priests were vigilant to watch that no "relaxation" should affect the service. When a man attended to anything outside his business, eyes were upon him; his credit was in danger—that is, his life was in danger. And the old priests were as ardent as the young ones; the million was as eager to be bigger as the thousand; seventy was as busy as seventeen. They strove mightily against one another, and the old priests were the most wary, the most plausible, and the most dangerous. Bibbs learned he must walk charily among these—he must wear a thousand eyes and beware of spiders indeed!

And outside the temple itself were the pretenders, the swarming thieves and sharpers and fleecers, the sly rascals and the open rascals; but these were feeble folk, not dangerous once he knew them, and he had a good guide to point them out to him. They were useful sometimes, he learned, and many of them served as go-betweens in matters where business must touch politics. He learned also how breweries and "traction" companies and banks and other institutions fought one another for the political control of the city. The newspapers, he discovered, had lost their ancient political influence, especially with the knowing, who looked upon them with a skeptical humor, believing the journals either to be retained partisans, like lawyers, or else striving to forward the personal ambitions of their owners. The control of the city lay not with them, but was usually obtained by giving the hordes of Negroes gin-money, and by other largesses. The revenues of the people were then distributed as fairly as possible among a great number of men who had assisted the winning side. Names and titles of offices went with many of the prizes, and most of these title-holders were expected to present a busy appearance at times; and, indeed, some among them did work honestly and faithfully.

Bibbs had been very ignorant. All these simple things, so well known and customary, astonished him at first, and once —in a brief moment of forgetting that he was done with writing—he thought that if he had known them and written of them, how like a satire the plainest relation of them must have seemed! Strangest of all to him was the vehement and sincere patriotism. On every side he heard it—it was a permeation; the newest school-child caught it, though just from Hungary and learning to stammer a few words of the local language. Everywhere the people shouted of the power, the size, the riches, and the growth of their city. Not only that, they said that the people of their city were the greatest, the "finest," the strongest, the Biggest people on earth. They cited no authorities, and felt the need of none, being themselves the people thus celebrated. And if the thing was questioned, or if it was hinted that there might be one small virtue in which they were not perfect and supreme, they wasted no time examining themselves to see if what the critic said was true, but fell upon him and hooted him and cursed him, for they were sensitive. So Bibbs, learning their ways and walking with them, harkened to the voice of the people and served Bigness with them. For the voice of the people is the voice of their god.

Sheridan had made the room next to his own into an office for Bibbs, and the door between the two rooms usually stood open—the father had established that intimacy. One morning in February, when Bibbs was alone, Sheridan came in, some sheets of typewritten memoranda in his hand.

"Bibbs," he said, "I don't like to butt in very often this way, and when I do I usually wish I hadn't—but for Heaven's sake what have you been buying that ole busted inter-traction stock for?"

Bibbs leaned back from his desk. "For eleven hundred and fifty-five dollars. That's all it cost."

"Well, it ain't worth eleven hundred and fifty-five cents. You ought to know that. I don't get your idea. That stuff's deader 'n Adam's cat!"

"It might be worth something—some day."

"How?"

"It mightn't be so dead—not if We went into it," said Bibbs, coolly.

"Oh!" Sheridan considered this musingly; then he said, "Who'd you buy it from?"

"A broker—Fansmith."

"Well, he must 'a' got it from one o' the crowd o' poor ninnies that was soaked with it. Don't you know who owned it?"

"Yes, I do."

"Ain't sayin', though? That it? What's the matter?"

"It belonged to Mr. Vertrees," said Bibbs, shortly, applying himself to his desk.

"So!" Sheridan gazed down at his son's thin face. "Excuse me," he said. "Your business." And he went back to his own room. But presently he looked in again.

"I reckon you won't mind lunchin' alone to-day"—he was shuffling himself into his overcoat—"because I just thought I'd go up to the house and get *this* over with mamma." He glanced apologetically toward his right hand as it emerged from the sleeve of the overcoat. The bandages had been removed, finally, that morning, revealing but three fingers—the forefinger and the finger next to it had been amputated. "She's bound to make an awful fuss, and it better spoil her lunch than her dinner. I'll be back about two."

But he calculated the time of his arrival at the New House so accurately that Mrs. Sheridan's lunch was not disturbed, and she was rising from the lonely table when he came into the dining-room. He had left his overcoat in the hall, but he kept his hands in his trousers pockets.

"What's the matter, papa?" she asked, quickly. "Has anything gone wrong? You ain't sick?"

"Me!" He laughed loudly. "Me *sick?*"

"You had lunch?"

"Didn't want any to-day. You can give me a cup o' coffee, though."

She rang, and told George to have coffee made, and when he had withdrawn she said querulously, "I just know there's something wrong."

"Nothin' in the world," he responded, heartily, taking a seat at the head of the table. "I thought I'd talk over a notion o' mine with you, that's all. It's more women-folks' business than what it is man's, anyhow."

"What about?"

"Why, ole Doc Gurney was up at the office this morning awhile—"

"To look at your hand? How's he say it's doin'?"

"Fine! Well, he went in and sat around with Bibbs awhile—"

Mrs. Sheridan nodded pessimistically. "I guess it's time you had him, too. I *knew* Bibbs—"

"Now, mamma, hold your horses! I wanted him to look Bibbs over *before* anything's the matter. You don't suppose I'm goin' to take any chances with *Bibbs,* do you? Well, afterwards, I shut the door, and I an' ole Gurney had a talk. He's a mighty disagreeable man; he rubbed it in on me what he said about Bibbs havin' brains if he ever woke up. Then I thought he must want to get something out o' me, he got so flattering—for a minute! 'Bibbs couldn't help havin' business brains,' he says, 'bein' *your* son. Don't be surprised,' he says— 'don't be surprised at his makin' a success,' he says. 'He couldn't get over his heredity; he couldn't *help* bein' a business success—once you got him into it. It's in his blood. Yes, sir,' he says, 'it doesn't need *much* brains,' he says, 'an' only third-rate brains, at that,' he says, 'but it does need a special *kind* o' brains,' he says, 'to be a millionaire. I mean,' he says, 'when a man's given a start. If nobody gives him a start, why, course he's got to have luck *and* the right kind o' brains. The only miracle about Bibbs,' he says, 'is where he got the *other* kind o' brains—the brains you made him quit usin' and throw away.' "

"But what 'd he say about his health?" Mrs. Sheridan demanded, impatiently, as George placed a cup of coffee before her husband. Sheridan helped himself to cream and sugar, and began to sip the coffee.

"I'm comin' to that," he returned, placidly. "See how easy I manage this cup with my left hand, mamma?"

"You been doin' that all winter. What did—"

"It's wonderful," he interrupted, admiringly, "what a fellow can do with his left hand. I can sign my name with mine now, well's I ever could with my right. It came a little hard at first, but now, honest, I believe I *rather* sign with my left. That's all I ever have to write, anyway—just the signature. Rest's all dictatin'." He blew across the top of the cup unctuously. "Good coffee, mamma! Well, about Bibbs. Ole Gurney says he believes if Bibbs could somehow get back to the state o' mind he was in about the machine-shop—that is, if he could some way get to feelin' about business the way he felt about the shop— not the poetry and writin' part, but—" He paused, supplementing his remarks with a motion of his head toward the old house next door. "He says Bibbs is older and harder 'n what he was when he broke down that time, and besides, he ain't the kind o' dreamy way he was then—and I should say he *ain't!* I'd like 'em to show *me* anybody his age that's any wider awake! But he says Bibbs's health 'll never need bother us again if—"

Mrs. Sheridan shook her head. "I don't see any help *that* way. You know yourself she wouldn't have Jim."

"Who's talkin' about her havin' anybody? But, my Lord! she might let him *look* at her! She needn't 'a' got so mad, just because he asked her, that she won't let him come in the house any more. He's a mighty funny boy, and some ways I reckon he's pretty near as hard to understand as the Bible, but Gurney kind o' got me in the way o' thinkin' that if she'd let him come back and set around with her an evening or two sometimes—not reg'lar, I don't mean—why— Well, I just thought

I'd see what *you'd* think of it. There ain't any way to talk about it to Bibbs himself—I don't suppose he'd let you, any-how—but I thought maybe you could kind o' slip over there some day, and sort o' fix up to have a little talk with her, and kind o' hint around till you see how the land lays, and ask her—"

"*Me!*" Mrs. Sheridan looked both helpless and frightened. "No." She shook her head decidedly. "It wouldn't do any good."

"You won't try it?"

"I won't risk her turnin' me out o' the house. Some way, that's what I believe she did to Sibyl, from what Roscoe said once. No, I *can't*—and, what's more, it 'd only make things worse. If people find out you're runnin' after 'em they think you're cheap, and then they won't do as much for you as if you let 'em alone. I don't believe it's any use, and *I* couldn't do it if it was."

He sighed with resignation. "All right, mamma. That's all." Then, in a livelier tone, he said: "Ole Gurney took the band-ages off my hand this morning. All healed up. Says I don't need 'em any more."

"Why, that's splendid, papa!" she cried, beaming. "I was afraid— Let's see."

She came toward him, but he rose, still keeping his hand in his pocket. "Wait a minute," he said, smiling. "Now it may give you just a little teeny bit of a shock, but the fact is— well, you remember that Sunday when Sibyl came over here and made all that fuss about nothin'—it was the day after I got tired o' that statue when Edith's telegram came—"

"Let me see your hand!" she cried.

"Now wait!" he said, laughing and pushing her away with his left hand. "The truth is, mamma, that I kind o' slipped out on you that morning, when you wasn't lookin', and went down to ole Gurney's office—he'd told me to, you see—and, well, it doesn't *amount* to anything." And he held out, for her inspection, the mutilated hand. "You see, these days when it's all dictatin', anyhow, nobody 'd mind just a couple o'—"

He had to jump for her—she went over backward. For the second time in her life Mrs. Sheridan fainted.

CHAPTER THIRTY-TWO

IT WAS a full hour later when he left her lying upon a couch in her own room, still lamenting intermittently, though he assured her with heat that the "fuss" she was making irked him far more than his physical loss. He permitted her to think that he meant to return directly to his office, but when he came out to the open air he told the chauffeur in attendance to await him in front of Mr. Vertrees's house, whither he himself proceeded on foot.

Mr. Vertrees had taken the sale of half of his worthless stock as manna in the wilderness: it came from heaven—by what agency he did not particularly question. The broker informed him that "parties were interested in getting hold of the stock," and that later there might be a possible increase in the value of the large amount retained by his client. It might go "quite a ways up" within a year or so, he said, and he advised "sitting tight" with it. Mr. Vertrees went home and prayed.

He rose from his knees feeling that he was surely coming into his own again. It was more than a mere gasp of temporary relief with him, and his wife shared his optimism; but Mary would not let him buy back her piano, and as for furs—spring was on the way, she said. But they paid the butcher, the baker, and the candlestick-maker, and hired a cook once more. It was this servitress who opened the door for Sheridan and presently assured him that Miss Vertrees would "be down."

He was not the man to conceal admiration when he felt it,

and he flushed and beamed as Mary made her appearance, almost upon the heels of the cook. She had a look of apprehension for the first fraction of a second, but it vanished at the sight of him, and its place was taken in her eyes by a soft brilliance, while color rushed in her cheeks.

"Don't be surprised," he said. "Truth is, in a way it's sort of on business I looked in here. It 'll only take a minute, I expect."

"I'm sorry," said Mary. "I hoped you'd come because we're neighbors."

He chuckled. "Neighbors! Sometimes people don't see so much o' their neighbors as they used to. That is, I hear so— lately."

"You'll stay long enough to sit down, won't you?"

"I guess I could manage that much." And they sat down, facing each other and not far apart.

"Of course, it couldn't be called business, exactly," he said, more gravely. "Not at all, I expect. But there's something o' yours it seemed to me I ought to give you, and I just thought it was better to bring it myself and explain how I happened to have it. It's this—this letter you wrote my boy." He extended the letter to her solemnly, in his left hand, and she took it gently from him. "It was in his mail, after he was hurt. You knew he never got it, I expect."

"Yes," she said, in a low voice.

He sighed. "I'm glad he didn't. Not," he added, quickly— "not but what you did just right to send it. You did. You couldn't acted any other way when it came right down *to* it. There ain't any blame comin' to you—you were above-board all through."

Mary said, "Thank you," almost in a whisper, and with her head bowed low.

"You'll have to excuse me for readin' it. I had to take charge of all his mail and everything; I didn't know the handwritin', and I read it all—once I got started."

"I'm glad you did."

"Well"—he leaned forward as if to rise—"I guess that's about all. I just thought you ought to have it."

"Thank you for bringing it."

He looked at her hopefully, as if he thought and wished that she might have something more to say. But she seemed not to be aware of this glance, and sat with her eyes fixed sorrowfully upon the floor.

"Well, I expect I better be gettin' back to the office," he said, rising desperately. "I told—I told my partner I'd be back at two o'clock, and I guess he'll think I'm a poor business man if he catches me behind time. I got to walk the chalk a mighty straight line these days—with *that* fellow keepin' tabs on me!"

Mary rose with him. "I've always heard *you* were the hard driver."

He guffawed derisively. "Me? I'm nothin' to that partner o' mine. You couldn't guess to save your life how he keeps after me to hold up my end o' the job. I shouldn't be surprised he'd give me the grand bounce some day, and run the whole circus by himself. You know how he is—once he goes *at* a thing!"

"No," she smiled. "I didn't know you had a partner. I'd always heard—"

He laughed, looking away from her. "It's just my way o' speakin' o' that boy o' mine, Bibbs."

He stood then, expectant, staring out into the hall with an air of careless geniality. He felt that she certainly must at least say, "How *is* Bibbs?" but she said nothing at all, though he waited until the silence became embarrassing.

"Well, I guess I better be gettin' down there," he said, at last. "He might worry."

"Good-by—and thank you," said Mary.

"For what?"

"For the letter."

"Oh," he said, blankly. "You're welcome. Good-by."

Mary put out her hand. "Good-by."

"You'll have to excuse my left hand," he said. "I had a little accident to the other one."

She gave a pitying cry as she saw. "Oh, poor Mr. Sheridan!"

"Nothin' at all! Dictate everything nowadays, anyhow." He laughed jovially. "Did anybody tell you how it happened?"

"I heard you hurt your hand, but no—not just how."

"It was this way," he began, and both, as if unconsciously, sat down again. "You may not know it, but I used to worry a good deal about the youngest o' my boys—the one that used to come to see you sometimes, after Jim—that is, I mean Bibbs. He's the one I spoke of as my partner; and the truth is that's what it's just about goin' to amount to, one o' these days—if his health holds out. Well, you remember, I expect, I had him on a machine over at a plant o' mine; and sometimes I'd kind o' sneak in there and see how he was gettin' along. Take a doctor with me sometimes, because Bibbs never *was* so robust, you might say. Ole Doc Gurney—I guess maybe you know him? Tall, thin man; acts sleepy—"

"Yes."

"Well, one day I an' ole Doc Gurney, we were in there, and I undertook to show Bibbs how to run his machine. He told me to look out, but I wouldn't listen, and I didn't look out—and that's how I got my hand hurt, tryin' to show Bibbs how to do something he knew how to do and I didn't. Made me so mad I just wouldn't even admit to myself it *was* hurt—and so, by and by, ole Doc Gurney had to take kind o' radical measures with me. He's a right good doctor, too. Don't you think so, Miss Vertrees?"

"Yes."

"Yes, he is so!" Sheridan now had the air of a rambling talker and gossip with all day on his hands. "Take him on Bibbs's case. I was talkin' about Bibbs's case with him this morning. Well, you'd laugh to hear the way ole Gurney talks about *that!* 'Course he *is* just as much a friend as he is doctor —and he takes as much interest in Bibbs as if he was in the family. He says Bibbs isn't anyways bad off *yet;* and he thinks

he could stand the pace and get fat on it if—well, this is what
'd made *you* laugh if you'd been there, Miss Vertrees—honest
it would!" He paused to chuckle, and stole a glance at her. She
was gazing straight before her at the wall; her lips were parted,
and—visibly—she was breathing heavily and quickly. He
feared that she was growing furiously angry; but he had led
to what he wanted to say, and he went on, determined now
to say it all. He leaned forward and altered his voice to one of
confidential friendliness, though in it he still maintained a tone
which indicated that ole Doc Gurney's opinion was only a
joke he shared with her. "Yes, sir, you certainly would 'a'
laughed! Why, that ole man thinks *you* got something to do
with it. You'll have to blame it on him, young lady, if it makes
you feel like startin' out to whip somebody! He's actually got
this theory: he says Bibbs got to gettin' better while he worked
over there at the shop because you kept him cheered up and
feelin' good. And he says if you could manage to just stand
him hangin' around a little—maybe not much, but just *some-*
times—again, he believed it 'd do Bibbs a mighty lot o' good.
'Course, that's only what the doctor said. Me, I don't know
anything about that; but I can say this much—I never saw
any such a *mental* improvement in anybody in my life as I
have lately in Bibbs. I expect you'd find him a good deal more
entertaining than what he used to be—and I know it's a kind
of embarrassing thing to suggest after the way he piled in over
here that day to ask you to stand up before the preacher with
him, but accordin' to ole Doc *Gurney,* he's got you on his
brain so bad—"

Mary jumped. "Mr. Sheridan!" she exclaimed.

He sighed profoundly. "There! I noticed you were gettin'
mad. I didn't—"

"No, no, no!" she cried. "But I don't understand—and I
think you don't. What is it you want me to do?"

He sighed again, but this time with relief. "Well, well!" he
said. "You're right. It 'll be easier to talk plain. I ought to
known I could with you, all the time. I just hoped you'd let

that boy come and see you sometimes, once more. Could you?"

"You don't understand." She clasped her hands together in a sorrowful gesture. "Yes, we must talk plain. Bibbs heard that I'd tried to make your oldest son care for me because I was poor, and so Bibbs came and asked me to marry him—because he was sorry for me. And I *can't* see him any more," she cried in distress. "I *can't!*"

Sheridan cleared his throat uncomfortably. "You mean because he thought that about you?"

"No, no! What he thought was *true!*"

"Well—you mean he was so much in—you mean he thought so much of you—" The words were inconceivably awkward upon Sheridan's tongue; he seemed to be in doubt even about pronouncing them, but after a ghastly pause he bravely repeated them. "You mean he thought so much of you that you just couldn't stand him around?"

"No! He was sorry for me. He cared for me; he was fond of me; and he'd respected me—too much! In the finest way he loved me, if you like, and he'd have done anything on earth for me, as I would for him, and as he knew I would. It was beautiful, Mr. Sheridan," she said. "But the cheap, bad things one has done seem always to come back—they wait, and pull you down when you're happiest. Bibbs found me out, you see; and he wasn't 'in love' with me at all."

"He wasn't? Well, it seems to me he gave up everything he wanted to do—it was fool stuff, but he certainly wanted it mighty bad—he just threw it away and walked right up and took the job he swore he never would—just for you. And it looks to me as if a man that 'd do that must think quite a heap o' the girl he does it for! You say it was only because he was sorry, but let me tell you there's only *one* girl he could feel *that* sorry for! Yes, sir!"

"No, no," she said. "Bibbs isn't like other men—he would do anything for anybody."

Sheridan grinned. "Perhaps not so much as you think, nowadays," he said. "For instance, I got kind of a suspicion he doesn't believe in 'sentiment in business.' But that's neither here nor there. What he wanted was, just plain and simple, for you to marry him. Well, I was afraid his thinkin' so much *of* you had kind o' sickened you of him—the way it does sometimes. But from the way you talk, I understand that ain't the trouble." He coughed, and his voice trembled a little. "Now here, Miss Vertrees, I don't have to tell you—because you see things easy—I know I got no business comin' to you like this, but I had to make Bibbs go my way instead of his own—I had to do it for the sake o' my business and on his own account, too—and I expect you got some idea how it hurt him to give up. Well, he's made good. He didn't come in half-hearted or mean; he came in—all the way! But there isn't anything in it to him; you can see he's just shut his teeth on it and goin' ahead with dust in his mouth. You see, one way of lookin' at it, he's got nothin' to work *for*. And it seems to me like it cost him your friendship, and I believe—honest—that's what hurt him the worst. Now you said we'd talk plain. Why can't you let him come back?"

She covered her face desperately with her hands. "I can't!"

He rose, defeated, and looking it.

"Well, I mustn't press you," he said, gently.

At that she cried out, and dropped her hands and let him see her face. "Ah! He was only sorry for me!"

He gazed at her intently. Mary was proud, but she had a fatal honesty, and it confessed the truth of her now; she was helpless. It was so clear that even Sheridan, marveling and amazed, was able to see it. Then a change came over him; gloom fell from him, and he grew radiant.

"Don't! Don't!" she cried. "You mustn't—"

"I won't tell him," said Sheridan, from the doorway. "I won't tell anybody anything!"

CHAPTER THIRTY-THREE

THERE was a heavy town-fog that afternoon, a smoke-mist, densest in the sanctuary of the temple. The people went about in it, busy and dirty, thickening their outside and inside linings of coal-tar, asphalt, sulphurous acid, oil of vitriol, and the other familiar things the men liked to breathe and to have upon their skins and garments and upon their wives and babies and sweethearts. The growth of the city was visible in the smoke and the noise and the rush. There was more smoke than there had been this day of February a year earlier; there was more noise; and the crowds were thicker—yet quicker in spite of that. The traffic policeman had a hard time, for the people were independent—they retained some habits of the old market-town period, and would cross the street anywhere and anyhow, which not only got them killed more frequently than if they clung to the legal crossings, but kept the motor-men, the chauffeurs, and the truck-drivers in a stew of profane nervousness. So the traffic policemen led harried lives; they themselves were killed, of course, with a certain periodicity, but their main trouble was that they could not make the citizens realize that it was actually and mortally perilous to go about their city. It was strange, for there were probably no citizens of any length of residence who had not personally known either some one who had been killed or injured in an accident, or some one who had accidentally killed or injured others. And yet, perhaps it was not strange, seeing the sharp preoccupation of the faces—the people had something on their minds; they could not stop to bother about dirt and danger.

Mary Vertrees was not often down-town; she had never seen an accident until this afternoon. She had come upon errands for her mother connected with a timorous refurbishment; and as she did these, in and out of the department stores, she had an insistent consciousness of the Sheridan Building. From the street, anywhere, it was almost always in sight, like some monstrous geometrical shadow, murk-colored and rising limitlessly into the swimming heights of the smoke-mist. It was gaunt and grimy and repellent; it had nothing but strength and size—but in that consciousness of Mary's the great structure may have partaken of beauty. Sheridan had made some of the things he said emphatic enough to remain with her. She went over and over them—and they began to seem true: "Only *one* girl he could feel *that* sorry for!" "Gurney says he's got you on his brain so bad—" The man's clumsy talk began to sing in her heart. The song was begun there when she saw the accident.

She was directly opposite the Sheridan Building then, waiting for the traffic to thin before she crossed, though other people were risking the passage, darting and halting and dodging parlously. Two men came from the crowd behind her, talking earnestly, and started across. Both wore black; one was tall and broad and thick, and the other was taller, but noticeably slender. And Mary caught her breath, for they were Bibbs and his father. They did not see her, and she caught a phrase in Bibbs's mellow voice, which had taken a crisper ring: "Sixty-eight thousand dollars? Not sixty-eight thousand buttons!" It startled her queerly, and as there was a glimpse of his profile she saw for the first time a resemblance to his father.

She watched them. In the middle of the street Bibbs had to step ahead of his father, and the two were separated. But the reckless passing of a truck, beyond the second line of rails, frightened a group of country women who were in course of passage; they were just in front of Bibbs, and shoved backward upon him violently. To extricate himself from them he stepped back, directly in front of a moving trolley-car—no place for absent-mindedness, but Bibbs was still absorbed in thoughts concerned with what he had been saying to his father. There were shrieks and yells; Bibbs looked the wrong way—and then Mary saw the heavy figure of Sheridan plunge straight forward in front of the car. With absolute disregard of his own life, he hurled himself at Bibbs like a football-player shunting off an opponent, and to Mary it seemed that they both went down together. But that was all she could see —automobiles, trucks, and wagons closed in between. She made out that the trolley-car stopped jerkily, and she saw a policeman breaking his way through the instantly condensing crowd, while the traffic came to a standstill, and people stood up in automobiles or climbed upon the hubs and tires of wheels, not to miss a chance of seeing anything horrible.

Mary tried to get through; it was impossible. Other police-men came to help the first, and in a minute or two the traffic was in motion again. The crowd became pliant, dispersing— there was no figure upon the ground, and no ambulance came. But one of the policemen was detained by the clinging and beseeching of a gloved hand.

"What *is* the matter, lady?"

"Where are they?" Mary cried.

"Who? Ole man Sheridan? I reckon *he* wasn't much hurt!"

"His *son*—"

"Was that who the other one was? I seen him knock him— oh, he's not bad off, I guess, lady. The ole man got him out of the way all right. The fender shoved the ole man around some, but I reckon he only got shook up. They both went on in the Sheridan Building without any help. Excuse me, lady."

Sheridan and Bibbs, in fact, were at that moment in the elevator, ascending. "Whisk-broom up in the office," Sheridan was saying. "You got to look out on these corners nowadays, I tell you. I don't know *I* got any call to blow, though—be-cause I tried to cross after you did. That's how I happened to run into you. Well, you want remember to look out after this. We were talkin' about Murtrie's askin' sixty-eight thousand flat for that ninety-nine-year lease. It's his lookout if he'd rather take it that way, and I don't know but—"

"No," said Bibbs, emphatically, as the elevator stopped; "he won't get it. Not from Us, he won't, and I'll show you why. I can convince you in five minutes." He followed his father into the office anteroom—and convinced him. Then, having been diligently brushed by a youth of color, Bibbs went into his own room and closed the door.

He was more shaken than he had allowed his father to perceive, and his side was sore where Sheridan had struck him. He desired to be alone; he wanted to rub himself and, for once, to do some useless thinking again. He knew that his father had not "happened" to run into him; he knew that Sheridan had instantly—and instinctively—proved that he held his own life of no account whatever compared to that of his son and heir. Bibbs had been unable to speak of that, or to seem to know it; for Sheridan, just as instinctively, had swept the matter aside—as of no importance, since all was well— reverting immediately to business.

Bibbs began to think intently of his father. He perceived, as he had never perceived before, the shadowing of something enormous and indomitable—and lawless; not to be daunted by the will of nature's very self; laughing at the lightning and at wounds and mutilation; conquering, irresistible—and blindly noble. For the first time in his life Bibbs began to understand the meaning of being truly this man's son.

He would be the more truly his son henceforth, though, as Sheridan said, Bibbs had not come down-town with him meanly or half-heartedly. He had given his word because he had wanted the money, simply, for Mary Vertrees in her need. And he shivered with horror of himself, thinking how he had gone to her to offer it, asking her to marry him—with his head on his breast in shameful fear that she would accept him! He had not known her; the knowing had lost her to him, and this had been his real awakening; for he knew now how deep had been that slumber wherein he dreamily celebrated the superiority of "friendship"! The sleep-walker had wakened to bitter knowledge of love and life, finding himself a failure in both. He had made a burnt offering of his dreams, and the sacrifice had been an unforgivable hurt to Mary. All that was left for him was the work he had not chosen, but at least he would not fail in that, though it was indeed no more than "dust in his mouth." If there had been anything "to work for—"

He went to the window, raised it, and let in the uproar of the streets below. He looked down at the blurred, hurrying swarms—and he looked across, over the roofs with their panting jets of vapor, into the vast, foggy heart of the smoke. Dizzy traceries of steel were rising dimly against it, chattering with steel on steel, and screeching in steam, while tiny figures of men walked on threads in the dull sky. Buildings would overtop the Sheridan. Bigness was being served.

But what for? The old question came to Bibbs with a new despair. Here, where his eye fell, had once been green fields and running brooks, and how had the kind earth been despoiled and disfigured! The pioneers had begun the work, but in their old age their orators had said for them that they had toiled and risked and sacrificed that their posterity might live in peace and wisdom, enjoying the fruits of the earth. Well, their posterity was here—and there was only turmoil. Where was the promised land? It had been promised by the soldiers of all the wars; it had been promised to this generation by the pioneers; but here was the very posterity to whom it had been promised, toiling and risking and sacrificing in turn—for what?

The harsh roar of the city came in through the open window, continuously beating upon Bibbs's ear until he began to distinguish a pulsation in it—a broken and irregular cadence. It seemed to him that it was like a titanic voice, discordant, hoarse, rustily metallic—the voice of the god, Bigness. And the voice summoned Bibbs as it summoned all its servants.

"Come and work!" it seemed to call. "Come and work for

Me, all men! By your youth and your hope I summon you!
By your age and your despair I summon you to work for Me
yet a little, with what strength you have. By your love of home
I summon you! By your love of woman I summon you! By
your hope of children I summon you!

"You shall be blind slaves of Mine, blind to everything but
Me, your Master and Driver! For your reward you shall gaze
only upon my ugliness. You shall give your toil and your
lives, you shall go mad for love and worship of my ugliness!
You shall perish still worshiping Me, and your children shall
perish knowing no other god!"

And then, as Bibbs closed the window down tight, he heard
his father's voice booming in the next room; he could not distinguish the words, but the tone was exultant—and there came
the *thump! thump!* of the maimed hand. Bibbs guessed that
Sheridan was bragging of the city and of Bigness to some
visitor from out-of-town.

And he thought how truly Sheridan was the high priest of
Bigness. But with the old, old thought again, "What for?"
Bibbs caught a glimmer of far, faint light. He saw that Sheridan had all his life struggled and conquered, and must all his
life go on struggling and inevitably conquering, as part of a
vast impulse not his own. Sheridan served blindly—but was
the impulse blind? Bibbs asked himself if it was not he who
had been in the greater hurry, after all. The kiln must be fired
before the vase is glazed, and the Acropolis was not crowned
with marble in a day.

Then the voice came to him again, but there was a strain
in it as of some huge music struggling to be born of the turmoil. "Ugly I am," it seemed to say to him, "but never forget
that I *am* a god!" And the voice grew in sonorousness and in
dignity. "The highest should serve, but so long as you worship
me for my own sake I will not serve you. It is man who makes
me ugly, by his worship of me. If man would let me serve
him, I should be beautiful!"

Looking once more from the window, Bibbs sculptured for himself—in the vague contortions of the smoke and fog above the roofs—a gigantic figure with feet pedestaled upon the great buildings and shoulders disappearing in the clouds, a colossus of steel and wholly blackened with soot. But Bibbs carried his fancy further—for there was still a little poet lingering in the back of his head—and he thought that up over the clouds, unseen from below, the giant labored with his hands in the clean sunshine; and Bibbs had a glimpse of what he made there—perhaps for a fellowship of the children of the children that were children now—a noble and joyous city, unbelievably white—

It was the telephone that called him from his vision. It rang fiercely.

He lifted the thing from his desk and answered—and as the small voice inside it spoke he dropped the receiver with a crash. He trembled violently as he picked it up, but he told himself he was wrong—he had been mistaken—yet it was a startlingly beautiful voice; startlingly kind, too, and ineffably like the one he hungered most to hear.

"Who?" he said, his own voice shaking—like his hand.

"Mary."

He responded with two hushed and incredulous words: *"Is it?"*

There was a little thrill of pathetic half-laughter in the instrument. "Bibbs—I wanted to—just to see if you—"

"Yes—Mary?"

"I was looking when you were so nearly run over. I saw it, Bibbs. They said you hadn't been hurt, they thought, but I wanted to know for myself."

"No, no, I wasn't hurt at all—Mary. It was father who came near it. He saved me."

"Yes, I saw; but you had fallen. I couldn't get through the crowd until you had gone. And I wanted to *know*."

"Mary—would you—have minded?" he said.

There was a long interval before she answered.

"Yes."

"Then why—"

"Yes, Bibbs?"

"I don't know what to say," he cried. "It's so wonderful to hear your voice again—I'm shaking, Mary—I—I don't know —I don't know anything except that I *am* talking to you! It *is* you—Mary?"

"Yes, Bibbs!"

"Mary—I've seen you from my window at home—only five times since I—since then. You looked—oh, how can I tell you? It was like a man chained in a cave catching a glimpse of the blue sky, Mary. Mary, won't you—let me see you again—near? I think I could make you really forgive me—you'd have to—"

"I *did*—then."

"No—not really—or you wouldn't have said you couldn't see me any more."

"That wasn't the reason." The voice was very low.

"Mary," he said, even more tremulously than before, "I can't—you *couldn't* mean it was because—you can't mean it was because you—care?"

There was no answer.

"Mary?" he called, huskily. "If you mean *that*—you'd let me see you—wouldn't you?"

And now the voice was so low he could not be sure it spoke at all, but if it did, the words were, "Yes, Bibbs—dear."

But the voice was not in the instrument—it was so gentle and so light, so almost nothing, it seemed to be made of air— and it came from the air.

Slowly and incredulously he turned—and glory fell upon his shining eyes. The door of his father's room had opened.

Mary stood upon the threshold.

THE END

QUESTIONS FOR STUDY AND DISCUSSION

1 Point out some features in any city that you have seen or read about, which are the result of the enterprise of men or women of the type of Mr. James Sheridan.

2 Point out those which are the result of the work of people whose viewpoint was similar to that of Bibbs and Mary.

3 What would that city be if either of these elements were lacking?

4 In what way could the thoughtful reading of this book give a more sympathetic and tolerant attitude toward other human beings?

5 Why do we call *The Turmoil* peculiarly a novel of American life? Why could it not have been written of England or France?

6 Make a brief study of the contrasts furnished by means of the following characters:

Mr. Sheridan and Mr. Vertrees

Mary Vertrees and Sibyl Sheridan

Bibbs Sheridan and his father

7 Select one of the main characters and make a study of it, based on the following suggestions:

Mary Vertrees

a What cause first brings together the families of the Sheridans and the Vertrees?

b What traits were alike in Mary and Mr. Sheridan, that served to give them mutual understanding?

c What service did Sibyl unwittingly do for Mary?

d Why did Mary write the letter to Jim?

e What characteristics were in Mary's nature that made her an inspiration to Bibbs?

Mr. Sheridan

a Wherein lay the force of Mr. Sheridan's character?

b Would you call him a cruel man? Why?

c Point out examples of his treatment of his wife that show his kindness of heart.

d What incidents show his generous nature?

e What was his shortcoming?

Bibbs Sheridan

a What causes produced the changes in Bibbs' character which appear during the course of the story?

b What force in American life does Bibbs typify?

8 Choose one of the following topics and learn all about it that you can:

a Trace the story of the growth and development of one of these Mid-Western cities:

Chicago	St. Louis	Pittsburgh
Detroit	Cincinnati	Cleveland

The Chamber of Commerce of any city will be glad to send you information.

b Find out what the American people owe to a great captain of industry.

John D. Rockefeller

Andrew Carnegie

Henry Ford

c Learn what our cities owe to one of our great American sculptors.

Augustus Saint Gaudens

Daniel Chester French

Lorado Taft

d Follow the life story of a great industry, with its effect on American life.

The canning of fruits, vegetables, fish and meat

The extension of railroads

The manufacture of steel

The making of farm machinery

The making of automobiles

OTHER NOVELS OF AMERICAN LIFE

BACHELLER, IRVING: *Cricket Heron*. Harper, 1909. A boy tells his own story of his wanderings and of life in New York as he saw it during the railroad and industrial development.

CANNON, LEGRAND, JR.: *Look to the Mountain*. Henry Holt, 1942. Whit and Melissa, young, strong, confident, went out before the Revolution to build their home in the New Hampshire Wilderness. A vital, truthful, and exciting tale.

CATHER, WILLA: *My Antonia*. Houghton Mifflin, 1908. Antonia is a Bohemian girl whose parents have come to Iowa in the great flood of immigration to the Middle West, to wrest a living from the unturned prairie soil.

EGGLESTON, EDWARD: *The Hoosier School Boy*. Warne, 1882. The story of an Indiana school boy, and his experiences as an early settler of that state.

FIELD, RACHEL: *All This and Heaven Too*. Macmillan, 1938. A dauntless young French girl, enmeshed in difficulties for which she was not to blame, flees to America, where her fortunes are interwoven with those of the Field family in the laying of the first Atlantic cable.

GLASGOW, ELLEN: *Vein of Iron*. Harcourt, Brace, 1935. The Fincastle family, endowed with iron-strong pride and integrity, settle in the Valley of Virginia. The story centers about Ada and her unhappy love, and old John Fincastle, a tragic but admirable figure.

HAWES, CHARLES BOARDMAN: *The Dark Frigate*. Little, Brown, 1934. A stirring and beautifully written tale of a fine and loyal boy who became involved with the pirates who in Colonial times infested the coast of North Carolina.

HOUGH, EMERSON: *The Covered Wagon*. Appleton, 1922. Pioneers leave their Missouri homes and make their way to Oregon. The story pictures the jealousies, the misunderstandings, and the dangers of the daily life of the travelers.

HOWELLS, WILLIAM DEAN: *The Rise of Silas Lapham*. Houghton Mifflin, 1884. In New England, about 1875, Silas Lapham makes a fortune in paint, and later suffers heavy losses. His efforts to guide his family arouse both mirth and sympathy, while his own uprightness wins admiration.

KREY, LAURA: *And Tell of Time.* Houghton Mifflin, 1938. Enterprising Georgia families, seeking new homes after the Civil War, journey to Texas and settle on the rich farming lands of the lower Brazos River. Their adventures reveal the difficulties of carpet-bagger days and the strength of heart and will of the pioneers.

MEIGS, CORNELIA: *Railroad West.* Little, Brown, 1937. This story presents in an authentic manner the almost incredible difficulties overcome in pushing our railroads across the Rocky Mountains and out to the West Coast. A young engineer encounters dust-storms and blizzards, land-grabbers and Indians, but succeeds in his enterprise.

MITCHELL, MARGARET: *Gone with the Wind.* Macmillan, 1936. Scarlett O'Hara is the daughter of a Georgia planter in Civil War days. Beautiful, headstrong, and selfish, she nevertheless loved the land with a love so strong it overcame all difficulties and rebuilt the ruins of the plantation. Long and repetitious, but the story is always interesting.

MITCHELL, SILAS WEIR: *Hugh Wynne.* Century, 1897. The story starts with Hugh Wynne as a boy in a Quaker family in Philadelphia. Upon the outbreak of the Revolution, the family is divided, Hugh joining General Washington. A beautiful love story is inwoven with adventures in the Continental army.

QUICK, HERBERT: *Vandemark's Folly.* Bobbs-Merrill, 1922. Vandemark, christened Jacobus and nicknamed "Cow," is a youth of Dutch extraction, who, about 1850, emigrates from New York State to Iowa to take up new land. The adventures of the long trip and of the settling of the prairies are vividly presented, incidentally portraying the frank and sterling character of the young American.

ROLVAAG, O. E.: *Giants in the Earth.* Harper, 1927. Per Hansa and his family cross the prairies from Minnesota and struggle to establish one of the first Norwegian settlements in the Dakota territory.

ROLVAAG, O. E.: *Peder Victorious.* Harper, 1929. The youngest son of Per Hansa goes to school on the prairie and grows to manhood during the stirring times when the division of the Dakotas occurred.

STEINBECK, JOHN: *Of Mice and Men.* Covici-Friede, 1937. The large grain ranches of California of the present day form the background for the story of two drifting, transient farm workers —George, the strong, compassionate protector and his half-witted companion, Lennie. A moving, tragic story, advancing swiftly, perfectly planned.

TARKINGTON, BOOTH: *The Magnificent Ambersons.* Doubleday, 1918. The Ambersons had been the leading family in a town of the Middle West, until new industrial life transforms the city, when the Amberson glamour fades. The story shows the development of the spoiled son and heir of the family under the stress of new conditions.

WHITE, STEWART EDWARD: *Gold.* Doubleday, 1913. Four young men make their way to California in 1849 by way of Panama. They find a fortune in the gold diggings, but disaster sweeps away all they have gained. Foreseeing the splendid future of the West, they start again, this time in business in San Francisco.

WHITE, STEWART EDWARD: *Wild Geese Calling.* Doubleday, 1940. A lively adventure story dealing with our very important remaining frontier, Alaska.

WHITE, WILLIAM ALLEN: *A Certain Rich Man.* Macmillan, 1909. A man rises to affluence as a wheat king in a mid-western town, which develops into a big and prosperous city.

WILSON, MARGARET: *The Able McLaughlins.* Harper, 1923. The McLaughlins are members of a Scotch community in the Middle West during the 60's. The hardships, perils, and stimulating adventures of pioneer life form the background for a love story involving several fine strong characters.

WISTER, OWEN: *The Virginian.* Macmillan, 1902. The Virginian was a young man who left his native state to become a cowboy in Wyoming. The life of the cowboys and ranchmen of Wyoming in the 70's and 80's was no easy one, but to their work they added fun and pranks that made life exciting during the development of that state. This book combines Western adventure with truth and a fine literary style.